GODDESS
IN
THE
MACHINE

Also by
LORA BETH JOHNSON

Devil in the Device

GODDESS
IN
THE
MACHINE

LORA BETH JOHNSON

RAZORBILL

RAZORBILL

An imprint of Penguin Random House LLC, New York

First published in the United States of America by Razorbill,
an imprint of Penguin Random House LLC, 2020
First paperback edition published 2021

Definitions for the following words are used courtesy of WordNet: An Electronic Lexical Database. Princeton University definitions of *belonging, stasis, exchange, cell, plan, control*, and *interface*. WordNet. Princeton University. 2020. https://wordnet.princeton.edu/.

Visit us online at penguinrandomhouse.com.

THE LIBRARY OF CONGRESS HAS CATALOGED THE HARDCOVER EDITION AS FOLLOWS:
Names: Johnson, Lora Beth, author.
Title: Goddess in the machine / Lora Beth Johnson.
Description: New York : Razorbill, 2020. | Audience: Ages 12+. |
Summary: Bound for humanity's new colony planet, seventeen-year-old Andra wakes up from a cryogenic sleep 1,000 years later than she was supposed to, forcing her to navigate an unfamiliar planet where technology is considered magic and its practitioners revered as deities.
Identifiers: LCCN 2019051799 | ISBN 9781984835925 (hardcover) |
ISBN 9781984835932 (ebook)
Subjects: CYAC: Science fiction. | Artificial intelligence—Fiction. | Cryonics—Fiction. |
Space colonies—Fiction.
Classification: LCC PZ7.1.J6287 Go 2020 | DDC [Fic]—dc23
LC record available at https://lccn.loc.gov/2019051799

Paperback ISBN 9781984835949

Printed in the United States of America

1 3 5 7 9 10 8 6 4 2

SKY

Design by Rebecca Aidlin
Text set in Iowan Old Style

NOV 29 2021

For Kelsey, Amanda, Taryn, Nadia, Kailan, Alex, and Bre—

my girl gang of goddesses:

I tolerate you.

GODDESS IN THE MACHINE

PART ONE

RESURRECTION

When you first awaken, expect some disorientation, sore muscles, shortness of breath, dimmed eyesight, and depression. These symptoms are usually mild. However, due to time constraints, no human trial has lasted the hundred years you will be in stasis. Symptoms may be aggravated by the extended length of time, as well as Mid-Stasis Relocation Disorientation (hereafter referred to as MSRD). Cryo'technicians and med'bots will be available to assist you after your unprecedented journey. Congratulations. You are making history.

—*Holymyth Colonist Handbook*, page 23, sponsored by the Lacuna Athenaeum Corporation

ONE

wake, n. or v.

Etymology: Anglo-Saxon *wacan*, "to be born"; possible adoption from Icelandic *vök*, meaning "an opening in the ice."

Definition: 1. to be roused from sleep; to revive, reanimate; to return to life.

2. the consequences of a body in movement.

3. a vigil by the body of the dead.

WHEN ANDROMEDA WOKE, she was drowning.

They'd warned her this would happen—that her lungs would burn and her eyes would sting and she'd have to fight for that first breath. *But you must take it,* they said. *If you don't, your lungs will collapse and we'll have to put you in a coma and just hope for the best.*

Okay, maybe those weren't their exact words.

She pulled in a breath, just like they told her. It burned. It stung. She fought. Water flooded her lungs, and the bitter taste of saline filled her mouth. Something was wrong. Something she couldn't quite place.

Her fist shot out, grasping for help, but it slammed into something solid. There it was—the wrongness. Ten-inch-thick metallic glass enforced with veins of diamond dust. Latched together with hinges of a tantalum-tungsten alloy. Supposed to be yawning open when she woke. But it wasn't. It was still closed, cocooning her in cold metal and melting cryo'protectant.

Calculations fired in her brain, searching for missing information, evaluating variables, solving for X. She'd just been put to sleep, and now she was drowning. No. It only *felt* like she'd just been put to sleep. It had actually been a hundred years. And now, she was waking up and (oh god) *naked*, but her chamber was still closed.

Something was definitely wrong.

They'd prepared her for this possibility—waking too early or crisis aborts or faulty latches—but it was hard to remember emergency plans in the middle of an emergency.

There was a button somewhere . . .

. . . or a switch?

She was too lightheaded. Her hands didn't work. Her brain was shutting down, synapses sparking, sending a single message:

air air air air air

She struck the glass again. It didn't even crack. It was meant to last centuries, meant to withstand zero gravity and a thousand times atmospheric pressure and two thousand degrees kelvin and zero degrees kelvin. But she kept pounding, each hit a bit weaker, a bit quieter.

She hit the glass until her strength gave out. Her arms fell to her sides. Just before her eyes slid shut, she saw a face above her. No one she recognized. There was no bright light. No life flashing before her eyes. No air. Just water and drowning and dying and water.

Then nothing.

WHEN SHE WOKE the second time, she was coughing up saline. This was an improvement.

Her throat was sore. It ached down into the recesses of her chest. She didn't want to breathe. It hurt too much. But she had to.

Just as soon as she coughed all the water out of her lungs.

At first, her senses didn't extend past *pain*. Then she heard shouts.

Murmurs. Whispers. Syllables that weren't words. Words without meaning. Strong arms held her, a rough hand patted her back. Not the cryo'tech—they weren't allowed to touch. Not her mom either—she didn't coddle.

The water was gone now, but the sting remained, the compulsion to cough. She gasped in a breath, and it dragged through her lungs, her throat, catching and tearing as it went. But it kept her alive, so she pulled in another.

And another.

Shivering. Shaking off flecks of ice.

So. *Cold.*

She thought about opening her eyes, but decided against it. Too much work. So she breathed, and then she slept, and then, for the first time in a hundred years, she dreamed.

Will I dream? she asked.

No, you'll be sleeping too deeply. Like a computer shutting down.

Will I know time is passing?

When they wake you, it'll feel like seconds from now.

When will they wake me?

When you reach the new planet.

So. You're the last person I'll ever speak to on Earth.

Don't be so morbid.

THE THIRD TIME, Andra woke to the tinny whirring of a fan. A blast of air hit her right cheek and shoulder, alleviating some of the oppressive heat. Sticky globs of residual cryo'protectant clung to her skin. She shivered and opened her eyes.

She was *awake.* She jerked into a half-sitting position. This was a new planet. A hundred years had passed. She had to find her family. She had to tell her mom she was sorry. She—

was in the dirtiest room known to man.

The floors were dirt, the walls crusted with something she *hoped* was dirt. It was like a cave, a single shaft of light filtering in through a high, thin window with no glass or holo'screen, and a plume of sand puffed in on an arid gust of wind.

The room was empty except for the bed she was sitting on, a metal table, and, on top of that, the fan—which looked like it was running on some sort of kinetic energy. It spluttered to a stop, leaving the room silent and stale.

This was no place for medical tests and routines, for purgative baths and reanimation therapy. Andra hadn't bothered to read the manual, but her mother had droned on about it enough that she knew the re-animation procedures by heart: once they arrived on the new planet, robots would wake the head LAC scientists—like Andra's mother—and a skeleton crew of cryo'techs. They wouldn't wake the colonists until mech'bots had constructed the hospitals and everything was organized and sanitary. Then, after resurrection, there would be sight tests, vocal tests, muscle tests, preliminary physical therapy, a nice hot bath, and finally: reconnecting with family.

The point was, all of this was supposed to occur in a pristine, sterile environment.

The harsh mattress beneath her groaned. The quilt covering it was gritty under her fingers, caked with sand. Without the fan, the heat was unbearable, and she was dripping in sweat and cryo'protectant.

But no longer naked, so there was that.

Her clothes: unfamiliar and uncomfortably hot—loose pants, cuffed at the ankle, and a rough tunic with a cowl-neck rucked around her shoulders. Everything was a little too tight, like the clothes her mom would buy to inspire her to lose weight. Her forearms were covered with a constricting, stretchy material, and her wrists itched where sweat pooled under the sleeves. The fabric was handmade; she could tell by the rough weave. These were no LAC-sanctioned medical robes, that was for sure.

On instinct, she mentally reached for her neural'implant, hoping she could use it to switch on an enviro'con, but found nothing. That was to be expected, since 'implants were known to glitch after stasis. She wouldn't be able to access any technology around her for an indeterminant amount of time. Andra hated that word—*indeterminant*. She liked for things to be determined.

She brushed her short, dark hair out of her face. Her fingers caught in the tangles just as the door swung open, and another gust of wind blew in, along with a man, who stood silhouetted in the doorway. A cryo'technician. Finally.

Andra tried to blink away the fuzziness. Right before the cryo'tech had put her to sleep, he'd told her to state her name, age, hometown, and CID as soon as she woke up. *Andromeda Yue Watts. Seventeen. Riverside, Ohio. 32-638-27.* That's what she was supposed to say, but all that came out was, "Huh?"

Because he didn't look like a 'tech at all.

He was young—probably only a bit older than Andra, maybe nineteen, twenty—but he looked . . . rough, haggard, raw. Blond. Crinkled eyes. His angular jaw was brushed with scruff, and his sand-colored tunic was deliberately disheveled. He leaned against the doorjamb, arms crossed, eyebrows lifted in a question.

And he was wearing leather armor.

Definitely not a cryo'tech.

"Show the toe, Goddess," he said, and though Andra understood each word individually, she had no idea what they meant put together in that order.

He pushed against the wall and sauntered over to the metal chair, twirling it around to sit backward. He winked, and Andra realized belatedly that she was gaping at him. Not because he was handsome—

though, he was—but because there was a boy in leather armor saying random words to her in a cave, and this was so not how she imagined waking up on a new planet.

"Evens, then?" he asked. "You slept *forever*. See?" He pointed to his chin. "I grew a beard while I waited. Makes me look charred, marah?" He tilted his head in a few different angles, so she could get the full effect. When she didn't respond, he patted the bed. "Show the toe. We need to peace. Sun's sinking quickish." His voice was richly reedy, and he spoke in an accent Andra had never heard before. It was hard to pick apart the string of phonemes into words. Even once she did, they didn't sound quite right. Mushy and rushed.

"I . . ." She trailed off, taking in her surroundings again. Dirt, dirt, a bed, an empty cup, more dirt. No clues as to where she was. Holymyth, obviously. That was the plan: to wake up when they got to the new planet. She could *feel* the distance. Like when she'd fallen asleep on the vac'train to visit her grandmother in the Maylarche and when she woke up, something in her body registered how far she was from home. That feeling—shaking, gnawing, unsettling—was a thousand, a million times more potent now.

She'd fallen asleep in one place and woken up across the universe.

No big deal. That was supposed to happen—waking up a gazillion miles away. But the rest of it—the dirty hut and the cryo'tech who wasn't a cryo'tech . . .

"Where am I?" she asked, her voice raw. "What's going on?" Rasping vowels, sticky consonants.

"You're at luck I speak High Goddess." He thrummed his fingers against the back of the chair. They were coated in sand. "No one else in this wastehole would reck your speech." He held out his hand. "I'm Zhade." The way he said it was halfway between *shade* and *jade*. "Been looking for you for nearish four years. There's a kiddun's game called Rabbit Rabbit—where one kiddun hides and the others have to find them, and you would be massive at that game."

8

Andra stared at his hand. It was wrapped with dirty bandages. He turned it over and looked at his palm.

"This is something you do, marah? The hand-shaking thing? Fraughted ridiculous custom."

Andra swallowed, her brain struggling to keep up, as though it were slogging through knee-deep mud. "Four years? What do you mean you've been looking for me?" The room grew dark, a cloud passing over the sun. The air didn't cool. "My family. I have to find my family. Is this Holymyth? Did something happen while we were in stasis? Where's the cryo'tech?" Again, she reached for her 'implant, hoping to ping her family, but found nothing.

"That . . ." The soldier frowned. ". . . is a lot of words I don't reck. I'll get Wead to fetch you something to eat, but then we need to go road-wise."

Andra swung over the side of the bed. Her legs ached, but not as badly as her throat. She wobbled as she got to her feet, but didn't fall. *Minimal muscular atrophy*, her mother would have said—was probably saying right now as she woke someone else up from stasis.

Maybe Mom was waking up Acadia or Oz or Dad. Maybe she was looking for Andra right now. Or maybe . . .

She hobbled to the door, her muscles stretching in ways they hadn't for a hundred years, even though in her mind, she'd used them just a few hours ago.

"Heya!" Zhade called. "Where are you peacing to?"

She pried open the door, expecting—

well, she didn't know what she'd been expecting, but it certainly wasn't *this*.

She stood at the top of a hill, in a village of rock huts. Not huts made of rocks, but huts carved *into* rocks. Enormous boulders, stories-high, with hollowed-out windows and doors and rooms. Dozens of structures sprouted from the ground. And beyond, as far as the eye could see: desert.

They were supposed to land somewhere subtropical. Somewhere lush, with moderate temperatures and low humidity, and enough trees to hide the horizon. Not a barren desert filled with boulders. The whole landscape was wrong.

But not as wrong as the people. Hundreds of them, all dressed like Andra—covered head-to-toe, despite the heat. As soon as they saw her, the crowd instantly quieted, and then, as one, they fell to their knees, murmuring a single word. Over and over. One Andra knew, but couldn't begin to understand. She looked back, and Zhade was standing in the doorway, arms crossed, a crooked smile on his lips. He raised an eyebrow and said the word the people were chanting, once and vivid and burning, and somehow, she knew he was talking about *her*.

"Goddess," he said.

Then, "How do you like your worshippers?"

Something was definitely wrong.

TWO

hell-mouth, n.

Definition: 1. used to denote the approach of that which lies
beneath.

2. the entrance to Hell.

ZHADE WAS WATCHING her, waiting. Just like the crowd of people who called her *goddess*.

Sweat dripped down Andra's spine, and she pulled at the stiff material of her borrowed shirt, searching the faces, recognizing no one. The Ark held a million colonists, and she only knew a few dozen, but surely there would be *someone* she recognized. Her friends, Briella and Rhin. An intern from her mother's office—Rashmi maybe. *Perhaps Cruz*, she thought with a blush. But there was no one. Just strange, haggard faces, dressed in heavy rags in the sweltering heat, murmuring *goddess* over and over, and staring at *her*.

Andra felt the tickle of nano'bots against her skin. The microscopic 'bots had been ubiquitous on Earth—used to transfer messages from 'implants to tech—and if they were here, the rest of the colonists must be nearby. The nanos were starting to 'swarm and would soon be thick enough to be seen by the naked eye. She wondered if it was because so many people were focused on her—if they were all using their 'implants to try to communicate with hers, sending the nanos to interface with it. But why would they want to?

A lot of things could have gone wrong in the hundred years she was in stasis, but there was no series of accidents she could fathom that would lead her to this:

A desert village. Surrounded by peasants. Who, she now understood, were praying.

To her.

Their *goddess*.

"I don't understand," she croaked. It felt like she'd been screaming.

She was considering running back into the hut, closing her eyes, and sticking her fingers in her ears when she saw it—nothing more than a glimmer in the crowd, but it stirred something in her. Something familiar. Something that reminded her of home.

A robot. On the outskirts of the crowd.

It was an info'bot. Class D. She could tell from its humanoid build and white paneling. It probably had a copper core and Corsairs drive, and she bet it was engraved with the Lacuna Athenaeum Corporation symbol—the infinity sign made from a DNA strand. Almost all info'bots were LAC models. Her mother's company covered the 'bot industry just short of a monopoly. And the med' industry. And the space travel industry. And the EPA. And, and, and.

An AI would have been preferable, with its brain-like CPU and ability to perform tasks beyond the programming of a standard 'bot, but this dusty model was all Andra had, and she hoped to hell it had at least been programmed to connect to the network.

She ran toward it.

Zhade called after her, but she had already disappeared into the crowd, which she quickly discovered had been a mistake.

Hands grasped her, tugging at her clothes, winding into her hair. People were everywhere, murmuring words she couldn't understand. Too close. Someone stepped on her foot. Another pulled a chunk of her hair. They were going to crush her, rip her apart. An arm grabbed her around the middle, and she cried out.

Suddenly, Zhade was there, pushing the people back, speaking in a language she didn't recognize. Slowly, reluctantly, the people backed away. Zhade tried to pull Andra toward the hut, but she wrenched out of his grasp.

"I need to get to the 'bot," she gasped.

"The what?"

"The 'bot." She pointed.

"Hmm." Zhade gave a wary look before shepherding her through the crowd, keeping the masses at arm's length with a harsh command.

The words didn't sound like any language Andra was familiar with—no dialect of English, not the bits of Hokkien her grandmother taught her, none of the European languages she learned in school. It was simultaneously mushy and clipped, filled with sounds she doubted she could mimic—and she could mimic a lot. There were hints of harsh consonants, voiced affricates, nasally vowels, some combination of Germanic and—

And it didn't matter. She should be focusing on what the hell had happened, not the architecture of a random language she'd never heard before.

They made their way down the hill, loose gravel shifting beneath them, but Zhade kept her upright while holding the people back. Faces peered through hollowed-out windows, behind stone structures. Whispers followed. Sweat dripped down Andra's back.

She was relieved when they reached the 'bot and the crowd drew away.

"Excuse me," she said. Standard greeting, if you didn't know the 'bot's domain.

It turned. 'Bots never looked completely lifelike—something about the dead eyes and the see-through skull-cap, revealing the wiring beneath—but this one looked especially mechanical, its movements jerky. Its paneling was muddied and scored with what looked like claw marks. Part of its face had been torn, exposing the gears that controlled the left eye and cheek. It walked with a limp, as though the joint in its right knee was rusted, but it appeared functional.

It tilted its head. "How may I help?"

Yet again, Andra mentally reached for her 'implant—the tiny piece of tech embedded in her brain. It was habit. She'd been implanted—as most people were—at birth, and she'd rarely used technology without it. Most people didn't even know how, except Andra's mother had demanded she have a basic understanding of manual technology and coding. Andra wasn't sure how long it would be until her 'implant was back online. Since she couldn't rely on a neural connection, she asked aloud, "Where am I?"

The 'bot started to respond, but shorted before it could get out a syllable.

"Switch to holographic display," she said. She preferred holo' displays to voice interfaces anyway. They were more discreet, and the rules of interacting with a visual interface were more straightforward than the algorithms for conversation.

The crackling of the voice interface silenced, and the 'bot upturned its hand, a holographic map shooting from its open palm. The data was too corrupted to make any sense of, and what Andra *could* see was nothing more than desert and more desert. A gust of sand scattered the pixels.

The transparent sheen of holo'keys appeared in front of her, and Andra typed her next question.

Am I on Holymyth?

A single word flashed across the screen: *Unknown.*

That was impossible. Or at least improbable. The 'bot should have known where it was. GPS was part of any 'bot's most basic programming, and even if LAC hadn't launched the satellites yet, it should still be linked to the Ark's mobile network. A tingle on Andra's skin reminded her that the air was filled with nano'bots, which typically communicated their location to one another. The 'bot should have been able to determine its whereabouts from the surrounding nano chatter at the very least.

What are the coordinates for this planet? she typed.

Slowly, sluggishly, the screen changed.

0-0-0

Andra ran a hand through her shorn dark hair, her fingers catching on the knots. She shouldn't have been surprised the 'bot was glitching. It had obviously seen better days.

Did we crash?

The screen blanked for a moment. *I'm sorry. I don't understand the question.*

You had to be so specific with these models. Andra wiped away a trickle of sweat before typing, *Did the Ark crash?*

No.

"Where is it?" she asked. The holo'display responded.

In geosynchronous orbit.

She took a deep breath. Okay. If the ship was orbiting the planet, she was on Holymyth and the rest of the colonists had to be here too.

The Ark was big. Big enough to hold a million people. Because of its size, it couldn't be built on-planet. It would require too much force to boost through the atmosphere, so it was built in space by a crew of astro'constructionists. After the colonists had been put in stasis, 'bots had shuttled them to the Ark, and then—because the ship couldn't land either—used the same shuttles to take them to the planet's surface once they reached Holymyth. They'd been in stasis the entire journey, so Andra never actually saw the inside of the ship that carried her across the galaxy, but at least it was still in orbit above her.

"The Ark colonists, where are they?" Andra asked.

The holo'display blipped, the harsh sun gleaming off the 'bot's open palm, and she heard the *kachunk, kachunk* of an overheated processor. She just hoped the data files weren't as corrupted as the 'display.

"Where is everybody? Are they still asleep?"

"Is who still asleep?" Zhade asked from behind her, and she realized she'd started speaking out loud. "The other goddesses? You're the last."

The *last*? The last what?

She turned to Zhade, narrowing her eyes, and examined him. He was a soldier. She could tell by the way he held himself, the calculating look in his eyes. The armor, of course. He was trying too hard to look casual, comfortable, but really, he was reading the situation, creating contingency plans. *Why would he need contingency plans?*

"Where are we?" she asked slowly. "What do you call this place?"

He shrugged, looking around the village. The crowd still watched, mesmerized. "The wasters call it the Hell-mouth." He gestured to his surroundings, as if to say, *Can you blame them?*

Andra tugged at the too-tight sleeves where sand had wedged against her skin. "Well, that's ominous."

"Scuze?" He laughed to himself. "No shakes. Now that you've woken, we can convo how you can—"

"You woke me up," Andra interrupted. She tried to ignore the fact that this random person—not a cryo'tech, not a doctor—had pulled her *naked* from her 'tank and then *dressed* her. She'd come back to that later.

He grimaced, annoyed, and ran a hand through his blond hair. "Certz. I've been looking for you for four years, and I had no plans to fork that grave all the way back to Eerensed. Have you tried lifting that thing?"

"You've been looking for me?"

He nodded.

"For four years?"

He nodded again.

Just as soon as Andra thought she'd fit all the pieces together, they fell apart in her hands. Maybe . . . maybe her 'tank had been lost once they reached the colony, and people had been sent to look for her. But how had she gotten lost? And how had she ended up here—in an obviously remote part of Holymyth? She swallowed her panic.

The soldier crossed his arms. "I've been looking ever since they peaced me out. You, my reluctant little Goddess, are my mark back acity."

"Zhade," a new voice said, a reprimand.

Behind Zhade stood a man dressed just like him—unkempt, sand-stained clothing beneath leather armor. His expression was kinder, though. He had a warm brown complexion, a tousle of chestnut curls hanging over piercing black eyes. Dimples beneath a thin beard.

He stood apart from the crowd, as though he didn't quite belong with them, and bowed to Andra. "Goddess."

She was really starting to hate that word.

"What Zhade *purposes* to say," the man said, straightening, "is that your people need you. Eerensed is dying. Without a goddess to sustain the gods' dome, it will fail. We were . . . sent to find you." His accent was formal and obviously didn't sit comfortably on his tongue.

"I don't understand . . . *any* of that," she said.

Zhade placed a hand on the other man's shoulder, pushing him back gently. "Scuze, Wead. Give her airspace. You overwhelm her." He turned back to Andra. "Soze, we need to go soon and sooner. *Four years*, Goddess. Time runs."

It didn't make sense.

Four years.

She'd been missing for four years.

Andra's stomach dropped at the thought of her family and friends living those years without her, moving forward while she was in stasis. Oz would be thirteen now. He had become a teenager while she was still one herself.

She turned back to the 'bot. "Where are the Ark colonists?"

It whirred, *kachunked*, and the light in its pupilless eyes dimmed as its humming devolved into a grinding whine.

"Damn it," Andra mumbled to herself, then turned to Zhade. "Do you have something long and sharp?"

He looked confused for a moment, but then reached for something—a dagger?—in a sheath at his side. Then, he seemed to think better of it and turned to his friend. "Wead? You hold a stick?"

His friend blinked, expression blank. "Neg. I'm not forking a *stick* in the middle of a Wastern village."

One of the villagers—a woman about Andra's mother's age, with stringy hair and paper-white skin—let out a startled cry and ran into a nearby boulder hut. Moments later, she returned with a metal spike. Resting it in her open palms, she bowed and offered it to Andra.

She took it hesitantly. "Uh, thank you?"

The woman beamed. Andra turned back to the 'bot. It was dark and still, but if it had truly died, its working nanos would have been released to find new homes. It probably just needed a reset. She turned the 'bot around, found the port at the base of the neck, and drove the spike home.

The crowd gasped.

"What are you doing?" Zhade demanded, and he sounded offended, maybe even scared.

Andra dug the spike in deeper. "This is a reset port. There's a cluster of nano'bots at the base that sort of act as the center to the circulatory system. Stabbing them is like giving it a jolt of robotic adrenaline."

Andra waited for a click. Ideally, this would be done with a reset pick, which would simultaneously reboot the 'bot while downloading any software updates it was missing. But in a pinch, any sharp object thrust into the port would at least restart it. She finally heard the click, and the 'bot hummed back to life, its hollow eyes flashing a yellowish white. The crowd behind her stirred with frenzied whispers. Andra handed the spike back to the villager, whose wide eyes remained unblinking as she took it and backed away from Andra with a terrified expression.

"Where are the Ark colonists?" she asked the 'bot again.

It hummed but didn't respond. The holo'screen lit from its palm but remained blank. Time to be more specific.

"Where is Isla Watts?"

The 'display blinked before giving an answer.

Dead.

"What?"

The screen remained unchanged. The arid air felt suddenly chilled.

"Elaborate," she choked out.

The colonists signed up for the generation ship Arcanum, commonly referred to as the Ark, are dead. Isla Watts is dead.

"Auric Lim." Dad.

Dead.

"Oz Watts." Her baby brother.

Dead.

"Acadia Watts. Cruz Alvarez. Briella Jackson. Rhin Valentino."

Dead. Dead. Dead. Dead.

They were . . . She couldn't even think it. It didn't make sense. How could everyone . . . And she . . .

A wave of dizziness hit her. She'd just seen them. Minutes before she was put to sleep, she'd left them in the waiting room. Her dad had mumbled something about being proud of her and patted her head like she was a child, or one of his bichons. Acadia, her older sister, didn't spare her a second glance, too busy pinging her instructors from her holo'band, making sure her credits would transfer interplanetarily. (They would.) Oz hugged her with tears in his eyes. Mom had given her a tight smile, still angry about their fight. *See you on Holymyth,* she'd said. Then, *You're going to regret not shaving your head.*

At the memory, Andra almost sank to her knees, but a hand caught her elbow.

Zhade cleared his throat. "Goddess?"

"Stop calling me that!" she snapped, pulling away from him. "I'm not a goddess!"

Rage shot through her, surprising in its intensity. Little realizations burst into her thoughts, faster and faster, like water coming to a boil. *She was alone. There'd been an accident. She'd slept too long. No one was coming to help her. The other colonists were gone. Her mother wasn't coming to check her vitals. Everyone she knew was dead.*

She didn't know how she knew these things, but somehow they felt real. No—they didn't feel *real* at all. They felt *true*.

She screamed, hands clenched at her side. The sound started low in her stomach, clawing its way through her throat and bursting from her lips. It drifted into the desert, falling flat on the wind.

The crowd cowered, and Andra sucked in a breath, taking in the frightened villagers. Sand stung her eyes, and she wiped away tears.

"Sorry," she muttered.

She had never made anyone cower before. She wasn't exactly intimidating. She was chubby and all dimples and too many teeth. But the people looked at her like she could snuff them out of existence with a thought.

"Evens, it's for certz you exist a goddess *now*," Zhade said. He walked over to the 'bot and slung his arm around it. "You just had a full convo with an angel. If the immortality did not convince me, *that* did. Only goddesses and sorcers can talk to angels."

Wherever she was, 'bots were angels and Andra was a goddess and her family was dead.

"You speak with angels. You rose from the grave. Admit it. You exist a goddess."

She gritted her teeth. She knew he didn't mean *grave* or *goddess* in the same way she understood it, but between that and her dead family and calling the planet the Hell-mouth—

She froze.

Hell-mouth.

Holymyth. Hell-mouth.

Maybe the people weren't being fatalistic at all. The villagers weren't speaking English, but maybe that was because English had changed. Words were living things. Shifting, adapting, evolving. Growing and shrinking to fill the space. Rising to meet needs, and falling away when obsolete. How long would it take for English to become unrecognizable to her?

"What year is it?" she asked.

Zhade narrowed his dark eyes. "I don't comp. It's *this* year. The year after last. The year before next, if it comes."

"That doesn't help." Andra turned to the 'bot. "What year is it?"

It groaned. The interface stuttered, a quick blip of data bytes firing, muffled calculations, and the 'display blinked back to life. A date spun in the 'bot's open palm.

3102.

"No," she breathed. "The *Gregorian* calendar. What year is it?"

She waited. The 'display refreshed, but the number remained the same.

"What's your malfunction, you piece of empty? I'm asking for the date." She struck the info'bot. It rang out, tinny and hollow. The mechanics inside whirred as it processed the insult, lights flashing rapidly along the exposed wires under its transparent skull.

I apologize for displeasing you.

But the year is still 3102.

The 'bot was tattered and decrepit, an inch away from a mechanical death, its processing speed slower than the old data'pads in Andra's school library, but if there was one thing a 'bot could do, it was tell time.

She was on Holymyth, the colonists were dead, and the year was 3102.

She hadn't overslept by four years.

She'd overslept by a thousand.

THREE

belonging, n.

Etymology: Middle English belongen: to long.

Definition: 1. a possession.

2. colloq.: a feeling of acceptance in a group or society.

ANDRA WAS GOOD with numbers, but she *loved* words. Numbers were black-and-white, never changing. One plus one would always equal two, from here to eternity, until the end of time, and the square root of 1,764 would never not be 42, and yes, Andra knew that off the top of her head. Words, on the other hand, were amorphous and fuzzy and fickle, and that made them infinitely more interesting. Words were alive. Numbers were tools.

343,568 days since she went into stasis.

987,432 colonists, now all centuries-dead.

8.2 trillion miles between her and Earth.

The numbers fell short of the reality.

The desert felt too large. The crowd felt too close. She broke out in a cold sweat, and sand clung to her exposed skin.

"I need to get out of here," she gasped.

"Certz . . ." Zhade said. "There's . . . not many spaces to peace to . . ." He looked around, as if something would suddenly appear.

Andra pushed past him. Her heart was racing, and blackness crowded her vision. Despite the frenzy happening in her mind, her brain seemed ultra-focused, dissecting and analyzing her new situation with brutal clarity. She ran across the ground of a desert planet, surrounded by people who thought she was a goddess, a millennium after her family had lived and died without her.

"Wait!" Zhade called, but she didn't listen. She had a singular focus: getting away from the gawking crowd and the stranger who'd woken her. Running from the 'bot that just told her that her family was dead, had been for a thousand years, and that Andra was alone.

She was halfway back to the hut when a glimpse of something stopped her. Up on a hill, overlooking the village, was Andra's empty cryo'tank.

IT WASN'T SO much a hill as it was a dune, and it took all of Andra's remaining strength to climb it. The sand was dark orange in the late-evening light, and the sky stretched in a cloudless expanse. She collapsed next to her empty cryo'tank, which had been left in a puddle of 'protectant residue, the tubing and life-support systems lying in tangles, spilled intestines of a complex machine reduced to its basic parts. She hauled herself up, examining the open 'tank, running her fingers over the now-warm glass casing.

She touched it almost reverently. It had held her for nearly a thousand years. That was fifty times the longest human trials. Ten times longer than her family had been in stasis. Longer than her family had been dead.

In the distance, children squealed and shrieked as they chased an animal that looked like a cross between a fox and a dog. Colonists' descendants playing with a space desert fox/dog in a society who worshipped her as a goddess.

She wiped the sweat beneath her eyes and tried to puzzle out what had happened, but she didn't have enough pieces to create a whole picture. The Lacuna Athenaeum Corporation had put together a plan to begin colonizing other planets. More specifically, Dr. Alberta Griffin, the founder of LAC and certified tech genius, had instigated everything: from cryonics to shuttles to generation ships to terraforming. To the 'bots and AI that would oversee it all. She was everything Andra wasn't. Tall, thin, blonde, intimidating, goal-oriented. Mom had introduced Andra to her boss a dozen times, and Dr. Griffin had been impressed with Andra's natural abilities in STEM disciplines. She was less than impressed with Andra's disinterest in them.

Words. That's what Andra wanted to study. Words.

Sweat trickled down her back, the heat suffocating, each breath sticking in her throat, right above her sternum.

She was utterly alone—there was no one to tell her what to do, or even explain what was happening. She couldn't rely on her mom to take care of everything, or even Acadia to boss her around. *Because they're dead*, she thought. She couldn't *fix* this; she could only understand, and there was only one place she could think to get any answers.

She bent over the data'screen at the head of her 'tank. If it had kept her alive for the last thousand years, surely it would still have all its data files intact as well. She fought the urge to use her currently useless neural'implant and instead lifted the shield panel that protected the 'display. It blinked to life, and the Lacuna Athenaeum Corporation's infinite double-helix swirled on the screen. Andra tapped the controls until she found the holo'display. Everything was recorded when it came to cryonics. A person in stasis was practically dead, completely dependent on the cryo'techs, which scared people enough to pass legislation that every cryonics company had to keep records of every moment spent in stasis. So there had to be recordings of what happened to the 'tank over the last thousand years.

What happened to *Andra* over the last thousand years.

The records folder was easy enough to find. She filtered through the time stamps, skimming through October 2161, but there, the files abruptly stopped. No records after the month she'd been put into stasis. There weren't even any spaces where the recordings had been. It was like they had never existed in the first place.

The squeals of the playing children faded, and a buzzing took its place. Andra stared at the empty folder long enough for the 'screen to blank and the now-holographic LAC logo to take its place.

Not that any of it mattered—the missing files, the broken 'tank. It wouldn't change the fact that she'd overslept, that she was abandoned on a desert planet in the future, that her family was dead. Had they lived long, happy lives without her? Had Acadia gotten five degrees and ruled the world? Had Oz grown up to become a drone racer?

Andra had to take deep breaths to steady herself. None of this should have happened. There was no way she shouldn't have woken up with the others, and it was next to impossible for there to be no record of what happened embedded into her 'tank. There were redundancies built into the system, checks and balances, fail-safes, protocols for every contingency.

Except, apparently, for this. Whatever this was.

She'd gone into stasis, flown across the galaxy, arrived at Holy-myth, and then . . . what? *Something* had happened.

The sun was getting low on the horizon. The shadows lengthened. It was still hot. There was a scuffle of sand behind her as Zhade's friend, the one with the kind eyes, made his way up the hill. When he reached her, he sat, cocking his knees and resting his arms on them. She thought she could wait him out, ignore him until he went away. But he sat in silence, watching the children play.

"I never wanted to come," she said, surprised the words were leaving her mouth, that she was divulging this truth to a stranger. "Mom and I had a huge fight about it, and I was tempted to just not go through with the process. What could she do? I'd be dead by the time they found out. And instead, they—"

She cut off, holding back tears.

She'd argued with her mother countless times over joining the colony. To Isla, it was a given. *Of course* they would go to Holymyth. It was, after all, her life's work. But it wasn't Andra's.

She wasn't sure what her life's work would be, but it felt tied to Earth. When she told her mother this, Isla had rolled her eyes. Andra's place was where Isla told her it was. They were a family, and they would stick together. Andra couldn't help but think her mom's adamance was less out of motherly affection and more about her need for control.

Now, here Andra was, on a planet she didn't even want to be on, alone, with no clue as to what happened or what to do next.

She dug her heel into the sand. "They're gone, instead," she finished.

The man beside her looked confused but nodded sympathetically. "Sorries, Goddess."

She winced. "Please don't call me that. It's Andromeda. Or Andra. Everybody calls me Andra."

"Andra," he repeated, misshaping the vowels, stumbling over the string of consonants. "It exists an honor. I'm Lew-Eadin. Wead as a shortcut."

Andra wrinkled her nose. "Yeah, I'm just going to call you Lew."

He laughed, though she didn't understand the joke. "Lew. Certz, then, Goddess." He shook his head. "Sorries. Andra."

Below, one of the children shouted above the rest, a long string of words Andra couldn't understand. She was starting to recognize patterns though, mining familiar syllables from the mush of elongated vowels and clipped consonants. She itched to write down what they were saying, to map it out.

The soldier laughed at something one of the children said.

Andra nodded to them. "How come you don't speak like they do?"

"I do," he said, raking his hand through his brown curls. "But when I convo with a goddess, I speak High Goddess. I learned it from the First, as did Zhade. As did most of Eerensed, which you will hear if you come with us."

The children dove for the fox/dog, their smudged faces lit with intensity.

"Come with you?" Andra murmured, but it wasn't really a question, just an absurd idea—tagging along with strangers to a place she knew nothing about. But on the heels of that absurd idea came the realization that she was low on options.

Lew-Eadin was quiet for a moment. "Firm, come with us. You can save us."

She snorted. "I'm not a goddess."

"So you say," Lew-Eadin said, smiling, though he gave her a sideways look. "But, full respect, I can't say I believe you."

Andra shrugged, tearing up a tuft of brown, crisp grass. "Suit yourself."

Lew-Eadin blinked, obviously confused by the phrase, but didn't comment. There was movement behind them, and Andra turned to see that Zhade had climbed the hill. His hood was pulled over his head, and the bandages on his hands had been replaced with fingerless gloves. He sat, wriggling between them and kicking up a cloud of sand in the process. Andra's eyes smarted.

"Wead, are you talking gnats with our Goddess here?" Zhade asked, then let out a cheer as one of the children launched themself at the fox/dog and missed, the animal slithering its way through the child's arms. He turned back to Lew. "She's had a day and a half. Leave her resting."

Andra fought back an eye roll. She was starting to make sense of Zhade's speech patterns, and if anyone was "talking gnats," it was him. She had the feeling he wasn't being honest or, at least, wasn't telling the whole truth.

"You woke me up," she said. It was an accusation this time. He had no right. And maybe she was still a bit mad he'd seen her naked. The paunch of her stomach, the heft of her thighs. The birthmark she hated—a starburst of dense freckles, like a pointillist painting, just under the left side of her collarbone.

"Firm," Zhade said slowly, then bit his lip. "We've convoed this already. Do you have no memory? We woke you. I'm Zhade, this is Lew-Eadin. You're the Third Goddess, the one who will save us all, stop the pockets, restore the forests and seas, which personalish, I don't believe ever existed. Just fishes and wishes. More importantish, you'll get me back to Eerensed."

She narrowed her eyes. It shouldn't have been possible—some random person waking her up. People went to school for years to become cryo'technicians. "You understand manual technology."

He leaned forward. "I don't comp what that means, but it sounds full good, marah?"

"How did you know how to wake me up?"

"I'm a sorcer, Goddess." He grinned. "Best there is."

"Where did you learn how to open my 'tank?"

He shrugged, his expression blank. "From another sorcer. In Eerensed. Where I once lived. Where I'm taking you now that I've found you, Goddess."

She scratched at the sand crawling down her neck. "My name's Andra, and I've told you, I'm not a goddess." She paused, cocking her head to examine him. He seemed arrogant and ridiculous, but his brown eyes were clear, sane. "Surely you can't believe I am."

Zhade picked up a flat rock and twirled it between his fingers, leaning back on his other hand. "I reck you were agrave for as long as anyone has memory. I reck you could probablish perform magic beyond the best sorcer." He leaned forward conspiratorially, his blond hair flopping over his eyes. "Which is me, beedub." He sat back. "I reck you speak High Goddess full flawless. And I just witnessed you come back to life. If you're not a goddess, what are you?"

Just Andra. Twenty-second-century teenager and all-around under-achiever.

"I'm from . . . the past," Andra said, wincing. Even to her ears, it sounded fantastical.

Zhade let out a bark of a laugh. "Me too. I traveled here from the moment before this one."

"That's not what I meant."

"I reck full well."

He watched her for a moment. Andra stared back, tugging at the tight material of the borrowed shirt where it had ridden up over her stomach.

"I'm not a goddess," she muttered.

Zhade waved his hand, dismissive. "Fortunatish for me, it doesn't import what you for true are. It's full good that people *believe* you exist a goddess. The Guv will let me in if I have you with me."

"So I'm a bargaining chip?"

"Neg. For certz not." He paused. "What's a bargaining chip?"

"You're using me to get what you want."

"Oh, then firm. You're definitish a bargaining chip."

Andra stood, beating the sand off her pants. "I'm not going with you to this Ear-and-sand," she said, though she wasn't so sure. What other options did she have? Stay here? In this town where she didn't speak the language, didn't know how to survive?

"Eerensed," Zhade corrected. "And I resurrected you. You owe me."

"She literalish just woke, sir," Lew-Eadin's voice was bored, per-functory, as though he were used to arguing with Zhade. His accent grew thicker, more natural. "She needs time and a half to adjust."

"Psh." Zhade ducked his chin.

"I don't know you," Andra said. "You could be anyone, and brag-ging about being banished from your hometown isn't a great recom-mendation."

Zhade looked affronted, started spluttering an argument, but Andra cut him off.

"I owe you nothing. Thanks for waking me, but I didn't *ask* you to, and honestly . . ." She took a deep breath. ". . . I probably would have been better off left in that 'tank. I'm not a goddess or a sorcer or whatever, and I certainly can't *save* anyone. I'm just a normal girl in a—" She laughed under her breath, kicking her foot lightly against her 'tank. "—a ridiculous situation, and all I want now is to figure out what happened to my family and try to get a ride back home—"

Her voice caught. She swallowed, thinking of home. Of Earth.

Earth: the blue-and-green ball hanging in space, third planet from Sol. But also Earth: the scent of rain in spring and the sound of leaves crunching in autumn. The park where she and Oz would race drones. Her favorite sushi restaurant. Getting hit with a blast of cold water when the shower temp'con glitched. The wall of pre-books in her room. Warm socks.

One thousand years. All of that would be gone now or changed beyond recognition. She didn't have a home to go back to. She felt the hot smart of tears welling in her eyes. Zhade didn't notice, and Lew pretended not to.

"I can't go with you," she mumbled. One tear slid free and she quickly swiped it away.

Zhade blinked into the desert wind, then nodded seriously. "Certz, certz." He stood up with a groan, dusting off his pants. "I was hoping, but fishes and wishes, marah? It's your fate to decide."

At the bottom of the hill, there was a high-pitched cry. One of the children had stabbed a knife into the fox/dog. The animal whimpered, and the child—a girl of about six—twisted the knife until the animal fell silent. Andra gasped, covering her mouth to hold in a scream. The other children whined words she couldn't understand.

"I spoze her fam will have meat tonight." Zhade didn't look at Andra. Instead, he watched the girl haul the carcass across the desert. "If she were in Eerensed, she wouldn't have to worry. We have full bars meat. Angels to cook for us. And a gods' dome to protect us from pockets."

Zhade turned to go, but one of the words in his strange dialect cut through the fog in Andra's mind.

"A, uh, gods' dome? Was it always there?"

On this strange planet where 'bots were angels and a girl in stasis was a goddess, a gods' dome must be a bio'dome. And this city Zhade talked about wasn't replete with magic—or gifts from benevolent gods—but with technology.

Zhade shook his head, a ghost of a smirk tugging at his lips, and Andra felt like she'd somehow stepped into a trap. "Neg. The First created it."

"The First what?" Andra asked.

"The First Goddess," he said simply. "Did you imagine you were the sole one?"

Andra's breath hitched, her heart stopped. Other "goddesses"? That could mean other colonists like her, who hadn't woken with the others. People from her time. From Earth. Too many questions sifted through her head, and she spluttered out the first one she could catch. "How many?"

Zhade shrugged, but the movement was anything but casual. "Three we reck. *The First was the goddess of knowledge and light,*" he recited. *"The Second brought us chaos and fright. The Third—"*

"And the other two? They were like me?"

"Impatient?"

"Frozen. In a 'tank."

The side of Zhade's mouth twitched. "Certz. Immortal and unchanging and powerful."

Maybe Andra wasn't the only colonist left. She didn't want to hope, but perhaps these other goddesses were women she knew. Whoever this First was, she'd *created* a fully functioning bio'dome. You had to be a certified genius to do that. There were a handful of people Andra could think of from her time who were capable of something like that. And one of them was her mother.

But the 'bot had said Andra's mother was dead. Maybe it was mistaken, or misinterpreting data. 'Bots weren't omniscient after all; they could only recite the information fed to them. And they weren't AI; they couldn't deduce. *Someone* had sent Zhade to find Andra, and who would do that, if not her own mother? It was too much to hope for—that she had some family left—and she tried to tamp down the thought.

"I'll go with you," she said, and watched Zhade's smile spread.

Something about it didn't seem genuine. Too many teeth.

"But you'll tell me everything you can about the goddesses on the way."

Zhade's smile twitched, showing a single dimple in his left cheek. He blinked slowly. "I'll tell you as much as I can." He gave Lew-Eadin a look Andra couldn't interpret, then started to descend the hill. "Full good. We'll peace in the moren. Decide your fate, Goddess," he called over his shoulder, and then he was gone.

Andra watched as his footprints filled back up with sand. "He's a bit . . . much," she said, but her mind was spinning with possibilities.

"He's intoleristic," Lew answered, but laughter tinged his voice.

The wind picked up and Andra was forced to cover her face or get a mouthful of sand. What little skin she had exposed started to sting, a million tiny pricks.

"We aged up together." Lew's voice was muffled by his sweater. "He's . . . more than he seems." After a moment, he asked, "Why don't you reck you exist a goddess?"

"The same reason you don't think you're a giant. Because I'm not one."

"Certz to full small creatures, I *am* a giant."

Andra laughed.

"Amid their own kind," Lew said slowly, "gods might not seem so special, but among mere mortals . . ." He let the implication hang in the air and stood. "I'd best make certz he doesn't set anything afire."

Andra eyed the rock town below. If anyone could set fire to stone, it would be Zhade.

Lew bowed slightly, just a dip of his head. "Goddess," he said, then caught himself. "Andra."

"Lew." She nodded back and he smiled before following his friend down the hill.

Andra waited at the top of the dune until the sun started to set. Not the sun she knew. Not Sol, but Andromeda. Her mother had named her after the star that supported Holymyth. With Earth's resources dwindling, the only option for sustaining the growing population was to spread across the galaxy, to travel to the nearest habitable planet, orbiting a sun not too different from their own. *Humanity's last hope*, her mother called it. *Andromeda will save us all*. What a joke, Andra thought.

She moved to the foot of the 'tank, where her belongings were kept. She pressed her hand to the scanner, and it beeped as it read her DNA signature. The drawer popped open with a hiss as the tech'stasis seal was broken. The compartment was the size of a standard suitcase— large enough for all the trinkets and 'bands and memories too precious to be parted from—and Andra had filled it to the brim with tablets and pre-books and clothes and the blanket she'd slept with until she was twelve. She'd filled it with home.

She reached in, her fingers grasping for the blanket, but instead, they met nothing but air. No 'band, no tablet filled with pics and music and books. No dress she was going to wear on her first day on Holymyth. Everything was gone.

"Looking for this?"

Andra whipped around to find Zhade had returned. His hand was held out, and dangling from his fingers was her holocket.

The faux-gold chain glinted in the dying light, ending in a star-shaped charm. It was stupid and pointless and sentimental, and Andra snatched it from Zhade's hands, hanging it around her neck with a sigh of strange relief.

It was a child's toy. Outdated years before she got it. So obsolete, even if her 'implant had been working, it couldn't have communicated with the 'locket. Cheap tech and even cheaper metal. There was no way it still worked.

"Where's the rest of my stuff?" Andra snapped. She thought about her security blanket and the first-edition pre-book copy of *I Think I Speak for Everyone* and the purple holo'band she'd gotten for her sixteenth birthday.

"That was all there was," Zhade said, his expression so disarmingly earnest, she actually believed him.

"Oh," she said. "Thanks."

He nodded. "Firm. Does it import?"

"Yeah," she said, her fist clenched around the 'locket.

She'd kept it because Oz had given it to her. He'd won it at a raffle at school when he was five, and even then, he was enamored with outdated tech. He'd carried that thing around for weeks, agonizing over how to use the memory slots. One day, Andra was upset about something—she didn't even remember what—but Oz had sneaked into her room, where she was curled up in a ball, crying silently, and he slipped the 'locket into her hand.

She didn't have the heart to tell him it was next to useless. 'Bands could store hundreds of petabytes. The 'locket had space for six single-gig memories. But she'd taken it from him, because she could tell he was proud of himself for his generosity. She'd used the memory slots to record random moments. They'd seemed mundane at the time, but now they were all she had of her past. Precious. Cruz was in there. And Briella and Rhin. Oz. Her family.

The wind picked up, almost a cool breeze. Zhade squinted into the sun, his hands in his pockets.

"I reck what it's like," he said, "to lose fam. To lose everyone." His eyes met hers. "Sorries. I wouldn't wish it on anyone."

Andra pursed her lips, swallowing her grief. Zhade nodded once, something serious and reassuring in his gaze, and then, without another word, he sauntered away, humming to himself as he descended the dune.

She turned to watch the sunlight fade to gray across the desert, 'locket clutched to her chest. It wasn't until her namesake disappeared below the horizon that Andromeda made her way down the hill.

FOUR

THE SOLDIER

ZHADE HATED THE Wastes. At least in Rocco, or any of the other desert villages he'd visited, he could pretend he was somewhere else— some obscure part of Eerensed where nothing grew and everything was falling apart—but once he left the shelter of civilization, it was glaringish obvi he was mereish a small speck in a vast sky of sand. *Oceans* of sand, the First had called the Wastes. Zhade tried to imagine all the sand replaced with water, but it seemed impossible.

Fishes and wishes, the Eerensedians would say. Meaning, *You might as well wish for the ocean.*

Zhade didn't believe the ocean had ever existed.

The desert spread out ahead of them, barren and endless. Nothing for miles except the road they followed, marked by a yellow line in the sand. Heat waves wafted in the distance. Zhade huddled in the back of their (borrowed) cart with the Goddess, while Wead led the (stolen) horse (*don't you dare tell the Goddess, Wead*) at an infuriatingish slow pace. Up and down dunes. Bell after bell. A dense fog of dust billowed ahead. Sandclouds. They were prominent in this part of the Wastes. Not dangerful, but not a piece of cuppins either.

It was a fault of his upbringing that he'd been full unprepped for the Wastes when he was exiled. He'd never been outside of the city til he suddenish was. He was clever, resourceful, a survivor. But navigating the streets and politics of Eerensed hadn't prepped him for making his march through the Wastes. There was no one to charm food out of, nothing to trade for protection, and nothing—full nothing—he could do to hide from the pockets. He was powerless.

He didn't like being powerless.

Most of his kidhood had been spent in hiding, tossed from cave to cave at the whim of others. His mam's whims, mostish. It was full rare he'd had any say in the meteor. She determined where he went and with whom and when. *For your own good*, she'd said. Zhade had yet to see this "good" of his she convoed. Still, he was following her whims, though she was dead and sunk into stardust. It was habit.

Take this, she'd said, giving him the icepick dagger, and he'd taken it. It still hung in a thin sheath at his side.

Find the Third, she'd said, and he'd spent his full banishment searching.

Don't let Maret have the crown, she'd said, and there Zhade had failed.

Maret already had the throne, and the best Zhade could do now was overthrow him.

Fishes and wishes.

At least he had found the Third—a nearish impossible task considering his searching radius was anywhere in the world. The Eerensedians would have called it fate. Zhade wanted to laugh at that. He had his own thoughts bout fate.

The cart rocked beneath them as Zhade looked over at the Goddess— *Andra*, she kept insisting. She'd salted him with questions, almost nonstop, since they'd peaced. *Why hadn't she woken earlier? Why did people worship her? Who stole her from Eerensed? What are the other goddesses like?* She got frustrated when he couldn't—or wouldn't—answer, stewing with her arms crossed and brow furrowed.

The Goddess had lain in the Yard for most of Zhade's kidhood— and for hundreds of years before he was born. He had memories of visiting her agrave, seeing her blurred shape through frosted glass, listening to the prayers and chants of the other visitors—the ones who *believed* in her and *hoped* she would wake soon to save them.

Zhade recked too much to believe or hope. But he'd gone with his mother once a turn to visit the Second and Third. He never prayed or chanted or took part in any of the rituals. Zhade's mam never prayed either, mereish watched, like she was waiting for something, but Zhade never recked what. Then the Second woke, and everything went to sands, and not long after, the Third vanished. Some said she'd woken. Others said she'd been stolen. It had always been Zhade's goal to find her eventualish—he'd trained on how to wake her, what to do after—but his mother's death and his banishment had sped up his plans a bit.

Neg. Not his plans. His *mother's* plans.

After the Third's disappearance, Zhade's memories of the Goddess had warped and faded. Now, faced with the reality of her . . . Evens. He'd always imagined if she came to life, she would be like the First. Wise, brilliant, and intimidating. But this girl—this girl was nothing like a goddess should be.

She was too unconfident, too uncomfortistic in her own skin. Shrewd and calculating, certz. But too uncertz of herself.

Easyish manipulated.

Zhade bit back a smile.

This had happened better than he imagined. Not sole could she get him back acity (he was certz of it—Maret wouldn't pass the opportunity to hoist his own popularity with a newish-arisen goddess), but he could use her to enact his plan.

This time, it was *his* plan, and his plan alone.

Decide your fate, the Eerensedians would say. It was hello and goodbye and the first part of an old saying fewer and fewer people had memory of. *Decide your fate, or fate will decide for you.*

Zhade had enough of fate deciding for him. He was determined to shape his own future. A future that required the Third Goddess accompanying him back to Eerensed and staying whole and full well til the time came for her to be of further use.

The cart jolted to a stop, and the Goddess slammed against him. He held back what he wanted to say—something bout her throwing herself at him. Flirting was its own kind of magic and there was a delicate balance to it—too much and it lost its power.

She scrambled away from him. "Why are we stopping?" Her accent made Zhade's stomach lurch. It was exactish like the First's.

He pushed himself up to see why Lew-Eadin had stopped, and then slumped back down with a groan.

"New one, sir," Wead said, as though Zhade couldn't see for himself. A pocket.

"What?" The Goddess scrambled to see over the side of the wagon. She froze when she saw what was afront of them.

A blackened, churning mass swallowed the road ahead, darkening the sky and sand and everything beyond. It reached past the clouds and across the desert, and now that Zhade recked it was there, he couldn't miss its droning hum. No one was full certz what pockets were. The opposite of existence. Void and fire and nothing. A single monster or an amalgam of roiling, cloud-like spirits. The Three's worshippers believed pockets were a corruption of magic. The sorcers sole recked they were death. Whatever they were, they appeared out of nowhere, with no warning. Living in the Wastes meant living in constant fear that one day a pocket would descend and you would blink out of existence. They always gave Zhade the fraughts.

This particular pocket was enormous. The biggest Zhade had ever seen, as a fact. The yellow road that led them disappeared into the pocket, swallowed by the darkness. It would take them bells and bells to go round.

Andra let out a low curse, voice trembling.

Zhade tried to hide his smile. Not that he hadn't felt the same kiddun-like awe and horror the first time he'd seen a pocket, but what was experience for, if not to deride those who lacked it?

He stretched, twisting and popping his back. Sweat trickled down Zhade's spine, and his full body was gritty with sand. He was used to it though. This had been his life for four years.

"Go round," he muttered, gnatted that Wead needed the instruction soon and sooner.

"What is it?" the Goddess asked, her eyes stuck on the seething darkness. That was a good march to insanity.

"A pocket," Zhade answered. "Places nothing can live."

She nodded, but he could tell she didn't full comp.

That was perfect. The less she recked, the more she would rely on Zhade.

Wead urged the horse forward and the cart gave another jolt as they turned off the road. The surrounding desert had grown more craggy and less sandy as they got closer to the city, and the cart jostled as they navigated the rocks.

Zhade saw the Goddess give the pocket one last look before she sat back down. Then her dark eyes met Zhade's, and he felt something most definitish not guilt twist his stomach.

THE WASTES DRAGGED on, a collection of jagged boulders and scragglish flora. Wead resolutish made his march round the edge of the pocket, looking for the gods' road, urging the horse to go as fast as it could, but many laps stood between them and their goal, and the horse was drained, both from distance and the desert heat. It got in their skin, and Zhade felt like groose wrapped in tin and put in the oven.

The night was another meteor. The Wastes grew intolerish cold at night, but over the years, Zhade had learned to tolerate it. The Goddess, however, had not. Where she was from—the land of the gods or wherever—apparentish did not experience extreme temps. She never complained, but as they huddled together under the bed of the cart, tangled in blankets, Zhade could feel her shiver, hear her teeth chatter.

She didn't sleep. Not full true. She pretended, never admitting she lay awake through the night while Zhade and Wead slept, but she would give herself away by fidgeting with the necklace he'd returned to her, and he wondered why it imported. She snapped it open and shut. Whispered *snick-snick snick-snicks* in the darkness. After several bells, her breathing would finalish slow, her body relax, but then she'd jerk awake, as though something had scared her. Zhade didn't say anything til the fourth night, when the *snicking* of the 'locket burnt his last end.

She lay between him and Wead, who had long since sunk off, full asleep with his head propped on his carry-with. She was shivering especialish hard tonight. He tried to huddle closer, but each time he did, she would shift toward Wead. Zhade tried not to take offense, unsuccessfulish. He was an exceptional snuggler.

snick . . . snick . . . snick . . .

He reached over to stop her. She froze before slapping his hand away.

He bit back his retort when he realized it was dark and they were basicalish strangers and he'd touched her without permission. "Sorries." He coughed. At least the snapping had stopped. "You're still awake, marah, Goddess?"

A night wind fluttered past, and he pulled his sweater tight round himself. He covered his mouth and nose, but still choked on sand. A barn loft, or even a smallroom, imagined awfulish good anow.

After a moment, she shrugged. "I don't feel like sleeping."

Zhade turned toward her, sand shifting beneath him, and huffed out a dramistic long-suffering sigh. "Close your eyes, I'll tell you a bedtime story."

The Goddess snorted. "Oh, this ought to be good."

"I'm a massive storyteller. What do you want to hear bout?"

She groaned, looking up through the slats in the wagon. Her eyes narrowed, and Zhade followed her gaze. Nothing but a dusting of stars—the sandclouds had finalish cleared. She was quiet for a time and a half, and if Zhade hadn't spent the last several nights next to her, he might have imagined she'd fallen asleep.

"What do people say about me?" she finalish asked.

Zhade stretched out, placing his hands behind his head, and held his voice low so as not to wake Wead. "That you're massive at parties, but not someone you'd ask to care for small kidduns."

She huffed, but he was certz she was holding back a smile. "Are there *legends* about me? About me being a . . . *goddess* or whatever. My powers, my history?"

For a moment, all he could do was watch her. She looked different in the starlight. Somehow both more and less. Her round cheeks were flushed, her dark eyes sharp and clear. She wore her hair short—not as short as Wastern women did, but much shorter than Eerensedians. It was a black and shiny, like the most expensive armor. He could see the goddess in her, but he could also see the fear. He turned back to the stars. "You're the goddess of virility, and your powers are—"

"If you're going to be like that, we can go back to that village."

He knew she was bluffing. Whatever she was looking for, it wasn't behind them.

"Why do you want to hear your own story?"

"Because," she paused. "I don't know it. I was asleep when my story happened. How on earth did I become a *goddess*?"

Zhade frowned at the phrase, but he comped her meaning. "Certz, *I* would march forward with it." He rolled the kinks out of his neck. "If people want to worship you, I say let them."

"But it's dishonest. I'm letting them believe a lie."

"Who says it's a lie?"

"Um. *Me*." She threw up her hands, almost smacking them against the cart, then dropped her voice when she realized she'd stopped whispering. "I do. I say it's not true."

"Who are you to decide what's true?"

"Apparently, I'm a goddess," she muttered.

"Ha!" Zhade tossed a grin in her direction. When he caught her glowering at him, he shrugged. "You said it, not me."

The Goddess pursed her lips, obvish holding in a laugh, and rolled away from him. Moonlight streaked across her hair.

"Once upon a time," he started.

"Zhade," she groaned, turning back and nudging him. He wanted to laugh at the way she said his name—like she had the sniffs, or a mouth full of butterjam. He wanted to hear it again.

"Do you want to hear this or not?" He didn't wait for a reply. "Once upon a time, there were three goddesses agrave. They were charred and immortal and unchanging. For hundreds of years, the world waited for them to wake, and as time ran, humans grew more desperate for the goddesses to save them. Finalish, the First awoke, and with her, the ability to sorcer the angels. She created the gods' dome and skooled us magic. When the Second woke, she was fiery and fickle and brought disaster. The people waited for the Third, but she vanished, never to be seen again. Evens—" He winked at her. "Til now. And the world grew darker and bleaker and it's said that sole the Third Goddess can save us from the planet trying to kill us." He paused, dropping the singsong quality of his voice. "But do you want to know what I imagine?"

"Not really."

"Stop interrupting." Another pause. "I imagine we did it ourselves. They blame the planet for not wanting us, but what's a planet going to do, marah? It's mereish a big chunk of rock and heat. We're the monsters. We're the ones with the power to destroy . . ."

His voice drifted off. *The power to destroy and create*, his mam had

43

told him, *is a responsibility no one should be burdened with, yet everyone has.* Then she'd given him a dagger and some jewelry and told him to save Eerensed.

That was the last time he saw her. Right before they killed her.

Right before *Maret* killed her.

The Goddess tilted her head, looking up at him under her lashes. "This is starting to be a bit of a downer."

He almost smiled. She could be funny, his Goddess.

"Who kidnapped me?" she asked, her voice drowsy. "And why?"

"Kiddun's naps? What?"

"Who *stole* me? Why did I vanish from the palace?"

"I told you, I don't reck."

The Goddess let out a long sigh, then stilled, as though she were waiting for something. "That rhyme you said back in the village, about the First and Second . . . how did it end?"

Zhade rolled his shoulders. Sand crept under his shirt. *"The First was the goddess of knowledge and light,"* he said slowish. *"The Second brought us chaos and fright. The Third will rise to save us all, if sole mereish before the fall."*

The Goddess was silent again, as though she were sorting through his words and choosing hers at care. "The other goddesses . . . they sent you to find me?"

Zhade hesitated. "Firm . . ."

"Does that mean *yes?*"

"Spoze."

"You're useless." She turned toward him, resting her head on her hands.

"Ah. You say that now."

She lifted a skeptical brow. "But I'll change my mind when we get to Eerensed?"

"Certz, probablish not." He nudged her lightish with his elbow. "Now go to sleep, Goddess. You'll need all your strength to save us."

She was bareish breathing. He'd grown used to the sound of her breaths.

"Save you? By getting you into Eerensed?"

"For starts," he said.

She huffed and turned away. After a moment, she murmured, "G'night."

"Dream well, Goddess." He smiled in the dark.

One more day, two at most, and he'd be home.

Home.

Listening to the hollow pitch of the time chimes. Walking next to the lazy flow of the River Sed. Eating hot, fresh butterjam dumplings under the shadow of the gods' tower. He would do it all. Then the real work would begin. He had the Goddess, and he had a plan. Zhade would decide his fate before fate decided for him.

FIVE

requiem, n.

Etymology: Latin *re-* + *quiēs*: rest.

Definition: 1. a hymn for the dead, a dirge.

2. colloq.: the dreamless sleep experienced by those frozen in cryonic stasis.

NIGHT WAS DIFFERENT on the new planet. It wasn't as dark as Andra thought it should be. The atmosphere on Holymyth must have been thinner than Earth's: the stars felt closer. They glittered, peeking through the slats of the wagon, watching, waiting for her to go to sleep.

They could keep waiting.

She lay between Lew and Zhade—perhaps a bit closer to Lew than Zhade—huddled under a mound of rough-spun covers. She'd heard the desert got cold at night, but this was ridiculous. Even wrapped in layers of knitted clothing, she shivered.

The blanket was rough against her cheek, the night unnaturally quiet. No traffic. No hum of electricity or the whir of security'bots. Not even animals calling in the distance or the wild moaning of wind as it wound its way through the desert. A soft snore rose from Lew's sleeping form. Zhade had quieted after telling her the ridiculous story of the goddesses, but it was impossible to tell if he was asleep without moving closer.

She reached under her shirt and pulled out the holocket, her thumb tracing the clasp. Its contents were all that was left of her family. Of Earth. She held all of human history in her hand. Six random memories. The 'locket was cold against her fingers.

She snapped her eyes open, not realizing they had drifted shut. She didn't want to sleep. She'd already slept too long. Her body felt weird, tingly, like her soul was too big, trying to seep out. Her eyes tried to close again.

No.

When she'd gone into stasis, there'd been no active nanos in her system. If there had been, her 'implant would have saved her when she woke drowning, collecting nearby nanos into a 'swarm, the sole purpose to protect Andra. But there'd been no nanos to collect, either around her or in her body. Just before stasis, they'd been purged from her, the risks of frozen tech outweighing the benefits. No one had even considered nanos would be necessary to save someone from drowning in cryo'protectant, alone, a thousand years late.

Andra hadn't even been given a sedative. Any medical nano'bots roaming around inside her would have been frozen where they were, their tasks on pause. If she'd gone into stasis sedated, she'd have come out of stasis sedated, and that would have been disastrous. So Andra was awake when they froze her.

She remembered.

Remembered being in a box that looked like a coffin, alone, naked. Each roll of skin, the blotchy starburst birthmark on her collarbone, all on display for the cryo'techs and scientists surrounding her. She felt the saline flood the 'tank. It lapped against her body, higher and higher until it covered her, tickling at first, and then all she could think of was holding her breath, closing her eyes. She was submerged. Then, for a split second, she felt herself freeze.

She felt herself die.

Less than a second later—less than an instant—she was waking up again. Drowning in the same water that had just killed her. Somebody pressed the pause button on Andra's life, and then someone else started her up again.

But in the meantime, the world had kept going.

Going and going and going without her for a thousand years.

She was dead for a thousand years.

Dead. Asleep. A matter of terms.

'Tank // Grave

Magic // Technology

Hell-mouth // Holymyth

Teenager // Goddess

Andra gasped awake, her heart pounding so hard it hurt. The stars winked at her. The rough texture of the blankets chafed her skin. She didn't move, only listened to Lew and Zhade's slow breaths, relieved they hadn't noticed her wake. The holocket pressed into her chest, the metal smarting against her sweat-slick skin. She shivered, blinking, her mind refreshing.

She stared at the sky, picking the sand from beneath her nails, counting her breaths.

SOMETHING WAS DIFFERENT. *Something was just as it should be.*

Andra was at her mother's office. At Lacuna Athenaeum headquarters. The sinking sun shone through floor-to-ceiling picture windows, the last rays escaping through the trees silhouetted on the horizon. Her mother's eyes were glazed as she composed a report using her neural'implant, its attached crown gleaming on her forehead, curved around her ear, wired into her brain. Every once in a while she would correct something using the keyboard. She didn't notice Andra slouched in the ergo'chair, clicking her 'locket open and shut. She didn't even look up when Oz started laughing. He had a high, frenzied laugh. A giggle run amok. It was a normal day, and for some reason Andra couldn't pinpoint, that fact filled her with relief. Relief and a strange sadness and the anticipation of disappointment.

Just a normal day. Her family was alive.

Of course they were alive. Why wouldn't they be?

"Oz, quiet down," Mom said. "I have to get these files copied."

"The other kids got to go to the Vaults today," he said. It wasn't a whine, and somehow that made it more pitiful. He, out of all the Watts kids, resembled their father the most. Dark eyes, easy smile, round cheeks. It made people love him without exactly knowing why. People had the urge to avoid Isla Watts, but they had the urge to hug Auric Lim—a trait he'd passed to his son. "They said they played old vid-e-o-games." He stumbled over the word. "Like sims, but you have to use a controller. With your hands."

"Mmm-hmm," Mom said, her eyes still out of focus. Her long, faded-red hair had fallen over one of them, but she didn't seem to notice. It hid the jagged scar that ran along her cheek. The one too deep for doctors to remove. That didn't stop her from trying, though she wouldn't even listen to Andra complain about her birthmark.

"One day I'd like to go." Oz slumped into the chair in the corner, kicking his feet when they didn't quite reach the ground.

Mom didn't bother to answer, and Andra suspected there was no real reason Oz couldn't have gone with his friends. No good one anyway. Mom was just too busy. Too busy making final plans for the Ark passengers. Too busy running tests and sucking up to her boss. Too busy thinking of Holymyth. Her body was still here, but Andra's mother had left Earth long ago.

Andra stared out the windows overlooking the Riverwalk. An entire wall of her mother's office was made up of windows with the best view of the city. She was pretty important at LAC. She had two doctorates: cryonic ethics, and astro-ecological theory. Plus, she was really good at computers. Well. Everyone was good at computers, but not everyone knew how they worked. Andra's mother did.

"And they have one room," Oz was saying, "that's all synth'trees, and an-

other with cos'masks, and you can look however you want, and Raj pinged me a pic of him with a rhinoceros face. Do you know about rhinocerosi?"

"Rhinoceroses," Andra corrected.

"I want to look like the Guardian, from 'Bot Wars." He turned to his sister. "I always play him in the sims. If I had—"

"Isla, I need you to come look at this," a voice interrupted.

Mom's boss, Alberta Griffin—the Alberta Griffin—stood in the doorway. She looked just like she did in the holo'coms, except maybe taller, sharper. Her blonde hair was pulled into a fishtail braid, brow furrowed over her modded left eye. The eye that allowed her to perform calculations and identify variables and foresee probabilities. The eye that lingered on Andra just a little too long.

Always recruiting, Andra thought. Only, Andra didn't want to be recruited.

Dr. Griffin stood tall and regal. Her neural'implant crown was the largest Andra had ever seen, silver and shining along her forehead, glinting from beneath her perfectly styled hair. Most crowns were just a slip of metal-coated tech embedded at the temple—little more than an accessory—but Dr. Griffin's took up an entire hemisphere of her skull. The skin across the left side of her forehead and scalp looked like it was made of precious metal. It was ostentatious, Andra thought. And unnecessary, considering Griffin had an 'implant and it basically did the same thing. Crowns were usually worn by those with religious objections to 'implants or tech allergies, but people like Dr. Griffin and Andra's mom used them to boost their own productivity.

Dr. Griffin waited at the door with a girl with dark waves and a gap between her teeth. Andra recognized her as Rashmi Bhatt, Dr. Griffin's intern, and Cruz's new girlfriend. Friend? Girlfriend? All Andra knew was that Cruz was spending more time with Rashmi, and less time with Andra.

"It's almost time, Dr. Watts," she said, her voice high.

They'd never actually met, her and Rashmi, but Andra hated her on principle. She was living the life Andra was supposed to be living, working for LAC as the perfect golden child, and attached at the hip to Cruz Alvarez, the boy Andra had been enamored with since he started interning with her mom two years before.

Mom got up. "Andromeda, do me a favor. Take your brother home."

"I'm meeting Briella and Rhin. Last time before my appointment. Acadia can—"

Mom was already halfway out the door. "I put credit in your account for a pizza. Make sure Osias is in bed by nine."

And then, she was gone, following Dr. Griffin and Rashmi out the door.

"Let's go home, Andra," Oz said, and this time he did whine. "Piiizzaaaaaa."

Home.

. . . home.

Time skipped forward. Suddenly, Oz and Andra were leaving through the back door of Lacuna Athenaeum, which led directly under the statue of Alberta Griffin. It was built out of glossy white marble, her head gleaming with real silver. Her right arm was pointing to the stars, her gaze following. The statue was surrounded by a circle of pristine Corinthian columns, like this was some sort of national monument. Perhaps one day it would be—when she was long gone with the portion of the population that had made the lottery for the first colony.

"Hey, Andra, watch this!" Oz cried, and she looked up to find him racing across the adjoining park, heading for the hover'swings.

Andra laughed and pulled out her 'locket. She pressed play.

ANDRA JERKED AWAKE in a cold sweat, her breathing harsh, her lungs burning. The wagon slats came into focus. The sky was lighter. The sun was coming up. *Andromeda is rising*, she thought wryly.

"Evens?" a voice said, and she turned to see Zhade kneeling, peering under the wagon. His blankets had already been gathered and it appeared he'd just given himself a shave.

She nodded, trying to keep her face blank, her breathing steady. He gave her a look like he didn't quite believe her, but just shook his head.

"Time to go road-wise," he said, and patted the side of the wagon before standing.

Andra took a deep breath. There was something cold in her hand, and she looked down to see her 'locket clenched in her fist, chain broken. Her thumb was pressed against the top button— the one designated to play the first memory. She should have been surrounded by the ghosts of her family, cocooned in a holographic rendition of home, reliving her past. Her truth. But instead, there was nothing but cold, hard reality. A pile of blankets, a rickety cart, and sand everywhere.

The holo'display was blank.

The 'locket was dead.

SIX

THE SORCER

THE SUN HAD risen on what Zhade hoped would be their final day in the Wastes. They were almost round the pocket, and the buttery tint of the gods' road glistened in the distance, miraged in waves of heat. The temp rose quickish. The cart rocked, and they sat in silence, the Goddess's bloodshot eyes narrowing on the pocket. Dirt smudged her face, and her black hair was a tangled mess, curling ever-so-slightish round her ears.

"We should convo bout what happens when we get to Eerensed," Zhade said. There were things he had to hold from her, but there were other things she *needed* to reck if they were going to survive.

The Goddess ignored him. "Is it getting bigger?" She leaned up to get a better look, prepping to push herself to her knees. She stuck out a hand.

"Neg, wait—"

She hissed, or her skin did, as it made contact with the burning metal of the wagon rails, and she jerked back.

"God damn it!" the Goddess gasped, cradling her burned hand to her chest.

"Which god? And what is she damning?"

"Your fucking wagon," she growled through gritted teeth.

Zhade's eyes widened. "I'm doing *what* to the wagon?"

She didn't respond, mereish shut her eyes, a single tear dribbling down her cheek, glinting in the sun. Even without seeing the wound, Zhade could tell this was not a bandage-and-goddess-level-healing wound. This was going to require some magic, and there was sole one conduit in his bag that would work.

When Zhade had been banished from Eerensed, he was peaced out with mereish the clothes on his back. Blessedish, the two gifts from his mam had been with Lew-Eadin, because Maret had taken everything from him. His conduits, his armor, his fam. At luck, they couldn't take what he carried inside his head, and he vowed never to be so unprepped again. A week into his life in the Wastes he found a tattered bag, discarded or perhaps carried on the wind from the rotting corpse of its previous owner. He tossed it over his shoulder and filled it with everything he could find—even if he wasn't certz how it could be useful.

He'd been building his arsenal ever since, and as his inventory grew, so did his plan. Finalish, the sole thing he'd needed was the Goddess. Now that he had her, he needed to keep her whole and full well.

He rooted round his bag til he found the wand at the bottom. He called it a wand, but it was bulkier than was typical. It was square and angular and ill fitting in the palm of his hand, but it did what he needed. Or, it would. Eventualish.

The Goddess grabbed it from him before he could explain.

"I've never seen anything like this," she said, her voice strained with pain, but liveish with curiosity. "I mean, it's obviously some sort of med'wand used for nano'plasty and cosmetic restructuring, but—" She held it up at different angles. "—this is incredible."

Zhade smiled, smuggish. "Certz it is. I made it myself."

The Goddess frowned. Her hair fluttered in the desert wind. "You *made* this? How?"

He didn't tell her he'd spent the last four years of his life perfecting it, coaxing supplies from angels at every village they passed, scavenging parts from discarded magic, and sorcering them together to create what he called a graftling wand, or grafter. He didn't tell her that with a few quick commands, it would release a slipperish sheet of mesh that could alter skin, shift bone, and reshape muscle. He didn't tell her that though he'd used it to heal minor wounds, that wasn't its intended purpose.

"I'm quite talented," he said, winking and taking back the grafter. "Now, give me your hand."

He expected a fight, but to his surprise, she held out her burned hand, eyes wide on the wand. A shiny red mark slashed across her palm. He started to place the grafter on her wound, then hesitated.

Last moon, he'd used it to heal a sun spot that had been giving him trouble. It had worked, but not without a cost: pain like Zhade had never imagined. When it was over, his skin was smooth and flawless. An ache still lingered, but the sun spot was gone.

"This—" He met her eyes. "—is going to hurt."

She bit her lip, then nodded. Zhade drew a few runes on the surface of the grafter, then tapped the wand against her skin, letting it sense her injury. Once it was done, a translucent netting slipped from the top and fit itself over the wound.

Firstish, it appeared nothing was happening. Zhade focused as hard as he could, willing the magic to begin, though he knew his sorcer abilities didn't work like that. Sole goddesses—and now Maret—could call things from thin air, commanding magic with nothing but a thought. Fishes and wishes. But Low Magic, *Zhade's* magic, needed a conduit like the grafter. He hoped the work he'd put into creating the wand had been worth it, and that its magic would break in soon and now. Perhaps it was already working. Perhaps the pain he'd felt had been a flute—

The Goddess screamed.

It wasn't a sound of pain or even agony, but something more, deeper. And it wrenched Zhade's stolid heart in two.

The wagon jerked to a stop. She scrambled to remove the mesh, but it had already latched on to her skin. Zhade could tell she was trying to speak—plead with him to remove the netting—but her screams didn't form words. Her eyes rolled back in her head, and she collapsed in a heap against the side of the wagon.

Wead jumped out, reaching over to cushion her head.

"Do something!" he snapped.

Zhade dove for her hand, but before he grasped it, the mesh . . . detonated.

He couldn't comp what he was seeing. One moment the silkish patch was fused to the Goddess's skin, covering her wound with a translucent glow. And the next, it burst into pieces. Pieces so small they were nothing but specks of sand glistening on the wind. They shimmered in the desert sun for a moment, then vanished.

The Goddess's breathing hitched and her eyes fluttered open. She met his stare, face flushed, chest heaving, lips parted.

"What. the fuck. was that."

Zhade pushed out his bottom lip. "You broke it."

Andra raised a brow, still gasping for breath. "I'll break more than that in a minute if you don't tell me what the hell you just did to me."

If she was full bars well to spar, she wasn't too badish hurt. Zhade felt a wind of relief.

"Zhade." It was Lew-Eadin, pacing. His voice was tight and low, almost threatening. "What was that?"

"I— Sorries," he pleaded. Both of their faces held matching expressions of anger. "It was mereish something I was working on. Magic to heal, alter flesh. It's painful, firm, but never— I never . . ."

The Goddess cradled her burned hand, squeezing the tips of her fingers til they turned red, as though that would stop the pain. She tilted her head back and groaned, and Zhade was momentarish distracted by the smooth amber skin of her neck.

He shook his head to clear it. "How did you do that?" he asked. "Destroy the mesh?" He'd never seen magic work like that before.

"I didn't," she said, eyes still shimmering in pain.

Zhade recked what he had seen, and he would ferris out her secrets later.

The Goddess's wound needed attention, and it was obvi he needed a more imaginative solution. Evens. There were other ways to tend to the burn without harming her further, and ways to get her to reveal her secrets. He leaned back and ripped off his shirt.

The flush on the Goddess's face was full worth the sun spot he was going to get.

"What are you doing?" she gasped.

He liked how raspy her voice was when she was flustered. And the flush on her cheeks was full charred. "Wrapping your wound."

He had plenty of bandages in his bag, but the Goddess didn't need to reck that. He ripped a strip of fabric from the bottom of his tunic. The material wasn't for true hard to tear, but he flexed a bit more than necessary. Her breath caught. He tied the cloth round her palm, at care to let his fingers dance across her skin. She opened her mouth to say something—a breathless thank-you, a flustered compliment. His signature grin was waiting to break free.

"Put your shirt back on," she said. "What are you waiting for? A mirror?"

Wead let out a laugh, then cut off. "Sir." His voice was tense. "Something happens."

Zhade followed Wead's line of vision. The Goddess had been right. The pocket was growing, getting closer, its shadowy mass swirling in agitation. A spark of lightning pierced a jagged path through it, briefish illuminating what looked like a hand reaching toward them.

"Is it supposed to do that?" the Goddess asked.

"I've never seen one do that before," Zhade said.

"We need to run," Lew added. He turned to jump back in the wagon, but before he could, the churning contents of the pocket shot out and severed his arm at the elbow.

SEVEN

Mortal, n. or adj.

Definition: 1. subject to death; human.

              2. incurring divine condemnation.

              3. one who is destined to die.

DISTANTLY, ANDRA WAS aware of someone shouting. Familiar words, urgent tones. But her field of vision was completely consumed by the pocket. By the nothingness, the lack of existence. By what she was certain was an immense 'swarm of nano'bots congealing into something corrupt and devastating, consuming everything in its path. It hung over her, a swirling mass of darkness, almost like it was watching her, sizing her up.

She was insignificant and tiny. She was real, she existed. Connected and apart. And she couldn't make the two thoughts fit together—

Someone grabbed her arm.

She blinked.

Zhade was in front of her, yelling something about Lew.

"What?" she choked out, but Zhade was already dragging her out of the cart, and for one wild moment, Andra thought he was going to throw her in, but right before they reached the pocket, she tripped over something.

Someone.

Lew-Eadin.

He lay writhing in the dirt, eyes clenched shut, groaning in pain. Lew's left arm was spread wide. Shoulder, elbow, then nothing.

They were so close to the pocket, Andra imagined she could feel the nothingness tugging at her, drawing her to it. Something in the back of her mind felt awakened.

"Help him!" Zhade shouted. He was frantic and angry and his eyes glistened.

"I—" She started to say she couldn't, that she didn't know how, but she couldn't stop staring at Lew. His brown complexion ashen, his unruly dark curls slick with sweat, his elegant face carved into something grotesque.

Zhade's eyes were wild. "Heal him. Now."

"I—I can't. I told you, I'm not a goddess."

"Mereish *try*," Zhade pleaded. "Like the others."

"I— Try what?" Andra spluttered.

"A miracle. I reck what the goddesses can do, what *you* can do." Andra opened her mouth to respond, but a low groan cut her off. Lew-Eadin.

Zhade knelt beside him in the sand, resting a hand on his friend's shoulder. The blackened nano'swarm still hung above, casting them in shadow.

"Evens?"

Lew mumbled something.

"What?"

"No fighting," he moaned.

Zhade murmured something in a dialect she didn't understand. Lew-Eadin let out a laugh that turned into a cough.

Zhade's jaw tightened. "Hurry. Help me get him acart."

THEY RACED ACROSS the desert, Andra clinging to Lew-Eadin in the back, while Zhade took the reins. The horse seemed to sense the urgency and galloped faster than Andra thought possible, the pocket growing smaller in the distance. They followed the road toward Eerensed—nothing more than a yellow line eco'grafted in the sand.

Andra imagined she could feel Lew-Eadin's life leaving him, slowly draining through the gruesome wound where his arm suddenly . . . stopped. She'd tied a tourniquet, relying on her memory of sims and old sight-and-sound films. She didn't have a clue if she'd done it correctly.

If Andra had any kind of technology—a phone, a 'bot, a 'band—she could have used a healing app. But all she had was the neural'implant.

She'd felt it come to life when Zhade had used the med'wand to put the nano'patch on her. It hadn't been trying to connect to the 'wand—Andra hadn't sensed the tech at the edge of her consciousness, like she would a light switch or sim or even nanos. Instead, she'd felt a spark, a panicked grab for something that wasn't there.

She flexed her hand, remembering the pain from the nano'patch.

Pain wasn't the right word for it. It was agony. It was torment. It was desolation.

It was like being torn apart into her smallest pieces and remade. Whatever the tech had been, it was *wrong*. She wasn't sure how she had destroyed it, *if* she had destroyed it. But she had theories. The pain, the threat of mortal damage had rebooted her 'implant, sending it into survival mode with a single focus: protect the host.

No, her 'implant hadn't interfaced with the med'wand, because if her body's response was any indication, the tech was fully incompatible with her own. So the question was: What had her 'implant used to destroy the 'patch? She was hesitant to ask, because she thought she knew the answer.

The pocket.

It had been the closest source of nanos. Corrupt and dangerous ones, yes, but definitely a 'swarm of nano'bots. Her 'implant had communicated to a small strand and they had attacked the 'patch to save her. But for some reason, the rest of the pocket had followed and acted on its own accord.

Attacking Lew-Eadin.

It had been *her* fault. *Her* 'implant had called the pocket nearer.

"How much farther?" she shouted, the wagon jolting beneath her.

The yellow road stretched ahead of them, vanishing over the horizon.

"Too far," Zhade growled, the wind stealing his words.

Andra hesitated just a moment before grabbing Zhade's bag.

"What are you doing?"

"Looking for that cursed 'wand of yours."

It was a desperate solution, but that's where Andra was. Zhade had implied he'd used the 'wand on himself and never experienced what Andra had. Her reaction to the 'patch had been because her 'implant thought it was malware and attacked, white blood cells neutralizing a foreign agent. If the only reason the 'patch didn't work was because of her 'implant, and Lew-Eadin didn't have an 'implant . . .

Andra found the 'wand, its metal casing rough and warm in her unburned hand. It had obviously been a slapdash job, a piecemeal of scraps. Rather than presenting a holo'display, a screen on its casing acted as an interface. She'd watched Zhade trace the symbols on it. One had looked like a broken square, like the scan symbol on her holo'band. The second had been harder to detect, but she'd noticed blue triangles with loops on top on some of Zhade's things—the symbol from her time that indicated a med'bot. She tried that now and pressed the 'wand to Wead's arm.

The nano'patch oozed its way onto the wound. It was nothing more than a collection of nano'bots, so thickly swarmed as to be solid. Each was programmed with a specific task, working together to heal Wead.

Andra hoped.

None of this was ideal, but she couldn't just watch Wead bleed out. Everything in her screamed to help.

The wind rushed past them as the 'patch dissolved into Wead's skin. The wound's ragged edges slowly knit themselves together, covering the blood and bone beneath. He writhed in pain, and Andra couldn't tell if it was from his injury, the lurch of the wagon, or the healing nano'tech. Whatever it was doing, it wasn't doing enough.

As far as Andra could tell, the skin wasn't healed, exactly. It had been remade—fundamentally altered from Lew's injured skin to new, undamaged flesh. It was genius, but inefficient, made by someone experimenting without precedent.

At most, what the 'wand had done was cosmetic. Wead still needed medical attention, and he needed it now. All Andra had been able to do was stop him from losing more blood.

She'd just have to keep Lew alive long enough to get him to the city. If the goddesses could create bio'domes from scratch, surely they could do something to heal him. Again, Andra considered her mother. Wouldn't it make sense that the only three colonists that hadn't woken with the others had something in common? Maybe a familial relationship? There were three women in Andra's family: Acadia, Andra, and their mother.

And if Isla Watts was waiting for them in the city, she could do something to help Lew. She was no doctor. However, she *was* a genius.

But the 'bot had said Isla and Acadia were dead.

It could be wrong. Andra tried to will it into existence. *It has to be wrong.*

On and on they flew. Through clouds of dust, over sifting dunes, across flat, barren stretches of land pockmarked with crisp, brown grass. Andra pulled the cowl-neck of her sweater over her mouth with one hand, using the other to mop up Lew's lost blood with Zhade's discarded shirt. Welts were already blossoming on Zhade's back, his skin fried to a deep red. A trickle of blood ran from one of the blisters, but he seemed not to notice as he pushed the horse faster.

The wagon jerked, and Lew let out a moan. The stump of his arm was beginning to swell, streaks of infection fanning out from the wound. His skin was on fire.

"You're pale, Goddess," he slurred. Then started murmuring too low for Andra to understand, his ramblings sporadically punctuated by a name that sounded like "Jenny."

Both his clothes and Andra's were drenched in blood, sticky and wet. She wondered how porous the cloth was, and how much blood it could hold, and was that more or less than Lew-Eadin could survive losing? He was well past the two pints that caused shock, but hopefully not close to the six pints that caused death. A square meter of material was probably soaked through, but then there'd been the blood lost to the sand. And the fabric wasn't cotton, it was some kind of rough—

She looked up and there it was.

Eerensed.

The sun kissed the horizon, its rays sifting through the wind-strewn sand to land on the city, encased in a giant bio'dome. The 'dome was nothing more than a sheen of transparent skin circling it like a snow globe, anchored by a titanium wall. Within it, teetering buildings spired into the sky, awash in vibrant colors. A single silver tower jutted up like a beacon.

Hope. But still too far off.

Andra felt Lew lose consciousness, felt the beat of his heart fall dangerously slow. What she wouldn't give for a defib app right about now.

"Hurry!" she shouted, keeping a finger at Lew's pulse.

Zhade didn't respond, only pushed the horse harder. They raced the rest of the way in a frenzied rush, not stopping until they were right up on the 'dome's base. It towered dark above them and stretched out in both directions. Andra almost missed the seam, the outline of a heavy door.

"What are you waiting for?" she shouted.

Zhade gave her a panicked look. "If they would open the gate for me, don't you reck I would have done that by now? You'll have to tell them who you are."

"Fine," she huffed, lifting herself out of the cart. "Take him."

Zhade did, and there was no time to think. No time to second-guess. Andra darted across the sand to the 'dome's gate, pounding her fist against the metal. It rang out tinny. Hollow.

"Let us in! I have an injured man who needs help!"

Silence.

She knocked again.

"You have to tell them who you are," Zhade called.

"This is Andra," she yelled. "Your . . . goddess."

She winced. Not only at the halting, unconfident way she spoke, but at the words themselves. The *lie*.

A lie that worked.

There was a creaking, a grinding of gritty gears. The whoosh of an airlock. Andra stumbled back. Hinges groaning, the door slid open, hissing as the vacuum seal popped. A plume of mist puffed out of the hole it left behind, and after a tense moment, a figure emerged. A soldier—dressed in all black. Glistening armor covered him like fish scales, and his face was hidden behind a dark mesh mask.

Andra sucked in a breath as he approached. She risked a glance at Zhade, who was watching the soldier, his expression tense, and Andra wondered if he had just led them to their deaths. The man's armor jangled as he pulled his mesh mask off, revealing a tanned face with an angular jaw, clenched. His eyes narrowed.

Andra stood frozen, her mind calculating the best escape route, the places to strike that would cause the most damage. She thought back on the strategies she'd learned playing sims and watching her little brother pretend to fight aliens and the one day of self-defense they'd had in her freshman social behavior class. Then Zhade said, "Gryfud?"

The soldier blinked, then his eyes focused on Zhade in the back of the cart.

"Zhade? You're you, boyo? I nearish recognize you." The soldier let out a long whoop. Then his gaze fell on Lew-Eadin and his blood sticking to Zhade's fingers, and the soldier cut off mid-laugh. His face paled. "Wead?"

"He's marching to badness," Zhade said. "Let us in, evens?"

The soldier shook his head. "They'll kill you, seeya."

Zhade nodded to Andra. "I don't reck so."

Gryfud's gaze finally focused on Andra and she saw the moment realization struck. His eyes widened, his mouth forming a comical O.

"For true, you're you?" he asked, voice rough.

Before Andra could answer, he dropped to a knee in the sand, head bowed.

"Forgive me, Goddess, I recked it was jokings. I didn't reck you were for true you."

There was an awkward silence, and Andra cleared her throat.

"You're . . . forgiven?"

"Thank you, Goddess, thank you." Gryfud rose and clasped her hand. "We hoped you would return. We prayed for it. I was convoeing the boyos yestereven—"

"Time runs, boyo," Zhade said, deftly slipping Andra's hand from the big man's grasp. He nodded toward Lew-Eadin, still unconscious in the cart. "Can you help?"

"Please," Andra added.

Gryfud nodded. "Certz. Certz. Anything for the Third." He gave her one last glance as he hopped into the cart. It groaned beneath his weight. "Where to, boss?" he asked Zhade.

"Tia Ludmila's place. Southwarden. She's a meddoc."

Gryfud nodded, and Andra moved to get back in the cart, but to her surprise, Zhade climbed out, leaving Lew alone with the strange soldier.

He grabbed Andra's wrist. "Not you, Goddess. You and I are going to the Rock."

Andra tugged away. She didn't feel right leaving Lew. Especially with this soldier who looked like he could tear him apart with his bare hands. But before she could stop him, he flicked the reins and they disappeared into the city.

Andra turned on Zhade. "You just let him take Lew?"

He waved a dismissive hand. "He'll be evens."

"He's *dying*, and you just let some random person take him. He's your best friend."

"He's my servant," Zhade corrected, striding through the gate without a backward glance. "And he's not dying. Tia Ludmila will heal him up for certz."

Andra bit her cheek but hurried to follow.

As soon as she passed into the 'dome, the world changed. The temperature dropped thirty degrees, the humidity rose. The air was breathable, and Andra's relief was overwhelming. But then the gate closed behind her, and it gave her the sense of being trapped. She cast one last look the direction the cart had disappeared, then turned to catch up with Zhade.

A tangle of streets spread out ahead of them, marked with patches of green. Buildings jutted up on either side, winding and twisting. It was an architectural miracle any of them were standing. The bleached-out facades shone in the sunlight. Those buildings lucky enough to have shade featured intricate designs in vibrant reds and blues and yellows, or tiles shaped into mosaics.

Andra shivered as the breeze cooled her skin, and then she felt the faint tickle of nanos. It was almost like a piece of home. She'd lived her entire life in a society where nano'bots were ubiquitous, the foundation of most, if not all, technology. 'Implants allowed users to cognitively interface with the nanos, and the nanos would interface with surrounding tech. Andra could turn on a light just by thinking about it. The electrical impulses of her brain would send the message to her 'implant, and then her 'implant would send the message to the nearest nanos, and then the nanos would send the message to the light. More complex technologies—like med'tech—required mental coding with an interface, but simple tasks were only a thought away.

But she only felt the nanos physically. When she searched for a mental connection, it was like stretching for something just out of reach. Whatever these nanos were, they were related to the tech she knew, but changed somehow. Like they'd been upgraded, and she had not.

Now that the adrenaline of the race to the city was ebbing, she felt the throb of pain in her burned hand. If she could just access the nanos around her, she could turn them into med'bots to heal the wound. She would worry about that later, maybe just ask the other goddesses.

A giddy thrill of anticipation passed through her, even though half of her mind was still with Lew in the cart. If the other goddesses really were colonists woken too late (and what else could they be?), then she would finally know what happened.

She hurried to catch up with Zhade. To their right, the silver tower she'd seen shone in the distance, at the northern edge of the 'dome.

"Is that where we're going?" she asked, pointing. Something about it called to her.

Zhade looked briefly over his shoulder, then shook his head. "Neg. Keep apace."

A clothesline hung over the road, and dust-colored shirts flapped in the breeze. Zhade grabbed one without breaking his stride and tugged it on. His gait was swift, his long legs carrying him faster than Andra could easily follow. She kept tripping over the uneven stone streets. Streets in a city on a new planet a thousand years in the future, growing out of the ruins of something the colonists built.

From what she could tell, the 'dome wasn't actually *preserving* the city. It had just been built around it to protect what was already there. Eerensed was like a vase that had been broken and glued back together over and over. New plaster on fallen ruins. Patched roofs and boarded windows.

Andra kept one eye on Zhade's back, while also trying to take in her surroundings. The streets were quiet, almost as though he was leading her purposely through alleys and abandoned neighborhoods. As they traveled farther into the city, the buildings grew nicer— detailing around the windows and above doors, more space between houses, vibrant paint covering the facades. They crossed a river. The water lapped at the banks, and she wanted to jump in and take a long drink. But not as much as she wanted to see the other goddesses.

Andra's shins were burning by the time the winding streets and tangled alleys fell away, revealing a building hewn into an outcropping of rock rising above the city. It twisted and spiraled higher and higher, a series of disjointed structures, teetering on a cliff. The walls were a pale pink stucco, and every crevice was adorned with sandstone carvings. It reached eight, nine stories into the sky, sectioned off into cubes wedged into the rock. Parapets wreathed the roof, and a single tower sprung up from the highest level.

"The Rock," Zhade said, pointing at what could only have been a palace.

Its shadow fell over Andra and Zhade as they followed the road to the front gate. Andra's body hummed with nervousness. They passed an open space of vibrant grass, immaculately groomed, lined with towering palms and ostentatious fountains. The road itself was sturdy brick, not the mismatched cobblestone of the city streets, and the metal spires of the gate shone gold in the fading sunlight.

Andra thought of the people of the decaying village that had hosted her frozen body for so long. There was so *much* here and it was so close to them. So why were they still in the desert?

As they approached, the gate opened, revealing stone steps ascending to the palace. A tall, thin woman in golden robes hurried down the stairs, her long brown hair streaming behind her. She was followed by a guard.

"Goddess," the woman said. The edges of her eyes crinkled in a grimace-like smile. Then her gaze caught on Zhade, and she froze. Her tanned skin went ashen, and her mouth tightened.

"Advisor Tsurina." Zhade's face spread into a grin and he gestured at Andra. "I brought you a gift."

A muscle in the woman's jaw twitched. Andra tensed at the theatrical power dynamics at play. She'd been so focused on finding the others like her, she hadn't considered the type of culture she was walking into. Everything about this moment felt . . . courtly.

The woman wore a neutral expression. She continued down the steps and stopped before Andra, bowing her head briefly. She was elegant, regal, a few strands of gray hair framing her high cheekbones.

"I'm Tsurina, Grande Advisor and mother of our Guv. We're surprised to see you." Her voice was smooth, pleasant, but something in her tone made Andra feel threatened. She offered her hand, and Andra shook it quickly, then pulled away before the woman's grip could tighten.

"But we're delighted, even so," she tacked on like an afterthought. She gave the figure behind her a quick nod.

In addition to the dark armor, the guard wore a gold breastplate and an elaborate sword in an ornate scabbard. He was handsome, but in an intimidating way, a serious expression carved into his deep brown skin, his head shaved, his nose hawkish. He held his jaw clenched, his dark eyes seeming to bore through Andra.

"Heya, Kiv," Zhade said, waving. The guard didn't respond.

"Please," Tsurina said. "The Guv is certz anxious to meet you. It exists a miracle you returned."

Her accent was close to Andra's, familiar, though peppered with future slang. She extended her arm in an invitation to follow, but Andra didn't move. She had expected to be taken straight to the other goddesses—to finally find some normalcy in all this strangeness. But things were just getting stranger.

"Can I come too?" Zhade grinned, shoving his hands in his pockets and rocking back on his heels. He winked at the older woman.

Tsurina's expression didn't change, but her voice turned ominous. "Oh, I wouldn't dream of stopping you." And Andra realized what the danger she felt was. This woman wanted to kill Zhade. Not metaphorically. Literally. Slowly and methodically.

Returning a dangerous smile of his own, Zhade offered Andra his arm, wedging himself between them. The advisor gritted her teeth, then turned swiftly and glided up the steps. Andra had no choice but to follow.

EIGHT

guv, n.

Etymology: possible abbreviation of millenial English *governor.*

Definition: 1. a ruler; one invested with supreme authority.

2. one with divine right of power.

DESPITE ITS PRECARIOUS position on the rock, the palace was as opulent as a postapocalyptic bio'dome-protected palace could be. When they reached the top of the steps, glistening silver mech'bots dragged open the intricately carved wooden doors, revealing the marble entry beyond.

Zhade tightened his grip on Andra's arm and hissed for her to wait. She pulled free and, stomach churning, followed Tsurina into the palace.

Her gasp echoed in the cavernous entry hall. Vaulted ceilings arched over marble columns and intricately tiled floors. Crystal vases held tropical flowers in pinks and greens and purples, and a constant bubble of water drifted from a series of fountains down the center of the hall. Before Andra, a handful of steps led down to a floor tiled with a repeating star design. On either side, a double staircase wrapped around the room, flowers and trees carved into its marble balusters.

Tsurina led them across the hall to a set of doors larger than the first. Gold-plated mech'bots waited for them, but didn't open the doors until the advisor nodded. Andra wondered if the woman had an 'implant, or if the 'bots were simply programmed to respond to ambiguous gestures. She tried to interact with them—get them to close the doors instead of open them—but they too were just out of reach, like they were running on different software. They grabbed the iron rings set into the double doors and pulled. The doors groaned open, and Andra's breath caught.

The room was larger than she expected, and she realized part of it must be hewn *into* the rock on which the palace sat. Columns lined the walls, carved from a blue-veined marble. Light flooded in through the windows in the arched ceilings, but some trick in the curvature of the glass directed most of the light toward this *Guv*.

He sat on a throne carved from a gnarled tree stump, its frayed edges blackened, pointed spikes of broken bark shooting off at odd angles. The tree had been broken, not felled, and it had been old. The Guv lounged lazily, catlike, one leg slung over an armrest, and he twirled something Andra couldn't see between his long fingers, watching them approach.

He wore a dark cloak lined with gold stitching. His ice-blond hair was slicked back from his pale, haughty face, and tacked to his left temple was a silver 'implant crown. It was larger than the models that had been in vogue in Andra's time, covering from forehead to just below his ear, curving behind the shell. Simple but elegant, and it glistened in the sunlight.

It was the first Andra had seen since waking, and she assumed it must be programmed to interact with the tech here—the tech out of Andra's reach. Maybe these people wore crowns rather than embedded 'implants. Or maybe just one person had that privilege.

The room was lined with 'bots of different shapes and sizes, though all were starkly humanoid. Presumably, the Guv could control every 'bot in the room. All of them were armed.

Outside of 'Bot Wars and the occasional sim, Andra had never seen a 'bot with a weapon. However these people were using technology, it was not what she was used to.

Andra self-consciously tugged at the blood-soaked shirt suctioned to her thick waist, pushed her hair out of her eyes. Her palm throbbed from the burn, but she ignored it as Zhade led her down the center aisle, his hand resting on the small of her back. Their feet slapped against the marble.

She came to a stop in front of the throne, craning her neck to see the man—*boy*, really; he wasn't much older than Andra—who decided their fate.

It was silent. The Guv sat forward. Andra felt exposed. The empty room was too large for her. She didn't fill the space.

"Hi." Her voice squeaked.

The Guv pocketed whatever piece of gold he was twirling between his fingers. "Goddess?" He didn't smile. Didn't frown. Didn't make any expression at all, just a tightening around the eyes, waiting for her to respond.

She didn't.

Zhade cleared his throat.

This situation was too ridiculous. She was stripped of everything she knew and thrown into this new world—literally—and expected to know how to interact with kings.

"You've returned," the Guv finally said, his voice low, and his eyes flicked to Zhade. "And, apparentish, brought home my brother."

Brother? Andra shot him a look. Would that make Zhade some sort of prince? Was Tsurina his mom? Andra definitely wasn't detecting any motherly affection there. Zhade kept his eyes resolutely from Andra's as he and the Guv stared each other down.

Zhade broke first, his grin brittle. "Miss me?"

Something more dangerous than anger flashed across the Guv's face. His pale skin flushed, and he took a breath, like he was about to breathe fire.

Tsurina coughed behind them, and his expression faltered.

The Guv stood. He was taller than he'd seemed on the throne, and thin. His robe was fitted, some kind of leather that crinkled when he walked. His eyes were molten lava, his sneer ice. He bowed and took Andra's hand, briefly touching her knuckles to his forehead in greeting, and when he rose, he didn't release her hand. His skin was cold.

"I'm Guv Maret kin Vatgha, Steward of Eerensed, Warden of the Easthand Gate, High Sorcer, and Protector of the Hell-mouth."

Andra looked at Zhade. He raised his eyebrows and gestured for her to respond.

"I'm, um, Andromeda Yue Watts . . ." Silence. She swallowed. "Daughter of Auric Lim and Isla Watts . . ." More silence. An awkward cough. "Reader of books, keeper of . . . secrets, and goddess of . . . you know, just general goddess . . . things."

The Guv's expression softened for a fraction of a second. So quick Andra thought she must have been mistaken. Then his eyes flashed, and warning bells were going off in her head. He held her hand too tightly. His posture was too stiff, his muscles too tense. There was anger in his eyes when he looked at Zhade. There was hunger in them when his gaze turned to Andra.

"Where have you been?" Maret snapped, and for a second, she thought he was talking to Zhade. He swallowed, and when he spoke again, his tone was softer, but it was too late. He'd already revealed the nature underneath. "You've been missing for nearish ten years."

Zhade cut in, pulling Andra's hand free from the Guv's. She was too blindsided to be grateful.

"I found her for you, Guv. I believe that means you owe me."

Zhade poked Maret in the shoulder. The guards' grips on their weapons tightened.

"You look different," Maret said quietly. His teeth were bared, and though his voice was soft, it quaked with something fierce. Something uncontrolled. "The desert has changed you."

Zhade looked down at himself. "Thanks." He flexed his muscles.

Maret drew close to Zhade and rested his hand on his shoulder. At a casual glance, the gesture looked harmless, but Maret's grip tightened, and Andra remembered the blisters beneath Zhade's shirt.

"You shouldn't be here," the Guv hissed. "Did you assume the Goddess would win your throne back?"

Zhade's grin spread wider, even though his eyes were glassy with pain. He tucked his hands in his pockets and shrugged. Blood blossomed under Maret's grip.

"Neg, actualish. I don't want the throne. It was never mine for starts, and sides, it looks good on you . . . uh, under you." More blood soaked his shirt. "I've learned my lesson, Guv Maret. The desert *has* changed me. I'm here to serve you soon and now."

"For certz?" Tsurina said coldly. Maret shot her a look that was part annoyed, part pleading, but she ignored it. "My dead husband's bastard son returns after four years, and we're spozed to believe what? That you want to behave? After what you did? After what *your mother* did?"

Zhade's eyes tensed, though his smile remained plastered on. "I have the Third, don't I? I could have used her powers to take the city myself, but I didn't. I brought her to you as . . ." His eyes glinted. " . . . an offering of peace." The words echoed hollowly in the giant space.

Andra's mind was spinning to keep up. She didn't like being referred to as an offering, but she'd known Zhade was using her. She was using him too. And she wasn't leaving until she saw the other so-called goddesses.

Zhade cocked his thumb, pointing to the massive door behind them, where more 'bots were stationed. "I can take her back adesert, if you want. No meteor to me."

For a moment, Maret didn't say anything. Time dragged forward, carrying the silence with it. Andra held her breath.

Zhade's expression was unreadable, but Andra saw his throat bob. "Evens, Mare. It's me. Do you have memory of the day we found the crow's nest? Or the boys in Eastwarden? Or the time"—Zhade chuckled—"the time in the lower city with the cabbage cart?"

A beat. Then Maret relaxed his grip and smiled. A predator ready to strike. He let out a laugh like breaking glass.

"It's good to see you, brother." His voice was tight.

Zhade relaxed as his brother finally released his shoulder.

The Guv's eyes flicked to his mother, then to Zhade. "I've regretted sending you away. For certz we won't have another incident." He tilted his head in question.

Zhade stared his brother down, the corner of his mouth raised in a smirk. He shook his head. "Certz not. We will be incident-free."

Maret's smile was nothing more than a sheer mask over his features. He took a step back, but the tension in the room remained.

"Welcome, Goddess," Maret said, turning to Andra. "Sorries and worries for the fam drama. By the look on your face, I reck you had no idea who you were allied with."

Andra trained her features. "He was a means to an end."

Zhade dramatically put his hand over his heart, feigning offense.

"Look," Andra said, deciding it was time to be direct. She'd always dealt better with bluntness. "I just want a chance to speak with the other goddesses so I can figure out what happened and maybe . . . go home?" She wasn't sure where or what home was anymore; she just knew it wasn't here. "I think we both know I'm not really a goddess, and I—"

Something about the way the room tensed, the energy that crackled around her, made Andra stop.

Zhade let out a forced laugh. "Goddess, you reck you shouldn't joke bout that, marah?"

"I—"

"Her humor is mereish like the First's," Zhade said to Maret. "I've tried to explain that's not what's best for our people, but, seeya, she just woke."

Maret's eyes narrowed. "You do realize," he said, smoothing back his hair, "that the punishment for impersonating a Goddess is death, marah?"

No. No, she did not.

Her heart rate picked up and she had the urge to round on Zhade, but she forced herself to meet the Guv's gaze.

"Yes," she managed to croak out. "Yes, I did. I did know that." The last words were no more than a whisper.

"Good," Maret said. "Because if you were allowed into this city under false pretenses, claiming to be our long-lost goddess, then I would have to execute not sole you, but also my brother, and anyone else who helped you."

Did they know about Lew? Or the guard that let them into the city?

"Well, I am most definitely . . ." Andra let out a shaky breath. ". . . a goddess."

The last word echoed weakly in the cavernous room.

"I believe you completish," Maret said, though his tone said otherwise. "But, we will require proof, you comp."

"Proof?"

"That you are the Third."

"Um." Andra's heartbeat was pounding in her chest, pulsing through her extremities. The burn on her palm throbbed uncontrollably. Did they expect her to perform a miracle? How the hell was she supposed to *prove* her deity?

When she didn't respond, the Guv nodded to her. "Your wishmark will suffice."

"W-wishmark?" Andra hated the way she stuttered. The decidedly ungodly fear in her voice.

"He means the mark on your collar," Zhade muttered.

Her birthmark. Of course.

Andra had tried to ignore the fact that for hundreds of years, she'd lain in her cryo'tank, fully naked. That they'd kept her *on display*. People knew her, prayed to her, studied her. They'd surely memorized the mark she hated yet was undeniably part of her.

Maret approached slowly, his robe swishing against the marble, footsteps echoing through the chamber. Andra willed herself not to tremble as she pulled aside the collar of her bloodstained shirt to reveal the starburst underneath. He drew nearer until he was so close that if she breathed, he would feel it on his skin. His eyes narrowed on her birthmark.

After what seemed to be eternity he stepped back, and Andra let out her breath. Maret sighed, almost as though he were disappointed. Or bored.

"Now," he said, ambling back to the throne, stepping through the beam of light. "You will remain apalace as our guest." He looked to Tsurina's guard. "Set the Goddess up in her awaiting suite. Tomorrow night we will observe her Awakening."

Andra cleared her throat. "Um, first, I'd like to see the other goddesses. Please."

The throne room fell silent. Not an empty silence, but one filled with tension and dread and something waiting to crack.

"The other goddesses?" Maret asked.

Andra's shoe squeaked across the floor. "Yes, the other two. I'd like to talk with them, let them know I'm awake, and I . . . we . . . you know, need to chat about . . ." She cast her eyes to the ceiling. "Goddess stuff," she said through a breath.

"Zhade didn't tell you?" Maret's eyes sparked dangerously.

Apparently, there were a lot of things Zhade hadn't told her. "Tell me what?"

"The other goddesses . . ." Maret said, an energetic tinge to his voice. "They're dead."

PART TWO

DIVINE
INTERVENTION

Even as we look to the future, we will never forget the sacrifices and achievements that allow us to move past what we are and become something more.

—Inscription on the Griffin Monument,

2159

NINE

assumption, n.

Etymology: Latin *assūmere*, noun of action:, to take, usurp.

Definition: 1. the taking up of a person into heaven.

2. the act of supposing without proof.

3. law: a promise or undertaking.

4. arrogance.

ANDRA SCURRIED THROUGH the palace, her shoes clicking against the marble as she tried to keep up with the long strides of the guard Zhade had called Kiv. The way he'd said it, Andra wasn't sure if it was a name or an insult. They'd separated her from him, and now she was alone with a man who could snap her in half with a flick of his wrist. She eyed the spear he used like a walking stick. The point glinted gold in the low palace light. She wished Zhade were with her.

Not that Zhade turned out to be much of an ally.

He'd lied to her about everything. The other goddesses were dead, and the last bit of hope Andra clung to was gone. There was no one else like her. And she had to pretend to be a goddess or she would be killed.

Learn, adapt, her mother's voice echoed in her head, and Andra could picture the disappointed expression that always accompanied those words.

"Where are we going?" she asked.

The guard's clanking armor was the only response she got.

"Can I have water? Is there food? A bath maybe?"

Nothing.

Her voice didn't echo here like it had in the throne room. The stone halls were too small and twisty. *Labyrinthine*, she thought. Such a great word. It left so much to interpretation, couldn't be quantified. Andra tried to quantify the twists and turns anyway, filing away their path through the palace in case she needed it later. She didn't know where she was going or how she would get there, but once she had a plan, she would need a way out.

They passed stone walls, filled with carvings of stars and coils and, oddly, snowflakes. Up stairs and down. Passing by people, some dressed like guards, others like servants, and still others like royalty. All of them staring.

The guard stalked forward, occasionally checking to see if Andra was keeping up, though her labored breathing should have told him so. They took hallway after hallway, weaving through passages, climbing up flights of creaking metal staircases, only to find another web of corridors. By the time they reached their destination, Andra was sure they were at the topmost point of the palace. She thought about the chunks of building, teetering precariously on the side of the rock spire, the single tower at its peak. The floor beneath her seemed to tilt.

The guard opened the only door in the hallway—ornate and wooden, surrounded by a rose-gold frame decorated with stars—and Andra stepped into an opulent suite entirely carved from marble. The floor, the walls, the ceiling. Marble columns, marble trim. A marble archway leading to a marble balcony surrounded by a marble banister. The balcony doors were thrown wide, and even from across the room, she could see out over the tangle of streets and stone and sand.

"This is my room?" she whispered. No. Not *her* room. A room she was supposed to stay in. A room borrowed from a goddess, a myth.

The guard grunted, and without a word, was gone. Andra stood frozen. She had to regroup, come up with a plan. But no sooner had the door clicked shut than there was a brisk knock, and three women entered with a Class B serve'bot—an opaque, bulky model that was nothing more than a glorified fridge.

"Um, hello?" Andra said.

The women averted their eyes. One was holding a new set of clothes, another carried what looked like a brush.

Lady's maids. How very . . . Victorian.

The third woman held a jug of water, and Andra snatched it from her without thinking. She chugged the whole thing. Then the youngest maid refilled it from the accompanying serve'bot, and she drank that as well. She didn't stop until the maid had refilled it three times.

Andra immediately regretted it.

She'd drunk too much, too quickly. She lurched forward, holding her churning stomach, and groaned. The first maid shot forward—a white woman probably Andra's mother's age, but with much grayer hair. No, not her mother's age. Her mother was dead.

Andra swatted the maid away. "I'm fine," she groaned.

The maid stepped forward again and started tugging at Andra's blood-soaked clothes.

"Jesus!" she spat. "I can dress myself!"

The woman paled and stepped back.

"Just—" Andra groaned. The room tilted. She was so tired. Her stomach hurt. "Just leave me alone, okay?"

Guilt washed over her, but she was covered in Lew-Eadin's blood and he might be dying and it was her fault and her stomach was killing her and she was exhausted and her family was dead and she just needed them to *leave her alone*.

"GO!" she growled.

Tears formed in the youngest girl's eyes, but Andra couldn't think through an apology. She would make it up to her later. As soon as the door closed behind them, Andra fell to the floor, her mind whirling. The 'bot in the desert hadn't been wrong. Her family had been dead for centuries, and even if her mother *had* been one of the other goddesses, she was dead now too. Andra was alone with no one to tell her what to do, and the only thing she wanted was *home*. Except home didn't exist anymore. She could figure out a way back to Earth, but what was even the point? *No*, she told herself. *Don't give up. Learn. Adapt.*

The room grew dark, and she reached for her 'implant, trying to turn on a light, before remembering it was no use. She tried to think of what came next, but couldn't move past the grief, and she lay crying on the cold floor of a goddess's room. Despite her best efforts, her eyes shut, and she fell asleep.

TEN

THE PRODIGAL

ZHADE WAS BEING followed.

He recked he would be. There was no way to avoid it, but there *was* a way he could lose Kiv, if he was at care. It was still prenight, and the palace halls were abuzz with servants and diplomats and angels. People always tried to use the darkness of night to do their sneaking, but to be true, crowds were the easiest way to disappear.

As soon as he'd left Maret's throne room—and how it galled him to see Maret sitting on his father's throne—he'd been separated from the Goddess. It had been apurpose. Divide and conquer and all that. He'd built an alliance with her, and despite her protests of him being a "means to an end," even Maret could see the Goddess relied on him. But his brother also saw that Zhade relied on the Goddess. Thank sands he didn't reck for what.

But he will, Zhade thought with a grim smile.

Even so, he didn't like to be parted from her. She was too valuistic to be left alone, and he didn't trust her not to get in trouble. He would just have to trust her to also get out of it.

He slid behind a marble pillar, and then a tapestry. He had to be quick. It wouldn't take Kiv time and a half to reck where Zhade had gone. Though once he did, there was nothing he could do. This was blood magic, and Zhade was the sole living person whose blood could activate the spell.

A panel bout the size of a crumb biscuit hid behind the tapestry. Zhade placed his thumb against it and tensed, waiting for the prick. The waiting was always the worst part. A quick stab, and a door appeared in the marble where there was none before. It slid back, then to the side, just full wide for Zhade to enter. He darted in, and let the door shut behind him with a groan.

It took a moment for the lights to click on, but when they did, everything was exactish as he had memory. He found himself on a translucent platform, hovering over a hole so deep he couldn't see the bottom. It would have frightened him except he was exceptionalish brave.

And he'd been doing this since he was a kiddun.

A layer of dust covered the conduit—another small panel floating afront of him by magic. He didn't stop to consider if the spell still worked—magic wore off sometimes; his mother had told him that. He placed his palm on the panel, and the platform began to descend.

When he was a kiddun, this was how he would visit his father apalace. The magic lift and the connecting tunnel had been confidential, as had Zhade's existence. Sole his fam, the Schism, and Wead— charged with his protection—recked who Zhade was for true. The bastard prince may have been a dirty secret, but his parents had still loved him, he spozed. Enough to sneak him in from time to time.

It had been his mam's decision not to tell anyone bout him. The blood magic had also been her idea. It sole worked for her and Zhade. Not even his father—and for certz not Maret—had access to this entrance to the palace.

Zhade had been born first, but Maret had been born legitimatish. Their father had married for a political alliance—back then, Eerensed was just as vulnerable as any other city, if not bigger. They relied on angels for protection, but sorcers to translate were few and fewer, so Guv Reiden married Tsurina kin Anloch for her family's sorcers and their absurd number of angels hoarded in Wastern caves. No one recked how the Anlochs had collected so many, but Reiden didn't care where they came from as long as they held Eerensed safe. Certz, soon and sooner, the First awoke, and brought with her magic beyond anyone's imaginings, including the gods' dome. Tsurina's access to sorcers and angels was no longer needed. And when the Guv fell in love with Zhade's mother . . . evens, Zhade happened. Maret happened not too long after, the assumed heir to the throne, but not the true one.

Zhade's mam recked that if the citians ever discovered Zhade existed, he'd be at danger, so she hid him in the Hive with a group called the Schism. They were powerful Low Magic sorcers, and to be true, where Zhade learned most of his magic, though he told people it was natural.

Part of Zhade wanted to run away to the Schism and never look back—even if they had betrayed him, they were nearish fam—but he'd promised his mother. *Find the Third, protect her, don't let Maret have the crown.*

The Silver Crown no one recked the origin of, but the power of which held such a terrible leader as Maret on the throne.

The magic platform finalish reached the bottom of the abyss. Zhade stepped off into a tunnel and pressed his palm to the wall, relying on muscle memory, and then realized he was a few inches taller than when he'd last been here and adjusted. When his palm reached a certain spot on the wall, the tunnel magicalish lit with a series of torches, each one sparking to life after the other, down the passage til Zhade could no longer see them. He set off toward Southwarden, the route achingish familiar, even after four years adesert.

The network of tunnels had been created from the excavated ruins of the civilization Eerensed was built upon, following the network of long-forgotten paths and roads. As a kiddun, Zhade would sometimes find artifacts that hinted at the ancient society—bits of metal and cords and glass. He'd had a stash of his findings in the Hive, but he doubted it was still there. Probablish divided among the Schism sorcers. Their protection had ended when his mother died—when Maret had killed her and banished Zhade, and the Schism had done nothing to stop it.

He made his march through the tunnels til he reached the peacing that led up to Tia Ludmila's house in Southwarden. From the outside, it looked like a sewer grate in her pantry, but it was actualish how Zhade's mam would take him to see the old meddoc whenever he was sick or injured.

He waved his hand, and the torches spluttered out behind him. Then he ascended a grimy ladder and lifted the grate. He moved it aside with a groan and dragged himself up, falling to a heap on Tia's pantry floor. She was waiting for him, arms crossed, foot tapping.

Tia was ageless in the way that she had always seemed ancient to Zhade. Her hair had forever been a translucent white, her skin always craggy. She offered him a brown-skinned hand, and for a moment, he mereish stared at it, confused.

"Get afeet, boyo," she snapped, her voice a low croak.

She loomed over him, blocking his view of her pantry, but he could see the metal shelves were far from full bars stocked and dust clung to every surface.

He finalish took her hand, and with surprising strength, she dragged him up. For a moment, Tia's weathered face drew into a soft expression. She was the closest thing to a grandmam he'd ever had, and he'd missed her. She pulled her hand from his and swatted hers together as though she were dusting them off.

"Fool boyo. Never had the sense of a skirl, darting front o' carts and stopping mereish in time to be killed. Now go see that other fool one. He's wellish. And I'm wellish too, thanks for asking. Now peace." She jerked her head toward the back room where she saw patients.

"It's good to see you, Tia," Zhade said. She grunted in response.

Zhade was through the door when he heard her mumble, "Decide your fate, Zhade." He grinned. That was exactish what he'd planned to do.

He found Wead stretched out on a patient's cot in the back. The infirmary was the largest room in Tia's house, long and narrow like a hallway and packed with a line of med cots hovering over the dirt floor. There were no windows, sole flickering magic torches that cast Wead's face into shadow. He had one hand resting on his stomach, and the other was made of glittering magic. Tia hadn't regrown Wead's arm—even magic couldn't do that—but she had given him a new one. It resembled that of an angel, and was probablish as hard and cold as well. If it was anything like the other magic-made limbs Zhade had seen, it would click and whir and take Wead time and a half to learn to use. But Wead was alive and full well. And they were home.

Wead opened one eye, and seeing Zhade approach, pushed himself up into a sitting position, the cot groaning beneath him. His movements were spry, natural. Zhade wondered if it would hurt Wead if he hugged him. Instead, he leaned against a med cart.

"Where's the Goddess?" Wead asked.

Zhade picked up one of Tia's conduits. It looked similar to the graftling wand. "Apalace."

Wead's eyebrows shot up. "Alone? Is that wise?"

"It was my decision, marah?" He set the conduit back, not meeting Lew's eyes.

"Hmm," Wead said. "Rare point." He stood, slowish, then stretched his new hand and flexed his fingers, awkwardish. "I'm magic-made now. Reck I'll have powers?"

It didn't seem as though he'd almost died yesterday. There was no indication that his life had almost bled out of him, that the Goddess had used her bare hands to stop up the wound, that Zhade had driven the horse to near collapse through the Wastes, convinced it was too late, certz his friend was already gone, sunk into stardust.

Zhade ran a finger through the dust on the med cart, searching for something to say.

"Wead!" A high trill of a voice echoed round the room, and a bundle of ganglish limbs and dark curls bounded into Wead's arms.

"They said you were back, but I never recked . . . It didn't seem possible . . . You . . . I . . . How . . ." She continued to mumble nonsense into his chest.

She was taller than Zhade had memory, but she'd been eight when they were banished, and that would make her . . . twelve now. Wead could bareish rest his chin atop her head.

"Heya, Doon," Wead said, as he hugged his sister tighter.

Their parents had died when Doon was mereish a kiddun, and Wead had practicalish raised her. If Zhade could bring himself to regret dragging Wead with him adesert, it would sole be because of the skinny dark-haired girl hanging on to the brother she hadn't seen in four years. She pulled out of the hug, but held her hands clasped in his, jumping up and down and squealing her excitement. She caught sight of Zhade and stopped.

"Ugh. You made it back too?" She scowled.

"Brought your brother back for you," he said, crossing his arms and leaning against the wall.

"Do you expect thanks? *You* took him away firstish."

"Doon—" Wead cut in.

She turned back to her brother, as though Zhade weren't even there. "Where are you staying? Does the Guv know you're here? I have friends—"

"Where's Dzeni?"

Her face fell. She still looked like a kiddun, her cheeks round, her forlorn expression almost a pout.

"Is Dzeni evens?" Wead's voice was frantic. He grabbed his jacket from the cot and moved toward the door.

"Firm," Doon said, stopping him. "Firm, she's evens."

"Are you not . . ." Wead frowned. "I recked after I . . . I recked you would stay with her."

"I . . ." Doon's gaze flicked to Zhade. "I stayed with the Schism. But that's not . . . I haven't for true talked to Dzeni since . . ." She took a deep breath. Let it out. "She has a kiddun, Wead."

"A—" Wead cleared his throat. "A kiddun?"

She ran an unconscious hand through her dark hair, not meeting her brother's eyes. "Firm. A boy. I don't reck. I've seen her round. She's always with someone. Cheska. Big boyo. A flamehead."

Wead was suddenish preoccupied with arranging his clothing: tucking in his shirt, straightening his collar. He picked at a hangnail. Doon was unnaturalish still.

"Sorries, Wead," Zhade said.

Dzeni had been kind. Strong in a way most people overlooked. She was quiet, but had yelled at Zhade on more than one occasion for getting Lew-Eadin into trouble. She wasn't imposing, but that somehow made it worse when he disappointed her. She and Wead had made promises just before he'd been banished.

"Cheska was always a good man," Wead said, dusting off his pants. "His shop did well. He'll take care of her . . . and the kiddun—"

His voice broke off and Zhade pretended not to notice.

"Are you staying with Tia?"

It took Wead a moment to comp Zhade's words, but when he did, his eyes widened. "She's terrifying."

Doon took his hand. The non-magic hand, Zhade noticed. "He's coming back to the Schism with me."

"The Schism is not what it once was, tiny warrior," Zhade said.

She scoffed. "What would you reck bout it? While you've been four years adesert, I've been working for them."

For the first time, Zhade noticed Doon wore swords—twin curved blades, strapped cross her back, hilts glinting in the dim torchlight. And she hadn't just gotten taller. She was still skinny and long-limbed, but she also looked strong. She'd always resembled her brother—the same bronze skin, the same tangle of dark curls, the same warm brown eyes. But now she also looked like her own person. With a story he recked nothing bout.

Her brother had been surviving the Wastes the past four years. What had Doon been surviving?

"And what is the Schism now?" Zhade asked.

Doon gave him a withering look. "Wouldn't you like to reck."

"Firm. I would. That's why I asked."

Doon rolled her eyes. She was definitish starting teenish years. "We mostish provide shelter for refugees. And there are . . . other missions."

The way Doon said it, he recked she meant illegal or dangerful. When Zhade's mother had been alive, the Schism had been more than a group of sorcers, but Zhade didn't reck exactish what. His mam never told him much, and what little she did, he wasn't allowed to tell his father. Zhade always assumed it was something subversive, something against the government. Reiden had been a mostish benevolent ruler (if somewhat oblivious), but now that Maret was Guv . . .

After Reiden died and they came after Zhade's mam, things in Eerensed got bad quickish. Maret was a massive sorcer, especialish with the mysteriful Silver Crown, but he was a dreadful ruler. He ignored what was best for the people, instead focusing on parties and appearances. He used up resources, leaving few for the citians. It was Maret's fault the gods' dome was failing. Maret's fault there was sole one goddess left. Maret's fault Zhade was an orphan.

The Schism reacted by dedicating themselves to protecting their city from its guv. Zhade recked things had mereish gotten worse since he was banished. What exactish was his tiny friend-sister part of?

"Where's the Schism hiding these days?" Zhade picked up a palmberry that was no doubt meant for Wead from a nearby table and bit into it.

"The easthand caves under the Hive," Doon said. "It's safe there."

Zhade doubted it. Nowhere was safe. Not anymore.

"Good." He pocketed the palmberry and switched it for the speak-easy he had stored there. He tossed it to Wead, who caught the small copper coin without looking. "Sorcered this from Fishy. You have memory of Fishy?"

A smile tugged at Wead's lips. It had been the angel Zhade's mam had sorcered the most. She hadn't named it Fishy—that had been a three-year-old Zhade. He was surprised to find it still apalace. He'd expected most of his mam's things to be destroyed or . . . repurposed. He'd found most of her belongings missing, but there were a few things left Maret must not have recked the power of.

Zhade nodded to the speak-easy—a flat metal disc bout the size of his thumb. "It'll glow when we need to meet. Use the southhand tunnel. That wing is blocked off anow."

Lew-Eadin frowned, and opened his mouth to say something, to argue probablish, but Zhade cut him off.

"We'll need to polish up our new goddess. Make her shiny for the Guv."

Wead blinked slowish. "Has the Goddess agreed to this?"

"Nearish."

He avoided Wead's gaze. He recked what his friend would say—that they needed to tell the Goddess the full plan, the full story. But Zhade was too used to holding secrets—to *having* to—and he wasn't bout to break habits now. Sides, even Wead didn't reck the full truth—mereish the instructions Zhade's mam had left, not how Zhade planned to fulfill them.

"We march forward," he said. "Make certz Maret trusts her."

"And the Guv's mother?" Wead asked.

Zhade shook his head. He had no proof, but he imagined Tsurina was the one who had killed his father. And it was her actions that led directish to his mam's death, though Maret did the deed. Tsurina was unpredictable, and he'd need to take an eye out. He would feel more prepped if he could mereish determine what she *wanted*. People were so much easier to manipulate when you recked their wants. It was usualish something simple like love or power. But Tsurina seemed to need neither. She never had friends or partners. Even with Maret, she bareish seemed to care for his feelings. As for power, she could have easyish taken the throne instead of Maret, but she didn't. Firstish, Zhade assumed Maret had held his mam from the throne using the Silver Crown, but now he wasn't so certz.

"We'll watch her, but we need to focus on holding Maret happy and making the Goddess more goddessish."

He could tell Wead didn't like it, but Wead didn't like much, so he spozed the less happy Wead was with a plan, the more likeish it was to work.

Wead gripped the coin in his magic-made hand before putting it in his pocket.

"You brought back the Goddess?" Doon asked, eyes narrowing. "Which one?"

"The Third. Why? Is there more than one?"

Doon shrugged, but a harsh smile tugged at her lips. "There's a rumor the Second is still alive."

Wead placed his natural hand on Doon's shoulder. "There's always a rumor. I wouldn't hope. Fishes and wishes."

Doon gave them both a level look. "I reck if the goddesses skooled us anything, it's that there are no fishes and wishes. Or hope."

Zhade didn't disagree, but Wead looked like he was bout to argue.

Doon tilted her head to the door. "Let's peace?"

Wead nodded, then gave Zhade a sorries look before following her back to the tunnel entrance, Zhade on their heels. They said goodbye to Tia Ludmila and lowered themselves into the underground passage, but it diverged in two directions—one to the Hive, one to the Rock.

"Tonight," Zhade said to Wead. "Have memory of the speak-easy. It'll glow when we're prepped to meet."

Wead nodded. They clasped forearms and traded decide-your-fates, and Wead and Doon disappeared into the dark.

Zhade twirled his own speak-easy round his fingers as he made his march back to the palace, plotting out contingency plans that accounted for Tsurina's unpredictability and the Goddess's misguidedness. He couldn't let anything come between him and his goals. Maret had taken everything from him. Both his parents, the four years he spent adesert, and his throne. Sole one of those things Zhade could get back, and so he would. There was work to be done and fate to be decided.

ELEVEN

lacuna, n.

Etymology: Latin *lacuna*: a hole, pit, anything hollow. Became synonymous with technology due to the prevalence of the Lacuna Athenaeum Corporation, a conglomerate under the direction of Dr. Alberta Griffin, which specialized in everything from cryonics to space travel to nano'meds.

Definition: 1. in a manuscript, an inscription, or text: a hiatus, blank, missing portion.

2. the hole left by something missing.

ANDRA WAS STUCK *in a loop. A recursive function swirling her from memory to memory. The third-grade spelling bee. Playing darz with Oz at the sim'porium on Twenty-sixth Street. Eating satay with Ah Ma.*

Her father, reading The Future's Historians *in his study, when she was eight. She hung in the doorway.*

Her mother, disassembling their first AI, and Andra crying.

"It's just an AI," her mother saying, the scar new and shiny on her face. "Not quite human."

She was in the kitchen, with her brother. He was laughing.

She was fourteen and in the school library. Rhin and Briella were whispering. Of course they were whispering—it was the library—but Andra wished they would whisper a little louder so she could hear. Her best friends were best friends with each other.

She was eating dinner at her house. Cruz was there. He caught her eye over a forkful of green beans and winked. She looked away, and blushed.

That night, she told Acadia about it. Back when her older sister went by Cadi. Back when she and Cadi were friends.

Her mother, downloading her report card. Her mother, disappointed. Her mother, yelling.

This is a dream, *Andra thought.*

Her mother was dead. They were all dead. All of them, except Andra.

She felt like she'd woken too early. Like something wasn't finished yet. But that wasn't it. She'd woken too late. Or perhaps she wasn't awake at all. Perhaps none of this was real. Perhaps she *wasn't real.*

There were numbers in her head. Numbers. Not words. And they were getting smaller, and the memories began to fade.

ANDRA WOKE IN the same position she'd passed out in, her clothes stiff with Lew-Eadin's blood, the tile smudged with crimson handprints. At least she wasn't drowning this time.

She hadn't meant to fall asleep, but her body had demanded it. She almost shot up with relief, wanting to prove to herself that she was awake, alive, but her muscles were too stiff. Her cheek lay cool and sticky against the floor of her new room.

Her back ached as she pushed herself to stand, her body screaming at her for the unideal sleeping position. If the nanos swarming around her had been compatible, her 'implant would have used them to work out the kinks, sending code that would switch them to med'nanos. But her muscles would have to heal on their own. Her burned hand no longer hurt, at least. She took in the room, looking for a place to wash up. The light was soft, casting a pink glow, and a slight breeze drifted from the balcony, cooling the sweat clinging to her skin. It sent a shiver down her spine. She vaguely wondered what time it was. The last time she'd overslept, she'd done so by nearly a millennium.

"Evens, it's been time and a half," said a voice behind her.

Andra whipped around. Zhade stood silhouetted in the doorway.

"What the hell are you doing here?" Her blood-soaked shirt was rucked up over her stomach. She tugged it down. "Were you watching me sleep?"

"Scuze," Zhade scoffed. "I was watching you *drool*."

She wiped her cheek before remembering the blood on her hands. It coated her like dark evening gloves. She pushed herself to her feet and began looking for a towel, one eye trained on Zhade.

"Get out," she said, tugging at her shirt again. "Wait. How's Lew-Eadin?"

She held her breath. The more she thought about it, the more she was convinced it had been her fault—that her 'implant had called the nanos from the pocket to protect her.

"Evens," Zhade said, and she could hear the shrug in his voice. "What did I tell you? Tia Ludmila healed him full bars. He has a new magic hand now." He raised his own hand and wiggled his fingers.

Andra waited for the relief, but it didn't come. She wasn't sure if she could trust Zhade to tell the truth, but surely he would show some grief if Lew hadn't survived.

"Good." She gave a single nod. "Now get out."

She had to clean off all the dried blood, and then she had to figure out what to do next.

Zhade grinned, sauntering into the room. He was dressed like the guards in the throne room, except he wore his uniform incomplete, his black shirt strategically unbuttoned at the top, his sleeves rolled up to his elbows. The ostentatious wrist cuffs were missing, as was the gold breastplate (so as not to defeat the purpose of the overlooked buttons), but a scabbard hung at his side. It was missing the ridiculous sword the other guards carried. They probably didn't trust him with a weapon. Andra didn't blame them.

"Sands," he cursed, looking her up and down. "Are you familiar with baths?"

"You used me." She stomped over to the vanity. Nothing to wipe her hands there. Then the wardrobe. She left fingerprints on the gold trim.

"That's what a deal is, Goddess," Zhade said. "We agree to use each other. Evens and odds, did you learn anything at goddess skool? Speaking of, we'll be starting one of our own. Tonight. It seems there are gaps in your education, and if you're going to survive, you need to fill in those gaps."

"Were you planning on telling me?"

"Bout goddess lessons?"

"About any of it!" She grabbed a dress from the wardrobe. It was silk. Handmade. Probably worth more than the entire village she'd been found in. She used it to scrub her hands. "Or was it all just a lie to get you where you wanted to be, *your highness.*"

Zhade's expression darkened for a moment before fading back into his usual grin. "Oh, I'm nowhere near where I want to be. Not yet, anyway." He crossed to the wardrobe and nudged Andra out of the way to riffle through the delicate clothes inside. "That's why I need your help."

"I'm done helping you."

Zhade rolled his eyes, pulling out a random dress. "Wear this. The bloodstains are dramistic, but I imagine you should choose something that says *ethereal deity*, and not homicidal psychopath."

Her eyes narrowed. "When in Rome."

"Don't reck what that means, but certz it's brill." He tossed the dress onto her bed. The material was light, made of a gauzy fabric that looked suspiciously see-through. It had a high waist, no sleeves. Mostly white, except for bursts of red. Despite what Zhade had said, it was obvious he was going for a certain imagery. "In the prenights after your goddess duties, Lew and I are going to skool you how to be a goddess."

Andra shook her head. "I'm not doing any goddess duties *or* goddess lessons."

"We'll see." He sank into a pink upholstered chair, swinging his legs over the armrest, and she fully saw his resemblance to Maret. She shivered.

"Why didn't you tell me the Guv was your brother?"

"*Half*-brother," he said, pointedly, relaxing into the chair, crossing his arms and ankles. "I'm illegitimate. A bastard." He lowered his voice to a stage whisper. "They say my mother was a whore."

Based on Tsurina's reaction to Zhade and her comments about his mother, Andra guessed that wasn't the full story. Unless this society punished cheating and prostitution by death. Of course, they might. She wasn't exactly sure what to expect from these people—warped descendants of the original colonists, distorted just like the tech around her.

Andra raised an unimpressed eyebrow. "Should we just add that to the list of things you neglected to tell me?"

Zhade scoffed. "Like what? I've been mereish honest."

She began counting off on her fingers. "That I had to *prove* I was a goddess or I'd get killed. That the other goddesses are *dead*. That you're related to the . . . *Guv* or whatever. Oh yeah, that Maret took your throne—"

"Evens, if you want to get magical bout it." Zhade groaned, leaning his head back and closing his eyes. A breeze from the balcony ruffled his hair. "And Maret didn't *take* the throne. It was given to him. No one recks I—"

"I don't care!"

He raised his hands, placating. "You were just yelling at me for not being forthcoming. I'm mereish trying to provide as much info as possible. I'm older, but Maret was the son of the Guv's wife. My mother was . . ." He stuck out his bottom lip, thinking. "Not the Guv's wife. I don't reck if you realized, but Tsurina doesn't like me full much."

"I. don't. care," Andra repeated. "I got you in your stupid city. Now all I want is—"

What *did* she want? Or, more to the point, what *could* she want? The deepest desire of her heart was to go back before any of this had happened and convince her family not to be colonists. To cry, argue, sabotage, whatever it took to prevent this from happening. Barring that, what she wanted was to go home. Only, Earth wasn't home anymore, not really. It would be unrecognizable to her a thousand years in the future. But compared to this planet, it seemed like the best option.

"Goddess?" Zhade prompted. "What do you want? Me? Don't be embarrassed. Most people do."

Andra ignored the comment, though it made her stomach flutter strangely. The question wasn't what did she want, but what did she *need*? If she was going to survive this city and get the hell off this planet, what would it take? She currently had no way to get back to Earth, but that didn't mean she couldn't create one.

"I want a mech'bot . . . *angel*," she corrected when Zhade looked confused. "One of the tall ones with the wide shoulders outside the throne room."

Mech'bots were tall, bulky, and strong, perfectly programmed for heavy labor. And this society was using them to *open doors*.

Zhade let out a bark of a laugh. "Is that all? Mereish one of the Angelic Guards? Why stop there? Why not Maret's personal angelic conduit? Or the buttons from his shoes?"

Andra set a hand on her hip. "Why not? I could always use extra buttons. And I also need any spare metal you can find." She started rifling through the drawers of her vanity, looking for supplies. "And any, uh, magic no one is using. Or, you know what, it doesn't even matter if someone's using it. I need it more."

A plan was forming in her head. Outrageous and risky, and if she could pull it off, she might just deserve to be called a goddess. All she needed were some scraps of metal, a mech'bot, and an AI. That last one was going to be tricky. On the surface, AI were indistinguishable from standard robots, but not all 'bots were AI. They'd been rare even in Andra's time.

"Seeya," Zhade snorted. "You want me to steal magical conduits for you? Sorcers' prized possessions? Their livinghood? And somehow procure one of the most conspicuous royal angels in the full of Eerensed?" He scoffed. "Stabbing me would be a quicker way to kill me, Goddess."

"Don't think I haven't ruled that out."

Zhade frowned. "Ruled . . . what?"

Andra stomped toward an alcove on the other side of the room. To her relief, it led to a bathroom. To her mortification, there was no door. And the indoor plumbing was nothing but a few pipes and a complicated pulley system.

Zhade followed, his hands jammed in his pockets. "Neg, for serious. Ruled what?"

Andra bit her lip. If the 'bot from the desert was correct—and it had been correct about Andra's dead family—then the Ark was still in geosynchronous orbit. An interstellar ship. All she needed was a short-range shuttle to get to it. She doubted any of those were lying around, but a mech'bot could be programmed to create one. Of course, assuming she found one and enough spare parts to create a shuttle, she would still be out of luck without a pilot for the Ark. And Andra would need someone—or some*thing*—to put her back in stasis. An AI could do it. But where was she going to find an AI in a place like this?

One step at a time, Watts.

First, she needed a mech'bot, and she needed to survive long enough for it to build a shuttle.

"How about this?" Andra said, turning on the faucet. It spluttered rust, then a burst of cold water splashed from the tap. "I'll take these stupid goddess lessons, *if* you find me the things I need."

Zhade grinned, but the expression was strained. He ran a hand through his hair. "Seeya, I can maybe, *maybe*, find you some spare magical conduits. Give me a list, and I'll do my best. But there's no march for me stealing an Angelic Guard from under Mare's chin."

"Fine. Then let's start with those spare parts." Andra ran her hands under the tap. The water turned a sickly pink, as she grabbed a nearby bar of soap. It stung, but she started to scrub. "You keep bringing me what I ask for, and I'll keep attending goddess lessons."

Zhade groaned, but it felt staged, like he was getting exactly what he wanted. "Evens. Magic for goddess lessons." He held out his hand. "Deal?"

They shook on it, Andra's hand still dripping with water and soap.

Zhade smirked. "This is a stupid custom, marah?"

She took her hand back, flicking water in his face. "Why do you even care if I pull off being a goddess? What do you get out of it?"

"Can't I mereish help you because I'm a nice boyo?"

"Not based on precedent."

"Hmm," Zhade said, flicking a towel from a nearby hook and offering it to her. "Let's just say my survival depends on your survival."

Andra grabbed the towel, a little harder than necessary. "Why are you even here? What are you trying to do? Take your throne back? Is that why Maret banished you? Because he wanted your throne? Or because you're a pain in the ass?"

Zhade pursed his lips, thinking. "Probablish a bit of both."

The towel had already turned pink.

"Maret was always . . ." Zhade shrugged. "Maret. Awkward. Stand-asidish. We were friendish when we were kidduns. Tsurina made a stop to that quickish. No one recked who I was, or even that Maret was a second son. He would have gotten the throne anyway, but apparentish it wasn't enough. They wanted me peaced adesert."

"Why didn't Maret just kill you?" Andra muttered, trying to make it sound like a veiled threat, but not quite pulling it off.

Zhade leaned against the wall, puffing out a sigh. "I imagine he recked the Wastes would do it for him." A grin spread across his face. "He's twice the fool, then, marah?"

His voice was light, even playful, but Andra thought she could detect a hint of sadness in his eyes.

She bit her lip. "How did the other goddesses die?"

Zhade was quiet for a moment, watching her with an unreadable expression. Finally he said, "You were asleep for time and a half."

"Not what I asked."

He seemed to weigh his next words carefully. "There's always a balance to things. Where there's worship, there's dissent. Everyone's god is a devil to others."

"They were murdered."

"Not what I said." Zhade took a deep breath and scratched the back of his head. "Hear. This is why you need me. I can help you. I comp Eerensed and Maret and how to hold you alive. I can skool you how to be a goddess people won't want to kill. Especialish Maret."

Andra hung the towel back on the hook. "Why? What's so important? What do you want from him?"

"The Crown."

"So you do want his throne."

"Neg—not—I want the *Silver* Crown." Zhade took the towel and refolded it neatly before hanging it back up. "The one on his temple."

The 'implant—the one that allowed him to control 'bots, and was probably the reason he governed the city. So no matter what Zhade said, he wanted Maret's position of power. He was going to be disappointed. Crowns couldn't be detached without a nano'surgeon.

"Full bars bout me," Zhade said. He rocked back on his heels, his mood suddenly shifting, and thrust his hands in his pockets. "Time for you to prepify for the ceremony. Certz you don't want help?" He winked.

She ignored him. "Ceremony?"

"Firm, it's an event where people—"

"I know what a ceremony is."

"Eight abell, then." He turned to go before Andra could ask any follow-up questions. "I'll send up your replacement maids."

"My replacement maids? What happened to the ones from last night?"

"The ones you yelled at and shoved out of your room?"

"I wanted to apologize." She picked at her fingernails.

Zhade clucked his tongue. "Evens, that will be difficult seeing as they're bout to be executed."

It took Andra a moment too long to process the words. Or one word in particular. *Executed.* It was harsh and archaic and she'd never heard it used outside of novels and period sims.

"What?"

"They displeased you, Goddess, what did you imagine would happen?"

Andra's mind whirled. She'd failed some test she hadn't even known she was taking. People were going to die because of *her*. It was like her brain couldn't . . . couldn't *process* that. The world dropped out from under her. She grabbed the sink to steady herself. Zhade was still talking, but she didn't hear the words. He was speaking through water. She was still in the 'tank, drowning, unable to breathe.

Before she could stop herself, she pushed past him.

"Where are you peacing to?" he called after her.

"To save them."

"What? Neg." Zhade hurried to catch up with her, his armor clinking, his movements stiff. "Neg. That is a fraughted idea. Whatever moral high dune you reck you have now, it won't meteor. Not against Maret. He's the Guv."

Andra threw open the door. "Yeah? Well apparently I'm a goddess."

TWELVE

THE INTERCESSOR

ZHADE FOLLOWED THE Goddess. It wasn't difficult to keep apace with her. Her stride was short, and she wasn't clued where she was going. The Rock was a maze even to seasoned servants and diplomats—stone staircases, brick hallways, tight winding passages. Although Zhade hadn't magicalish aged up here, his mam had made certz he recked the layout of the palace full well. The little Goddess did not.

"This is bad magic," Zhade said, but he comped no argument would convince her. Sides, it might be good for her to see what she was marching toward. It would be a thin string they'd half-walk if Zhade was to get Maret to trust her. She couldn't seem weak, because then the Eerensedians wouldn't follow her and she'd be useless to the Guv. But if she appeared too powerful, she wouldn't survive the day. She needed to see what the consequences were if she stepped too far aside.

After several woefulish wrong guesses, Zhade took pity on her and began to lead her in the direction of the Yard. It was where all executions took place. Including his mother's.

It was also, not by accident, the same place the goddesses were held agrave.

The angels and servants ignored them as they wended through the palace. The diplomats stared. It probablish had to do with the blood-stains on the Goddess's shirt, but also, Zhade's new uniform was brill.

He wasn't for certz why Maret had made him a guard. Like the Goddess had said, it would have made more sense for Maret to have killed his half-brother long ago, and now, he was not mereish *not killing* him, but he was trusting Zhade to *protect* him. Maret had a thing in his sleeve.

But Zhade had several.

He took the Goddess down to the base floor on the westhand side of the palace. A small, unassuming door was tucked beneath a stair. This was mereish a side entry to the Yard, but Zhade certz as sand wasn't going to take her through the main entrance.

"Are you certz you want to do this?" Zhade asked, recking the answer.

She glared.

He shrugged. "It's your fate to decide."

The First had been too powerful—a leader, rather than the servant the people wanted in a goddess. The Second had quiet ire and un-contained passion. Neither had decided their own fates. If any of the Goddesses could be what the people wanted, what Maret wanted, it would be the Third. It *had* to be.

He opened the door, revealing the Yard beyond.

The side entrance opened to an alcove behind the alters; so firstish, they didn't see anything, mereish heard the murmur of the crowd. Fraughts. Zhade hadn't been expecting an audience. It was one thing for the Goddess to confront Maret with a handful of guards present. It was full another for her to do it with citians there. This was sud-denish full bad magic.

The people had already started praying, and Zhade felt the stardust circling round them. It reminded him of cathedzal with his mam when the dust would swarm thick enough to see. Evens. Maret had turned this into a religiful ceremony. Zhade should have been expecting this. A religiful execution prepped Maret's intro of the Goddess tonight.

Zhade would have to imagine this through at care. If he couldn't convince the Goddess to give up trying to save her maids, maybe he could skool her the right words to say to prevent her from joining them.

The Goddess took a deep breath and let it out. That was the mereish warning Zhade got before she marched out of the alcove. She stopped short when she saw the graves.

On the other side of the wall were three daises, one for each Goddess. The First's was decorated with Coils, the Second's with Crystals, and the Third's with Celestias. The graves of the First and Second still stood on their platforms, shining in the moren light. There was a darkened outline in the stone where the Third's grave had sat before she disappeared.

Zhade put a steadying hand on the Goddess's back. She was breathing too quickish.

The crowd beyond were faced away, packed shoulder-to-shoulder, dressed in Rock uniforms and the bright fabrics of Southwarden and the fraying threads of the Hive. Maret must have wanted as many people present as possible. But without the Goddess as witness, what charges was he executing the maids on? Or did it meteor? Maret didn't even have to play benevolent ruler with the Silver Crown on his head. Fear ruled.

Without the crowd, the Yard was full charred, a perf place for honoring the goddesses. The outer walls of the Rock hid behind ivy and crawl-plants. The floor was tiled in mosaics, and rare flowers sprouted from every corner. The garden fitted itself round the Yard's centerpiece—a three-tiered fountain featuring a mythic swan. It had been his mam's favorite.

This should have been a place of peace, but Maret used it for displays of power. In front of the crowd was a metal platform. On it, the three maids stood, hands bound behind their backs. They were surrounded by angels ready to follow the command of the Silver Crown.

A sandstorm of memories swept over Zhade, and he tensed. He

couldn't let them blow him over soon and now. He had to stay focused on the full alive Goddess afront of him. He had to make certz she stayed that way.

Maret stood to the side, his face flushed and grim. It was the same expression he'd had when he'd ordered Zhade's mother's execution. It almost looked like he didn't want to do it. As though this were all for the good of the people, a necessary burden he would bear.

The maids were still in their white servant uniforms, their faces streaked with dirt. Zhade bet they had spent the night in the cells below the Rock. When his mother had been executed, they had done it quickish. They'd dragged her straight to the Yard, angry mobs of people already pressing at the gates, prepped to watch her final moments. She'd recked it was coming and had taken the time to braid her hair. It was an odd detail to have memory, but Zhade held on to it like it was the answer to every question he'd ever had.

The youngest maid was crying. She was mereish a few years younger than Zhade. Her fam was probablish from the Hive and sent her to the Rock to earn a few extra Silver Seconds. The others were more stoic. Nearish resigned. The oldest was trying to chant along with the people, her chapped lips bareish forming the words.

"What are they saying?" the Goddess asked, breathless.

It wasn't a prayer Zhade had heard before. He hadn't memorized . . . *any* of them, but he could have easyish translated a standard prayer into High Goddess. Instead, he had to strain to listen, to make sense. He'd grown too used to Wastern dialects. It had been time and a half since he'd spoken Eerensedian.

"These are punished . . . neg, *to be* punished. The goddesses will it. Sunk into stardust. The goddesses demand it. Sunk into sand. Just like the sacrifices—"

He cut himself off, not wanting to translate the rest.

The Goddess frowned. "That's . . . really creepy. Why are they chanting?"

Zhade had memory of his mam first explaining the chants to him. That was when he stopped saying them. "It's a ritual. They believe when they get enough people saying the same thing, imagining the same thing, they can control the stardust."

"The stardust?" The Goddess held her voice low, following Zhade's example.

"It's . . . a bit the essence of things? It surrounds us and responds to High Magic—like yours or the Guv's. Most sorcers use Low Magic. We need a conduit. But High Magic bypasses that and works through the stardust."

It wasn't odd that she was asking—the first two goddesses had different names for everything too. It *was* odd that except for saving herself from the grafter, she'd done no magic at all.

The chanting got louder, covering whatever the Goddess said next. Zhade tensed, prepped to stop her if she made a move toward the Guv. She should see this, maybe even fight Maret bout it. But later, without an audience. When Maret felt in control.

The air above them thickened. Zhade had always imagined stardust had a cloud-like quality, but now that he'd been adesert, he recked it looked more like a sandstorm. The dust glittered, and as the people looked up in awe, they chanted louder.

Three angels stepped forward, one for each of the maids. They were bright white, polished for the occasion. Zhade imagined he could see magic sparking the coils in their skulls, though they were too far away to see crystal. They stood behind the maids, holding them aplace. Maret controlled them, standing tall, arms outstretched. It was mereish flash, not full necessity. High Magic was done with will, not movement. But Maret was always trying to prove his power, rather than mereish use it.

"What are they doing?" the Goddess whispered, her face close to his, her breath warm. She hummed with energy.

"You'll see."

She was quiet for a moment. Then, "No. I won't."

She darted forward before he could grab her.

"Wait!" she screamed over the chanting voices, and firstish no one heard her. "Stop!"

It was too much to ask that she would mereish be ignored and give up. She pushed through the crowd, yelling for them to stop. Zhade tried to follow, but though he was thinner than her, he was taller and broader, and the people were too tightish packed. He edged along the side of the Yard, hoping to cut her off.

He recked better than to hope. Fishes and wishes.

She made it to the edge of the platform, knocking into a plant pot, spilling its contents on the ground.

"Stop!" she screamed, and Maret's eyes met hers.

He held his expression surprisingish blank as he willed the stardust to coalesce into three ghostish spears, suspended and sparkling in the moren light. He paused mereish a second. Then plunged the spikes into the maids' chests.

The crowd silenced. There were no cheers at an execution.

Nausea roiled Zhade's stomach. He steadied himself against the ivy-covered Rock wall but couldn't block the memories.

Zhade's mam on her knees.

A spray of blood.

Her blank stare as she toppled forward.

She hadn't seen him in the crowd. Her last words to him had been the turn before. *Find the Third, protect her, don't let Maret have the crown.* It was sole later that Zhade realized his mam had been talking bout the strange Silver Crown, not the gold one his father had worn.

She would be so disappointed. The Crown on Maret's head, and the Third marching forward into disaster.

The silence was broken by the Goddess's scream. Zhade shook himself and pushed ahead. Her scream cut short, her eyes fixated on the dead maids.

An excited hum rose through the crowd. Zhade heard the words *Third* and *Goddess* amid the murmurs, and recked it was too late to move anywhere but forward. It seemed Maret had come to the same conclusion, as he reached the Goddess before Zhade and pulled her onto the platform. It groaned beneath them. She stumbled, but Maret's grip held her upright.

"People of Eerensed, our Goddess has returned!" he shouted in what was bareish a passable imitation of excitement.

The crowd roared. This is what they'd been waiting for. The Third Goddess. Their last hope. The other two had failed them, but for certz this one would not. Maret pulled her closer. She cringed at the contact, but her body was moving as if by rote. It wouldn't be long before the shock and politeness were blunted, and Zhade needed to be there before she did something stupid that decided both their fates. He rushed forward, at care not to sprint and pose a threat. But his guard's uniform let him be both ignored and feared, and no one stopped him as he mounted the platform and stepped behind the Goddess.

"Whatever you do," Zhade whispered in her ear, "do *not* confront him here."

He expected a fight, but she mereish nodded. He felt her shallow breaths, saw her hands shake. Maret met his eyes over her shoulder, and his expression was carefulish blank. He was getting better at hiding his emotions.

The crowd's cheers didn't wane, mereish got louder and stronger, til the full mob was in sync, crying the same word over and over.

"Goddess! Goddess! Goddess!" The stardust swirled round her.

She was grubby and dirty from days adesert. Blood soaked her clothes and even congealed in her tangled dark hair. At her feet were three corpses. This was not the intro Zhade had hoped for. But the people cheered on.

THIRTEEN

mask, n.

Etymology: perhaps from Latin *masca*: evil spirit.

Definition: 1. anything disguising or concealing the face.

2. a pretense; a masquerade; subterfuge.

3. colloq.: when preceded by an apostrophe, refers to a bionic facial covering that allows the wearer to enhance or change facial features; short for cosmetic mask, or cos'mask.

ANDRA NUMBLY FOLLOWED Maret through the halls of the Rock, his midnight robes swishing against the marble floors. Zhade's grip on her arm was tight—not so tight as to hurt, but enough to warn her she was in dangerous territory.

As if she needed the reminder.

She'd just seen three people killed in front of her. Because of her. She'd never seen anyone die before, but even more disturbing was the manner of their deaths.

They'd been murdered by nano'bots.

That should have been impossible. In Andra's time, there were overrides that prevented nanos from acting on commands that caused humans harm, barred 'bots from using dangerous objects, required special 'implant software for weapon use. There were accidents of course—technology was never perfect; there was always human error. However, they were few and far between, and there had never been an account of *intentional* harm.

But as Andra had observed, the tech around her had been updated countless times in the past thousand years until it had morphed into something else. Something not quite right.

The Guv had used his crown to command the nanos to kill.

The maid's faces were permanently etched in Andra's brain—the way the oldest welcomed the blow, the grimace of the one Andra's mother's age, and the surprise on the youngest's face as she died. There'd been a moment Andra felt something rise inside her, and she thought maybe, just maybe, she could turn the coalesced nanos to healing tech and bring the women back. But it was a ridiculous thought. Even if her 'implant had been compatible with the nanos, she couldn't reverse death.

So Andra had watched them die, watched the spears disperse back into an invisible force in the air, watched Maret use her presence to unite the people, watched the hungry expressions in the crowd.

Behind the horror, she was starting to piece together bits of how this society functioned. They no longer understood the tech left over from the original colonists, so they'd created a religion around it—around the nanos they called stardust, and the 'bots that seemed all-powerful and immortal, and the three colonists who had slept unchanging in glass coffins. And it was more than just Andra's and her predecessors' perceived immortality that gave them god status. Zhade had said the others could do magic with no more than a thought, which meant they were cognitively interfacing with the nanos rather than manually coding the 'bots. They could use the nanos to perform what the people would see as miracles. So why couldn't Andra? What was different about the first two goddesses that made them able to use their 'implants while Andra couldn't?

She shook off the thought. She could worry about that later, but right now, she had to focus on how to keep the Guv from killing her like he'd just killed her maids.

"Goddess," Zhade muttered under his breath. A warning.

They were at the far end of a long mirror-lined hall. One wall was entirely made of windows, and the late-morning sun shone in, bouncing off the reflective surfaces. Ahead of them was a door painted a violent shade of red. Dark tapestries lined either side, and Kiv took his post next to it, eyes straight ahead, spear held tightly in his fist.

"Welcome to my suite, Goddess," Maret said, and she felt anything but welcomed.

If she had been in her right mind, she would have run, but she was too shaken by the maids' executions to think straight. And besides, it was probably best to do as the Guv said, or she would be next.

He pressed his finger to a small pad by the door and winced. The space he'd touched glowed red, then green, and the door slid open. A crude DNA scan, but something these people probably saw as blood magic.

He entered the room, and Andra followed.

"It's peaches, Kiv," she heard Zhade say behind her.

The room beyond was a cave. The walls were a black marble, streaked with red. The furniture was overlarge and brutish. A dozen upholstered chairs were situated around the room, all facing a single velvet couch the same color as the blood-red veins in the marble. Maret gestured for Andra to have a seat. Zhade sat beside her, and Maret took the couch.

"Would you like something to drink, Goddess?" a voice said, and it was only then that Andra realized Tsurina was in the room. Her dress was a royal blue and it matched her long, pointed nails. She was pouring a dark liquid into a cup, steam rising from the rim.

"No, thank you," Andra croaked, her heart hammering.

"I'll take some of that," Zhade said.

Tsurina ignored him and handed the cup to her son.

Zhade leaned closer to Andra. "She probablish would have poisoned it anyway."

Tsurina's eyes cut to him. "Probablish."

Maret took a sip, looking over the rim at Andra. "I was surprised to see you at the ritual today, Goddess."

"The ritual?" she asked, her voice flat. "That was *murder*."

She heard Zhade suck in a breath, but he made no move to stop her.

Maret groaned. "They were *executed*." He set down his cup, eyes flicking to Tsurina.

"No," Andra said through gritted teeth. The passive voice set her on edge. *They were executed.* As though it had been an accident, or their own fault. "You *killed* them."

Tsurina made a noise in the back of her throat and sat in a nearby chair. Her posture was stiff, a sad smile tacked to her face. Maret abandoned his cup of tea, moving to an ornate liquor cabinet Andra noticed was out of the advisor's line of sight. It also brought him closer to a plasma'dagger. A few laser'guns were mounted on the walls, and Andra didn't understand why guards carried swords and spears when they had technology like that. Unless, of course, they didn't have 'implants. But Maret had a crown, so it would only take a thought to bring the 'gun online or the 'dagger crackling to life.

Andra was suddenly aware of all the 'bots stationed around the room. The handful of guards were dangerous, sure, but it was the 'bots that frightened her. The guards had minds of their own, free will, and they might think twice before murdering a goddess. The 'bots, however, had no autonomy. They were merely extensions of Maret's every whim.

His fingers brushed against the 'dagger, but skipped over it to reach for a bottle of liquor instead.

"I did nothing," Maret said, unstoppering a crystal decanter. His voice was bored, patronizing. He poured the brown liquid into a glass. "It was the stardust, the angels, the will of the goddesses." He nodded toward Andra, rolling his eyes. "You must have wanted them dead, or you would have stopped it."

"You think I don't know my own mind?"

Maret smirked. "Do you?"

"You were heard screaming," Tsurina said, her voice a hypnotic purr, somehow both rich and thin, quiet and strong. "The maids rushed out of your room, and when a guard went to investigate, you were found lying unconscious on the floor. We were protecting you, but it is unfortunate you had to witness the incident."

"*Unfortunate*? The *incident*?" Andra snapped, the numbness fading and anger rising in its place. She gripped the edge of her chair cushion. "Were they given a trial? What were they even supposed to be guilty of? If the guards were so worried about me, why did no one wake me up to see if I was okay?"

"That's not how things happen here," Maret said, shoving a glass in her direction. She wrinkled her nose at the sharp scent. "Justice and punishment happen quickish. The gods' dome mereish sustains so many people. We can't allow thieves and murderers to take the place of good people. Innocent people. Your maids died so you and your . . . *friend*"—he glanced at Zhade—"could live here."

Andra didn't know how to argue with people like this. All she wanted was to stay alive long enough to find a mech'bot and an AI, and then get off this planet. Whatever had happened since the colonists had landed, whatever their descendants had become, it was warped and inhuman and evil, and Andra wanted no part of it.

Maret gave her a pitying smile. "Soze you see my side."

"They should have been given a trial," she said, her voice small. She crossed her arms over her stomach. "Why kill them? If you're so worried about the population, why not just make them leave the 'dome?"

Maret clenched his jaw and looked down at his drink, his face red.

"Mercy," Tsurina answered. Her elbow rested on the armrest, her long nails skimming her cheek. "You've seen the Wastes. It was kinder to give them a cleaner death. An Eerensedian wouldn't last a turn outside the gods' dome."

"Scuze," Zhade said, gesturing to himself.

"You've always been the exception," she said, her tone light, but teeth bared. "For many things."

"The exception, and exceptional." Zhade winked at Andra. Her cheeks burned. How could he be so cavalier after what happened?

Maret ignored him, but his expression was taut. "It's my job to hold the citians of Eerensed safe, to hold as many of them alive as possible. You haven't been here time and a half, but you'll lose that naivete soon and sooner. Sacrifices must be—"

"I can fix the 'dome," Andra blurted, a half-baked plan rising in her mind. This was a risk. She didn't even know what was wrong with the 'dome and definitely not how to fix it, but if she played this right, she wouldn't have to. "I just need something in return."

Maret frowned. "An offering?"

"Goddess," Zhade cut in. He placed a hand on her forearm in warning.

She pulled away. "No, not an offering."

"Then what?" Maret asked, running a hand through his hair. The white-blond locks were starting to fall into his eyes. "You have the ability to fix the gods' dome, but require something in return? Are you holding our lives hostage?"

"No!" Andra felt a surge of guilt. "I just need to inventory the, uh, magic of the angels . . . All the angels in the palace. Their magic can . . . supplement mine to fix the 'dome. But I don't know which ones. So I need to . . . check them." She inwardly cringed and hoped it didn't show on her face.

Maret's eyes narrowed. "The other goddesses didn't need angels to do their work for them."

Andra swallowed. "The other goddesses left you a faulty 'dome. Maybe they should have." Was that sacrilege? Did it count as blasphemy if she was a god herself?

If she'd offended them, they gave no indication. Tsurina only coughed, and asked, "How much time will this take?"

Andra sucked her teeth and shrugged. "It depends. On the angels. On the state of the 'dome." *On how long it takes me to find a mech'bot to build me a shuttle and an AI to fly me the hell off this planet.*

"You will have other responsibilities, Goddess," Tsurina said, and though her tone was polite, her eyes blazed. "The people will want to see you. There will be ceremonies and meetings and—"

There was a *thunk* as Maret slammed his glass down on the table. Liquid sloshed onto his hand.

"For certz she can have a bell each day, *mother,*" he said through gritted teeth. His hair was no longer slicked back, but hanging in strands across his face. "Between bells after dinner. We will do what we can to help you."

His words were for Andra but his eyes were on his mother. There seemed to be a struggle of wills, and then Tsurina sighed.

"Certz," she said, her smile slow and disconcerting. "I'll have Kiv bring a selection of angels to your suite after dinner."

"Thank you," Andra croaked, but she got the distinct impression that she wasn't actually getting what she wanted.

"Perhaps"—Tsurina stood, dabbing at the corners of her mouth with a cloth napkin—"the Goddess should be cleaned up before her Awakening Ceremony." She eyed the bloodstains on Andra's clothes.

The dismissal was clear. Andra wanted to keep arguing, to keep pushing. Nothing had been solved, and she felt like this conversation was setting a dangerous precedent. She should demand more time with the 'bots, free rein of the palace, no more killing. But Zhade nudged her arm.

"Time to peace, Goddess," he said. "You have a ceremony to prepify for." He stood and offered Andra his hand.

She ignored it but stood as well. "It seems I have *a lot* to prepare for." She gave an awkward curtsy.

Maret's smile was a sneer. "Decide your fate, Goddess."

Andra nodded. She would have to endure goddess lessons and political negotiations, but eventually she would get out of here. Deciding her fate was exactly what she planned to do.

ANDRA SAT AT a small table in her room, the balcony doors thrown wide and a breeze rustling her hair as she picked at her food. She moved her eggs from one side of the plate to the other in a way that would have made her mother snap when Andra was younger, and then, once Andra started gaining weight, would have left a glint of relief in her eye.

Andra needed to eat to keep her mind sharp. It would be easy to wallow in grief, but there were things to do if she wanted to survive. As long as Maret believed she was trying to fix the 'dome and Zhade believed she was trying to get him the crown and the Eerensedians believed she was a goddess, she would stay alive.

She needed her strength. So she ate.

A ceramic plate stacked with flatbread had been waiting for her when she got back to her room, along with an egg bake and reddish vegetables she didn't recognize. So had Kiv. He stood stoically by the door, his eyes never meeting hers. Even when Andra mumbled under her breath, "I don't eat with murderers watching," Kiv didn't even blink.

Andra was trying the pot of tea—it was cold, and she wished she could have used her 'implant to command the kettle to heat some more water—when there was a knock at the door. Before Andra could answer, a girl with brown skin and long dark hair waltzed in.

"Goddess," she said, her voice breathless. "I'm Lilibet." She bowed her head, dipping into a swift curtsy, then teetered as she rose. "Your new maid."

The girl was shorter than Andra, and skinny as a rod'bot. Her bronze skin was flushed, and a tiny hoop pierced her left nostril. When she smiled, she revealed a row of crooked white teeth, her tongue pressed against them as though she were holding back a squeal.

Andra wanted to tell her to leave, to run as far as she could. But if she dismissed her, and with Kiv watching, the girl might end up with the same fate as the other maids. Her dark hair hung to her waist, swaying as she skipped over to the table. She poured Andra some more tea, overflowing the cup when she noticed the guard standing silently by the door.

"Hi, Kiv!" Lilibet waved. Her cheeks darkened in a blush.

Kiv didn't respond, only stared at her with an intensity that made Andra want to step between them. His eyes narrowed, his dark complexion deepening. He nodded. Just once. The maid lowered her head shyly, biting back a smile.

"I priorish worked akitchens," Lilibet said, taking away Andra's eggs before she was finished and replacing them with flatbread. "Mainish stirring stuff—seeya, stews and things. It was always full hot, because, seeya, it's *fire*. And you don't for true get to dress nice, and I like dresses, and so when they said they needed maids for *you*, I volunteered *soon and sooner*, but they didn't pick me, but then this moren, Tarna said they needed someone else, and I begged and begged and *begged*, and they let me, and gave me this dress, and it happens *so charred*, marah?" She twirled for Andra. It was a simple white smock. "And to say truth, I imagine Tarna was glad to see me go, because she recked I talked too much."

Andra's eyes were wide, chin tucked.

"I've never seen a goddess up close before," she continued. "My fam worshipped the Second—neg offense—but I never got to see her. Except for the monies. One time, I got to hold a Silver Second because I was scrubbing dishes out back and a man said to give it to Tarna for—evens I don't have memory for what—but I took it to her. I didn't hold it for myself! But I did look at the pic of the Second on the front and then made a sketchings of it and then stitched it in a leftover burlap from the kitchens and sent it to my fam. They like my stitches."

Andra wanted to ask what the Second looked like, but Lilibet kept going.

"I sole saw the First once. And I've *never* seen a Gold First, but I don't reck it has her pic. I heard stories she recked the monies were silly. Will you let them put your face on Bronze Thirds? Or maybe the Celestia? Evens, I reck that would be charred either way."

By the time she was done with this speech, she'd rearranged the plates half a dozen times, and Andra had only gotten the most cursory taste of each dish before they were stacked back on the silver tray. Lilibet looked so pleased, Andra couldn't bring herself to say anything. She didn't feel like eating anyway, though her stomach rumbled as the maid took the tray to Kiv.

"Out, you spoon," she said, swatting him with her free hand.

His eyes narrowed at the contact, and Andra braced herself, but after a tense moment, he took the tray from Lilibet, and left without a word.

She called, "Bye, Kiv!" as the door fell shut, then turned to Andra, placed a hand on her hip, and pointed to the washroom. "We need to clean you. Your dress for the ceremony happens to come soon."

"Dress for the ceremony?"

Lilibet frowned. "It happens"—she made an ambiguous gesture with a dainty brown hand—"like a religiful occasion—"

"I know what a ceremony is. Why do I need another dress? Isn't this my banquet dress?" She picked up the gauzy clothing Zhade had pulled from the wardrobe, displaying it for Lilibet.

Its delicate fabric must have cost a fortune. This wasn't something 'bot-made. There were too many imperfections, the fabric too sheer—a synth'bot would snag and tear right through it. Someone, not some*thing*, had made this.

Lilibet laughed. "Neg, you spoon. That's a *day* dress. The stitchers are still working on your Awakening dress. All night. All day. Seven stitchers all at once. I asked to be a stitcher before you came, even though the stitchers only made stuff for the Guv, and it happens all black, always black, and that's so *boring*."

She pulled a pair of long sewing needles out of the ends of her sleeves, as though she'd hidden them like weapons.

"I practice, seeya. Stitch, stitch, stitch." She made a sewing motion with the needles, then jabbed one in Andra's direction. "Now, into the bath, Goddess. Tonight, you shine."

WHEN ANDRA FINISHED her bath, her new clothes were waiting on the bed. Cream-colored leggings adorned with delicate gold lace, a matching sheer skirt, and a beaded bodice that wrapped around her torso in such a complicated fashion, Lilibet had to help. The lace was scratchy, and the beads made the whole thing heavy. The fabric was much too clingy, but at least the dressmakers had gotten her size right.

The evening's ceremony sounded exhausting, though Lilibet chatted about how amazing it would be and how she wished she could go. It sounded like Andra just had to stand there and be prayed at. After what she'd seen this morning, she wasn't too keen on the idea. But she just had to get through the Ceremony and the following dinner, and then she would have an hour all to herself to sort through 'bots. Of course, then she would have to go to Zhade's stupid goddess lessons, and then start everything all over again the next day.

"There," the maid said, as she placed the last pin in Andra's hair.

Andra sat in front of her vanity and Lilibet stepped back to admire her own handiwork, holding up a mirror so Andra could see the back. "I recked I would make a good maid. I did my sister's hair before"— her ecstatic expression faltered for a moment, but she recovered quickly—"before I came here. I told Tarna I'd do better higher on the Rock. I'm a waster at stirring stews. They forever burn on the bottom. And *then*, I have to scrub the pot too. I happen small, certz, and I have to climb *into* the pot to scrub it. I recked one day they'd forget I was inside, and serve me as the day's stew."

She giggled, but Andra was too busy looking at the design Lilibet had pinned into her hair to respond. She'd woven strands of synth'hair and golden twine into Andra's own locks, twisting and pinning until she'd created a single design in gold, against Andra's naturally dark hair.

It was a starburst, twelve lines spewing from the middle, each a different length. And suddenly, Andra recognized the same design everywhere. Sewn into the stitching on the bedspread, hewn into the marble walls, carved into the wooden furniture. And now Andra realized what it was, and why it was all around her.

They'd re-created her birthmark.

"Do you like them?"

Andra jolted, realizing she'd been staring at the starbursts for far too long.

"The Celestias?" Lilibet said the word with a hard *C*. She pointed to Andra's collarbone, where her birthmark was hidden under the gown.

Andra swallowed, nodded. "Yeah, they're great."

Lilibet looked satisfied, and then reached into a drawer in the vanity. "One last thing," she said, and pulled out a cos'mask.

Andra deflated. She hated 'masks. They were fine when you used them like Oz (like Oz *used* to, she reminded herself)—just for fun, pretending to be his favorite character or laughing at a lion's face superimposed over his own. But when they were used like this—to *fix* her—it was just a reminder of all the ways she wasn't good enough.

"Where did you get that?" Andra asked.

Lilibet pointed at the drawer.

"No. Before," Andra said. "Where did it come from?"

Lilibet blinked. "The angels," she said simply, placing the cos'mask on Andra's face.

'Bots making 'bots. An endless cycle of technology creating and repairing itself. The same function of technology that allowed a thousand-year-old ship to orbit in perfect condition also made it possible for the Eerensedians to keep using technology even though they couldn't create it. The technology sustained itself. Though it seemed that some of this tech had been created by the other goddesses or . . . whatever Zhade was.

"You're a . . . sorcer," she said, remembering the word Zhade had used.

Lilibet giggled. "Neg, you spoon. The spell's already inside." She pressed a hidden button on the side of the 'mask.

Afternoon light shone in from the balcony as Andra watched the 'mask scan her face, and then seamlessly transform it into sim-star perfection. Vanishing blemishes, evening her skin tone, thinning her brows. It took what it thought were the best aspects from either side of her face and transferred them to the other, making her features nearly symmetrical. It was only an illusion—one that would fall apart the moment someone got too close, but from a distance Andra looked nothing like herself.

Lilibet didn't seem to notice her disappointment. The maid droned on about stitching while she helped Andra into her silk slippers, sash, and fur cape.

It wasn't long before Zhade returned, sauntering in with his hands in his pockets, not sparing Lilibet a glance as her wide eyes flitted between Zhade and Andra. Though there was curiosity on her face, there was no recognition. He was just a guard to her. His true identity must have been kept a tight secret. Lilibet curtsied and scurried out of the room, leaving Andra alone with the bastard prince.

He was clean-shaven, his uniform pressed. He had all the accoutrements now: breastplate, saber, dust-colored pants tucked into recently shined boots. His hair was still a mess, but a nice mess. He held his shoulders back, standing tall, and his face was set in a grim expression, even as his eyes twinkled.

"You look like a real Eerensedian in those clothes."

"Is that bad?"

Instead of answering, he pulled a rose-gold circlet from his bag. Not a crown or a tiara—more like a wreath, gold strands twisting into delicate vines and flowers, so intricate Andra was afraid to touch it. Zhade set it on her head. It weighed practically nothing, but the elaborate detailing pricked her scalp, sending a tingle down her spine.

"It's a bit much, don't you think?"

He paused, taking in Andra's dress and hair and 'masked features. After a brief hesitation, he reached for her face. She tried to at swat him, but he grabbed her wrists. "Stop," he whined. "I'm fixing it."

He activated the holo'display of Andra's cos'mask. A few swipes of his fingers, and he pulled away.

"Better," he said.

She gave him a shocked look before leaning over and glancing in the mirror.

Holy shit.

Not only did she look amazing—and she *did* look amazing, not like a sim star, but like the best version of herself, her round cheeks glowing, her eyelids dusted with gold—but Zhade had made the changes manually. Even in her time, it was difficult to program a 'mask from scratch. Most people just downloaded the look they wanted, keeping a catalog of them in their 'bands, and used their 'implant to activate them. But Zhade had made drastic changes to the algorithm with a few simple commands, as casually as though he were tying a shoe.

"How'd you do that?" Andra lightly pressed her fingers against the node at her ear. With the 'mask and her new clothes, in front of a backdrop of pink marble and velvet furniture, she almost did look like a goddess.

Zhade shrugged. "I keep telling you, I'm a sorcer. Working with magic is a bit what we do."

Andra gave herself one last look and followed him to the door. Before he opened it, he met her gaze. His eyes were a deep brown, and mixed with his blond hair, they made him look like a puppy. A mischievous puppy. He looked like he was about to say something, but all he did was adjust her crown and nod to himself in approval.

They exited the relative safety of Andra's room. The hallways were now lit with torches, and guards were stationed around every twist and turn. A few servants scurried past, averting their gazes. When they occasionally passed someone whose attire suggested they were relatively important, Zhade would bow to them, and they would bow to Andra.

As they made their way through the palace, Andra lagged a half step behind Zhade, dread knotting her stomach.

She cut him a sideways glance. "So . . ."

"Soze?"

"Ceremony?" she asked. "Big ritual in celebration of me? What does that entail? What should I do?"

Zhade shrugged, not breaking his stride. "Don't make eye contact too long. Respond to questions, but give vague answers, and don't provide info on the voluntary. If asked to make a speech, make it short, and make it import. And don't eat the stew. It'll give you gas for days."

He stopped and watched her, and she realized he was waiting for her to respond. She nodded, swallowed her fear, and lifted her chin.

"Can you have memory of all that?" he asked.

"Well, you're my escort," she said. "You can remind me."

He took her chin in his hand, and what should have been an aggressive gesture, or an intimate one, was neither. Instead, it felt desperate. "*You* are not escorted. *You* enter unaccompanied, because *you* are a goddess, and will lean on no one."

Zhade released her, his face relaxing into his cocky grin.

"Now, let's meet your worshippers, Goddess."

She shivered in the drafty corridor. "But what about goddess lessons? And when are you bringing me the supplies I asked for? And what about—"

He grabbed her hand and brought it to his lips. Her breath caught, and she watched him watch her through his dark lashes.

"Did I mention you look beautiful?"

Dear god, he was serious. There was no hint of amusement on his face, no sense of irony in his voice, not even the teasing lilt that permeated his every word. He was paying her a genuine, heartfelt compliment.

"That's terrifying," she whispered.

He drew back, brow furrowed. "What?"

"You, being serious. It's disturbing. What's your malfunction? Are you dying?"

He faked offense. "I can be serious. I'm mereish saying, you look nice without the bloodstains, and seeya, all . . ." He waved his hand to gesture at all of her. " . . . agowned. You should always remind people who you are. It imports to set yourself apart." He tucked a stray hair under her tiara.

"Really? Is that the advice I get from an exiled p—"

Prince. That's what she was going to say: that he was supposed to teach her how to be a goddess, how to decide her fate, and whatever else nonsense he spouted, nonsense *he* wasn't even following as he lurked in his brother's shadow. But none of that came out, because his mouth was suddenly covering hers.

She panicked, her muscles stiffened, and she stood frozen, but his hand was on her cheek, his thumb doing something that could only be called caressing, and she was suddenly kissing him back. His other arm snaked around her, drawing her close so her front was crushed against his. And he was so gentle, and it was not at all what she expected, and her hands were threading through his hair, messing up its carefully disheveled appearance, and it wasn't enough. She wanted to dishevel all of him.

She'd kissed boys before. *A* boy. Jay, behind the bleachers, freshman year. Neither had been into it. They'd just done it because they were both considered the "fat kids" and it seemed to be expected of them. Andra remembered thinking it was wetter than she'd anticipated and that lips felt weird.

This was nothing like that. She wasn't waiting for it to be over or overly aware of her limbs. She wanted to keep kissing him, wanted him to keep kissing her. She *wanted*.

Zhade's arms clenched, and she thought he was about to deepen the kiss, but he pulled away, looking down at her. The thumb on her cheek traveled to her lower lip, tracing it, and oh—

"You should be at care," he whispered, and she watched his lips, "with what you say in these halls."

Oh.

He'd been shutting her up.

She stood back and nodded, and fought the impulse to wipe his kiss from her lips because suddenly it felt dirty—unearned.

"Evens, Goddess, time to peace." His voice sounded as it usually did—lazy, arrogant, indifferent.

He extended his arm, but she didn't take it.

ZHADE DROPPED ANDRA off in a brightly painted alcove, telling her to wait, and leaving with a wink before she could ask what she was supposed to wait *for*. The tiny nook made her claustrophobic, even though the walls were pockmarked with holes, like dozens of small windows. A cool breeze drifted in, but it did nothing to calm her nerves. She was close to wandering off to find out what she was supposed to be doing, when Maret appeared. He gave her a cursory glance, then turned away and started pacing.

She stood stiffly against the far wall, the ghost of Zhade's kiss still on her lips, as his brother prowled back and forth across from her. He held his hands behind his back, leaning slightly forward as he walked, his face pinched into a severe expression. His light hair was perfectly slicked back from his forehead, where his crown gleamed silver every time he passed a window. His feet created a syncopated rhythm on the stone floor, over and over until Andra wanted to snap at him to stop. But she needed to play nice so he would believe she truly was a goddess and not execute her.

She watched as his pacing quickened, his jaw tightening. She swallowed.

"So . . ."

He stopped, his back to her, and Andra hurried on before she shorted out.

"What's this Awakening Ceremony like?"

"Short." He started pacing again.

Andra took a steadying breath. "Right. Right."

Click-click click-click went Maret's footsteps.

"What should I expect?"

This time he didn't even pause his movements. "To be worshipped, Goddess. Isn't that enough?"

"Are you nervous?"

Maret froze. He squinted into a beam of light. "Scuze?"

"You're pacing. It's often a nervous tic. I just don't know what you'd be nervous about."

"I—nothing—habit, I spoze."

Andra shrugged. "Well, I'm nervous."

That's what people did, right? Empathize? Surviving this planet would be easier if Maret was on her side. Or, at the very least, thought she was on his.

His expression relaxed, but didn't soften. "I don't see why *you* have anything to be nerveful bout." He leaned against the wall. It didn't look nearly as natural as when Zhade did it. "You mereish have to stand there. I have to do all the work."

"What do you have to do?"

"I have to speak."

"That's it?"

"That's it?" he sneered. "Would you like to do it instead?"

She blanched. "No thank you."

"I recked not." Maret started pacing again, and this time, Andra heard him muttering something under his breath.

He seemed different than he'd been in the throne room and in his suite. Less confident. More whiny. Even his speech patterns were altered, and she wondered if he put on an act when the Advisor was around.

Andra coughed. "Your mom didn't seem to want to give me access to the 'bots—angels. Is there a reason?"

Maret whipped around, and Andra was certain she'd gone too far. His gaze was intense, his muscles taut. She stepped back. For a moment, she thought he would attack—not with his crown but with his fists. He took a deep breath and smoothed his hair. "My *advisor* recks what serves the citians best. She wants to make certz you have time to accomplish that."

"And what serves the citians best?" Andra asked. "Shouldn't it be fixing the 'dome that keeps them safe, so you don't have to kill so many people?"

Maret's hand lifted again to his hair, hovered above it, clenched, then drifted back to his side. "I said you would have access to angels, Goddess," he said through gritted teeth. "They can also address what is crystal a problem with your hearing."

Andra crossed her arms and plopped into a nearby chair.

Maret scowled. "Stand up. You'll wrinkle your dress."

She glared until he turned away. There was only so much *nice* she could play. She could hear the hum of voices on the other side of the alcove's door, and nerves were overtaking her.

"So," she said, "you go in, make a speech, they clap, and then we're done?"

Maret was breathing slowly through his nose. "Firm. Just a few minutes of being worshipped, and then we're done."

It should have been a relief, but something about Maret's tone made it sound like a threat.

FOURTEEN

THE SPY

ZHADE WAS BOTH stressed and bored as the crowd filled the room, buzzing excitedish.

He was stationed plastered to the cathedzal's back wall, fake saber at his side. He'd been to oozhles of these ceremonies, and he'd hated every tick of them. The chanting, the incense, the prickle of stardust.

There were dozens of chapels throughout the city dedicated to each of the goddesses, but there was sole one cathedzal in the Rock, and it was one of the largest rooms apalace. The space was thin, but tall, and any echoes it might have produced were released by the numerful holes pockmarking the ceiling and three of the walls. These were said to let in the stardust, though Zhade noticed the dust could move through walls just evens without them, and the room needed days of drying out after every rain.

Everything was deep shades of red and mahogany, and the stardust vents did little to brighten the room. There were a few benches up front for the olds, but mostish people stood. It was one of the things Zhade hated bout the ceremonies. Stand up straightish. Don't slouch. Mereish talk when you say the prayers.

Today's ceremony would be blessedish short. Maret would intro the Third to the people, and fin would be fin. Later ceremonies would take longer, and the Goddess would need to be prepped on how to behave.

He'd sent word through the speak-easy to Wead. The Goddess's lessons would have to begin tonight.

Zhade recked full well this ceremony was a test. While Maret was introing the Goddess, he was also watching to see how the people responded. They needed to adore her in a way that made them worship Maret, not her. To survive Eerensed—to survive *Maret*—she needed to half-walk the thin string between immortality and sacrifice.

He had the urge to check the tracking spell in his pocket, but resisted. The scrying ball he carried was spelled to locate the rose-gold tiara he'd found in the First's rooms yestereven. He was surprised Tsurina hadn't melted it down, but it was in the First's abandoned jewel chest. From there, it wasn't hard to cast the tracking spell, and now he just needed the Goddess to get attached to the thing, so he would always reck where she was.

"Bodhizhad."

He stiffened, turning toward the honeyed voice. "Grande Advisor."

Tsurina wore a silver dress and tapped one of her razor-sharp nails against her cheek.

Zhade flashed her a grin, hiding his nerves. She had always given him the fraughts. "Shouldn't you be astage?"

She tilted her head. "Shouldn't you be dead in the Wastes?"

He forced out a laugh. "Hear, hear. Just because you wish for something doesn't make it true."

She lifted a single brow, looking down her nose at Zhade though she was bareish taller. "Full true. Wishes don't, but actions do."

He smiled as though she hadn't just implied she was going to kill him. "Decide your fate, marah?"

"Hmm," Tsurina said non-commitalish. She gave Kiv a brief glance. He nodded back, and she moved on without another word, gliding toward her seat astage.

He'd forever recked the Grande Advisor wanted him dead. At times he wondered why he was still alive, because not even Zhade could avoid death if Tsurina wanted it so. She hadn't killed him for a reason. He just didn't reck what it was. Or why she was letting Maret rule in her place. Or where the Silver Crown came from.

"Not the advisor's shadow today, Kiv?" Zhade muttered, leaning against the stone wall, arms crossed.

"Neg. Yours," Kiv grunted, and Zhade looked up to find Kiv watching him.

Zhade winked.

Before Kiv could respond, the back door opened and Maret entered to the fanfare of trumpets. A hush fell over the cathedzal. The Guv was dressed in his normal drab colors, the silver stitching glittering in the sunbeams sifting through the stardust vents. The mysteriful Crown winked in and out of the light as he made his march to the podium. Behind him was a backdrop of stained glass forming the First's Coil overlaid with the Second's Crystal and the Third's Celestia.

"People of Eerensed," Maret started. His voice echoed hollowish, the crowd absorbing every word. "We have been blessed with the awakening of two goddesses in our lifetime, and when the Third disappeared, we recked we would not see another."

What Maret didn't say, and what the people chose to forget, was what had *killed* the first two goddesses, but it was full bars smart of Maret not to remind them.

"But our fate has been decided yet again. We're here today to celebrate the Third's awakening and return."

Energy thrummed through the crowd. Cathedzal wasn't the place for cheering, but they wanted to.

"Eerensed has never been stronger," Maret continued. He touched the Silver Crown at his temple, as though anyone needed to be given memory it was there. In adds to the guards, angels were stationed round the room, waiting to respond to Maret's High Magic. "I will continue to protect our city from the pockets, and all outside forces that threaten us. No meteor what our new and *final* goddess brings, we will be safe. Sole this moren, the Goddess has already promised me her help."

Zhade bit back a groan. Tonight's first goddess lesson would be bout not making promises she couldn't keep.

"Many of you have noticed the gods' dome weakening," Maret continued, and Zhade's stomach plummeted. If Maret was admitting something was wrong, that meant he couldn't hide it anymore. And now, he had someone to shift the blame to. "We've had reports of increased winds in Southwarden, decreased rain in our farming districts, and for certz, the black ley lines that so often precede broken spells are spreading."

Zhade had bareish noticed when he arrived, but imagining back, there had been something strange bout the gods' dome. If he'd looked closeish, he probablish would have seen lines of black rot creeping cross it like naked trees against the sky. He'd seen it before in some of his mam's spells. Though some magic sustained itself, not all lasted forever. So many of her spells must be dying without her.

The Guv continued. "But now that our Third has returned, there is nothing to worry bout. She will work with me not sole to strengthen the gods' dome, but also to expand our borders, and protect us from invasion."

Maret's words had a rehearsed rhythm. He was not an engaging speaker, didn't care to be. Didn't *need* to be when the people lived in fear of the magic he wielded. Tsurina sat tall behind him, and Zhade imagined she was mouthing the words with her son. Zhade bet his butter she'd written this speech.

As Maret droned on, Zhade scanned the room, watching the crowd fidget. They were packed tight as a rock tin, kidduns settled on parents' shoulders, olds leaning against youngers. There were people from every section of Eerensed, all their faces raised in anticipation of their Goddess.

All but one.

Cross the room, a woman was staring straightish at Zhade.

One of her eyes was magic, shining bright against her black skin. Her head was shaved like a waster's, and she wore the thick-knitted clothing Zhade had come to associate with the desert. He stared back, but her gaze didn't waver. He recked he saw something shiny flicker in her hand.

"And now—"

Maret's voice got louder, drawing Zhade's attention to him momentarilish. When Zhade looked back, the woman was gone. *You're growing paranoid, boyo.* Zhade should be used to people staring at him. He was, after all, full charred.

"—I would like to intro our Third Goddess."

Maret stepped aside, just bareish. The door in the vestibule opened, and the Goddess walked out.

By the look on her face, Zhade imagined she was going to be sick, or at least trip. He recked she'd been shaking in the Yard that moren because of the dead women at her feet. But maybe it also had to do with every eye staring at her. She took a few steps forward, smiling politish at the people, and her eyes sought out Zhade. He'd have to put a stop to that. She couldn't appear to rely on him. He held her gaze anyway.

She looked regal in her new clothes and tiara, and though Zhade recked the bloodstains and tangled hair gave her a formidistic aura, he liked the glamourful Goddess as well.

She stood awkwardish, but it didn't meteor. The people were enamored with her mere presence.

She startled when the priest appeared aside her to start the prayer. Zhade recked this one. It had been said at many of the First's ceremonies. It was basicalish the phrase "worship the Goddess" over and over, with a few variations to hold things interesting. Zhade didn't join in. Kiv, who nudged Zhade til he stood up straightish, wasn't chanting either.

Like Zhade had memory, the stardust shimmered in the air as the chanting gathered it, and slowish began to surround the Goddess, giving her an otherworldish glow. She looked more uncomfortistic than ever. As a fact, she looked scared.

The prayer was almost at its end when Zhade caught movement out of the corner of his eye. Everything happened so fast. A thin mustached man rushed the stage; someone let out a scream.

Instinct pushed Zhade toward the Goddess, but there was no march he would make it in time. There was a lightning dagger in the man's hand, raised high, blue streaks of light crackling at its edges.

Zhade's heart stopped.

He saw all his plans turn to sand. Another goddess killed. His own banishment (again) (or worse). Maret still on the throne. All the while Eerensedians kept dying and his final promises to his mother remained unfulfilled. And the poor Goddess, who didn't even want to be here. She didn't see it coming, didn't see the man rushing toward her, didn't see the glint of the dagger.

It was over as quickish as it began.

There was a sickening squelch. A spray of blood.

The man stopped. The Goddess's eyes widened, finalish aware of what was happening.

An angel's spear stuck cleanish through the attacker's chest, in through his back, out right below his breastbone. With a jerk, the angel pulled the spear free, and the man fell face-first onto the platform. Dead.

Leaving the Goddess whole and full well.

There were screams and gasps, but the people were too enthralled to flee. A hectic thrill rushed through the crowd, along with disappointment for not seeing an assassination. Zhade recked they would turn on the Third in a tick for a bit of excitement.

He watched as Maret stepped forward, Silver Crown gleaming in the light of the stained glass, and Zhade comped what had happened.

Maret had used his magic to save the Goddess.

The crowd realized a tick later and began to cheer, their disappointment vanishing. To them, this was better than witnessing the Goddess martyred. Their Guv saved their Goddess, and it charmed them.

The Goddess looked as shocked as Zhade felt. Eyes flitting between the dead man and the Guv, she took a few stumbling steps back. Maret, an annoyed sneer on his face, helped her to a nearby chair.

Zhade wound through the crowd, pushing past dignitaries and diplomats and peasants. He accidentalish jostled a woman, but didn't stop, even when she cursed after him.

He was vagueish aware of Maret speaking again, directing everyone out of the Rock, but he didn't listen, focused soleish on his prey. He found the spot the night-skinned woman with the angelic eye had been standing, but she was gone. He turned in a circle, as citians rushed past him. It would be impossible to find her in this crowd, and she could have already left the cathedzal.

A shine caught his eye, and he looked down. A small coin lay at his feet. He bent to pick it up, even as the people pushing past threatened to knock him over. It wasn't a Gold First or a Silver Second. It would be worthless aboveground, but he recked exactish where someone could use this as currency. The symbol on either side gave it away.

A ladder, twisting in on itself to form the shape of a half-moon.

The symbol of the Schism.

FIFTEEN

duty, n.

Definition: 1. that which one is bound by moral obligation
to perform.

2. respect, regard, reverence.

3. an obligation; any assigned service.

4. a euphemism for defecation.

ANDRA COULDN'T FEEL *her body.*

That was her first hint it was a dream.

She was running.

That was her second.

She was nothing but thought and energy and time, but somehow she was running toward something. There was a clock beeping or a bomb ticking or her heart beating. Whatever it was, it was counting down. Something was almost over. Something was about to begin.

As she ran, the scenery shifted, a swirl of colors and shapes and instinct. Everything was a blur until she focused on a single detail.

A stack of books.

The Griffin Statue.

Her father's dogs. Her mother's disappointment.

They nipped at her heels as she passed.

She was flying.

Something rose ahead of her. Something big and dark and important. She couldn't see it. Not with her eyes. She was going to hit it. She was going too fast, flying too straight.

She couldn't slow, couldn't swerve.

She was a drone—the kind her brother raced when he could hide it from their mother. She was being controlled. Faster and faster she flew, drawn forward, pushed forward. By fate or kismet or predestination.

She was going to crash.

ANDRA JERKED AWAKE to the scraping of metal against brass as the gauzy pink curtains were thrown wide. She groaned, squinting into the sudden beams of sunlight haloing Zhade's silhouette. She couldn't have gotten more than a few hours' rest—if she could call it that. She'd almost been murdered yesterday.

And that hadn't even been the weirdest part of the day.

She'd been introduced to the colonists' descendants as their goddess and they'd worshipped her as she was submerged in a shimmering nano'swarm.

It was so awkward.

She'd never been religious, but she was sure that twenty-second-century holy rituals hadn't been anything like this.

The nanos had tickled, but they weren't technically doing anything. The people looked at her like they expected her to perform some miracle with the nano'swarm, but there wasn't anything she could do. Even if she *could* use her 'implant, she wouldn't do so to impress the people. She'd use it to track down a mech'bot and AI.

Andra had barely had time to take in the variety of skin tones and racial traits in the crowd. She'd glimpsed the red hair prevalent in her mother's family, and even recognized some of the features she had inherited from her father's side—though she wasn't sure she could call them Southeast Asian, a thousand years in the future on a planet that had never had an Asia. In fact, so much time after colonization, she suspected the descendants had formed their own racial constructs, and not necessarily the ones she was familiar with.

The diversity of the city was surprising considering Eerensed was a closed society. The city must not have always been sealed off to the Wastes. It almost reminded Andra of Riverside—lots of races living together, though only certain ones had power. It didn't escape her notice that Tsurina and Maret and the diplomats had much lighter skin that the average Eerensedian. Though looking at the crowd, it had been hard for Andra to pinpoint what the average Eerensedian would be. She hadn't had time to ponder it before someone tried to kill her.

The attempted assassination had shaken her, but only after the fact. She hadn't even known what was happening until the man lay dead at her feet, slaughtered by a 'bot controlled by the Guv.

Maret had killed again, with nothing more than a thought. But he'd also saved her. And when he'd helped her afterward, he seemed almost as shaken as she was. Zhade had been nowhere to be found. So much for him trying to keep her alive.

She hadn't seen Zhade again until she was back in her room. He'd been waiting for her, leaning against a marble wall and twirling a piece of metal between his fingers. There had also been a host of 'bots lined up, left there by Kiv or one of Tsurina's other guards. They were all variations of models Andra recognized, altered just enough to be unfamiliar. She'd fallen face-first onto her bed, sinking into the mattress as she listened to Zhade ramble about how hard the piece of tech in his hand had been to find. In the end, they hadn't started goddess lessons that night, because Andra had fallen asleep before Zhade had finished speaking.

"Show the toe, Goddess," Zhade said now. "The day happens."

"It can happen without me," she grumbled, pulling the pillow from behind her head and throwing it at him. He caught it and tossed it back.

"Not this day. Goddess duties await." He tore away her covers and darted out of the room before she could retaliate.

Lilibet brought in breakfast, narrowly dodging Zhade's exit. She giggled and gave a knowing look. Andra scowled.

ANDRA USED WHAT little time she had to skim through the 'bots that had been left for her. Though none of them were mech'bots, she checked their programming anyway, and it quickly became obvious that not just any 'bot would do. Most of them ran on the upgraded Eerensedian tech that had been designed for battle, not manual labor. She needed something that still had colonial programs in its memory banks—something that still remembered how to construct a shuttle.

She found no AI either. If the 'bots' skullcaps were clear, Andra could easily see if they had the silicon CPU of a standard 'bot or the wetware brain of an AI. But most were opaque, so she was left with giving each a Neo-Turing Test. She'd gotten through half the 'bots by the time Kiv came to collect her.

"Are you taking the angels too?" she asked, tugging at her silk clothing. Today, she was wearing a jumpsuit, but between the sheer material and the way the bodice wrapped around her torso, it was hardly practical.

Kiv merely grunted and turned, expecting her to follow. She did, not wanting to be on the other side of that spear.

They made their way down a number of stairways Andra hadn't seen the day before and ended up in a small stone room on one of the lower floors of the Rock.

Maret sat at the head of a long wooden table filled with various older men and women. Tsurina sat to his right, dressed in gold and black, her brown hair falling in waves over her shoulders. Behind them, two gleaming black mech'bots stood against a wall of windows, giving Andra a view of the courtyard below. Her stomach lurched, both from being near the site of her maids' executions and from the surety that Tsurina wouldn't give her access to these particular 'bots.

"Goddess," the man to Maret's left said. He was balding, white tufts of hair sprouting above his ears. "We have so much honor for you to join us."

He stood, his chair scraping against the floor. The rest of the meeting attendees followed suit, all except for Maret.

"Please, have a seat," the man said.

Maret rolled his eyes. "Firm, firm, sit so we can start this meeting." He gestured to the empty seat at the far end of the table and added under his breath, "Finalish."

Andra sat, careful of her embroidered jumpsuit against the grain of the wood. The others sat too, a chorus of scraping chairs and groaning joints. Maret met her gaze, expression annoyed, and she couldn't tell if it was directed at her, or a shared secret over the silliness of the decorum.

As soon as everyone was seated, the man who had welcomed her spoke. "Firstish, Guv, is to convo security for the Goddess."

Maret sat slumped in his seat, forehead resting on his fingertips. "Certz, Prezdin. I'm disappointed. We've prepped for this for years, and yet the Goddess's first day here, you've allowed an assassination attempt. It was at luck I was there. Must I do your job for you?" Again, he slid into his courtly speech patterns, his mother seated at his side, eyes narrowed.

His fingertips grazed his crown as his gaze landed on a man halfway down the table with pale skin that turned blotchy under the Guv's scrutiny. This must be the head of security. He visibly swallowed.

"Firm, Guv," he said, his voice strained. "Security will tighten. We will do better. The unforeseen event—"

"It shouldn't have been *unforeseen*," Maret spat. "We can assume the Goddess's life is at risk at every tick. But especialish during religiful ceremonies."

Andra bit her lip. She'd just started coming to terms with pretending to be a deity or else risking execution. She wasn't ready to accept that she might be killed anyway. She couldn't wrap her mind around the fact that people wanted to *murder* her. She'd barely been noticed in her previous life.

Maret gave the head of security a dark look. "Sfin, are you so incompetent you didn't even consider a possible threat?"

The mech'bots behind Maret both raised their spears in Sfin's direction. The movement happened so fast, Andra almost didn't catch it. Maret lounged lazily, as though bringing two huge 'bots to attention cost him no effort.

"I will do everything in my power to protect the Goddess, Guv," the man said, bowing his head meekly, a visible tremor in his hand.

Tsurina cleared her throat and seemed to communicate something to her son.

"Good," Maret said, and the 'bots relaxed their weapons. "Now, assuming that these attempts on the Goddess's life will be numerful and frequent, what are your plans to prevent them?"

Despite his insistence that Andra *not* be assassinated, Maret didn't seem actually interested in the suggestions. Andra, on the other hand, listened intently, itching to take notes. The advisors provided strategies, all in the dialect Zhade had called High Goddess. It was easy for Andra to pick apart the sounds and meanings, and she found herself almost slipping into the accent—even if she didn't use the slang itself—as she responded to the proposals, most of which required her to be escorted at all times. She was beginning to wonder if she was even going to be able to go to the bathroom by herself.

"Um, excuse me?" She raised her hand.

Maret drummed his fingers against the wooden table. "Firm?"

"This is all fine for during, you know, business hours, but I'm not comfortable being followed around twenty-four seven."

Maret sighed and pinched the space between his eyes. "Scuze?"

"I don't want someone following me around all the time. I want . . . alone time. Time to myself. Surely I don't need an escort every moment of the day. It's a waste of resources. As long as you make sure the palace is secure, then there's no reason to have someone tailing me."

Maret gritted his teeth, his eyes heavy-lidded. "But what bout threats from *inside* the palace?"

The room was silent, all eyes directed at her. It was a good question, and one she didn't want to ponder. Any person in this room could want her dead—*would* want her dead if they discovered she had no godly powers. She couldn't replicate whatever magic the first two goddesses somehow had. People had already tried to kill her, and Maret was talking about it happening again as inevitable.

She took a deep breath. She just needed to survive long enough to get out of here. Find a mech'bot, find an AI, build a shuttle, and return to the Ark. She'd get back to Earth, where—even though it was a thousand-years changed—people wouldn't actively try to assassinate her. She couldn't do all that if she was being followed all day, every day.

She met Maret's gaze. "I assure you. I can deal with any threats that come from within the palace."

She wasn't sure she'd been convincing. She'd never delivered an ominous threat before. But a shiver went through the room. Even Maret looked taken aback, before his bored/annoyed expression slid back into place.

"Evens," he said, then turned to the man at his left. "What's next to convo?"

THE MEETINGS LASTED all day. Andra survived by giving vague answers and repeating lines from the wisest characters in her favorite sims. The one tricky moment was when someone asked about the 'dome and what she planned on doing. Since Maret had brought it up at the ceremony yesterday, Andra had paid extra close attention to the skin of the 'dome. It was true about the ley lines, though they weren't called that. They were just rotting nanos. The connection between the individual panes of glass was breaking, the seams becoming more visible. If she stared long enough, and the light was just right, she could make out each hexagonal link in the 'dome. That wasn't good, and she definitely didn't know how to fix it. In Andra's time, whenever nanos began to rot, you would just run an update, or they would automatically be replaced by nearby nanos. Andra couldn't run the update manually, and she didn't know why the 'dome wasn't healing on its own. She'd smiled tensely and said she was working on it.

After a dinner with some of the palace dignitaries, Andra returned to her room almost too exhausted to look through the new crop of 'bots Kiv had left. It was eerie in a way she hadn't realized the night before, a line of humanoid 'bots, eyes blank, holding spears. Only one was a mech'bot, but it didn't have the programming she needed. It had been either created or updated recently. She checked the others for AI capabilities, but they were all standard 'bots.

Andra powered down the last one and sank into her bed. This was completely inefficient. She should be actively searching, not waiting for the 'bots to come to her.

Despite her exhaustion, she pushed herself up. She wasn't a prisoner; she was a goddess. She could go out into the city and search for a 'bot herself.

Tucked in the back corner of her wardrobe, she found dark, durable pants and a black shirt that was tighter than she was comfortable with, along with a sturdy pair of boots. She donned them, left her room, and ran straight into a dark figure in the hallway.

They grabbed her wrist, and she jerked back, flailing, arm swinging out, and by some miraculous accident, it made contact. There was a crunch, a spray of blood, and the person—whom Andra now saw had broad shoulders and tousled blond hair—rolled to the floor moaning.

Both hands covered his face, but it was unmistakably Zhade curled into a ball. "I think you broke my nose!"

She let out a sigh of relief and rolled her eyes. "You're fine, you big baby." She wasn't that strong.

He sat up and tilted his head back, stanching the flow of blood with the sleeve of his jacket. "What an absurd insult." It came out: *What ad abturd intuld.* "Would you hit a baby?"

"If it were you, I might," she said dryly.

"Peacing somewhere?" he asked from the floor. She hadn't encountered him all day, and it was an odd relief to see him whole and unscathed—well, except for the bloody nose—even if she was still annoyed with him for not being there when she was almost killed.

"Uhhh . . ." Andra scrambled for an answer, but wasn't sure exactly what Zhade would approve of. But what did it matter what Zhade approved of? "I'm going out."

"Out?"

She gave a one-shouldered shrug. "I'm not a prisoner."

Zhade stood, moving past her into her darkened room. He jostled out of his bloodied jacket and tossed it over the back of one chair, and then settled himself into another, his gold hair sticking out in a perfect mess. He raised an eyebrow. "Aren't you forgetting something?"

Andra looked around the room, grabbed her 'locket from the bedside table, and then clasped it around her neck. She gave Zhade a forced smile and started to leave, but he cleared his throat.

"We had a deal. Goddess lessons."

She sighed. "Fine." She drew out the word. "Where's the piece of magic you promised me?"

He nodded to the tiny circuit board he'd brought her last night. It was sitting, untouched, on her vanity. "One piece of magic for one goddess lesson. I brought that to you last night and you *fell asleep* while I was talking. I'm not certz if I should be offended or concerned."

Andra crossed her arms. "I doubt you're ever either."

"Let's peace." Zhade stood. "You say you're not actualish a goddess, but we have to hold up this ruse for time and a half, so your lessons start tonight. Wead's waiting for us."

Andra was relieved. She would actually *see* Lew-Eadin and know for sure that he was all right, that she hadn't accidentally killed him. She groaned though, just for show.

Zhade put his hands up in protest. "I'm mereish trying to hold you alive."

She was going to argue that he wasn't doing a very good job, but there was a tiny cough behind them, and a small voice said, "You're not actualish a goddess?"

Andra turned. Lilibet was standing in the doorway.

"SHUT. UP," ANDRA hissed as they sneaked down a secret passage through the center of the palace rock. It was dark and almost too narrow for Andra, and she kept feeling things skitter past her feet.

"Sorries and worries," Lilibet tittered. The vowel sounds had changed enough in the last thousand years that the words rhymed. "I'm mereish excited. I've never been a part of a secret *scheme* before! Plans, firm, but never a *scheme*. It's nearish like we're story heroes and, seeya, Goddess, you can trust me. Should I still call you Goddess? I should probablish still call you Goddess. Out of habit. I don't want to accidentalish call you Andra afront of the Guv. It's such a charred name, marah?"

Her ramblings were muffled as the passageway got smaller and they had to duck and crawl single-file under a fallen stone archway.

"It's not too late to kill her," Zhade said.

"It's not too late to kill you either," Andra shot back.

Zhade's lips tightened, like he was holding back a smile.

The passageway opened behind a faded tapestry in what Zhade

said was an abandoned wing of the palace. He helped her to her feet, then Lilibet, whose incessant chatter trailed off as she took in the room they were now in. Her mouth fell open.

The ceilings were high and arched. Glass skylights let in the stars and faint green aurora trails. Though the furniture was coated in dust, Andra could tell it was every bit as opulent as her own. A plush settee, a gilded glass table, an enormous canopy bed set on a pedestal. Like Andra's room, there was a balcony on the far side. Unlike Andra's room, it was boarded shut. Flickering candles lit the space, and something about being here in the candlelight, under the stars, with Zhade, made Andra blush.

"This belonged to the First, marah?" Lilibet breathed.

"Zhade! Andra!" Lew emerged from the shadows, alive and well, wrist flicking as he extinguished a match. His eyes fell on Lilibet. "And guest."

Andra nodded to the smaller girl. "This is my, uh, maid, Lilibet."

"Co-conspirator," Lilibet corrected. "Spy for the rebellion."

Andra winced. "This isn't really a . . . never mind."

Lew laughed. "Honors, Lilibet."

They touched palms, as she'd seen Eerensedians do in greeting.

Zhade had warned her about Lew's modded arm, but it still caught her by surprise. It wasn't synthesized from organic matter, like most mods. It shone like the metal casing of a 'bot. Whoever had healed him had done an incredible job, but they were working without the entire history of human ingenuity to support their work. The word *cyborg* had never been used in Andra's time, even with people who were over 50 percent modded. But with Lew and his metal arm, it was the only word she could summon.

She felt a surge of guilt.

"I'll bring actualish lights next lesson," Lew said. "Candles were the best I could do for today."

Andra made her way around the settee and threw her arms around him in a tight hug. He seemed surprised, but hugged her back.

"I'm so glad you're okay," she said. "I mean, I'm glad you're evens."

"Never better," he said.

Zhade coughed. "Candles will do. Is Doon coming?"

Lew swallowed, pulling away from Andra, but not before she felt him tense. "Neg, she's . . . busy with the Schism."

She had heard the word before, but she couldn't remember the context. The way Lew said it didn't sound nice. "What's the Schism?"

Zhade glowered. "Doesn't meteor. They hate the goddesses and their magic. It's something Doon shouldn't be involved in."

"Who's Doon?"

"My sister," Lew said.

Zhade nudged Andra. "She thinks I'm charred."

"She doesn't." Lew rolled his eyes. "She's twelve."

"I'll let her down easyish."

Andra plopped onto a nearby sofa, stirring up a cloud of dust. She tensed, until she realized it wasn't a nano'swarm. "What are we working on today?"

Lew handed her a small tablet. It glowed in the candlelight, and on it, Lew had typed a list. No, a schedule.

"You made me a syllabus?" she asked.

Lew pursed his lips. "I don't reck that word, but I spoze."

Andra skimmed the tablet. The dates were unrecognizable to her—whatever calendar system the Eerensedians were using, it wasn't one she was familiar with. Next to each day was a lesson topic: dining, religiful ceremonies, greetings, public appearances, etc. She glanced at the top of the list, the lesson that was scheduled for this evening.

"Dancing?" She groaned.

Lilibet paused her inspection of the room to clap and squeal.

Andra tossed the tablet onto the couch and leaned her head back. "Why?" she whined. "When am I ever going to be dancing?"

"Parties, banquets, festivals," Zhade said. He was leaning against a tapestry-covered wall, arms crossed. He'd already discarded most of his guard accoutrements and unbuttoned the top of his shirt. "You are expected not sole to save the people, but to interact with them as well. That includes dancing."

"I can already dance," Andra said.

"Oh? Then show us."

Andra pushed herself to her feet and started a half-hearted group dance that had been popular when she was a freshman. Heel. Toe. Butt jiggle. Jump turn. Hands up. The next part involved her 'implant, so she just did another butt jiggle.

"That was awful," Zhade said.

"You have . . ." Lew shot him a chastising look. "Space for improvement, Goddess."

Lilibet nodded sagely.

Lew picked up what looked to Andra's eyes like a guitar. Its surface gleamed, polished and cared for. He cradled it like it was a child and lightly strummed the strings as he sat on the nearby settee. His left hand was awkward, but the mod work had been good. He was acclimating to his new limb quickly. The sound he produced was higher than a guitar, the tuning of the strings somewhere between a jazz scale and an eastern mode. It was haunting and delicate, and the sound grew and shrank as Lew refamiliarized himself with the instrument. Then a song began to form.

Something about it almost seemed . . . familiar. The rhythm, the short melody, and sparse chords. It almost sounded twenty-second century. It almost sounded like home. Then she realized—

"Is that . . . *The Sun and Other Stars* by Vichey?"

Her mother's favorite song to work to, though she tried to hide it. Sentimental nonsense, her mother called music. She considered it a waste of time, but Andra couldn't count how often she'd walked by her office and heard the four-note melody seeping under the door. If they knew the song here on Holymyth, a thousand years in the future, perhaps the First *had* been her mother, and she'd reintroduced it.

Or maybe it was just an old folk tune now.

Lew smiled over the instrument. "Zhade's favorite."

He nodded to Zhade, and the prince stepped forward, arms outstretched, ready to dance.

Andra hesitated, remembering the fake kiss in the hallway. "Could I learn with Lew instead?"

Lew's smile turned apologetic. "I never learned to dance."

"Much to Dzeni's disappointment," Zhade said.

Andra could tell Zhade immediately regretted his words. The sadness in Lew's eyes deepened.

"And sides," Zhade went on quickly, "even if Wead could skool you, I play the strings bout as well as you dance." He gave Andra one of his rakish smiles and stepped toward her again. He was taller than she thought. She had to look up to meet his eyes. He placed her left hand on his shoulder, took her right in his, and then snaked his remaining arm around her waist, pulling her close.

For a moment, Andra didn't breathe. Her muscles tensed, and as Zhade began to lead her in the dance, she fought the urge to pull away. She fought the urge to lean in to him.

One, two, three, four. She counted in her head, moving her feet as little as possible, letting Zhade guide her.

She stared resolutely at a snag in his shirt. It was dangerously close to his revealed collarbone. The creak as Lilibet sank into a chair made her jolt. Zhade laughed, and pulled her tighter.

"You look tired," he said. His voice was soft. Their feet tapped against the marble floor. Andra could feel each individual finger on her waist through the thin fabric of her shirt. "Day and a half?"

One, two, three, four. Such simple numbers, but she couldn't translate them to her feet.

"Just boring." A waste of time. "And it's tiring being nice and godly all day. Who knew being worshipped was such hard work?" Andra tried not to let the anxiety seep into her voice. "These were the First's rooms?"

"Firm."

"Do you think there's anything left from her?" Any clue that the First could have been her mother. "Maybe an ancient angel? Like one of the Angelic Guards?"

Zhade shook his head. "I already checked. Nothing left. Maret must have raided the room before he boarded it shut."

"Why did he close off this part of the palace?"

"Probablish so he could forget what he did."

"What did he do?"

"A lot of things."

"You're always so cryptic."

Zhade smirked. "What's this *cryptic*? I don't reck this word."

"Means mysterious. It comes from a Latin word that refers to hidden caves where they buried their dead."

"Oh." Zhade twirled her, her feet almost stumbling as the floor moved from marble to carpet, but he drew her back. "What does *Latin* mean?"

One, two, three, four.

"It's an old language that—you know what, never mind."

Zhade laughed. "You gods and your languages," he said, almost to himself. He nudged Andra. "No shakes, Goddess. Decide your fate. Do your best, and all happens evens."

"You mortals and your languages." Her laugh caught in her throat.

"For true. No shakes, Goddess." Candlelight flickered across Zhade's serious expression. "I reck you have fear, but all you have to do is sit there and look charred. For now."

"What's charred?"

A smile spread across his face. "Means beautiful. It comes from a Zhadian word that means absolutish delicious."

She rolled her eyes. "You're a scoundrel."

"I don't reck that word either, but it sounds like a compliment."

"Yeah, well, to you it probably would be."

"You reck you like me," he said, his grin almost shy.

One, two.

"I . . ." She sighed. " . . . hate you less than other people."

Three, four.

The corner of his mouth twitched. "And I tolerate you."

He was so close, she couldn't breathe. His eyes were not as brown as she once thought. A little bit of green lined the edges. There were the beginnings of crow's feet at the corners, and a small scar at his temple that she could only see when they twirled into the moonlight.

Lew-Eadin coughed. Lilibet snickered.

Zhade and Andra pulled apart. He gave her a half smile and scrubbed the back of his neck.

"Rare form, Goddess," he said, looking away.

For a moment, she didn't say anything. Only tried to control the blush that was rising to her cheeks.

"I don't know those words, but they sound like a compliment."

Zhade grinned, meeting her eyes. "Oh, they are."

SIXTEEN

THE LIAR

THE GODDESS WAS a terrible dancer.

Her movements were almost angelic: stiff and exact, but somehow the precision made her awkward, not graceful. It was like there was a time chime ticking in her head, forcing her to stay on beat. There was no room for interpretation. No room for passion.

At least in her dancing.

The rest of her, though . . . the rest of her was passionate and smart and caring and—

No distractions, Zhade reminded himself.

He splashed cold water on his face, then leaned onto the sink and watched it drip off his cheeks, down the drain. He'd scuzed himself soonish after their dance and found an empty smallroom—one designated for the First's servants. It was also the entrance to one of the tunnels he and Wead had used as boys to escape the palace. A series of loose tiles in the corner gave way to a trap door. It was now the easiest way for Wead to meet them, and the sole reason Zhade was evens with using the First's suite for the Goddess's lessons.

The Goddess.

His hand on her waist, her laughing at his jokes, relaxing into him—
She's just a tool. Just a way to get revenge.

Neg. He had to be honest with himself. He was attracted to her.

That wasn't saying much. He was attracted to most people. It was more than that. She was kind. She wanted to help. She was funny. She was awkward, but in an endearing way, and she had a dimple in one cheek when she smiled full wide or pressed her lips together in exasperation.

When he'd kissed her to shut her up, he'd wanted to keep kissing her. Just because he *liked* her.

That was problemistic.

She's just a tool.

It didn't import that he liked her. There'd be others—there always were. Vengeance imported more than . . . whatever this was.

He shut off the faucet and watched the last of the water swirl and vanish. There was no towel, so he wiped his face with his untucked shirt.

No more lessons today, he decided. The rest of the night would consist of Zhade pilfering what was left in the First's suite and then scoping out the Rock—watching, learning its rhythm, leading Kiv on a wild moose chase. He needed the Goddess far from him so he could get his head straightish.

He followed the dark hallway back to the First's suite, where the Goddess was waiting. (His face felt warm. Was he blushing? Certz not. He never blushed.) He was bout to open the door when he heard Wead's voice.

"Favor me? Don't tell Zhade."

He froze. His hand hung suspended, knuckles brushing the knob.

"He won't help me if he knows?" The Goddess's voice was muffled by the door.

A pause. "Perhaps. But also, I worry if you change Zhade's past, you'll change his future too."

His best friend and his . . . whatever she was . . . plotting together? Keeping secrets. He wished he could reverse time like he did on the scrying boards and catch the beginning of the convo.

"Well . . ." The Goddess sighed. "I won't tell Zhade if you think it's best, but . . . I didn't understand a word you said."

Lew-Eadin's laugh wafted under the door. It was the laugh he'd used with Dzeni. "Thanks."

"No, thank *you*. I needed to talk."

Zhade had been standing there time and a half enough. He entered the room, making as much noise as he could.

The Goddess and Wead pulled apart. She looked flush. He looked guilty. Had they been . . . ? Certz not. Not with the maid-girl there. Certz it was nothing more than a cheek-kiss. Or a hug. A one-armed one at that. Full friendish.

For a moment, the tension hung in the air, thick as a sandcloud between them. Then Zhade stretched, plastered on his best grin, and scratched his stomach.

"Bout time to get abed, marah, boyo?" he asked. His tone sounded too forced. Was he talking too loud?

She's just a tool.

Wead visiblish relaxed and nodded to Zhade. He picked up his pack, then tossed Zhade's bag to him.

Zhade approached Andra's skirlish little maid. What was her name? Something Hivish.

"Charling, could you take the Goddess to her room?" He took her hand and kissed her knuckles. He expected a giggle or for her brown cheeks to darken, but she mereish stiffened and looked at the Goddess. Zhade did too. "And make certz she stays there."

"Certz," the maid whispered.

Mereish a tool.

"Decide your fates," he said. The Goddess scowled. Wead coughed. Zhade left.

SEVENTEEN

confession, n.

Definition: 1. an acknowledging of a fault, wrong, crime, or guilt.

2. obsolete: the tomb of a martyr.

EVERY DAY WAS the same pattern, even though the details shifted. Andra would wake from her restless sleep and Lilibet would help her into her newest ridiculous article of clothing. She'd then be escorted to meetings—mostly with important members of the government, though sometimes with select Eerensedian citizens. Sometimes they'd ask for things Andra couldn't give, but wished she could— better crops, healing for a sick relative, more food. Sometimes they asked for spiteful things—for their neighbor's rosebushes to die or for a business competitor to fall ill. No matter what, she gave them all the same answer Zhade had given her.

"I'll think about it."

She hated the response for several reasons, but mostly because it was a lie. She did her best *not* to think about all the things she couldn't give them, not to focus on the people at all.

The more she learned about the 'dome, the more she realized it wouldn't be standing much longer. Apparently, there was a section southwest of the palace where the deterioration was so bad, people could see the links in the 'dome's skin on moonless nights.

Granted, the stars were bright here, but still. Once the 'dome failed, the Eerensedians would be just as vulnerable to the corrupted tech of the pockets as the Wastes. But if Andra started to feel sympathy for them, she would start to doubt her objective: to get to Earth. To no longer be in danger. To no longer be a goddess.

She was already starting to feel guilty about leaving Lew-Eadin and Lilibet, and maybe even about leaving Zhade. She met with them each evening, after sorting through the 'bots Tsurina had sent her. They never included a colonial mech'bot, nor an AI, and she started to notice after a week of searching that Tsurina was sending her 'bots she'd already checked. Andra was going to have to come up with another way to find what she needed.

Each night, Zhade brought her another piece of tech before goddess lessons. She had a vague idea of what she needed, and she understood the coding, but shuttle hardware was somewhat of a mystery to her. She'd put together a short-range one with her classmates in her sophomore engineering workshop, but they hadn't done it manually. They'd programmed mech'bots to do it for them. She kept everything Zhade brought her, just in case.

They continued to meet in the First's rooms for the lessons, but Andra had yet to find anything to suggest the First had been her mother—or *any* identifying characteristics. It had been a fool's hope anyway—that she would *happen* to know the two out of a million who had accidentally woken late with her.

There was a different lesson every night. After dancing, they covered table manners, then Eerensedian history, then language. The last one was her favorite. The slang of High Goddess was easy to pick up, but the speech of the common Eerensedians was completely unrecognizable as English. At first glance, at least. The more Andra dissected it, the more she could see how one word evolved into another. How *house* had led to *howz* had led to *ousz*. How the grammar had simplified and verb tenses became implied. When she was done with a language lesson, her brain ached in a good way, like a muscle just exercised. If that was all her life was here, she wouldn't have minded it so much.

But it wasn't. Her life was a labyrinth of royal etiquette and deific pretense, a parade of endless meetings and futile searches. It would have been boring, except she was always aware of the danger of messing up, of swaying even a little. She threw herself into goddess lessons, if for nothing else, as a distraction.

Every lesson had a moral, a phrase Zhade wanted her to memorize, quoting it over and over, like his little sayings were pure brilliance.

Answer a question with a question.

Don't make promises you can't keep.

Always pretend you're one move ahead, even when you're not.

Lew and Lilibet rolled their eyes behind Zhade's back while cheering Andra on. She'd started to feel a certain kinship with them. They formed inside jokes and communicated in shorthand. Zhade was stand-offish. He flirted and bantered, but the friendship that had been forming between them was gone. That was fine, Andra thought. She didn't need to be friends with him. She didn't need to stare at the jacket he'd left in her room that first day in the palace. She didn't need to remember what it felt like to kiss him.

She needed to get out of here.

One night, after lessons, Andra stopped Lew-Eadin on his way out. She noticed Zhade pause at the door, but only for a moment before hefting his bag over his shoulder and leaving.

"Firm, Andra?" Lew said. Lew was the only one who actually made any effort to call her by name.

"I was wondering if you knew anything about the Angelic Guard?"

Lew nodded. "A bit. When I was training with the Guv's guard, we had to work closeish with them."

"The ones outside the throne room. Are they always the same ones? Or do they rotate?"

Lew thought for a moment. "It's diff to say. Many of the Angelic Guard look alike, but I reck that sometimes, as angels grow ancient, their magic decreases, and they're sent out into the city for other use."

Bingo.

Colonial 'bots would definitely be considered ancient, which meant a mech'bot with the capabilities she needed could be somewhere out in the city. She just needed a way to find it. Andra had yet to go outside the palace since her arrival. It was "too dangerous," according to Zhade and Maret's advisors. Lew, however, had no such restrictions. She hated asking—he would say yes because she was a goddess, because he was a nice person, because she'd already confided in him that she was leaving.

She didn't know why she'd told him, only that she'd felt tingly and light-headed after dancing with Zhade during that first goddess lesson, and she needed to remind herself what she was doing.

So she'd told Lew-Eadin everything. Not just reiterating that she wasn't a goddess, but giving him specifics. About Earth and the Ark and her mother's disappointment and the cryo'tanks and being forgotten. That the Goddesses before her had been just like her—if not unremarkable, at least unmagical. She told him all the particulars she'd told Zhade in sweeping vague statements a hundred times, but he'd brushed aside. Lew had listened even though she knew he didn't understand. He believed her—not in the way she wanted to be believed (literally, not metaphorically), but it was enough.

Then he'd asked her not to tell Zhade.

Lew seemed sad she was leaving, but there was something else there as well. It was almost like he was guilt-ridden. Which meant that Andra leaving messed up Zhade's plans. She knew Zhade wasn't telling her everything, but she'd been hoping Lew might. He hadn't.

He had promised to help her, though, even at great personal cost. Even though by leaving, she was betraying him.

The guilt didn't keep her from asking for his help finding a mech'bot though.

He agreed, and she'd checked with him every goddess lesson since, but he hadn't found anything, and the 'bots from Tsurina turned up nothing. Her chances of making it off the planet before she did something that got her killed were slimming.

As her hopes began to dwindle, she grew more familiar with the cadence of the palace. Her life here was starting to fall into rhythm. Then one night, she came back from dinner, expecting to find a collection of useless 'bots in her suite, and found Maret instead.

He was sitting in an upholstered chair, Zhade's discarded jacket tossed aside. For a moment, she thought he *was* Zhade, and her heart did a funny lurch. But the figure shifted and the moonlight fell on his pinched face and pale hair, and her heart jolted for a different reason.

"Guv," she said, trying the bow Zhade had taught her the other night.

Maret seemed unimpressed. He stood and made his way to the door. "Walk with me."

Andra froze. "No . . . thank you?"

Maret was already out the door, but he called back over his shoulder. "It wasn't a request."

Andra wanted to debate whether or not a guv could command a goddess, but given Maret had access to weapons, it was probably best not to antagonize him.

"Where are we going?" she asked, catching up.

"The 'dome," was all he said, and Andra felt her stomach drop.

She'd been searching the 'bots for colonial programming, giving them the Neo-Turing Test for artificial intelligence. She hadn't been looking for other capabilities, like 'dome maintenance.

She didn't speak as she followed Maret, and he didn't seem uncomfortable with the silence. He probably would have been more annoyed if she'd spoken, and the thought made her wish she could think of something to say. But her brain was too busy calculating risks and preparing for possibilities. Surely he wouldn't demand she fix the 'dome right now?

Zhade would be expecting her for goddess lessons in a few hours. She wondered if she would be back in time. If she would be coming back at all.

Maret led her through the palace and out into a courtyard. As soon as Andra realized where they were, she took a step back.

The place her maids had died looked different in the dark. The fountain was no longer bubbling, and though the tiled pathway was lined with candles, they had been extinguished. The metal platform was gone, but Andra remembered where it had been.

It took the Guv a moment to realize he was no longer being followed. He turned and gave Andra an exasperated look.

"What?" His silhouette was unmistakable in the dark, his figure tall and lean. His clothes blended perfectly into his surroundings, but his pale face shone in the moonlight.

"Where are we going? Actually?" Andra asked, taking another step back.

"To the gods' dome. Actua*lly*." He drew out the last syllable, mockingly. "Like I said."

"Why are we going this way?"

"It's peaceful." He shrugged. Then flicked his hair out of his eyes. It wasn't slicked back as it usually was, and it was surprisingly long— down past his chin. It didn't look as effortlessly tousled as Zhade's.

"Peaceful?" Andra asked. "The place where you execute people?"

Maret gave her a blank expression. "It relaxes me."

Despite the derision in his voice, he looked more comfortable than she'd seen him. In fact, he almost carried himself like Zhade, and if he'd had pockets, she bet his hands would have been stuffed inside.

It was easy to forget they were brothers, but if she were to see them side by side right now, there would be no question they were related.

She wanted to ask him about his guards—if he was just going to wander around outside at night without them—but she didn't want him to think she was planning to take advantage of that. Even though she was. But did he even need his guards? The crown was dull in the darkness, his unkempt hair mostly covering it, but she still felt its presence like a weight. Just a few weeks ago, he'd used it in this very courtyard to murder. He could easily use it to attack her with a nearby 'bot. Hell, he could probably just overpower her physically.

"Should we really be going to the 'dome at night? Weren't you the one who said I shouldn't leave the palace for safety reasons?"

"That was Prezdin actualish." He patted down his hair, mimicking the chief of security's nervous tic. It almost surprised a laugh out of Andra. "Scared off by one assassination attempt?"

Was that a threat? It felt like a threat.

"All part of being a goddess." She swallowed. "I guess."

The courtyard fountain bubbled away.

"You promised to fix the 'dome, and you can't do that if you never see it." Maret huffed. "Are you scared? For certz? You're a Goddess and I have this." He pointed to his crown. "We'll be evens."

The crown was exactly what she was worried about, but she couldn't say that without revealing she had no godlike powers with which to protect herself.

As though reading her mind, Maret said, "You've yet to perform a miracle. What good is a goddess without them? Sides, don't you want to save all those people you say I murder needlessish?"

Andra swallowed. Perhaps she should have been focusing on the 'dome. Amid all his pithy advice, Zhade had mentioned miracles several times, but Andra had blown it off. She'd decided to put all her efforts into her escape plan, but maybe she should be figuring out how to perform one so she wouldn't be killed before she had the chance to leave. And even though Andra hadn't seen an execution since her maids', she didn't doubt Maret would use her inaction as an excuse to kill again.

"Sure," she said. "I'll go with you."

"Finalish," he muttered, and led her through the garden.

THE CITY WAS a study in contradictions. Carts lined the streets instead of cars or hovers. Horse-like creatures drowsed, tied to posts at front stoops and in alleys, while overhead, drones flew rooftop to rooftop, window to window. Andra heard no steady hum of electricity or ambient noise of enviro'mods, but the tingle of passing nanos pricked her skin. It was habit to reach out with her 'implant, as was the disappointment that inevitably followed.

Maret walked in silence. At first, Andra was surprised he wasn't using some kind of carriage, but she got the impression he was sneaking around too.

He took the easiest route to the 'dome, if not the quickest. The palace was on the edge of the city, but craggy hills of rocks and forest stood between it and the 'dome's wall. Instead, they walked in the direction away from the silver tower.

The streets were mainly deserted, except for the stray drone or 'bot, which Andra mentally cataloged. She didn't see any mech'bots, but there were definitely sections of the city that were more populated with 'bots than others. Occasionally, she saw someone smoking a pipe in an alley or gazing at the moonlight from their front stoop. The desertion, coupled with her current company, gave the city an eerie feel.

"A magic bean?"

Andra started. The voice had drifted from the shadows, coarse and aging, half grinding stone, half whispering ghost. Her gut reaction was to run, but her curiosity got the best of her, and she stepped toward it.

Maret grabbed her arm, but she pulled away. She heard him mumble something under his breath.

An old man sat huddled on a sheltered stoop. A craggy grin spread across his face, revealing a row of crooked teeth, rotting and yellowed like the keys of an old piano. He held out a tiny serve'drone. The moonlight shone down on the man's modded arm, gleamed off the fluttering mini'drone hovering over his open palm. "A good price for a charred lady."

His modded arm was decorated with a design that felt familiar, but she couldn't place it. She drew forward.

Maret tried to usher Andra away. "No deal, boyo," he said, his voice masked by the accent she'd heard Zhade use with the soldier at the gate.

They'd barely taken a step before the old man wheezed. "I reck what you are, witch."

Andra froze, and she felt Maret tense beside her.

The man stood, his legs wobbling beneath him, but his eyes never left her, hard as flint. "You exist a fraud." His voice rumbled, his accent thick. "You use the people and corrupt our leaders, just like the others. There exist no goddesses, no gods. No angels or sorcers or magic. Sole tricks of light and sleight of hand. You happen dangerful. A liar and a thief, and you deserve what comes."

Andra hadn't seen him move, but he was suddenly in front of her, his arm raised, a knife glinting in his clenched fist. And she knew she should run or fight back or do something, but she couldn't. She just stood there, because part of her believed him—that she did deserve what came. For lying. For being a disappointment.

For not being the Goddess these people needed.

Just as the man was about to bring the knife down, he froze. His eyes widened, his mouth gaping like a fish. At first, Andra didn't understand what was happening, but then the man made a choking sound, and she turned to see Maret, his brow furrowed in concentration and his crown gleaming beneath his hair in the moonlight.

He was choking the man with nanos.

There weren't enough nearby to form into spears, as Maret had done with her maids. There were, however, enough of the microscopic 'bots to block the man's airway, and that was exactly what Maret was doing. Then, the man's hand slowly began to turn, until he was pointing the weapon at himself. His eyes widened further in panic.

"Guv," Andra whispered, needing to stop this, but afraid to startle him into action.

Maret's face was contorted, and what Andra thought was a trickle of sweat was actually a bead of blood running down his cheek. Either something was wrong with Maret, or with the crown.

The man's hand arced further, the edge of the weapon grazing his throat. His face was a bright red.

"Guv," Andra said again, but Maret seemed not to hear her. She took a step closer and put a hand on his arm. "Maret, stop."

He blinked, and it was like he was coming back to himself. As quickly as he had captured the man, he released him. The old man fell to his knees, sucking in a breath, and his weapon clattered to the cobblestone.

Maret stooped in front of him, picked up the knife, and used it to lift the man's chin. The man's face lit with recognition.

"Sorries, Guv," he croaked. "Sorries. I didn't reck . . ."

"If you," Maret said, his voice low, "or any of your ilk, come near the Goddess again, I will find you and fillet you as you breathe. Do you comp?"

The man swallowed, attempting to nod with the knife still caught against the soft spot under his chin. "Firm. Firm, Guv, sorries."

"Neg, you're not." Maret pulled away, flipping the knife in his hand and pocketing it. "But you will be."

The man scrambled back, not waiting to be dismissed, and hobbled down the nearest darkened alley.

Maret turned to Andra and offered her his hand. "Shall we?"

Andra ignored him, her pulse still racing. "What was the symbol on his arm?" It had been a ragged hollow circle, lit in a web of circuitry. It reminded Andra of a coffee cup stain, or an eclipse. A ragged red slash tore through it, like someone had tried to cut it out.

Maret was quiet for a moment. "He's with the Luddites. Or dunno they call themselves something different, but that was what the First called them, and it snagged. They hate angels and everything to do with High Magic. And . . . the Goddesses." He pushed his bottom lip out in thought. "You."

"But his arm was modded . . . magic. He was trying to sell me magic."

Maret laughed without humor. "People are always against something til it favors them." He was quiet a moment. "And not everyone has a choice bout what's done to them. Bout what they are."

Something about his tone—the softness, the vulnerability—kept Andra quiet. He shrugged and walked on, footsteps gritty against the cobblestone. After a moment, she followed him in silence.

They took the street past a teetering neighborhood, and there, the buildings ended abruptly. There was a small grassy area, and then the edge of the 'dome.

The base formed the black titanium wall encircling the city. It was taller than Andra, and she had to look up to see where it gave way to the plastene/metallic glass hybrid of the 'dome. In the sunlight, the glass had a faint rainbow sheen, but in the dark it was nearly invisible. Or it should have been. When she twisted her head, she could see where the hexagonal plates converged. Stark black lines ran in between each panel, bleeding into the glass itself. Dead nanos. They stretched along the skin of the 'dome like greedy fingers, fading into the night sky.

Maret gestured for her to take a look. "Evens. Can you fix it?"

"Give me a minute," she muttered.

Andra approached the 'dome and reached out, feeling along the cold titanium surface for a seam. It was for practicality's sake—it was too dark to see—but Andra realized the movement made it look like she was doing magic.

"Where is it," she mumbled.

"Here," Maret said, and a light flicked on.

She turned to find him holding a T-16 Prime Tablet. Andra's breath caught. She couldn't believe it.

Did Maret have any idea what he had?

It was the same model her mother, Dr. Griffin, all the LAC elites had used. It had the most powerful processor on the planet, but it was a miracle it had survived this long and Maret was using it as a flashlight.

Something must have shown on her face, because Maret asked, "Are you evens?" At first his voice sounded concerned, but then he added, "To be true, you're the most squeamish goddess we've ever had."

"I'm fine," Andra whispered, reluctantly turning back to the 'dome anchor.

That tablet must have been the First's. But how did she get access to something only LAC officials used? *Stop it*, she told herself. *It wasn't Mom.* It was probably just handed down by the original colonists. But she didn't believe that either. She shook away the thought and continued her search.

Andra found a tiny crack, a hinge, but her mind was still focused on that T-16 Prime. Her hands shook as she flipped open a plastic cover to reveal a palm'lock beneath. She pressed her hand to it and a holo'display emerged asking for a pass code. She circumvented it using a hacking method she'd picked up in school, when the students would break into each other's logins.

Once past the security, she filtered through the files until she found a program for maintenance. And here, she was lost. Though she could detect patterns, she couldn't make sense of them. But one thing jumped out at her. A file about the 'dome's construction. She sucked in a breath.

"Can you fix it?" Maret asked again, and Andra couldn't tell if he was curious or just reminding her he was there.

She didn't answer right away. No, she couldn't fix it. But she knew who—or what—could. Halfway down the file were the words:

Rather than relying on human care, maintenance will be provided by a corresponding AI.

An AI.

Andra's heart pounded with adrenaline as she pressed her palm to the 'lock, shutting down the 'display, and turned back toward the palace. "I think so." The words were a whisper.

The 'dome was failing because the AI assigned to reprogram its nanos was missing. But luckily, a homing beacon showed where it was being kept.

The palace.

An AI. In the palace.

The 'display hadn't said exactly where in the palace, but Andra had a way to find out. AI gave off a specific tech signature, which Andra hadn't considered since her 'implant was incompatible. But now, she had another option. Maret's tablet had a scanner that could lead her right to it.

She still needed a mech'bot, and more scraps of tech for the shuttle, but for the first time in a long time, Andra felt something like hope.

She was going back to Earth.

EIGHTEEN

pishogue, n. or adj.

Definition: 1. a spell or charm.

2. belonging to witchcraft.

3. a story of unbelievable elements.

ANDRA DIDN'T REST at all that night. It had been tough for her to make herself sleep since coming out of stasis, but now it was nearly impossible. She'd gotten back from her excursion with Maret in enough time to make it to goddess lessons, albeit a little late. Zhade didn't seem to notice—just handed her a busted circuit board, then started teaching her the miracles of the First (her awakening, the great stardust migration, the building of the 'dome . . . was there anything this woman couldn't do?). He called it a night when Lilibet started listing the miracles of the Second, which were more fire-and-brimstone oriented. Andra would have to do something miraculous soon if she wanted to keep up this ruse. Unless she could get off-planet before she needed to prove her goddessness.

After lessons, Lew-Eadin told her he had a lead on an old Angelic Guard somewhere in a place called Southwarden. A possible mech'bot. Her collection of scraps was growing. And now she knew there was an AI somewhere in the palace. And possibly a way to track it down.

The tablet she'd seen Maret with could do a lot of things, but the only thing Andra was interested in was its ability to scan for AI. She needed to get that tablet, and Maret gave her the perfect opportunity.

After they'd returned to the palace the night before, he'd told her to take the morning off goddess duties. He'd made it sound like a favor, playing the kindhearted ruler, but Andra shouldn't have had to perform goddess duties in the first place. And if she *had* been a deity, shouldn't she be allowed to set her own schedule?

At any rate, while Maret thought Andra was sleeping in—or preparing to fix the 'dome, or whatever he thought goddesses did in their off time—he was in the throne room, doing whatever guvs did, his guards stationed around him. Nobody thought to protect his empty chambers, because they were sealed with "blood magic." And Andra had a hunch about how to get around that.

She sneaked through the palace, using some of the hidden passages Zhade had shown her, and found herself on Maret's hall. It was a cloudy day, and the light shining through the windows was muted. Dust particles and nanos sparkled in her path, brushing her as she passed. She hadn't been to his quarters since the day of her maids' executions, and a wave of memories washed over her. She shook them off.

She stopped short once she reached the end of the hall, the security DNA scan blinking to the right of Maret's blood-red door.

If Andra was right, these hadn't always been Maret's rooms. She guessed they'd once belonged to the former Guv. Which meant the scan not only opened for Maret, but had once opened for his father. It responded to those who shared his DNA.

Which included Zhade.

Fortunately, she didn't actually need Zhade with her. She just needed his blood. And thanks to her reflexes when he'd sneaked up on her, she had it. He'd left the jacket he'd wiped his bloody nose on hung over one of her chairs. If she was lucky—and she was overdue for some luck—there would be enough remnants of Zhade's DNA on the jacket sleeve for the scanner to read and let her into Maret's suite.

The scanner came to life. Andra held her breath and let the sleeve hover over the target. She tensed her muscles to run. If this didn't work, the best-case scenario was that it just wouldn't let her in. Other, more likely scenarios included an alarm going off or a trap springing.

For a moment, nothing happened.

Then the door clicked open.

She released a sigh and stepped in. Maret's rooms were just as she'd seen them before. The same extra-large furniture in dark shades of black and red. The same weapons hanging around the room. A half-drunk glass of alcohol lingered on the side table. Without the Guv and Tsurina to fill the space, the room looked less intimidating and more . . . sad. She didn't know where to begin, but instinct told her to start with the door to the far right.

It led to Maret's bedroom.

It was shrouded in darkness, thick black curtains pulled taut over the windows. The bed was perfectly made, but on the floor was a nest of blankets, twisted and disheveled. The room was filled with nanos, thick as fog. Andra felt like she was inhaling them as she crossed the room and threw open the curtains.

The window let in minimal light, but it was enough to search by. Andra felt with her 'implant. There was nothing there—or rather, there was something just out of her reach. Like her fingers were only skimming the surface.

Andra started with the desk closest to the door. At first, she tried to be inconspicuous, but soon she was rifling through its contents with little regard for secrecy. She found a lot of mutilated technology—sparked-out cyber implants, broken 'bands, a crushed force-field diode—but no T-16 Prime Tablet. She'd considered Maret might keep it with him, but she hadn't seen him with it until last night.

She checked the ornate wood cabinet next, but it was nothing more than weapons storage. Nothing in the bedside table, and she was about to go diving under the mattress when something caught her eye.

Aha.

It was beneath the pile of blankets. Sleek and thin, its silver casing scored with scratch marks and dusted with dirt. She picked it up, careful not to disturb the blankets, and all but cradled it to her. This was a bit of familiarity, a bit of home. And it could have been her mother's.

No, Andra chastised herself. *Don't think that.*

She was worried there would be some sort of security feature, but it opened right up for her, displaying in a flattened hologram. It was definitely a T-16 Prime Tablet, which meant it should have been compatible with her 'implant. But when she tried to interface with it, nothing sparked. It was a mystery, but not an obstacle.

Andra manually opened the 'scanner app and asked it to scan for an AI techno'print, kind of like a human's heat signature. The scanning program was efficient, and it only took a few minutes for the progress bar to go from empty to filled. Those few minutes felt like a thousand years, and Andra's heart sped up as the scan neared its end.

87%

94%

99%

Right before the results appeared, there was a noise at the door.

"Shit," she hissed, then cursed herself silently for cursing out loud.

Andra closed the program, hesitating less than a moment before placing it back where she found it. She rushed to the window to close the drapes just as the doorknob turned. She closed herself behind them and held her breath.

Footsteps. Someone entered. The hair on her arm bristled.

The person—Maret, she supposed—moved further into the room. The tread was light, slow. She was paying close attention, so she noticed when the steps changed from something casual to something alert.

A pause, then a quick tread to the desk, the bureau. The same places Andra had just searched. She prayed to whoever was listening—the

First, the Second (and herself, she thought dryly)—that she'd put everything back where she found it.

The footsteps grew closer to her hiding place. Andra held her breath, trying to make herself smaller, invisible.

Closer.

Closer.

Until Maret was a breath away from her, and if the curtain vanished, she would be staring right at him.

The curtain twitched, as though he was running his fingers along it.

Andra was smart. Clever. An excellent problem solver. But nothing in her life prepared her for what to do when faced with this: being hunted. It was too primal, when Andra had lived nothing but a life of sims and dehydrated meals and indoor plumbing. She was grasping for explanations, for plans and contingencies, but coming up desperately short. Dozens of calculations fired in her brain, but kept fizzing out, a spark extinguished before it could even catch. She could fight, but with what? She could run, but to where? She could talk her way out, but how?

She was shorting out. No fight or flight, just freeze.

A portion of the curtain bunched, like Maret was grasping it. Light filtered through the bottom, and if he looked down, he would see her feet. She bit her lip until the coppery taste of blood filled her mouth. The frantic rhythm of her heart thumped wildly behind her eardrums. Her breath threatened to spill out of her. All these reminders that she was alive, and that, if Maret found her, she wouldn't be for long.

The curtain started to open.

"There it is." Maret's voice, muffled.

The curtain swung back into place, heavy enough to flap against Andra's thighs.

She heard his footsteps retreat. Stop. Something rustling. And then more footsteps. The door opened.

Then closed.

Andra didn't move.

Was it a trap? Had he merely pretended he was leaving to draw her out? He had to have known someone had been in his rooms. She'd left evidence of her presence everywhere. Was Maret leaning against the door as Zhade would have been, waiting for her to reveal herself?

She waited a full ten minutes, ticking the time off in her head, straining to hear any indication of another presence in the room. A breath, a cough, the shifting of weight. But soon, her legs started to cramp, and she felt silly hiding behind a curtain, if the room was truly empty.

She peeked out. No one. Her eyes did a quick sweep of places someone could hide—under the bed, behind the bureau—but she was alone in Maret's room. She started to dart out, when she remembered the reason she'd come in the first place. She rushed over to Maret's nest, but the tablet was gone.

She pushed the blankets over, looking under and between, until she'd made a complete mess, bedding strewn across the room, but it was nowhere to be found. Her answers. The scan. The thing she'd risked her life for. Maret had taken it.

ANDRA DIDN'T FULLY release a breath until she was back in her suite. She didn't know when it had happened, but she'd come to think of her room as home base. The safety was an illusion, she knew, but it was familiar and comforting all the same.

She threw herself on her bed. Despair threatened to overtake her. She tried to remind herself it was just a setback. Lew could still find a mech'bot for her, she had a pile of scrap metal and tech stored on her balcony, and she had proof there was an AI *in the palace*. But all she really wanted to do was sulk.

There was a knock on the door and the sound of Lilibet's dainty feet. She expected the maid to scold her for still being in bed. *Show the toe, you spoon. Goddesses don't pass all day abed!* But instead there was just a small cough.

She lifted her head and saw Lilibet staring at her, eyes wide and watery. Andra shot up.

"What's wrong? Did someone hurt you?"

Lilibet sniffed. "Neg, Goddess, but you happen kind to ask." Another sniffle. "I just came to tell you I heard from Lew-Eadin."

"Is something wrong?" Andra immediately started collecting things and shoving them into a silk purse. Canisters of water, bandages, anything an injured Lew might need. She almost grabbed the tiara Zhade had given her to barter with, but thought better of it. As soon as she tried to sell it, people would know who she was. "Is he okay?"

"Evens?" Lilibet asked. "Firm. He's evens. He has an angel for you to look at."

Andra dropped her things. "An angel?"

Lilibet nodded. "One of those . . . what did you call it? Mech . . . bots?"

"Lilibet, that's awesome!" After Andra's failure to find the AI and almost getting caught in the process, she needed a win. But Lilibet still looked on the verge of tears. "Why are you so upset?"

Was it because Andra was leaving? Maybe Lilibet realized she was abandoning them all to death.

The maid took a deep breath. "I have . . . something to confess, Goddess."

The pit of Andra's stomach dropped. Was Lilibet a spy for Maret? Was she part of that group—the Luddites?—who hated the Goddesses? Had she told someone Andra's identity? Or was it something more *Lilibet*? Maybe she would confess she didn't actually know how to sew, or that she didn't really like the color of Andra's newest dress.

"What is it?" Andra asked. She sat on the bed, hands clamped on either side of her. She nodded for Lilibet to have a seat.

The maid sat in Zhade's chair, running her long sleeve over her eyes. "I'm not who you reck I am."

Andra held her breath.

"I didn't ask to be your maid because I was tired of stirring stews. I came to the palace because . . . because . . ." She hiccupped. "Because I was looking for the Second!"

She burst into tears.

Andra sat silent for a moment, trying to process what she'd just been told, but there was too much missing information.

"Okay . . ."

"Seeya, we reck she's still alive," Lilibet said, voice wavering. "No one saw her die, and me and the others, we reck she's hidden somewhere apalace, or they moved her to a safe location in the Wastes . . . evens, safeish, marah? I came here to gather info, but then I became your maid, and even though you're not a real goddess, I full bars like you. You're such a good friend, and now you're going to diiiiieeeee." The last word devolved into sobs.

Andra stood. "I'm going to do what?"

Lilibet said something, but through the tears, Andra couldn't distinguish it. She knelt before the girl.

"Lilibet. You have to calm down. What are you talking about?" She tried to say it gently, but her panic was rising.

Lilibet blew out a shuddering breath, eyes rolling back to look at the coffered ceiling. She dabbed at the last few tears to leak out.

"Sorries and worries," she said, her voice slightly stronger. "You need to peace soon and now." Lilibet looked around the room, her voice lowering. "Tonight even. If you can."

"Why?"

"Has Zhade told you what happened to the First?"

"He told me she died."

"Did he tell you how?"

Andra shook her head.

"She was sacrificed."

Andra's blood ran cold. "She was what now?"

Lilibet tucked her hands beneath her knees. Another tear dribbled down her cheek. "I was a kiddun, but I have memories. The First, she gave us so much, but it was never enough for some people. She saved Eerensed, but she didn't save the neighbor villages. We have fam out in the Wastes. Or fam that were eaten by pockets. Or murdered." Lilibet's voice grew quiet. "The First didn't waken to save us. I don't reck what she was doing, but whatever it was, all this was mereish the cuppins frost. The people got tired of waiting for miracles. So they decided to make one."

"Make one?"

Lilibet nodded. "There was a rumor that . . . that when a goddess died it would be just like when an angel dies, but more powerful."

Andra didn't need her to go on. When 'bots died, they released their nano'swarm, so any functioning nanos could serve surrounding systems. It was simple conservation. An algorithm to prevent waste. For a short time after the system absorbed the 'swarm from the dead 'bot, it would look like it was performing at top speed. It was a quick high, while the system acclimated itself to the additional moving parts.

For a people who worshipped nanos, it would look like a soul escaping a body, and then dispersing to a nearby source of magic. The 'dome probably actually worked *better* after a 'bot died. But not *that* much better.

There were two things that didn't make sense though. One: 'implants didn't actually hold nanos. They just commanded the nanos around them. So how were the other goddesses housing them to release upon death? Two: Andra's 'implant proved colonial tech wasn't compatible with Eerensedian tech. So, even if the goddesses *did* somehow release nanos, how did they boost the tech around them?

The goddesses had been different, though, able to use the Eerense-dian tech to perform miracles, where Andra could not.

Lilibet bit her lip. "They sacrificed the First, and for time and a half, everything was evens. The gods' dome protected us, and magic was stronger. But when it didn't last, they sacrificed the Second as well . . ." Lilibet trailed off, twisting her dark hair around her fingers. "Or said they did. I recked she was alive, but the more I look, the more I believe . . . she's gone too, and I have fear you'll be next."

Andra was having trouble breathing. Her mind was spinning, calculating the implications, fitting together all the disparate pieces of what she'd just heard with everything she'd experienced so far.

Holy shit. Once the Eerensedians thought the goddesses were more helpful dead than alive, they killed them. And so far, Andra had been anything but helpful.

"Why?" Andra croaked. "Why are you telling me this now?"

"Because," Lilibet said, "the Third Festival is soon and sooner."

"Yeah, I know." It had been mentioned in a meeting several days ago. Each of the goddesses had a festival dedicated just to her, and Andra's festival was in a few days. Apparently, there would be fireworks and sparklers and star-shaped butter cookies, all in tribute to her stupid birthmark. Unlike all the other religious rituals and ceremonies, all Eerensedians would be invited, instead of just the diplomats and government officials. Part of Andra—a very small part—was looking forward to it.

"We don't celebrate the First's and Second's festivals anymore. Because . . ." Lilibet hiccupped, her shaking hand pushing back her hair. She met Andra's gaze. "Because it was during their festivals that they were sacrificed."

NINETEEN

forget, v.

Definition: 1. to cease or fail to remember.

2. to overlook, to neglect, to leave behind.

3. archaic: to be guilty of that which is unworthy.

ANDRA DIDN'T WAIT for Zhade or ask Maret for permission. She ducked out of the palace through a side door and nobody stopped her. Apparently, she was running out of time, so she would go out into the city, following the directions Lilibet had given her, and find Lew-Eadin and the mech'bot he'd discovered. A tiny spark of hope lit in her chest. Regardless of what Lilibet said about the goddess sacrifices, she couldn't help but feel something was about to go right.

Please let something go right.

She should have done this long ago. Even with the fear of the unknown, leaving the palace was freeing. She wore nondescript clothes and she'd programmed her cos'mask to a random face. No one even looked her way as she followed the winding streets, the 'dome looming above, the palace towering behind. The silver tower shone to her left, and she had the urge to head toward it.

There was no logic to the city layout, and Andra had to rely on instinct as much as Lilibet's directions. It wasn't that Eerensed was large space-wise. It was that it was packed in tight. Too many buildings and people crammed into a too-small space. It made Andra claustrophobic, but it was worth it to leave the palace.

She followed cobblestone streets and alleyways, weaving through markets and ducking past guards. She crossed a brick bridge that led over the river into another tangle of neighborhoods. And still she kept going.

Too many thoughts were fighting for dominance in her mind. Lew-Eadin had a mech'bot. An AI was in the palace. The other goddesses were *sacrificed*.

The threat of death had loomed over her since she'd arrived, but Zhade had talked her through how to avoid Maret's wrath. He *hadn't* told her about the sacrifices and that she had to curb Eerensedian resentment as well. The Third Festival was in a little over a week, and it could be her execution date. Sure, the First had lived through many festivals before the one they'd killed her during, but she had also given the people numerous miracles. Andra had provided them with none. She would have to change that. Even if this mech'bot was exactly what she was looking for, it would take at least two weeks to build the shuttle. She would need a miracle to survive until then.

It took almost an hour—or a bell, as the Eerensedians called it—for Andra to find the place Lew-Eadin was staying. Southwarden was a blend of richly adorned apartments and fancy shops. Andra found herself on a winding street full of restaurants. The scent shifted from savory to sweet, and Andra finally located the bakery Lilibet said Lew was living behind.

She pushed open the shop door and a bell rang a discordant chime. The bakery was free of customers, and most of the baked goods were picked over, leaving only a sprinkling of crumbs and misshapen scone-like pastries in the case. A single worker leaned on the counter, biological hand clasped with a modded one. Lew-Eadin.

He looked up, and it only took a moment for him to recognize her. So much for her disguise.

"What are you doing here?" he whispered, urgently ushering her in, then drawing the shades and locking the door behind her.

"I came for the mech'bot," Andra said. "You told Lilibet—"

"I didn't convo her to send *you* for it. I was going to bring it to goddess lessons. Does Zhade reck you're here?"

No. "Yeah," Andra said. "It was . . . his idea."

A few weeks pretending to be a goddess, and she'd become an expert at lying.

Lew looked skeptical—maybe not an expert then—but didn't argue. He shrugged and pulled back the curtain that led to the back room. There were pots and pans and an old stove cobbled together from disparate parts, but Andra didn't care to take in her surroundings, because right in front of her stood a mech'bot.

It was almost seven feet tall, its black casing polished to a shine even with deep silver scratches running along its torso and arms. Its left forearm sported a silver LAC logo. It looked mostly humanoid, except for the multijointed limbs.

She approached the 'bot and it came to life, its flat eyes sparking and glowing white. Suddenly, she was *aware* of the 'bot, like she used to be aware of light switches and sim controllers and open-access tablets. She couldn't control it with her 'implant—it was still just out of reach—but it was close.

"Excuse me," she said. "What is your make and model?"

"I am pleased to comply with your request," the 'bot said, its voice thin and crisp. "I am a LAC-sanctioned mechatronics and engineering robot, Class B, with a Corsairs-Veridian drive and Coppercell core."

"Year?"

"2162."

Andra felt a rush of dizziness overtake her. That was the year after she'd gone into stasis. The year the colonists had left for Holymyth. This 'bot had been created just before they'd departed, or perhaps even on the ship. It had been among the very first colonists. Maybe even interacted with her family. Whatever the 'bot had been used for since, it had been first designed for building things: hospitals, roadways, trains. Shuttles.

Andra swallowed. "Will you please display . . ." Her voice was no more than a whisper, so she cleared her throat and tried again. "Will you please display your protocols?"

The 'bot lifted its palm, projecting a holo'display containing a list of the tasks it was designed for. Andra filtered through until she got to the *T*'s, then gasped, tears springing to her eyes.

"Is everything evens, Andra?" Lew asked. "Is this what you were looking for?"

Right under the topic *Transportation* were the words *Shuttle construction and maintenance.*

Andra took a steadying breath. "Yeah," she whispered. "Yeah, it's perfect."

ANDRA TOOK A different route back to the palace, this time getting caught in the late afternoon rush. She'd managed to convince Lew to let her return by herself.

"I'll be fine," she'd said. "I have Mechy here to protect me." She patted the 'bot's shoulder and then realized that was something Zhade would have done.

Not that she minded Lew's company, but she needed time to herself, time to think. She'd expected to feel joy when she finally obtained a mech'bot, and there was some. But there was also fear of the festival, and strangely, guilt for planning on leaving. And on top of all that, disappointment that she wasn't only feeling euphoria. It was too much to untangle with someone by her side.

She got lost in the crowd, the mech'bot following behind. She picked up bits of language as she passed. It sounded different from the pieces Zhade, Lew, and Lilibet taught her, the accent thicker, the rhythm too fast.

She followed twist after turn, dodging barkers selling their wares and swerving past what was apparently a school letting the student sorcerers out for lunch. She kept turning back to make sure the mech'bot was keeping up. It was. People parted to let it pass, barely giving it a glance. Andra was exhausted, but she kept going, until the buildings fell away and the noise of the city muted, and she found herself standing at the edge of a clearing.

The river flowed on the far side. The ground was sandy as the desert, and nothing—no rocks, no plants, no buildings—were within a two-hundred-meter radius. Except for a grove of ruins in the very center.

A circle of columns stretched out of the earth and broke off suddenly, their edges worn and cracked. A crumbling statue was buried in the middle, the head and shoulders of a humanoid figure jutting out of the ground, so worn down, it looked like a decaying body. These ruins were old. Perhaps from the first colony, just like the mech'bot. The colony she was supposed to be a part of.

Something more than curiosity pulled Andra toward them. A tug, a nag. She gave the mech'bot a command to stay where it was and crossed the clearing, gravel crunching beneath her feet. When she made it to the first stone, she reached out cautiously, wanting to touch it, to feel what had been created possibly by people she knew. Oz might have stared up at the statue, clinging to his sister's hand. Acadia's, instead of Andra's.

Right before she made contact, she heard a voice behind her.

"How you happen here, girl?"

It was not a friendly voice. The threat was evident. Andra spun.

The man in front of her was dirty, hair hanging in stringy clumps, a sinister leer revealing several missing teeth. He wasn't alone. Two others stood behind him.

They had dark reddish tans—the kind of permanent sunburn that people who worked outside got, only visible on their exposed forearms and torsos. The rest of them was completely covered in ragged sand-colored clothing, crusted with dirt and twigs. Their faces were hidden, wrapped in rags, and curved horns protruded from their temples. One snarled, and where his teeth should have been were metallic pieces filed down to points. Andra wasn't sure if they were bio'mods or decoration. Her heart thundered. She cast her gaze to the mech'bot, but it was too far away to help, and she wasn't sure what one unarmed 'bot could do against three men.

The man in front laughed and scratched his uneven beard. "Hear, boyos. It's the *Goddess*." He spat the word. Seriously, her disguise was terrible. "All alone in the Small Wastes. You should reck better, charling."

Andra took a step back, the sand shifting beneath her feet, and poised herself to run, but she knew she wouldn't be fast enough.

She was right.

They were on her before she could think, knives clutched in their hands. They jabbed at her, and she barely danced away.

The leader said something to the others in Common Eerensedian, and Andra knew just enough to understand he was telling them not to kill her. To keep her alive for now so she could be sacrificed later.

That was only slightly reassuring.

Andra ducked behind a column, but one of the other men had guessed her intentions and cut her off on the other side. His knife slashed, catching her in the collarbone. She gasped, feeling the sting a moment later, then the hot rush of blood. She meant to run, to fight back, but the pain overtook her and she fell to her knees.

Neurons fired, delivering messages. *Pain, pain, pain*, they said.

It's not real. It's in your head.

Someone was laughing.

Not real.

Pain.

The synapses are blocked, rerouting . . .

Pain.

PAIN.

Andra blinked, shaking away whatever was happening to her head, to her 'implant. She couldn't focus. She couldn't *think*. It was almost like she had fallen asleep. Had started dreaming. But the men were where they had been just a moment before. Poised to pounce. Poised to take her away, to hurt her some more.

The leader bore down on her, and she kicked out on instinct, making contact with his face. She heard a crunch as his head jerked back. His groan morphed into a growl as he turned toward her. He spat a globule of blood into the sand, his face bright with rage.

"No one round here," he rasped. "No one to hear your screams. And no one would come running if they did."

She tensed, trying to stay conscious, trying to focus, trying to come up with something to say, something to do, just *something*. But it was almost like her mind had shut down for a moment, her body frozen in fear.

Then there was a new voice behind her.

"Unless they were tracking her."

The men jerked their heads up, but Andra didn't need to. She would recognize that arrogant drawl anywhere.

"We dared each other as kidduns to come up here," Zhade said, still out of Andra's line of vision—she didn't dare take her eyes off the attackers—but she could hear him coming closer, his footsteps making slow, lazy thuds against the sand. "If you made it to the closest column without wetting yourself, you were considered brave. I made it all the way to the center and rubbed the Buried Man's head for luck." She heard two thumps, as though he were patting the statue like a dog. "For certz, I screamed the full march, and I swear a ghost grabbed my ankle. Neg, hear, I still have the scar."

A rustle of clothing. The idiot was actually showing them his ankle.

"I come up here sometimes to ponder, seeya. Clear my brain of all the murder and stuff we do at the palace. That's actualish in the job description: murder and stuff."

She could now see him out of the corner of her eye. He'd drawn level with her, his hands in his pockets, his belt free of weapons. He shuffled his feet, spraying sand as he went.

"Almost didn't come today. My friend here would have been all alone, except *someone* went looking for her, because *someone* recked she would do something reckless and stupid eventualish, and now *someone* is going to hand you your teeth for bread."

The men stayed frozen. Zhade took another step forward.

"I'm—" He pointed at himself. "I'm the someone. Was that not crystal?"

Zhade pulled something out of his pocket. It was a thin dagger, almost translucent. Andra had never seen a weapon like it. No hilt, like the tip of an icepick, and made of no metal she recognized. It could almost be glass, or an icicle. It shone in the sun, a myriad of colors. It was beautiful, but useless against the weapons the attackers were wielding.

"Wait!" Andra shouted, but it was too late.

All three men lunged for Zhade. Two aimed high, the other low. Zhade danced out of the way. It became obvious pretty quickly that fighting was not Zhade's forte, and whatever techniques he had were cobbled together from a handful of controlled training sessions— probably with Lew or some palace official in charge of the bastard prince. Luckily, his opponents weren't that skilled either. But there were three of them, and one Zhade.

Andra tried to push herself to her feet, but pain coursed through her body, her mind still fuzzy, and she toppled to the ground.

With a spin, Zhade managed to dodge the first two men's attacks, but not the third's. His rusty weapon caught Zhade on the cheek, and a thin line of blood ran from temple to chin.

Zhade touched the tips of his fingers to the wound, then looked down at the smudged blood. He paled.

"Sands," he breathed. "Not the face."

The first man darted forward, knocking Zhade's translucent dagger to the ground. It skittered across the sand and landed by Andra. She grasped it. Pain shot through her, as sudden as a burst of adrenaline, but not nearly as focusing. She tried to push to her feet. But it was too late. The second man—the one with the pointed teeth—held a knife to Zhade's throat, as the third pinned his arms behind his back.

"You're all words, boyo," the second man growled. "And words are nothing."

Zhade took one last look at Andra and winked.

She had no clue what he had planned, but there were three men holding him, and one had a blade to his neck. The man's muscles tensed, and Andra had the sympathetic sensation of the bite of metal against skin. The warmth of spilled blood. Time slowed. She screamed.

"NO!"

The man started to choke.

Even as pain coursed through her body, Andra watched the attacker's hand waver and, as though against his will, draw the knife away from Zhade's neck and bring it to his own. Andra knew what would happen before it did, but it still shocked her as the man slit his own throat and fell, dead before he hit the ground.

The two others were stunned, but Zhade was ready. He drove his elbow back into the one holding him, crushing his nose. Blood spurted everywhere.

The other met Andra's eyes. "Witch," he hissed, and then he was running, his companion scampering to catch up.

For a moment, it was still, nothing but the sound of their breathing, and the crunch of gravel as Zhade shifted his weight. His face was coated with blood, his hair mussed. His carefully disheveled look was just chaos. There was nothing intentional about him now, and whatever arrogant mask he constantly wore had slipped, and Andra saw he was scared and relieved and maybe a bit confused.

"What was that?" Andra asked. "How did you do that?"

Did he have an 'implant? He'd used the same trick she'd seen Maret use the other night—choke the attacker with nanos, then use the technological components of the dagger to turn it on its wielder.

"Do what? That wasn't me."

Andra's heart stuttered. She looked around. They were alone. There was nowhere for anyone to hide, and surely Maret couldn't control nanos over large distances. She hoped.

Zhade scratched the back of his head, grinning to himself. "Some magic."

"Some magic," Andra agreed, though not as delighted. Was Maret somewhere nearby? Just out of sight? And why had he saved Zhade but not her? "Wait. But if you didn't know what would happen, why did you wink at me?"

Zhade grinned. "Because I like making you blush."

"That—but—you could have *died*."

"Hear, there you go again." His gaze dipped to her collarbone, and his smile vanished. "What's this?" he said, darting forward.

He drew the torn flaps of shirt from the wound. Before she could protest, he pulled out some bandages from his bag and started dabbing the blood from Andra's collarbone.

She held out his translucent dagger, and he paused his ministrations just long enough to take it back.

"I'm sorry I wasn't more help," she said.

"Psh." He scoffed. "And deny me the chance to show off?"

She pointed at his face. "Shouldn't we take care of your face first?"

"Neg." Zhade shrugged. "I have hope it'll scar." The blood was already starting to clot, but he needed a med'bot.

"Your perfect face?"

"Ah! You reck I have a perfect face?" Zhade said, helping her to her feet. The movement pulled at her wound, and she hissed through her teeth.

"Be at care," Zhade said, holding her up. He waited until she was steady before he started helping her toward the riverbank. "Aren't you going to thank me for saving you?"

She cut him a glance. "How did you know I was here?"

"Wead sent me a message. I've been following you for time and a half."

"Well, you certainly took your time rescuing me."

"Ah, so you admit I rescued you."

"For the sake of argument."

"I was waiting for the most dramistic moment. *You* should apologize for making me worry."

She stumbled, and Zhade caught her. "You were worried?"

"For the sake of argument."

Andra's skull ached. Her arms and legs felt heavy.

"Let's get away from here," Zhade said. "This place gives me the fraughts."

She nodded, glancing back at the statue. Then paused.

"Wait."

Something about the place felt both foreign and recognizable, like a familiar room with the furniture rearranged. Andra took a step back up the hill. Then another. And another. Her thighs burned as her feet sunk into the sand. She trailed her fingers over the nearest column.

Zhade groaned, then followed her.

She knelt in front of the statue. "Why do people think it's haunted?"

He plopped down onto the dirt beside her and pulled a canteen from his satchel. He took a swig and wiped his mouth with his arm before answering. "How does any legend get started? Probablish with a little bit of truth and a lot of good escapist storytelling. The truth is probablish boring, so each time someone told the story, they added a bit of flash so it made sense."

He offered her the canteen, but she shook her head.

"I'd suspect the real story, the *true* story, makes more sense than the place being haunted."

Zhade snorted. "Real life rarish makes sense, Goddess. And there's *never* any truth in it." He nodded to the statue. "What are you looking for?"

"I don't know yet."

He rolled his eyes and pushed himself to his feet, sauntering over to the nearest column and patting it as though he were complimenting it on its sturdiness.

Andra tried to imagine what the statue had looked like new. If the top of its head hadn't been cut off, it would have had hair. Some remained at its nape and around the ears. A single strand fell down what was left of its right cheek. The face was so weathered, there were no distinguishing features. Just two sunken eyes, a bump for a nose. The ears had been eroded down to nonexistent nubs, and the mouth had completely faded into the chin. Andra ran her hand over the ridges; then her fingers landed on a clump of some black substance at the base of the neck, like tarnished silver. Her stomach dropped.

She started to brush away the dirt covering the stone at her feet. "Help me, will you?"

Zhade knelt beside her, gently pushing her aside. "Rest yourself," he said, taking over for her. "What are you looking for?"

She didn't answer, because she was afraid she already knew. Was hoping she was wrong.

Zhade removed enough of the dirt to make out what was beneath, and Andra peered over his shoulder. The stone was part of a longer piece, curved like it used to run around the top of the pillars. It was etched with letters.

They were so familiar to her, she almost missed what was odd about them.

She *knew* them.

They were hers—hers in a way that they belonged to no one else alive. She brushed more dirt off, and more of the letters came into focus until they formed a word.

forget

Her fingers frantically cleared the gravel from the grooves, leaving the letters clean and legible. Little by little, she uncovered the entire stone, and with it, its inscription. Tears pooled in her eyes.

She knew these words. Not just the language, but the specific words, in that specific order, carved into that specific stone.

we will never forget the sacrifices and

The next word was *achievements*.

How many times had she read those words? How many times had she walked past them, skimmed over them, heard them quoted? Listened to Oz recite them when he was first learning to read?

We will never forget the sacrifices and achievements that allow us to move past what we are and become something more.

The Griffin statue. Andra had stood in this very place. Stood under that very chunk of rock, passed under it when it had been suspended as an arch over the entrance to LAC headquarters. The buried man wasn't a man at all, but Dr. Alberta Griffin, now forgotten under centuries of sediment. That river. That was the same river she'd walked along to the Vaults with her little brother. The same city, the streets reorganized, built on top of the old ones, sunk further into the earth.

The *Earth*.

She thought back to when she first woke up, asking the 'bot where she was. It never said *which* planet she was on.

Except it had.

The coordinates of the planet Andra stood on—it hadn't been a glitch or a malfunction. Galactic coordinates indicated where a planet was in relation to Earth, so Earth's coordinates would be—

0-0-0.

Just like the 'bot said.

It had given her everything she needed to know that first day, and she hadn't even realized it. It told her where her family was—dead on Holymyth. And where she was—awake on Earth.

She had her answer. She knew what had happened to her family, had happened to *her*.

They'd gone to Holymyth like they were supposed to. Like she was supposed to. Except she hadn't.

She'd been left on Earth.

PART THREE

JUDAS KISS

Requesting update on subject 3263827. I have concerns about the AI's progress. I wonder if its attachment to humans stunts its learning curve. I've received similar reports of subject 3263826. Not quite human, you always say. It seems that gap is shrinking, and humans, as much as I hate to admit it, are limited. We don't want AI to be limited as well. Of course, if they don't learn to love us, they could easily be the end of us all. Let's look into psychological theories of conditioning and manipulation.

And please stop publicly referring to the Arcanum as the Ark. You'll give people the wrong (right) idea.

> —Excerpt of memo to Isla Watts, from Alberta Griffin,
> founder of the Lacuna Athenaeum Corporation

TWENTY

arcanum, n.

Etymology: Latin, neuter of adjective *arcānus*: that which keeps a secret. Postmodern primary use: proper noun, name of ship commissioned by the Lacuna Athenaeum Corporation to transport humanity's first interplanetary colonists (often shortened to *The Ark*, a reference to the Biblical Ark, which saved Noah and his family from a global flood).

Definition: 1. a sacred secret, a mystery.

2. a marvelous elixir or remedy.

"THIS IS EARTH," Andra wheezed. She fell to her knees. The earth was dry to the touch, crumbling beneath her fingers. The sun warmed her back, gleamed off the statue of Alberta Griffin.

"Certz," Zhade said. "Where did you reck you were?"

"Holymyth," she choked. "The 'bot told me people called this planet the Hell-mouth."

"Firm, have you seen this place?" He gestured to their surroundings. Across the river, sand-colored buildings towered under the 'dome, its sheen a thin veneer of safety. Blackened fingers of rot were stark against the washed-out sky.

Andra let out a sob. She felt the sand pass through her fingers, sand where there had once been lush grass.

"Heya." Zhade steadied her as she swayed. "What's wrong?"

Her eyes brimmed with tears, and her throat burned. It was

bad enough thinking she'd been forgotten, but to have been left behind . . .

Nothing about this planet resembled Earth. The barren deserts, the pockets, the lost technology. She hadn't even known Earth was dying. Maybe that's what the Ark had been for—to save humanity. Maybe it had never been about conserving resources, but about escape. They'd saved a million and left billions behind. All the pain, the horror these people went through—were still going through— for centuries, and they'd just been *left*.

Andra stomped toward the statue, then her fist slammed against the stone. *Crack.* Her knuckles. *Snap.* The statue's nose. *Crunch.* Andra's blood ran down Alberta Griffin's stone face. Her fist stung and then went numb. She cocked her arm back for another hit, but something stopped her.

"Heya, heya, what are you doing?"

Zhade turned her toward him and took her hand, easing her fingers open. She felt nothing. Not the sand stinging her wounds, or her crushed knuckles, or the cloth he used to wipe away the blood.

Not the grief tearing her chest in two.

Her family was dead. Dead across the universe, which somehow made it worse. Separated by time and space. Somewhere humans were still alive, not fearing for their lives, not waiting for the planet to swallow them whole. Because they'd saved themselves and left everyone else to die. She yanked her hand from Zhade's and started toward Griffin's stupid face again.

He pulled her back. "Leave that statue alone. You've done full bars damage, and I reck he's sorries."

No, she wasn't. She was dead, like the rest of them, and this was the closest thing Andra had to revenge.

"Heya, none of that now," Zhade said, pulling her into his chest, and she realized she was crying.

His arms tightened around her, his hand cradling her head. He threaded his fingers through her hair, combing out the Celestias Lilibet had woven that morning. She sniveled into his chest, her head tucked under his chin, and she couldn't stop the words as they tumbled out, over and over.

They left me.

They left me.

They left me.

THE NEXT FEW minutes were not her finest. And she'd spent the last millennium naked in a box, so the bar was already set pretty low. The sun—sol—beat down as Zhade held her until she calmed, settling into the sand by Alberta fucking Griffin, his fingers brushing Andra's hair. It was nice, necessary even.

She noticed he'd grown slim, losing muscle mass, despite now living in relative comfort. His hair had been getting lighter, turning almost white. Was he stressed? Was he eating enough? She didn't want to be thinking about Zhade right now—who cared if he was wasting away, when she had been *left*. She scuttled out of his lap and sat next to him, silent. He let her, without comment.

There was a good view of Eerensed from where they sat, the river cutting through, the winding streets sprawling toward the palace. Her mind kept overlaying the city she knew on top of the city in front of her. That wasn't a row of houses—that was the drone field where Oz played. That wasn't a market square—that was the Academy. That wasn't the palace—that was the Vaults.

The Hell-mouth was Earth, and Eerensed was Riverside. All this time, she'd been trying to get home, and she was already there. Her city. Her planet. This was no longer some strange world across the galaxy. This was the remains of everything she'd ever known.

Her family had *left her behind*.

Andra huffed out a long breath. "We should go back to the palace."

She stood, wiping the sand from her pants, and caught sight of the mech'bot Lew-Eadin had given her just a little while ago. The mech'bot that was going to help her build a shuttle. Its polished surface gleamed, its LAC marking stark against its black paneling. It was useless now.

"For certz." Zhade scratched the back of his head. "Soze, I've been snapping a few pieces of information together, and—"

"I thought I was somewhere else."

"Firm, oddish I did reck that." Zhade tapped his finger against his temple. "Not just a charred face." He nodded toward the statue of Alberta Griffin, his blond hair falling into his eyes. "Soze, do you reck him? I'm mereish asking because you broke the poor man's nose. Just broke it clean off. Seeya, the stone is old and fragile, so don't get full egotistic bout it."

"Her. And yes. We met a few times. She deserved more than a broken nose."

What should Andra even *do* now? She had nowhere to run, and even if she escaped death at someone else's hands, when the 'dome failed, she'd die alongside everyone else.

Zhade pursed his lips. "Evens. Evens . . . Soze, you've been full vague bout all this and, seeya, that's your prerogative as a goddess, but if you want to tell me anything . . ."

The wind picked up, stronger than should have been possible inside a fully working bio'dome. From here, Andra could see the palace, teetering on the rock, the city in its shadow. There was an AI somewhere in there, she was sure of it. An AI that could fix the 'dome, and protect Eerensed. Riverside. Her city.

This was her home now, whether she wanted it or not. Where she was worshipped as a goddess, whether she wanted it or not.

So much had been decided for her. What did she have left to choose for herself? How could she decide her fate?

"I want you to take me back to the palace," she said.

Zhade groaned as he got to his feet. "Evens then, Goddess. Firstish, let's figure a way to hide that wishmark."

She looked down. There was a gash through her birthmark, where one of the men had cut her. She'd wanted rid of the unsightly mark, but this seemed an extreme solution. Now, it was her proof that she was a goddess—or at least, the same girl who'd lain for centuries in a box—and she couldn't go around flouting its injury.

Zhade helped her to her feet and led her toward a stone bench at the water's edge. There had been a hover'bench about two meters to the left during her time. The mech'bot trailed over without being given a command, ready to be of service. If it had been a med'bot, it could have done something about their wounds, but its fingers weren't fine enough for delicate work.

The river lapped against the bank, giving off the scent of fish and algae. Across it, there had once been a park, a few restaurants clustered nearby. Sometimes her mom would work late, and they'd meet her for dinner at the sushi restaurant. During the summer, she and Oz would race drones there. The memories blurred, running together like dyes bleeding through cloth. She was having trouble focusing. Perhaps she'd lost too much blood.

Zhade helped Andra onto the bench, surprisingly gentle. Instead of pulling away, he paused, his arms caging her in. His gaze started at her temples, but then shifted across her face—her eyes, her nose, her chin, then ended on her lips. She held her breath. Zhade leaned closer, and lifted one hand to her cheek, and—

Ripped off the cos'mask.

She'd forgotten she was wearing it. Her cheeks heated, and Zhade did a poor job of hiding his smile. He hummed to himself, turning the 'mask over in his hands, then held it up to Andra's collarbone, right above her birthmark.

"This will hurt, but we need to cover the wound til we get an angel to heal it."

She nodded, wincing as he pressed the 'mask to her skin. Once the edges had faded to a thin line, he started programming away the blood and superimposing the birthmark as it had been before being slashed. The fit wasn't perfect. The mesh screen was designed to be flexible, but with faces in mind, not collarbones. It was too large for her birthmark, and the holes designed for eyes, nose, and mouth roamed, trying to find where they were supposed to be, until Zhade finally programmed them away completely. The mesh melted into a single round 'mask.

"How did you do that?" she asked.

"I keep telling you I'm a sorcer," he said. "This is what we do."

Even Andra, brilliant as she was at technology, didn't know how to do that. She hadn't even known it could be done.

Once the fake birthmark was in place and the lines of the 'mask had faded, Zhade stood and nodded at his work.

"Evens. Time to sneak you back apalace."

She took a deep breath and nodded. She would go back to the palace. She would inventory her resources and count her assets. She would make a plan. Then, she would be a goddess.

TWENTY-ONE

THE DIRTY SECRET

ZHADE WAS GOING to kill her.

The air was damp and chilled as he hurried through the underground tunnels, scratching at the wound on his face. He'd seen an angel as soon as they returned apalace, but what he for true needed was Tia Ludmila and her med sorcery. Guards sole had access to small-magicked angels, and he would have a scar if he didn't see Tia soon and sooner.

He'd left the Goddess in her tower, warning her to stay apalace, and then marched forward straight to the tunnels. He felt the need to hurry. Who recked what the Goddess would do in his absence? What had she been imagining? Wandering acity alone? Thank sands Wead had sent him a message. Zhade had bareish gotten there in time.

His speak-easy had gone off in the middle of training with Kiv. He'd had to fake an injury and semi-fake losing the sparring match so he could find her. Wead's message said the Goddess had left the palace. Alone. In the mid of the day.

He was going to kill her.

If someone else didn't get to her first.

His plan had been sloppy; he knew that now. By tracking the tiara he'd given her, he'd overestimated her attachment to her divinity, assuming she'd be like the other goddesses—reliant on symbols of power. But she never wore the thing, so he'd need a better method of tracking her soon and now.

Zhade quickened his pace, his footsteps making heavy thuds, his armor clinking. His nose crinkled at the smell of mildew in the air.

The one good thing that had come out of the Goddess's little day trip was that Zhade had chance to listen to pieces of convo as he passed through the city. Rust had grown on his Common Eerensedian, but he had memory enough to comp the people were growing impatient. The Goddess had promised (or the Guv had promised on her behalf) to fix the gods' dome, but it was still weakening. As the ley lines grew, so did their fear. Most of what Zhade overheard was frustration, but some of the citians already had anger with their new Goddess for not acting full quickish.

And Zhade had memory of what happened to Goddesses who didn't do what the people wanted.

Zhade recked it was going to be an issue eventualish, but they'd been here all of what? Less than a moon? He needed a plan if he was going to save the Goddess from sacrifice. The Third Festival was in a turn—eight days. Good sands, would she not even last til then?

He needed a miracle. And there was sole one place he recked where to get one.

Zhade headed toward the Schism, going faster and taking less care than some of the more unstable sections warranted. Hardcrete crumbled neath his feet and he bareish caught himself as he edged round a sinking hole. The tunnel forked, and he hesitated sole a moment before taking the path veering southeast. He hadn't gone this direction since before his mam died. Even with the Schism coin heavy in his pocket, he wasn't certz he'd be welcome.

He had to try, though. His need was dire. Otherwise, he wouldn't have risked leaving the Goddess alone. For the first time in four years, he would seek their help. He would ask the people who betrayed his mother for a miracle.

Wead met him before he reached the entrance, walking briskly, his magic hand gloved. He looked healthier than he'd ever looked in the Wastes—dark curls curlier, rich complexion richer—but his full demeanor had changed. Adesert, he had something he was trying to get back to. Now, Zhade wasn't certz what Wead had.

"You're for certz you want to do this?" Wead asked.

"When am I certz bout anything?" Zhade held back his irritation at Wead for letting the Goddess leave the bake shop alone, for getting her an Angelic Guard—which was full obvi counter to Zhade's own plans. "You know I mereish make stuff up as I march."

"Firm. I do." Wead sighed, and there was more than the norm resignation in it. Zhade didn't have time to ponder why. They'd reached the entrance to the Schism.

He tightened his grip on the coin. "Prepped?"

"Neg."

They entered the cave.

Since the days Zhade's mam had been a part of the Schism, they'd met in secret. Mostish in homes, but then later, in caves located off the tunnel system that ran under Eerensed—the ruins of the civilization Zhade's mam told him bout. Now, the Schism was located in a cavern that had once been too dilapidated to live in, but was currentish teeming with life. Despite Doon telling them how strong the Schism was, Zhade was surprised at how many people there were.

As big as the cave was—and it was the largest Zhade had seen—it was overcrowded. People were *everywhere*, spilling into the space like water in a pot. Wood and metal structures formed markets. Magic orbs lit the space. People called to one another across makeshift paths. There was a full city under Eerensed, and no one recked.

"Bodhizhad kin Vatgha."

He winced at the sound of his full name and reluctantish turned toward the familiar voice. He'd expected some kind of welcome, probablish guards or soldiers. He'd hoped for a parade. But it was mereish the universe being a giant fraught that it was Skilla meeting him. Doon had said she would set up a meet. He imagined she meant with someone in the Schism, not with the Schism itself.

"Skilla," Zhade greeted her through gritted teeth.

She strode toward him, decked out in fighting gear and weapons, her raven hair pulled back into a high knot atop her head. Her cheekbones could cut glass, and she was full charred in the most intimidating way possible. A few people at a nearby stall stared as she passed.

She was several years older than him, and his mam had relied on her, confided in her in a way she never did with her own son. It still singed Zhade that his mam had chosen Skilla to prep for leadership, while she'd trained Zhade as nothing more than an amateur sorcer. She'd left Skilla a veritistic empire, and to Zhade, she'd left an obscure message bout saving the Goddess and a few worthless hand-em-downs. In the end, Zhade was the one carrying out his mam's legacy, while Skilla sat hidden with her cadre of Low Magic sorcers.

She was flanked by two people—Doon on one side, and the woman he'd seen at the Goddess's Awakening Ceremony on the other. Her magic eye gleamed against her dark skin, her face smooth, expression blank.

"I have something of yours," he said, tossing the Schism coin, watching it flip a few times before catching it. He did it again, but this time, quick as a sandstorm, the girl snatched it out of the air.

"Took you time and a half," she growled, teeth bared. Her magic eye was trained on him, and could probablish target the exact location of his heart and the speed and trajectory needed to throw the coin and kill him instantish.

"Xana," Skilla snapped, and immediatish the girl went still. She looked around. Several people were watching them. "Let's get away from this crowd."

She nodded to a nearish alcove empty of people. It was nothing more than a smallish round room carved into the wall of the larger cavern. The rock ceiling didn't look full stable, but Zhade followed her there anyway.

"So you've finalish come to visit us," she said once they were out of the main cave. It didn't allow much privacy—there was no door—but the curve of the walls made it easier to hear. "What do you want, Zhade?"

That was a loaded question. He wanted to go back in time and make certz the Schism didn't betray his mother. He wanted to never have been banished. He wanted the Goddess safe. He wanted to decide his own fate. He *wanted*.

"What do *I* want? You're the one that left me breadcrumbs." He nodded to the coin in Xana's hand. "Seems likeish you wanted something from *me*."

"We never want anything from you, Bodhizhad. We were checking on you out of respect for your mother."

Zhade's anger rose hot. "For true? You for certz didn't show her respect when you helped Maret kill her."

If Skilla felt anything at the accusation, she didn't show it. "We did nothing."

"Exactish: You did nothing and let her die, when you had resources to stop it." He gestured to the cave beyond, bright with magic, and filled with people.

Skilla took a deep breath, but it seemed less that she was calming herself and more that she was waiting for Zhade to do so. She raised her eyebrows as if to say, *Are you done?* "If this is the sole reason you came, the meeting is over."

This was one of the things that irked Zhade bout Skilla. She always played the role of emotionalish-detached leader. As though emotions weren't full useful. His mam had been like that too, and it made sense she would bond with Skilla more than Zhade, who saw feelings not as a hindrance, but as a tool.

He tried to mimic Skilla's stance, arms crossed, feet shoulder-width apart. "Did Maret hire you to kill the Goddess?"

Skilla's poised exterior came down mereish long enough for a burst of laughter. "Why would you imagine that?"

"Your charling here was at the ceremony."

"So were a lot of people," Xana snapped. Her magic eye went red.

Zhade ignored her. "You don't exactish have a crystal record when it comes to goddesses."

Skilla gave him a pitying look. "We may have been at differs with goddesses in the past, but that doesn't mean we want the Third dead. And we would never work *with* the Guv. Everything we do is to take down that monster."

"You swear?" Zhade asked.

Skilla sighed. "If you don't believe me now, why would you believe me if I swore?"

"Rare point."

Zhade scratched the back of his head, considering the evens and odds. It was true the Schism had turned their back on him. They'd been his home, his fam for so much of his life, and they'd done nothing to stop his mother's murder. They'd refused to hide him when it became obvi Maret would banish him. They'd shifted from a group of secular sorcers practicing Low Magic to some sort of rebellion. But if Maret was for true their enemy, that meant they could be useful. He didn't have to trust them to use them.

"I need your help," he said.

Skilla cast Xana a sidelong look like they were sharing a joke. Xana seemed pleased.

"That must have been hard for you to say."

"Neg. Super easy. I didn't even have to practice. Not like I would have to if I was saying, oh, seeya, *I forgive you* or *I won't kill you the firstish I have chance*."

Xana's eyes narrowed, hand going to her sword, but Skilla nodded, as though she were expecting this, and let out a sigh. "If you hate me so much, why come here?"

"I brought the Third back from the Wastes."

"So I've heard. Were you expecting a parade?"

"For certz, but that's not why I'm here. The people are growing restless. They expect the Goddess to perform miracles, but she's not like the others. She's magicless." He paused to let that sink, but Skilla didn't react. "I've seen her do two miracles, and she didn't reck she was doing either. Both times her life was at danger, and during the second one . . ."

Zhade hesitated. He wasn't certz how much he should reveal to Skilla bout what had happened in the Small Wastes. He hadn't even told the Goddess his theory. *She'd* killed the man. Choked him and slit his throat. It had to have been her. It for certz wasn't Zhade. And though he was full grateful she'd saved him, he recked the Schism wouldn't feel the same, considering she'd ended someone's life. He had to take full care what he told them.

" . . . during the second miracle she controlled the stardust, but it was sole because she was holding this."

He took the icepick dagger from his pocket. It must have had something to do with what happened at the Small Wastes, the Goddess using it like some sort of conduit. When his mam had given it to him, he'd assumed it was for his own protection, but maybe it was for the Third. Maybe his mam had sorcered it for her. He didn't comp how or why it worked, but considering how close his mam had been with Skilla, maybe the Schism General did.

Her dark eyes remained unimpressed, though, as she took in the dagger.

"It wasn't apurpose," he said, pocketing it. "Her magic is unreliable. But if she doesn't prove her goddessness soon and sooner, if she doesn't make herself indispensable, the people will call for her sacrifice. We need to fake a miracle."

Skilla chewed on her lip, hand resting on the battle axe strapped to her side, and nodded. "Be at luck. Xana, see our guests peaced."

She turned back toward the cavern, but Wead stepped forward. "General. I'm Lew-Eadin, Doon's brother."

Doon had been quiet during the full convo, but now she beamed.

Skilla paused, groaning as she faced him. He nodded his head deferentialish, and she reluctantish nodded back. Zhade probablish should have let Wead do all the convo from the beginning.

Skilla's eyes narrowed. "I see the resemblance." She placed a long-fingered hand on Doon's shoulder. "Doon has been a great help to us. She's special."

Wead smiled softish. He'd always been full proud of Doon, but neither of them had wanted her to end up with the Schism. "Firm. She is. And I want to hold her safe. The Third is special too. She can save us. We can't let her be sacrificed like the others."

Skilla's gaze bore into him, and Zhade was familiar with her expression. It was carved into something ferocious, but it was just a mask she held in place while she was considering. She never let herself appear vulnerable or indecisive. That—more than anything except Maret's hunger for power—was what had gotten his mother killed.

Finalish, she said, "Neg. If she's so special, she can save herself. There's too much at stake soon and now. I won't risk exposing ourselves."

The sounds of the crowded cave muted as Zhade's anger flared. "You're all selfish cowards," he spat. "At least that hasn't changed."

He recked it was futile. It was mereish him and Wead soon and now. They'd survived the Wastes together, for certz they could protect the Goddess as well.

Skilla nodded to herself, her smile patronizing. "You sole ever see mirrors of yourself, Zhade. Now, I have somewhere to be. Despite the fact you reck where to find us, I won't have you killed. You're welcome. Don't make me regret it."

With that, she left, disappearing into the cave and Xana following in her wake. They were soon swallowed by the crowd. Doon remained behind, gnawing a fingernail, avoiding her brother's gaze. Her foot scraped against the cave floor, rearranging the graveled hardcrete.

"*That* is what you work for now?" Wead asked, and it was the angriest Zhade had ever seen him.

Doon scowled, still not meeting his eyes. "They took care of me when you didn't. They skooled me how to survive when you chose *him* over me. Chose that *Goddess* over me."

"I didn't choose," Wead argued. "I did my *job*, and I did it *because* of you. We need the goddesses to survive. They made a better world for us. A safer world. That's a world I want you to age up in. I reck you're not old enough to have memories, but we used to have hope."

"You left me," Doon said. "I'm old enough to have memories of that."

Wead's face was pained, and he opened his mouth to argue, but a voice cut him off.

"Lew-Eadin!"

Wead froze. Footsteps thudded toward them, and Wead's face drained of blood as Dzeni threw her arms round his neck.

She gripped him tightish, her small frame clinging to his, sobbing into his chest. He stood stiffish, but his arms twitched as though they wanted to wrap round her. His eyes scanned the cave, no doubt searching for Cheska and the kiddun.

Dzeni pulled back, looking a bit confused, but overwhelmed with happiness. She reached up and grabbed Wead's face, staring at him in disbelief. Her black hair was pulled back, her heart-shaped face framed with wisps of curls. Her full lips were open in a gasp, and her blue eyes shimmered, brimming with tears.

"They told me you returned, but I didn't believe it." Her voice was hoarse. "Why didn't you come see me?"

Zhade shuffled his feet. "Seeya, I feel full awkward."

Dzeni shot him a playfulish chastising glance. "Oh, hush, you rogue. You'll get your hug soon and sooner." She turned back to Wead. "Where have you been?"

He took her gentlish by the wrists and lowered her hands from his face. She didn't even react to his new magic arm. "I . . ." Wead's voice cracked, and he cleared it. "I didn't want to . . . intrude . . ."

He released her and took a step back. She took a step forward. He took another step back. Zhade tried to catch Doon's eye, but she'd become suddenish captivated by picking the dirt from under her nails with a knife, the blade glinting in the torchlight.

"Where did you get that?"

Doon pushed him away. "Get your own. It's mine."

Dzeni gave Wead a confused look. "How could you ever think you were intruding? Why didn't you come see me? Why did I have to hear bout it from Cheska's uncle?"

At the sound of Cheska's name, Wead tensed, and Zhade scoffed. He had always liked Dzeni—adored her actualish—and he'd never considered her stupid or cruel. But she was being one or the other anow.

"Oh, you heard bout it from *Cheska's* uncle, marah?" Zhade snapped. "What else has Cheska's fam told you? Do you chat after fam prayers? Cheska, Cheska, Cheska. Can you convo anything else?"

Dzeni looked to be at the edge of tears again—not the happy kind this time—but Zhade couldn't bring himself to care.

"I . . . what? I mentioned him once. What is this bout? Wead?" She stepped toward Lew-Eadin, reaching out for him, and this time he flinched. Dzeni gasped. "Do you no longer love me?"

"Sands, Dzeni," he sighed, running a hand over his face. "I will always, *always* love you. Til I'm sunk into stardust. Even after. That is the one thing in life I reck for certz."

She hiccupped. "Then why—"

"*Because* Cheska. Because of the kiddun you have with him. It's too . . . fraughts, I reck it's selfish, but I mereish can't, Dzeni. I mereish can't."

For a moment, she stared at him, mouth agape, her eyes shining. And then she laughed.

This time, when Zhade tried to meet Doon's eye, she frowned and shrugged.

"I'm not with Cheska, Wead." Dzeni laughed again.

"What?" His voice was rough.

She erased the distance between them, rushing into his arms. They went round her automistic, and Zhade suddenish felt like he was intruding.

"Cheska helps, is all," she said, her voice muffled, head tucked against his chest, and Zhade didn't mean to listen. "With mam and da gone, Cheska offered helpings. He's with Swan, actualish. He's full good with Dehgo."

"Dehgo?" Wead croaked.

Zhade watched as realization hit him. They'd been gone four years. Four years, and Doon said the kiddun looked to be round three. He thought she'd just moved on to Cheska quickish, but she hadn't. That meant the kiddun . . .

"Is yours, you spoon." Dzeni looked up at Wead, her chin resting against his chest, and Zhade felt a sharp pain above his heart.

He wandered back toward the tunnel entrance, allowing Dzeni and Wead their privacy, leaving the laughing and kissing and planning behind. His feet scraped against the floor, and cold sweat ran down his spine. He was almost back to the tunnel entrance, when someone pulled on his sleeve. Doon was there, round face looking up at him.

"What do you want, little assassin?"

Her eyes were wide. "Why did my brother go with you? Why didn't he stay with me? Or at least stay for Dzeni?"

Zhade recked what the girl was asking. *Why wasn't I enough?* But that was not a question he wanted to answer. Not a question he wanted to ask himself.

"Because . . ." He leaned against the wall, rolling his sleeves up to his forearms. A rock jabbed his shoulder. Back in the alcove, Wead and Dzeni were still locked in an embrace. "Because I ordered him to. And his job is to follow my orders."

"Bullshit."

"Heya." Zhade frowned. "Don't you believe I'd order someone to leave their fam and promised to wander the Wastes for an indefinite period of time mereish so I wouldn't be alone?"

"Neg, I full believe you would. But I don't believe my brother would obey. Soze, why did he go?" She narrowed her eyes. "Why did *you* go? There are places inside the city to hide."

"Not good ones."

"Better than waiting to be swallowed by a pocket."

Zhade shrugged. "True convo. Maybe we were looking for something."

"The Goddess?"

Zhade didn't answer. He turned to go, but Doon's hand on his arm stopped him.

"What, tiny warrior?"

"Does she import that much?"

Did she? Zhade wasn't certz how much she imported to Eerensed. He doubted she would save them the way Wead recked she would. But to him? His plan full hinged on her.

He placed a hand on Doon's shoulder. "Firm. More than you reck."

She gave him a disconcerting smile and brushed his hand away. "Can I borrow your dagger?"

"Neg. Why?"

"I have an idea. A way to fake a miracle for the Third. You said that both times her life was at danger?"

216

Zhade nodded slowish, not liking where this was going.

"Evens. You give her the dagger, and I attack her afront of a crowd of people. With the dagger in her hand, and her life at danger, she'll automistic perform a miracle for true. You won't have to fake one."

"Neg. Absolutish not." Zhade shook his head emphaticish. There was no guarantee the Goddess's magic would work, and Doon might hurt the Goddess. And if her magic *did* work, the Goddess might hurt Doon. Or worse.

"Hear, Zhade, I bet you a Silver Second I can do it."

"I have no doubt you can, tiny friend-sister." He ruffled her hair, and she glared at him and pushed him away. They had such fun together. "But there are too many variables. No shakes. I'm full brill, seeya. I'll imagine a plan soon and sooner."

Zhade turned away from her scowl, but worry knotted his stomach.

TWENTY-TWO

frenemy, n.

Etymology: rooted in Millennial English, a portmanteau of *friend* and *enemy*.

Definition: 1. a person with whom one must make an alliance, despite intense mutual dislike.

ANDRA SAT IN her suite with the useless mech'bot. A breeze fluttered the gauzy balcony curtains, and the morning light cast a soft glow on the 'bot's midnight surface. She tucked her feet under her, sinking into the vanity's accompanying velvet chair. But instead of looking at her own reflection, she was staring down the 'bot. Its blank face gazed back, expression fixed and empty. Andra put her head in her hands and sighed.

She finally had what she needed, and it didn't matter. The Ark was gone. In geosynchronous orbit around a completely different planet.

Andra was stuck on Earth.

Over the last thousand years, those 'swarms of corrupted tech in the desert had destroyed the planet, leaving its residents struggling to survive this hellscape. Andra had been left on a dying world to die with it. Her family, LAC, all the colonists, had saved themselves and ignored everyone else. She felt a strange kinship with the people left behind. She didn't understand their culture or religion or speech, but she was one of them. One of the forgotten.

"What am I going to do with you, Mechy?" Andra asked the robot.

It tilted its head, eyes flashing, but didn't respond. It wasn't AI, so it couldn't answer such an open-ended question. It could only reply with programmed responses to explicit requests.

She'd restored it as much as she could. Some of the scraps Zhade had brought her fixed the worst damage. She replaced most of its casing and did what she could to keep its software running smoothly. It had thanked her, as though it could feel any gratitude. At least its manners algorithms were still intact. As for its shuttle construction capabilities, there was no use for them now.

She scratched at what was left of the wound over her birthmark. It had healed quickly, but it itched like crazy. She rested her head against the back of the chair, stretching out kinks. This was her future now—pretending to be a goddess forever, or at least until someone inevitably decided to kill her.

She couldn't accept it. Wouldn't. She wasn't made to just give up when things were tough. If she had to be a goddess, she was going to be the best damn goddess these people ever had.

And she would start by fixing the 'dome.

In so many unfortunate ways, this was her home. It was Eerensed, where she was a goddess; and it was Riverside, where she'd grown up. It was up to her to keep it safe. Luckily, she still had the hidden AI to fall back on. If only she could find it.

She was jolted out of her thoughts by a knock at the door. The only people who visited her were Zhade and Lilibet, and neither of them was fantastic at knocking. She hurried to pull the mech'bot behind the balcony's velvet inner curtain, but it didn't move. It was far too heavy for her to carry or drag.

"Mechy! Don't just stand there," she hissed. "Help me!"

It walked jerkily to the balcony and let Andra throw the curtain shut, hiding it from view. She opened the door, expecting Kiv or another guard. Instead, she came face-to-face with Maret.

"Guv," Andra said, dipping into the awkward bow Zhade had taught her.

Maret raised a brow. "Goddess." He brushed past her into her room. He was wearing a black high-waisted robe, angular collar climbing up his pale neck. His blond hair was only partially slicked back, stray strands brushing his cheek. "We need to convo."

Andra stiffened. She'd hidden the mech'bot, but not well. She hadn't anticipated the Guv just waltzing into her room. She tried to catalog the other contraband she had in here—the cos'mask still tuned to her birthmark, the heaps of broken tech Zhade had brought her. None of it had been expressly forbidden, but she had a feeling Maret wouldn't like it. It was more than just Andra at stake—it was Zhade and Lew-Eadin and Lilibet.

"Please," Andra said dryly, "make yourself at home."

Maret tossed himself into the chair Zhade usually occupied. He slouched, where Zhade would have lounged, but it was impossible not to see the similarities between them. Their voices, their expressions. Their insecurities. Zhade thought he hid his better, but he was just louder.

Maret squinted, the thumb of his right hand tapping each of his other fingers in turn. "Why did my brother come back?" he asked without preamble. "For the throne?"

Andra turned the vanity chair so it faced him and positioned herself between the Guv and the 'bot. "I can honestly say I have no clue why your brother does anything." She felt the urge to defend Zhade. "But he did tell me once that the throne was never his to begin with."

Maret let out a mocking laugh. "Evens, did he? Magicalish, the throne is his alone."

Andra blinked, stunned. She hadn't expected him to admit the throne he occupied wasn't his.

He shrugged, kicking off his boots with his heels. He leaned farther back into the chair. "There's a reason Bodhizhad is not guv."

"Bodhizhad?"

A smirk tugged at Maret's lips. "He didn't even tell you his full name?" He threw an arm over the back of the chair and exhaled. "My brother is many things, and a liar is one of them. Don't ever forget that, Goddess."

Zhade was a liar, but Maret was a murderer. His temple gleamed with the crown. Even if he didn't notice the hidden 'bot, all he needed were some well-placed nanos to explode her lungs or stop her heart.

He sat forward, steepling his fingers, eyes glazed. "My mother wants to kill Zhade." He glanced up at Andra. "I won't let her."

"What?" She tried to hide her shock, but her face gave away everything.

Maret smiled. "Surprised I care to stop her?"

"A bit," Andra admitted. "I want to kill him most days, so I figured you would too."

Maret tilted his head in agreement. "I banished him to save him, and the fraughted bastard came back. My mother wants him dead. She would prefer I do it, but she'll march in if I stall much longer. Whatever else he is, he's my brother. I can't let her kill him."

"Just like you didn't let her kill my maids?"

"That's not fair." He started fidgeting again. *Tap-tap-tap* went his thumb against the tip of each finger. He twisted his neck as though working out a kink.

"Just like you're planning to sacrifice me at the festival?"

"I . . . what?" He froze, hand paused at his neck.

Andra took a steadying breath. "I know you sacrificed the other goddesses. And I know you did so at their festivals."

Maret's shock was replaced by annoyance. "You've been convoing with the *common* people, haven't you?"

"Common people you're supposed to protect."

Maret sighed. "Whatever you were told, it's a half-truth at best."

"A half-truth? What creative excuse are you going to use to justify murder this time?"

He pinched the bridge of his nose, his hand dangerously close to his crown. Andra shifted in her chair, wondering if she should have taken the time to shut down the mech'bot completely.

"Hear," Maret said. "We can argue bout morality, or I can swear I have no intention of sacrificing you."

"And why should I believe you?"

"Because I want to make a deal."

"A deal?" She thought back to the deal she'd made with Zhade—a piece of tech for every goddess lesson. It had all been for nothing.

Maret watched her for a moment over his clasped hands. "You do something for me, and not sole will I promise *not* to sacrifice you, but I'll also give you what you're looking for."

Her heart was in her throat. "What am I looking for?"

Answer a question with a question.

"Do you imagine I don't reck the truth?" he asked.

Damn it. He knew that trick.

"I'm not sure you can give me what I'm looking for."

"Can't I?" Was he flirting? Or threatening? Or were they one and the same to him? He stood and approached her. Andra's heart sped up and she grasped the armrests of her chair with strained fingers. She tensed as he leaned in close and lowered his voice. "I reck you were in my room."

Andra's blood chilled. She tried to formulate a response, but her thoughts were glitching, cycling through the memories of hiding behind Maret's curtain, of Lilibet telling her of the sacrifices, of Maret threatening her with death that first day in the throne room.

"Did you reck I couldn't see the trail you left behind? Your presence was all over the place." His breath was hot against her cheek. "I reck you were there, and I reck why."

Andra was frozen in fear, but after a moment Maret backed away. He crossed to the balcony, his stiff clothes creaking with every movement. She held her breath, willing him not to sense Mechy like he'd sensed her in his room.

He didn't look at her when he said, "You were looking for an AI."

Andra's breath left her in a rush.

He turned. "Surprised I reck the term?"

She swallowed, still recovering from her fear. "Surprised you know about it and haven't done anything."

"I haven't had a reason to yet."

She stood and faced him. "People dying isn't reason enough?"

"Not particularish."

Andra glowered.

Maret put up a placating hand, a gesture that mimicked his brother. "Hear, I reck you need an AI to fix the dome. I reck more than you imagine—bout you, bout the other goddesses. But I don't reck everything—like how to use the AI to fix the gods' dome."

"How do you know so much?"

"My mother," he said flatly. "She told me a lot of things."

"Where did she learn it? The First?"

"I don't reck where she gets her info." Bitterness tinged his voice. "Suffice it to say I have an AI and you need an AI."

"Why didn't you tell me earlier? Hell, why has Tsurina *always* known about the AI and kept it hidden while letting you *kill* people and blame the 'dome?"

Her room grew darker as the sun started to set. The last vestiges of light silhouetted Maret against the open balcony doors.

"Because she hates it," he said. "She hates the 'dome and High Magic and everything that has to do with the goddesses. She hates it all so much she's willing to let Eerensed be destroyed if it means ridding it of the Three's influence."

Andra thought back to her walk to the 'dome wall with Maret. The old man with the serve'drone and the modded arm.

"She's like that man you choked," she guessed. "She's part of that . . . what did you call it? The Luddites?"

Maret nodded.

A fitting name, but even in Andra's time Luddism was considered a joke. How could someone exist in the world apart from technology? How could Tsurina hate the goddesses so much that she would be willing to live like the villagers in the Wastes, with no protection from the pockets?

Although, the pockets were also technology. Maybe Earth would have been better without any of it.

"What about you?" she asked.

He scratched the skin beneath his crown, glowing orange in the light of the sunset. "What bout me?"

"You're her son. Where do you fit in?"

"I . . ." His eyes glazed over. His hair fell into his face, and his expression relaxed for a moment. Andra almost pitied him. His mother wanted to kill his brother and destroy his city, and she was using her own son to enact some sort of revenge on the goddesses. But then Maret's familiar sneer snaked back into place. "I'm the Guv. I ruled where she couldn't, because I have *this*." He gestured to the crown.

This was more than she had signed on for—navigating Maret's family problems. She could deal with all that later. For now, she needed the AI.

"This deal," she said, circling her chair, and leaning back against it like Zhade would have. "What do you want me to do?"

Maret waved a dismissive hand. "Mereish convince Zhade to leave Eerensed. The method is your decision."

"And why would he listen to me?"

Maret smirked. No, it was less cruel than that. It was almost a smile born out of . . . fondness. "My brother always had a weakness for a pretty face."

His chapped lips stretched into a grin at Andra's stunned expression.

Never let your surprise show, Zhade had advised. *Always pretend you're one move ahead, even when you're not.*

"Get Zhade out of the city," Maret said, "and I'll give you the AI."

She couldn't go home. She couldn't get her family back. All that was left for her was to protect the ruins of her hometown—this city that thought she was a goddess.

"Okay," she said. "I'll do it."

Maret smiled and stretched out his hand. Andra hesitated just long enough to steady her nerves, but then reached out as well. The day's last ray of light shone on their clasped hands.

"Fraughted ridiculous custom," Maret muttered.

TWENTY-THREE

manifest, n.

Etymology: classical Latin *manifestus*: evident clear, plain, palpable; probably *manus*: hand + *-festus*: the second element also of *infestus*: hostile, harmful.

Definition: 1. a list or inventory.

2. a public declaration; a public statement, a manifesto.

THERE WAS LITTLE time to enact her deal with Maret. Andra was ushered from meeting to meeting, from appearance to appearance. Though she no longer needed to inventory the palace 'bots, new ones were still brought to her every evening. She checked each for tech'scanners and AI abilities, even though she knew it was futile. The sole AI in the palace was hidden by Maret, and he wouldn't give it up unless she got Zhade out of Eerensed.

The only times she saw Zhade were goddess lessons, which continued even though she no longer needed tech scraps in return. Each evening they met in the First Goddess's rooms, dust sparkling in the light of kinetic orbs, and each evening Andra tried a different approach.

The first tactic she tried was subtlety—even though she'd never been good at it. They'd just finished goddess lessons, and she'd sidled up to Zhade, heart skipping. He was packing the set of sim'drones they'd "sorcered" to perform fake miracles—crude visual and auditory sims of lightning and thunder.

"Good for smiting," Zhade had said. It was a desperate solution. Any sorcer could program a sim. It was nothing the people hadn't seen before and wouldn't necessarily prove Andra's deity. They needed something bigger, something unique, but the Third Festival was four days away and Andra was running out of time. Apparently, if Tsurina had her way, Zhade would be running out of time too.

"So," Andra said to Zhade.

Lilibet was looking through the First's collection of dresses. Lew-Eadin hadn't joined them since reuniting with his girlfriend.

Zhade looked up from what he was doing, eyes narrowing. "You want something."

Andra coughed. "Why would you say that?"

He set down his pack and leaned against the bedpost. He held up a finger. "One, because you didn't complain once during the full lesson. Two." He added another finger. "You complimented me on my hair when you arrived, which you never do though always should. And three." Another finger. "I'm a full brill sorcer and mereish reck things."

Andra showed him one of her fingers, a gesture that was lost on him.

She sighed. "I was just wondering why you came back to Eerensed only to be a guard in a palace that belongs to you."

His eyes cut to Lilibet, but she was holding a gold gown to herself and twirling in front of a mirror. As far as she knew, Zhade was nothing more than a palace guard who happened to know Andra's secret lack of deity.

"Why would I rather live under a gods' dome and sleep in a real bed and be among my old friends than wander the Wastes running from pockets and pirates? Is that what you're asking? Why do I want to be safe?"

But you're not safe, Andra thought.

"The 'dome won't last much longer."

"Ah, but I'll still have the bed." Zhade turned back to the sim'drones. "Are you trying to be riddens of me?"

"No!" she said a bit too quickly. If he'd been looking, he would have seen guilt cross her face. "No. It's just . . . I don't know what's in this for you."

He was still for a moment, and then went back to packing. "Maybe I don't reck yet either," he said, but Andra didn't believe him. "Can't I mereish want to protect my city?"

Andra turned to go, then stopped. "What if . . . what if instead of the 'drones performing the miracle, they caused a disturbance. What if the miracle was me stopping them?"

Zhade nodded, eyes glazed. "Like an attack on the city. An army that you defeat, but is actualish mereish a glamour spelled to dissolve at magic words. That could work." He gave her a smile that almost seemed proud.

It was risky. Sims were never quite believable as reality, but if the attack was short and Andra's response swift, it would be a start to securing her deity.

"And . . ." Andra scratched the back of her neck. "You could launch the sims from outside the 'dome?"

Zhade gave her a suspicious look, but didn't respond.

He seemed done with the conversation, so she tried again the next night, this time mentioning the idea of rescuing people from the Wastes. She hoped to appeal to his sense of humanity, but he merely shrugged and asked why. The third night, she planned to flirt with him, but before she'd built up the nerve, he'd turned to her, arms crossed.

"I don't reck why you want me to peace, but I'm not. So drop the convo, seeya?"

So by the night of the festival, she was no closer to getting Zhade to leave. No closer to getting access to the AI and fixing the 'dome. She just had to trust Maret would give her more time.

At least the "miracle" was ready. Halfway through the festival,

Zhade would release the sim'drones, programmed with synchronized projected simulations. To the crowd, it would look like a group of Wastern pirates was attacking the courtyard. In order to sell the illusion, they'd included tactile sims as well as visual and auditory, but Andra made Zhade promise no one would be really hurt. She still didn't like it. Any simmed pain the people felt would be real enough to them.

The sims were set on five-minute loops, but Andra would stop them with her "goddess powers" long before then. They were programmed to dissolve at her command, pixels scattered on the wind, the attackers disappearing before the people's eyes.

Andra was filled with nerves as she entered the courtyard for the Third Festival. It had been decked out for the occasion. Flickering candles lit a glossy tile path through the lush oasis, littered with red and purple fringed pillows. Palms and ferns sprouted between tropical plants, and a porcelain fountain sat at the center of the courtyard, water trickling over its shell-shaped basins from the mouth of a swan (with dragon wings—Andra wasn't sure anyone here had actually *seen* a swan).

The courtyard teemed with the citizens of Eerensed, the cast-iron gate thrown open to allow the party to continue in the city streets. The warm smell of butter cookies drenched the night air, and the hum of thousands of voices was occasionally punctuated by the shrieks of playing children or a high chorus of laughter.

Andra sat with her back to the palace wall, and several feet in front of her was a barricade of guards and armed 'bots prohibiting people from coming any closer. Citizens waited in a long line, approaching one at a time to make requests. She predicted she would get a third of the way through the line by the time Zhade released the sims. Her stomach clenched in anticipation.

The festival was open to the entire city—even the poorer sections— and most of the people were just happy to see her. She did, however, notice groups of people who eyed her suspiciously, a few getting in line to ask her pointed questions about when she intended to fix the 'dome. They were usually ushered away before she had a chance to respond.

The line of those waiting to meet her slowly proceeded, and Andra tugged at the diaphanous material of her dress where it cinched at the waist. She imagined Lilibet slapping her hand away.

Stop fidgeting, you spoon.

The time chimes struck eight abell. Fifteen more minutes. She tried not to look at Zhade. For once, he was stationed as part of *her* guard, rather than the Guv's. Andra wondered if Maret was doing it on purpose—trying to get them to spend more time together so Andra could convince Zhade to leave. The bastard prince stood next to her, surveying the crowd, his face carved into a lazy almost-grin. His muscles were tight as though he had forced them into position, trying to appear relaxed though he had a remote trigger in his pocket for fifty sim'drones. Andra sighed, turning back to the queue of people, and recognized the next person in line.

At least, for a moment, she thought she recognized her. There was something familiar about her features. A girl, probably around twelve. Bronze skin and a pile of brown curls knotted on top of her head. Her dark eyes were wide as she stepped forward, wringing her hands. The people nearby fell silent as the girl drew closer. She hunched over, shrinking under the gaze of the people. Andra felt Zhade stiffen beside her.

"I have a gift for the Goddess," she said.

Another guard stepped forward and held out her hand. The girl looked between the guard and Andra, fidgeting with a bouquet of wildflowers.

She swallowed. "I wanted to give it to the Goddess myself." Her voice was small.

"It's okay," Andra said.

"Goddess, I don't reck—" Zhade started, but Andra cut him off.

"Guard. Let her pass."

The guard stood back and let the child through. The girl took a few timid steps, then the light from a passing kinetic orb reflected on something shining at her shoulders.

A voice cried, "She has a knife!" And everything went to hell.

The girl pulled out two matching swords hidden beneath her tunic. She dropped the flowers. Before they hit the ground, Kiv was there, shielding Andra. The girl slid between his legs. There was a flash of silver, then a spurt of red at Kiv's ankles.

She took another guard out at the knees. As he fell, the girl used his thigh and shoulder as stepping stones, propelling herself forward. She grabbed the next approaching sentry, twisting his body. His outstretched sword nicked his comrade's shoulder.

Andra couldn't move.

The guards lay at the girl's feet, unconscious or incapacitated. For a moment, she was still, her swords splayed at her sides, blood dripping from the tips onto the tile mosaic below.

Zhade stepped in front of her, weaponless, hands outstretched, pleading. But before he could get a word out, the girl had thrown her right sword at Zhade. It caught the fabric of his sleeve and pinned him to the wall. The girl darted forward, following through with her fist, but instead of landing a blow, she reached into his jacket pocket. In the same movement, she jerked her elbow up, catching him in the jaw. She turned, arm raised, and in her hand was Zhade's icicle dagger.

The glittering spike came down on Andra. She raised her hands, catching it just before it reached her chest. The girl raised her other sword, ready to strike, and for a brief moment caught Andra's eye.

The girl's expression froze, then a blade sliced across her neck, splattering Andra with blood.

The sword clattered to the floor, and the girl fell.

She lay still, her blood coating the jeweled Celestias. Maret stood behind her, his own dagger dripping red.

He'd just killed her.

It was silent for a moment, then the courtyard erupted in chaos. People screamed. Someone pulled Andra back. She kicked, thinking it was Zhade, but it wasn't. He was still pinned to the wall, mouth gaping, eyes strangely wet. He stood frozen for a second, then his gaze fixed on Maret and he lunged, sleeve ripping as he pulled himself free.

"STOP!" Andra cried, but her voice was lost to the chaos. Kiv staggered to his feet, pulling Zhade back. Maret still stood over the girl's body. She was just a little girl, and suddenly Andra realized what was familiar about her.

She looked just like Lew-Eadin.

Andra pulled free and rushed toward the crumpled body, nearly tripping over her own feet. She drew the girl into her lap—the girl who could be, might be, Lew-Eadin's sister. Something about the way she'd looked at Andra—right before the dagger had sliced her throat—told Andra the girl hadn't been trying to kill her. This was something else. Andra just didn't know what.

The girl's eyes were still open, filled with tears. One slid down her cheek. Her lips were slightly parted, but no breath expelled. Andra noticed a slick film covering the girl's skin as she frantically searched for a heartbeat that wasn't there.

Of course there wouldn't be. Maret had split open her throat, but unlike the assassination attempt at the Awakening ceremony, he hadn't done it through his crown, with a 'bot. He'd done it by his own hand.

Anger coursed through her, and she picked up the dagger. It glistened in the low candlelight and sparked to life in her hand, a burst of rainbow colors dancing across its surface. She expected a shock, but all she felt was its power, something rising up inside it. Inside her.

"Goddess," someone murmured. Maret. His voice was soft. Too soft for a murderer. He was silent for a moment, then gave a startled shout and backed away. Something tugged at the edge of her consciousness.

The people closest to Andra noticed before she did. They exclaimed and knelt, and that's when Andra saw it.

A nano'swarm coalesced in the air, glittering in the flickering light. Roughly human shaped, it hung suspended for a moment, and then dove into the girl. Her back arched, and Andra scuttled back, watching as the wound in the girl's throat knitted itself back together, slowly, purposefully, until the fatal cut was nothing but a puckered scar and dried blood. Andra had never seen nanos work so quickly or cleanly. It was incredible, but ultimately useless. The girl was already dead; the nanos couldn't change that.

But they did.

The girl gasped, her eyes flying open. Andra dropped the icepick dagger and it clattered to the tile. The girl met Andra's stare, gulping in heaving breaths. Andra sensed the 'swarm leaving the girl's body, but slowly, not as dramatically as it had entered.

The girl wiggled away from Andra, eyes still set in defiance, hands grasping for her swords, which were now out of reach. It was like no time had passed for her. Like . . .

Like she'd been in cryonic stasis.

Maret was still beside her, his 'implant gleaming on his forehead.

Andra was too stunned to move, but her brain was flying through the implications. In order to bring someone back to life, they couldn't have been dead in the first place. The girl had dropped like a stone, almost as though she had died instantly. Even the deepest cut to the carotid artery would have incurred some kind of reaction as she died. But if she had been put into stasis first . . .

It would require portable cryo'technology, which should have been beyond Maret's capabilities, beyond *anyone's* capabilities. But Andra saw the evidence in front of her. The girl had been put into stasis right before Maret slit her throat, then she'd been healed and woken up again. All in a matter of seconds.

The crowd gasped. Every single person fell to their knees, bowing to Andra, and suddenly she realized what they saw. What they *thought* they saw.

She'd brought someone back to life.

Well shit, she thought, and glanced at Maret. Had he just proven she was a goddess?

She had to make the most of it, use it to her advantage. It had to look like she'd done it on purpose. She stood, willing her legs not to give out. The people were bowing, trembling, and Andra opened her mouth to speak, not sure what would come out.

"This planet is dying," she said, keeping her voice firm but quiet, so that the crowd had to lean forward to hear. "The protection the gods have given you will not last forever. The gods' dome must be sustained with . . . magic that is beyond any of your sorcers, even that of your beloved Guv."

She heard Maret's breath falter, but she didn't care. Something churned inside her. Something dark and wonderful and heady. The tips of her fingers tingled with power, and she loved it. And she hated it.

And she loved it.

She was used to being too much: she was too fat, too analytical, too sarcastic, too *Andra*. So she'd learned to make herself smaller, to take up less space—physical and otherwise. To stay out of the way until needed. But here. Here she could make herself as big as she wanted. As *much* as she wanted.

She raised her voice—just a bit, not enough to make it look like she was trying to hold their attention, but enough that none of them would miss her next words. The stars shone above. Twinkle orbs reflected off the colorful tile and the thrill of nano'bots brushed her skin.

"But it's not beyond me." She took a deep breath. "I am your goddess. And I will save you all."

The crowd was silent, and Andra felt a thrill of light-headedness as they stared at her in awe. Like she was some great and terrible thing. And Andra realized they saw in her both their salvation and destruction.

She turned to go, but not before pausing to hiss at Maret, "What did you do?"

"I didn't do anything, Goddess." He stared at her, just as awed and frightened as the people. "That was all you."

TWENTY-FOUR

THE BROTHER

ZHADE CREPT THROUGH the First's suite like a thief—moving as silentish as possible despite being in a hidden corner of the palace. He didn't even light the candles, mereish searched by starlight. Outside, the wind howled under a fading moon bandaged in tattered clouds.

No meteor how many times he'd hit the button on the speak-easy, Wead still hadn't responded. There were a palmful of possible reasons. Perhaps he'd lost his device. Or maybe he was busy. He and Dzeni had been apart awhile, and perhaps they had the ridiculous need for space. But Zhade couldn't shake the sense something was wrong. He hadn't heard from Wead in a turn, and now, news was spreading bout the girl who had died and been resurrected by the Third, as was her identity. If Wead recked his sister was being held captive in the palace, nothing would stop him from saving her.

So what was stopping him?

As stunned as Zhade had been in the Yard, he'd had enough sense to snatch the discarded icepick dagger before anyone noticed. It now hung heavy in his pocket as he rifled through the First's suite, looking for bits of magic he'd yet to explore. A few fractured spells littered the ransacked drawers. Discarded casings hid under the bed. He was full certz he'd already gathered anything useful, anything

Maret had missed, but if there was something left that would help him get Doon out of prison, he would find it.

Zhade should have seen this coming. The little warrior was changed, for certz, but she'd always been impulsive. He should never have told her bout the dagger. He should have taken an eye out for her. He should have done more to stop her. There had been oozhles of opportunities to prevent this, but he'd been too focused on his own plans to see them.

Wead was going to kill him.

When they had left four years ago, Doon was still playing Stone's Throw with the other Hive kidduns. She was smaller, and weaker, and if she hadn't been so fraughting sweet, she'd have been a target for bullying. Now, she was a trained killer who'd died and been resurrected.

Zhade had paid so much time planning to *fake* a miracle, and then the Goddess had gone and done a real one.

He didn't reck how to describe what he'd seen. Doon had been dead—that was for certz. No one could survive an injury like that—not even with an angel nearish to heal them soon and sooner. Zhade's mind had blanked, and then flooded with images of Lew-Eadin finding out his sister was dead. At the hands of Zhade's brother.

Evens. It wouldn't be the first time they'd lost someone to Maret's knife.

What Zhade couldn't shake was that through all the grief and shock of seeing Doon dead on the floor, he also felt . . . *grateful* to his brother for saving the Goddess—even though she'd never been at danger. And everything bout that was unforgivable.

Zhade spotted two sensor spells and a glamour mask tucked under hair threads in the gilded vanity, and shoved them in his satchel. That would have to do. He didn't have time for an intricate plan—the long con, the marathon: those were his specialties. This slapdash, hurried kind of mission always went wrong, and if he ever needed Wead here to sort things, it was soon and now.

He tossed his bag over his shoulder and strode across the plush carpet to the metal servants' door, swinging it open—

And ran straight into the Goddess.

Her short hair was free from ornament, and for once she wore no face glamour. She was dressed in the dark clothes she usualish wore when sneaking round the palace, because she recked they made her invisible. As though anything could do that.

"Miss me?" He tucked his hands into his pockets and leaned against the doorframe.

"Terribly." She scowled, but Zhade recked it was just to hide her true feelings. "How did you know?"

"Evens, it was either that, or you're here to ask for my help breaking the little assassin out of prison."

The Goddess blinked. Zhade grinned.

"I'm full brill. Didn't you reck?"

ZHADE'S PLAN WAS brash, and he'd prefer that the Goddess not be involved, but he was running out of time to save Doon, so here they were. The first thing they needed was a disguise. It would be hard enough to sneak into the dungeon, even harder with a recognizable goddess at his side. So he smuggled a uniform about her size from the laundry and brought it back to the First's rooms.

Zhade turned his back as Andra changed, scrunching his eyes shut as he listened to the rustle of fabric over skin. Once she was done, he sat on the First's bed, spelling the glamour mask to make her features mimic a guard named Ahloma, whose clothes she now wore. It wouldn't fool anyone who looked closeish. But no one tended to look closeish at those wearing uniforms. He was aware of the Goddess watching him as he nimblish cast the spell, picking out features from the scry that best suited Ahloma.

"Seriously," she said. "Where'd you learn to do this?"

"Magic hands," he said, wiggling his fingers.

A single streak of moonlight shone across her face as she rolled her eyes.

She liked him, he could tell. And not just physical attraction, either, though her response to his kiss in the hall had been enthusiastic enough. She found him charming, wanted to pass time with him. He couldn't blame her. Most people did.

But most people didn't make him feel the same way.

He lifted the hem of his shirt to wipe off the sweat from his brow. He flexed his abs. She looked.

Certz. The Goddess was in love with him.

"Evens," Zhade said. He motioned for her to sit on a nearby chair and knelt before her, lifting the glamour mask to her face, sealing it against her skin with extra care. He sat back on his heels, admiring his work.

At a quick glance, she looked just like Ahloma. But at closer inspection, there was no mistaking her for anything but the Goddess. Through the glamour, he could see her dark eyes and amber skin. Her full lips pursed together, like they did when she was lost in her head. Every time she blinked, her lashes fluttered against her cheeks, and Zhade found himself drawing forward.

The Goddess cleared her throat.

"What's next?"

Zhade blinked. "Uh . . ." He sat back, running a hand over his face. "Ahloma has the day shift, so we shouldn't run into the real Alohma for a good six bells. But shifts change all the time, so nobody should question why you're—*she's* with me."

The Goddess nodded, and Zhade grabbed her hand.

"How did you do it?" he asked. "You keep saying you're not a Goddess, but I saw you. Everyone saw you. You brought someone back from the dead. What are you?"

Zhade had seen the First do miraculful things, but he'd never seen her bring someone back to life. For true, he'd sole ever seen goddesses resurrected, and Doon was no goddess.

Andra hesitated, and something like fear flashed over her features. "I don't . . . know." She let out a long sigh. "I have an 'implant . . . in my brain." She touched the back of her head, tenderish, like she would touch a bruise. "Sort of like the one Maret wears, but it's inside me. I didn't think it could interact with the nano'bots—the stardust. But somehow, it did. And it did something it *shouldn't* have been able to do, even with compatible tech. Maybe whatever happened with the little girl is the same thing that happened when I accidentally destroyed the nano'patch. I didn't *mean* for it to happen, it was just instinct. Or maybe it's a fluke of how tech has evolved." Her eyes glazed over. "I thought it was Maret who brought her back."

Zhade rubbed his neck. "Maret was the one who killed her."

The Goddess shook her head, eyes still thoughtful. "I don't think she was ever dead. My 'implant wanted to protect me from her, so it did. It was like it put her into stasis—like I was, but without the box. That shouldn't be possible though."

Zhade let out a breath and pulled the icepick dagger out of his pocket. "I reck it was this."

She looked from him to it. "What is it?"

"Dunno. I recked it was mereish a dagger, but now I imagine it's something more. Something to do with you. Both times you held it, you performed a miracle."

He didn't want to convo this—he recked the guilt the Goddess would feel when she realized she had killed the man in the Small Wastes. But keeping it a secret had cost them both. He saw when it hit her, the grief that overtook her face.

"You think I killed the man by the statue?" she choked.

"Sorries and worries. I reck you didn't do it apurpose," he said.

"That doesn't matter!"

Zhade took her hand. "You saved my life. Thank you."

She bit her lip, and her eyes grew red and wet. For a moment, she did nothing but stare, and Zhade could all but hear her thoughts. Under her glamour, her face was ashen and her eyes shimmered. He held her gaze til she nodded, then turned the dagger over in his hands.

"Whatever this is, it releases your magic."

She swallowed. "It's . . . possible, I suppose. My 'implant doesn't interact with the tech here. Maybe this is some kind of . . . translator? An upgrade patch?" Her voice was still rough.

Zhade didn't comp what she was saying, but one thing was for certz—the Goddess was teetering on the precipice of something. Whatever it was, it was wild and dangerful, and if Zhade didn't pull her back from the edge, he'd lose her.

And then what would happen to his plans?

And her?

"You should hold it," he said, offering her the dagger.

She immediatish recoiled. "No. No way. If what you say is true, I *killed* someone with that, Zhade. You can't let me near it."

"You also saved someone."

She hesitated for a moment, but then shook her head again. "No. I can't risk it."

"Evens." He stood. He would find another march to protect her, after they saved Doon. "Soon and sooner, let's peace and break the tiny warrior out of the palace dungeons, marah?"

Andra stopped him with a hand on his arm. "She's Lew's sister isn't she?"

Zhade nodded once.

"And she wasn't trying to kill me, was she?"

He shook his head.

"Then why—"

"Rescue anow, convo later," he said, shouldering his bag.

He handed her a sword, which took her a few tries to get into Ahloma's scabbard. He promised her she wouldn't need it, though it was a promise he couldn't keep. The plan was to casualish walk to the dungeons, then casualish walk out with Doon.

Terrible plan, for certz. The Goddess told him as much, and he agreed.

"That's why it'll work," he said. "But it'll sole work once."

Zhade led Andra down the hall. He'd visited the dungeons a handful of times, back when he was a kiddun. They weren't used as dungeons then—mereish storage. They made their march downstairs, and the farther they went, the dimmer the light grew, the more twisted the halls. Guards and servants let them pass, giving them mereish passing glances. Occasionalish, someone would nod to Zhade or ask the Goddess how she was doing. Ask *Ahloma* how she was doing. She'd shrug, and Zhade would smoothish provide some excuse bout Sfin changing Ahloma's shift, and fin would be fin.

They entered the dungeons by descending a flight of cracked, narrow stairs. At the bottom, two guards stood blocking their entrance. Zhade wouldn't have recognized them, but he had memory of the rotation and recked they were Legra and Dzon.

Legra nodded to Zhade. "What happens?" Her tone wasn't accusatory, just curious.

"Sfin sent Ahloma and me to relieve you," Zhade said.

Dzon frowned. "We've been down here mereish half abell."

If some of the other guards had been down here—Pin or Ricado perhaps—they would have jumped at the chance to be relieved of duty soon and sooner. But Zhade had to take a different tack with these two.

"Evens," he said, thrusting his hands into his pockets. "Sfin's not too happy with you pair after prior eve."

Their eyes widened. Yahtzee.

"He recks bout that?" Legra asked.

Zhade nodded graveish. "Firm. And you happen at luck that all he asks is you clean out the barracks smallroom."

The guards sighed in relief, nodded their thanks to Zhade, and hurried up the stairs.

"Don't return til it shines!" he called after them.

"What did they do last night?" the Goddess asked.

"No idea." He opened the door and gestured for her to go first.

Zhade grabbed a torch from where it was mounted outside the door and lit the room. It was a cavernous space, the walls a hodgepodge of rocks and hardcrete and metal, jagged and muddied. The cells were cages, the metal rods disappearing into the walls and ceilings, like they grew from the rocks themselves. Somewhere, water was dripping, hitting the floor with incessant *pings*. Doon was huddled in the corner of the far cell, a pile of rags curled in on itself.

"Little assassin?" the Goddess whispered, weaving her arm through the bars. Something bout the image made Zhade's heart clench. "Are you okay?"

"Evens, it's bout time," said Doon's voice, but it was coming from the ceiling, and definitish not from what turned out to be an actual pile of rags.

Doon dropped from where she was perched, fingers clinging to minute grooves, legs forming the splits, each of her feet wedged against a wall. She landed with an *oof*, but quickish straightened.

"I was nearish to finding my own march out." She gave Zhade a pointed look and held her hand out. "And I'll take that Silver Second now."

Zhade flicked her a coin. She caught it with ease.

The Goddess turned on him, arms crossed. "You planned this? For Lew's sister to get caught?"

"I did nothing of the sort," Zhade said, leaning against the dingy dungeon wall, then realized what he was doing and cringed, wiping the grime from his shoulder. "How very dare."

Doon tapped her temple. "I planned it."

"Hear?" Zhade said, pointing at the girl. "Andra, Doon. Doon, Andra." He waved his hand between them in intro.

"Did you plan for Maret to kill her too?"

Zhade winced, but Doon sighed, crossing her arms over her chest. "Sands, you said she was smart."

"I said no such thing. You reck I don't give out compliments."

She tapped her forehead. "You also said she was charred."

"Firm, but I say that bout everybody." He waved away the comment.

The Goddess pinched the space between her eyes, and for a moment, Zhade had a fear she would pass out. "Is anyone going to explain to me what happened? Was there a reason you wanted Lew's sister to try to kill me and then get put in prison?"

Doon looked offended. "If I had actualish been trying to kill you, you would be killed."

"Then what was the point of attacking me?"

"Zhade said we needed to save you from being sacrificed. The best way to do that was to make you . . . what was the word?"

"Indispensable?" Zhade supplied.

"Firm. Indispensable. The people haven't seen you do magic yet, but Zhade has. You saved him from bad boyos in the Small Wastes. You made his dagger come to life."

"Firm, she did," Zhade interrupted, a smirk on his face.

Doon gave him a flat look, then turned to Andra. "If the people could see you do that, then it would be bad magic for them to sacrifice you. Soze, I put your life at danger and made certz you were holding the dagger."

Zhade raised a finger. "I would like to interject to say I had no reckonings of her plan."

Doon crossed her arms. "I told you the full thing."

"I had no reckonings she would follow through on her plan."

"But I *didn't* do anything to the dagger," the Goddess protested, but it didn't sound full hearted. "I don't know what happened. And that's a terrible plan! I *killed* the dude by the statue! I could have killed Doon too!"

"Ah!" Zhade said. "So you admit it was you."

"Not—I—" she stammered.

Doon stood and clapped the dirt off her hands. "Time runs. Are we going to do this?"

The Goddess sighed, giving Zhade an exasperated look. "What's the plan, mastermind?"

"*Master*mind? I like that." Zhade grinned. He turned to Doon. "That's what you'll be calling me soon and sooner."

Doon shot the Goddess a glare.

"Now," Zhade said, "we escort her out of the palace."

"That's it?" the Goddess asked. "That's not a plan. That's a goal. A plan is *how* to accomplish a goal."

"Hear?" He looked at Doon. "Smart." He tapped his forehead. "I reck where guards are stationed this time of night. I made certz any along our route will be busy elsewhere. Walk confidentish, and no one will ask questions."

"That simple?"

"That simple."

Zhade pulled a key out and fidgeted with the lock. A palmful of prisoners occupied the other cells and started pleading for help as soon as they saw the key. The Goddess had to step away from hands grasping through the bars. Zhade tried to ignore them, but he recked their fate. If he didn't save them, they would die. The prisoner in the cell next to Doon's didn't even look up, resigned to their fate.

The door clinked open, and Doon climbed out. Zhade handed her back her swords. It had taken him time and half to locate them, but he'd eventualish found them tucked in Sfin's bunk chest. The head guard had apparentish taken them as trophies. And for good reason. They were brillish balanced and massive craftsmanship. Doon weighed them in her hands, then with a quick twirl, sheathed both behind her back.

"If it's that simple," the Goddess whispered, "what about the others?" She nodded to the pleading prisoners. "Why not release them? Why didn't you save my maids?"

Because it wasn't part of the plan. Because this will sole work once. Because even this one time is jeopardizing everything I'm working toward.

"I wasn't trying to impress a charred and exasperating goddess before. Beauty works marvels for motivation." He winked.

The Goddess opened her mouth to respond, but then frowned. "What was that?"

"What?"

Then he heard it. A beeping coming from his pocket.

Zhade cursed, pulling out the sensor. It flashed red, a warning. Someone was heading their way, and there wasn't enough time to cover their sandprints.

"Sands," he hissed, then turned to the Goddess. "Heya, I need you to stab me a little."

"Stab you?"

"Firm, mereish a little." He pinched his fingers together. "Seeya, don't kill me or anything. Mereish enough to make it look like I tried to fight."

"What? No! I'm not going to stab you!"

Doon groaned. "I'll do it." She pulled one of her own swords from its sheath, ready to stab.

"*Ah!*" He lifted a finger. "Not the face."

"You're an idiot," Doon said, then plunged the blade into his shoulder.

Zhade had been stabbed before, but something bout recking it was coming made it hurt even worse. The sword made a meaty sound as

Doon drew it out. Blood seeped from the wound, soaking a stream down the front of his shirt, and he fought not to pass out.

"Rare form, little warrior," he gasped, fisting his hand over the wound.

"I've always wanted to do that," she said.

The Goddess jolted forward, grabbing at the ends of her guard jacket, her fingers fumbling as she tried to tear the fabric into bandages.

"What . . . why would you . . ." Her voice was high, frantic. And for some reason, her concern didn't warm Zhade. He mereish felt guilt for worrying her.

Her eyes began to shine, and it could have been tears, but he had memory of what she said bout healing Doon on instinct, and he didn't want to have to be stabbed again. He grabbed her arm with a bloodied hand.

"You're going to have to get her out of the palace without me." He squeezed her wrist til she met his gaze. "Walk. Don't run. Or they'll reck something's wrong. Escort her out through the westhand stairwell and into the First's smallrooms. There's a hidden door in the floor. Once she's atunnel, wait for me there, and I'll get you back to your room."

Her gaze kept drifting down to his wound.

"Heya," he said, pulling her chin up. She flushed. "I'm evens. An angel will heal me right up. As long as you hurry and get the fraught out of here before I bleed to death."

Andra nodded. Zhade had a million other things he wanted to say, but he mereish slipped the icepick dagger into her pocket and gave her a little shove. She pulled herself away and grabbed Doon's hand. Zhade watched as they darted up the stairs, and then he slumped to the stone floor and let darkness take him.

TWENTY-FIVE

stasis, n.

Definition: 1. a stagnation or stoppage; inactivity resulting from a static balance between opposing forces.

2. archaic: sedition, rebellion, revolution.

3. biotech: The state of (non)being experienced by those put into cryonic sleep; the cessation of biological activity without the consequences of death.

A CHILL RAN up Andra's spine, and a burst of adrenaline sent her heart into a frenzy. She and Doon had managed to sneak out of the dungeon before the guards arrived, but they still needed to make it through the palace, out the secret exit, and to the Hive.

They'd left Zhade bleeding.

Andra hoped Doon knew how to stab nonlethally, but there'd been so much blood, and she'd seen the pain in Zhade's eyes. It would have been wasted if they hadn't run, but she still didn't like leaving him.

The palace was dark and silent, and Andra couldn't help but feel clunky running alongside the small girl, who seemed to slip through the stone halls like a ghost. They didn't slow until they reached the main arteries of the palace. They needed to get to the First's room— on the south side—but there was no way to *get* to the south side without first going west, around the Rock. Which led directly past the throne room.

"You're too tense," Doon whispered. "People will notice."

"People are going to notice anyway," Andra hissed back. "We're about to go through the most populated part of the palace."

Granted, it was in the middle of the night. There wouldn't be many people around. No one but a handful of guards and maybe a few servants. But what if the guards Zhade had tricked had already sounded an alarm?

Doon muttered under her breath, "People sole see what they expect to see, unless you give them reason to see otherwise. Walk like you belong. Hold my arms behind my back, like you're escorting me. You're a guard now. Believe you're a guard, not a goddess."

Okay. She could do this. Guard, not a goddess.

They continued down the hall as Andra pulled Doon's arms behind her. She kept her head high and her expression blank, so people could interpret it how they wanted—a move she'd seen her mother do plenty of times. Sweat built up under her cos'mask. The main hallway appeared ahead of them. She counted her breaths. In-two-three. Out-two-three. The throne room foyer opened up before them. A dozen guards. Three or four servants.

"This is worse than I recked," Doon muttered. "Any side passages?"

"No. What do we do?"

"Keep walking. Hope for the best. Be ready to fight our way out."

"Horrible plan."

Doon nodded. "The worst."

The girl dragged her ahead, Andra's hands still tight around her wrists. At a cursory glance, people would see a guard leading a prisoner. *Here's to cursory glances*, Andra thought, lifting her chin. They passed a servant. No response. Halfway through. The 'bots ignored them completely. One guard nodded, and Andra nodded back.

Her armor clanked with each step. Her breath was too loud.

Almost there.

Almost.

There.

They passed out of the foyer and into a side hallway.

Empty.

"Don't relax. Keep going," Doon whispered.

Andra didn't relax—couldn't.

About halfway down the hall, she realized someone was following them. She sucked in a breath, searching for a way to tell Doon without saying it out loud. She still held the girl's wrists and gave them a squeeze. Doon wiggled a hand free and reached for one of her swords.

"Wait," Andra whispered.

There were no footsteps behind them, and when Andra risked a glance back, there was nothing, only a shadow out of place, only the feeling of eyes on them. Little details Andra processed without realizing it. Her spine tingled. They kept moving forward, turned a corner.

"We can't lead them to the secret passage," Doon hissed.

Andra took stock of where they were. First floor. Western wing. She knew of one exit, but it was a risk.

"Follow me," she whispered to Doon.

The first glints of morning light were peeking through the windows when they finally made it to the small back entrance to the courtyard. Andra breathed a sigh of relief as she swung it open. The fountain bubbled. Birds sang. Dew was already collecting on the flowers, and the morning was quiet enough to hear their footsteps slapping against the tile. They swung around the corner behind the daises and froze.

Maret was waiting for them.

He stood straight, his robe impeccably tailored, not a hair out of place. Still, something about him seemed disheveled. Perhaps it was the bruise on his cheek, beginning to yellow, its edges cloudy, lining the silver crown. Maybe it was the tic in his hand, his thumb tapping the pad of each finger, then making the circuit again. Or it could have been the look in his eyes—a little unfocused. A little *unhinged*.

Andra had forgotten what he'd said the other night, about the garden feeling peaceful. It had been stupid to deviate from the plan, and now she was faced with a very angry Maret.

She took a step back.

"You betrayed me, Goddess." His eyes didn't even flick to Doon as she unsheathed her blades, one still wet with Zhade's blood. They'd been caught, and he'd been stabbed for nothing.

Maret was alone. His midnight robes outlined his thin, strong build. The pleats blended right into the scabbard at his side, holding a gilded sword Andra had never noticed. His hand rested on the hilt. Dangerous, yes, but in the way of an animal chewing itself free from a trap.

She held a hand out in Doon's direction. "Wait."

She'd never grown to fully trust Maret, but over the past few days, they'd built up a rapport. Sure, it had been strategy. And sure, his humanity and vulnerabilities couldn't erase all the terrible things he'd done. But he wanted to save his brother. And he'd saved Andra multiple times. He could be reasoned with.

"I did what I had to do," Andra said. "I didn't want her to die like my maids."

Maret's jaw clenched. "She tried to kill you."

"But she didn't." Andra tensed, surreptitiously taking in the courtyard, looking for something that would get her and Doon out of this without resorting to swords. There was only one path out of the garden, and Maret was blocking it. "We chatted. It was all just a big mistake."

"Mistake? If I hadn't—"

"Thank you for protecting me. But it wasn't necessary." Andra swallowed. There was a sword at her side, but she wasn't sure she could use it. Doon was inching her way around the garden. A few more meters, and she could attack Maret from behind.

"Wasn't necessary?" Maret sneered. "She was trying to *kill* you. She deserved it."

"Deserved it? She's a child!"

"So was I!" Maret roared. He blinked, as though he hadn't meant to say it.

The birds had stopped chirping. The fountain bubbled on.

"What do you mean?" Andra asked, her voice gentler. Out of the corner of her eye, she saw Doon ready to strike. Shrubs and potted plants stood in her way, but they would obviously be no obstacle for the girl.

"It doesn't import."

"It does."

"It doesn't," he gritted out.

Doon tensed to spring. Andra got ready to run. Then, with a flick of his wrist, Maret unsheathed his sword and pointed it in Doon's direction. Swift. Firm. He didn't even look her way. "Don't. I studied the same arts as you. And time and a half as long."

Doon raised both hands in the air, but didn't drop her swords.

Maret never looked away from Andra. "The people are scared."

They should be, Andra thought. But not because of her. "Sorry?"

Maret smirked. He looked like Zhade then, but only in the way Andra looked like Acadia. The resemblance was there, but no more than a cheap imitation.

"You raised the dead. That's too much power for one person. They want you sacrificed to the gods' dome."

So Doon's plan had backfired. Instead of making Andra indispensable, Doon's resurrection made her a frightening unknown. She wondered if the people would change their minds if she fixed the 'dome. Not that it mattered. There was no way Maret was giving her the AI now.

Maret's face tightened into a grim smile. "You may be a goddess, and you may have lived for centuries. But I reck you're not immortal."

"Because Tsurina killed the other two?"

His expression blanked, but Andra didn't miss the tightening around his eyes.

"Did you have a hand in that?" she goaded, careful to keep her eyes off Doon. If she could distract Maret enough, perhaps the girl could strike. "Or did she do that without telling you as well? Who really rules Eerensed?"

"I do," Maret growled. "*I* hold this city safe, *I* protect its people. The Hell-mouth is activeish trying to kill us, and we're trapped inside ancient magic none of us comps or recks how to maintain. Every day, the gods' dome can sustain fewer and fewer people. *I* bore that burden while you were nothing but a *girl in a glass box*." He spat the words. "And whether you want to believe it or not, I'm the sole thing standing between Eerensed and my mother."

There was a mad gleam in his eye. Andra tried to stay focused on Maret, even as she saw Doon take a step forward in her peripheral vision. The Guv had drawn closer. Closer than Andra had realized, close enough to impale her with his sword if he wanted.

"I do what I have to do to hold as many people as possible alive. If that means killing, so be it. Someone has to make the hard choices."

Andra swallowed, willing her fear not to show. "That would be Tsurina. You're nothing more than a puppet."

He grabbed her by the throat, his grip bruising. Doon darted forward, but Maret slashed his sword in her direction, never taking his eyes off Andra. Doon froze.

"You're a naive little girl," he growled. "You're the weak one. I was a fool to ever put my trust in you."

She tried to pull out of his grasp, but his blunt fingernails dug into her skin.

"I have power," he whispered. "And I will do what it takes to keep it. That doesn't make me evil; it makes me human."

Maret had never felt so dangerous. So out of control. Something had happened, and he had snapped. Andra's mind was whirring, but some instinct led her hand to her pocket, almost unconsciously.

Maret pulled her closer, painfully, muscles tightening. His breath was heavy as he lowered his mouth to Andra's ear. "You'll see. You've sole had a taste of power, but that's all it takes."

Andra's hand closed on the icicle dagger in her pocket, something in her unsurprised to find it there, had known all along. Calm washed over her.

She felt it this time—something burgeoning up inside of her. In her and of her. Some extension of herself that had always been there, but she'd never known. It was as natural as breathing. As thrilling as flying. She called. She answered. She soared.

"You'll see," Maret snarled. "One day you'll make the same choices as me."

With nothing more than a thought, Andra rallied a 'swarm of nanos. For a moment, they hung in the air above them, a glittering fog. Maret's eyes widened in fear, and Andra's mind sent them a single purpose. Attack. And they did.

TWENTY-SIX

schism, n.

Definition: 1. a breach of unity.

2. the division into separate and mutually hostile organizations.

MARET DROPPED LIKE a stone at Andra's feet.

Oh shit.

What had she done?

It hadn't been conscious thought. It had been intuition and will and fear, and now Maret lay unmoving at her feet.

She looked down at the dagger in her hand. It shone, the first rays of the morning sun glancing off it, sending sparks of color through it like a prism. Zhade had been right. Every time she'd been holding the dagger, she'd been able to use her 'implant. It must somehow be translating her 'implant's colonial code into the updated Eerensedian code.

It *had* been her who killed the man by Dr. Griffin's statue. And it looked like she'd just killed again.

She knelt next to Maret.

Maret's body.

Maret.

His skin was cold and slick, like Doon's had been the night before. Tiny dots covered his skin, his pores expanding. Except they weren't pores.

They were nano'clusters.

The Guv's expression was frozen, like there was still something going on in his brain. Except there wasn't. Whatever synapses that had been firing were suspended. He wasn't dead. He was on pause.

She'd put him in stasis.

And based on the tight feeling in her chest and the wave of exhaustion overtaking her, it was costing her.

"I reck that's a bit problemistic, marah?" Doon asked.

Andra had forgotten she was there.

Doon raised a sword in question. "Should we?"

Andra didn't answer. The tile path was cool against her skin.

The street-side door swung open and Andra jolted. A black girl with a modded eye and shaved head stood in the open gate, an arsenal of weapons strapped to her person.

Andra tensed, ready to fight, but then remembered the dagger in her hand. The wrong thought at the wrong time, and she could accidentally kill or freeze someone else.

The girl looked between Andra and the Guv's body. "That's not what I was expecting."

"Xana?" Doon asked. "What are you doing here?"

The girl rolled her biological eye, while the modded one zeroed in on Doon. "I came to save your ass, what do you reck?"

Doon sheathed her weapons. "All these rescue attempts. I could have gotten myself out evens."

"Fishes and wishes," Xana muttered, approaching Andra and offering her a hand. Andra hesitated. "I had full opportunities to kill you if I wanted. Several times."

Andra let the other girl help her up. A cool breeze fluttered through the garden. Maret lay unconscious at their feet.

"Prepped to peace, Goddess?" Xana turned back to Doon and clamped a hand on her shoulder. "Skilla is going to feed you to a pocket."

Andra tensed.

"Relax. It's mereish a figure of speech." She tapped the Guv's prone body with her toe. "Congrats. You killed the bastard."

"Actually, no." Andra bit her lip. "He's just . . . temporarily dead. I mean, yes I killed him, but I can bring him back."

That got Xana's attention. "How? And why would you want to?"

Andra swallowed. "I put him in stasis . . . I mean, to sleep. I can wake him up later. It's kind of like what happened with Doon."

"For certz?" The younger girl bent over the body and poked it. "Massive!"

Xana watched Andra, her eyes narrowing like she was trying to sort something out. "You want to bring him back?"

Not really, no. But she had to. Maybe Maret was right, and he was the only thing standing between Eerensed and his mother. His rule was oppressive and cruel, but Tsurina would be worse. She would let the 'dome fall, destroy all the technology keeping Eerensed alive.

"I *need* to bring him back," she said. "I can't leave him dead."

"Why?"

Andra let out a long breath, running a hand through her hair. "If he dies, Tsurina takes over." She didn't have time to explain why that would be such a bad thing, but Xana seemed to understand.

"Rare point. But you can't stay here. You attacked the Guv. Even if you bring him back, your life is forfeit."

Andra turned the dagger over in her hand. It was beautiful and deadly, and if she could understand how and why it worked, she would be able to protect herself. She could force Maret to tell her where the AI was. She could fix the 'dome and avoid being sacrificed.

Of course, she could also accidentally kill someone.

Again.

"I can take you somewhere safe," Xana said.

Andra didn't look away from the dagger. "Where?"

"The Schism."

"Uh, no thanks. Aren't those the people who hate me?"

"If I said neg, would you believe me? If you stay here, Maret *will* kill you. Even if you bring him back to life. This is your sole option."

The AI was here. As was Zhade, probably bleeding out on the dungeon floor. The palace was dangerous, but familiar. *Better the devil you know*, Andra thought.

Maret stared unseeing at the sky, his pale hair stark against the bright-colored tiles.

"We can't just leave Zhade." Andra looked to Doon, but it was Xana who answered.

"You don't have a choice."

Andra didn't trust her, but she was right. A few feet away was the space where her maids had been killed. It could be her next. She just had to trust Zhade had known what he was doing.

She sighed and held out her hand. "Andra."

"Scuze?"

"My name. It's Andra."

"Xana."

Xana stared at her hand, but didn't move to shake it.

"Follow," she said, and Andra did.

On the other side of the gate, she paused, gripping the dagger tightly. The city spread out ahead of them, and it was early enough that no one was around to witness their departure, or what Andra was about to do next.

She didn't really know what she was doing, but something did. Instinct or intuition. She told the nanos to release Maret, and it was like letting her heart beat. It was like running a marathon.

She gasped for air.

A masculine scream rent the air. It had worked. Maret was awake.

They took off running toward a nearby alley, but it was too late.

There was a shout behind them and then the sounds of a laser 'gun. Shots pinged off the cobblestones at their feet. Doon reached for her swords, but Xana stopped her.

"Neg, let's go!"

They ran, and several realizations bubbled to the surface of Andra's mind.

Swords were ineffective against 'guns, so why did the guards and soldiers use them? Because, Andra knew, complex tech could only be controlled by Maret's crown. Her mind went back to the day of the Awakening ceremony. The assassin's attack that Maret had stopped. Just in time.

It had been a setup. Maret had sent someone to kill her, bringing the weapon to life with his crown, just so he could be the one to save her.

Andra's memory skipped forward to the man in the alleyway, the one Maret claimed had been a Luddite, just like his mother. Had that been a sham too?

All of this ran through her head in an instant, and on its tail, the reminder that Maret wasn't the only one who could control technology right now.

Shots rang out around them as Andra pulled the dagger from her pocket and stopped, standing her ground. Maret stood silhouetted in the courtyard gate, pale hair hanging limp, black robes disheveled, a silver 'gun pointed at her.

"Don't!" Xana said, grabbing Andra's arm, pulling her out of the path of the 'gunfire. A shot pinged off the icepick dagger, shooting it out of Andra's hand. It clattered against the cobblestone.

"Wait," she shouted, but Xana pulled her away. "I need that!"

"Do you need it more than your life?" Xana growled.

Doon grabbed Andra's other arm, and together, they dragged her through the empty streets of Eerensed, leaving the icicle dagger behind.

ANDRA AND DOON followed Xana through the city, the Rock looming behind them, a dark silhouette against the 'dome. Andra felt hollow. Extra aware of her faulty 'implant, like one of her senses was misfiring. The sounds of 'gunfire had long faded, but Andra still felt a prickling sensation on the back of her neck.

The sun peeked over the horizon, pricking the rainbow sheen of the 'dome. She could now see clearly the black decay of dead nanos, thousands of jagged scars running across the 'dome's surface. Wind pounded against them as they ran, and Andra thought she could hear a distant groan, as though the 'dome was straining against the weight of just existing. Andra ran faster. Sweat slicked her skin and she peeled off the cos'mask that made her look like Ahloma, tucking it into her pocket.

The farther they went, the tighter the streets, the smaller the houses, until suddenly they found themselves at the edge of a cliff.

Not a cliff of rock, but houses. Dark ragged homes were stacked one on top of the other, rising up in jagged, tilted levels, the floor of one home's porch forming the roof of another. Like a hive. Xana tilted her head, gesturing for them to follow, and then with a leap, she descended onto the top level.

They had to zigzag from one platform to another, sometimes dropping farther than Andra would have liked. The ground groaned when they landed, unstable. It wasn't made of rock, but of compacted dirt. It felt like one good leap would level the entire cliff.

"The Hive!" Doon chirped, hopping from porch to porch (or roof to roof, depending on how Andra looked at it). She landed deftly, as though she were a rock skimming across a pond. "This is where I aged up. Before Wead left."

Andra followed awkwardly, her feet unsure, the nagging sensation of danger getting stronger, a dull throb in the back of her skull.

The sun had breached the horizon by the time they arrived at the bottom, and the Hive was starting to come alive. People were calling to their neighbors across rooftops. An old man beat a rug into submission, plumes of dust sparkling in the sunlight. Kids chased one another, hopping from porch to porch, their mothers yelling after them.

Andra didn't know what she was walking into, and she'd already second-guessed herself a dozen times since they left Maret at the palace. This didn't actually solve anything, except allow Andra to live another day. She needed to come up with a plan that got her back into the palace to find the AI, to fix the 'dome. For now, all she could do was run.

"Hurry," Xana hissed, and Andra realized she'd been staring.

Xana led them to the edge of the Hive. Behind a large boulder lay a small, unguarded entrance, nothing more than a glorified sewage drain. Xana brushed off an overgrowth of vines and trash, revealing a rusty grate underneath. It lifted with a squeal, and Andra winced. They climbed down a ladder into the dark. The rungs were both gritty and slimy, and Andra tried not to think about why as they descended into the black underbelly of the city. When she reached the bottom, her feet landed with a squish. It was too dark to see, but she imagined they were in a tunnel of some sort. It was murky and dank and smelled like sick. She followed the sound of Xana's squelching footsteps.

Within a few steps, her boots were drenched with . . . whatever she was walking on. The hem of her pants grew heavier. Then started clinging to her legs.

But you're alive, she told herself. She wouldn't be if she'd stayed at the palace.

Her eyes slowly adjusted to the dark, and after a while, she could almost see Xana ahead of her, this stranger leading them to god-knows-where.

"I wish Zhade were with us," Andra mumbled.

"Why?" Doon whispered. "He'd just get us into trouble."

"He *rescued* you," Andra hissed back, cutting Doon a sideways glance. She could just make out the girl's shape in the dark. "You didn't have to stab him so hard."

"Scuze. He'll be evens. Sides, you imagine he did that for *you*? He could have come with us. The stabbing was to give *him* an excuse. He wanted to stay."

Andra bit her lip. A few weeks ago, she would have agreed—that this was just some grand plan of Zhade's, that he was being selfish. But now, she wasn't so sure. He'd saved her from the men by the ruins, he'd held her while she'd cried, he'd taught her how to survive Eerensed. More than that, it almost seemed like they were building a friendship, tossing jokes back and forth, giving each other support. If he'd needed to stay in the palace, it must have been for a good reason. At least, Andra hoped.

Their footsteps quieted as the ground grew firm under their feet. Andra followed Xana's silhouette, until she realized she could distinguish the color of her jacket, see the stubble on her shaved head. Doon turned and grinned—the expression either cheerful or foreboding—before skipping ahead, her swords still sheathed. There was light in the distance. The end of the tunnel.

It took longer than she thought it would to reach, but not long enough. Xana gave her an appraising look, or maybe a warning, her modded eye glowing in the dark. She stepped out of the tunnel and Andra followed.

She found herself in a huge underground cave lit by flickering torches and crude kinetic lamps. People were everywhere, the soft murmur of voices filling the space, punctuated by raucous laughs. The air was crisp and chilly and stale. Most of the cave was a giant open space, filled with kiosks and carts and scrap huts, but a few structures were built into underground ruins. The whole place had a slapdash, hurried feel to it, and Andra didn't have time to take it all in before someone saw them and gasped.

A murmur built up among the people, and then suddenly they were backing up, hands pressed over their mouths or hearts, eyes wide with fear.

At least they weren't trying to kill her. Yet.

"You're always bringing back strays," a husky voice said.

Andra barely had time to register the shame on Xana's face before she was shoved against the wall of the cave. Jagged rocks dug into her back, and she gasped as a hand tightened around her neck.

"What is this?" the woman choking her asked. Andra coughed. Damn it, this was the second time she'd been grabbed by the neck in as many hours.

"It's the Third," Xana said.

The woman raised a perfectly shaped brow. "I can see that. What is she—"

Before she could finish, a sword landed at the base of the woman's neck. Andra saw a single drop of blood, but otherwise the woman was unhurt.

"Let her go," Doon gritted through her teeth, her other sword poised to strike.

If the woman was nervous being held at sword-point, she didn't show it. Her expression only changed by a fraction, just a bare curling of her lips.

She relaxed her hold, and Andra fell to her knees, gasping. No one came to help. Xana didn't seem particularly fond of her, and Doon was busy holding their host captive. Andra spluttered and propped herself up against the cave wall.

A crowd had gathered, their eyes fixed not on Andra, but on the woman who'd choked her. They seemed ready to jump to the woman's defense, but only if she asked. No—*commanded*. Something about the way she held herself, about the look of adoration in the crowd's eyes—in Xana's eyes—made it clear this woman was their leader. She wore formfitting pants and a tight tank top. Some kind of dagger was strapped to a thigh holster, a sword hung at her side, and a battle-ax was slung across her back. Her dark hair was pulled sharply away from her pale face, revealing a myriad of scars and fading bruises.

"Put down your swords, Doon," she said. "You're outnumbered."

A few members of the crowd tensed, hands drawn to their sides, to hidden weapons. Guards, or perhaps a militia. They were dressed in plainclothes, and there weren't many of them, but the undisciplined gleams in their eyes felt more dangerous than even Kiv's intense stare.

"Outnumbered, dunno," Doon said. "But not outmatched."

Something flashed in the woman's eyes, and Andra tensed, but she just huffed out a short laugh and raised her arms in surrender.

"We'll convo later," she said, and Doon relaxed her stance, but didn't put away her swords. The woman crossed her arms and surveyed Andra. "So you're the new goddess." She gave her a look that said she wasn't impressed. "And the Guv's new pet."

Andra was about to argue, but Xana beat her to it.

"She killed the Guv," she said, turning a cold eye on Andra. "And she's not exactish a goddess. She's a fake."

Xana pulled something out of her bag and threw it to the dark-haired woman. In the dim light of the cave, it was hard to make out at first, but the woman turned it over, and suddenly Andra recognized it.

Her cos'mask. The one Zhade had programmed to look like her birthmark.

"I can explain that," Andra said, but she was more interested in how they'd found it. Last she'd seen it, the 'mask had been in a drawer in her bedroom at the top of the palace. Apparently, Xana and the Schism had been keeping an eye on her.

"I'd rather you explain bout killing the Guv."

Andra bit her lip, shivering in the cool damp of the cave. "I didn't kill the Guv. I mean, I did. But not really. Only temporarily. I brought him back."

"Now why would you want to do that?" Skilla murmured, weighing the deactivated cos'mask in her hand.

Andra was about to answer when, in one swift movement, the woman tore the neck of Andra's guard uniform, revealing her birthmark. Skilla's eyes narrowed, then softened as they landed on Andra's necklace.

"A holocket," she breathed. She gave Andra an appraising look, then stepped back, and Andra wondered why this time it was the 'locket and not her birthmark that saved her.

The woman assessed Andra, her piercing eyes narrowed. Andra tried to appear both confident and innocuous, neither a look she was able to pull off. She felt the stillness in the cave like a physical weight. The woman stepped forward, with the grace of a cat. Long, lithe, silent movements. Her eyes remained locked on Andra as she offered her hand.

"I'm Skilla."

Andra shook it. "Andra."

Skilla laughed without humor. "I know."

With that, she turned and walked off. Without breaking her stride, she called back, "Follow," and Andra did.

Skilla led Andra through the cavern, Doon and Xana falling in step behind, past the crowd of people eyeing them warily. They were dressed like the desert villagers had been, in rough-knit clothing, and there were even more skin tones than in the city above. She imagined not all of these people were Eerensedian, but from elsewhere.

Once Andra got past the shock of how many people were hidden down here—almost a shadow of the town above; no wonder the 'dome was failing—Andra realized *why* this underground city felt so comfortable. Familiar.

Technology was everywhere.

Not just 'bots, though there were plenty of those. But also data'screens and holo'displays—projecting all sorts of information, playing advertisements for stitches, synth'protein, 'bot repair. People had 'bands on their wrists and tablets on their laps. They were communicating. There was a *network* down here. It was glitchy—'screens flickered as they passed and lights stuttered—but it *worked*.

"You have technology," Andra breathed. It wasn't sacred. It wasn't some mystical remnants of the gods. It just *was*. She tried to access it with her 'implant, but it was useless. She thought longingly of the dagger.

Skilla smirked. "You have no idea."

Despite being cut off from the sun, the cave glowed like midday, lit by the active devices, and the further they traveled, the more familiar it felt, and Andra realized why.

These were the excavated ruins of a grocery store.

Or it could have been a hardware store or a sim'porium. Whatever it was, it was from Andra's time. The floor was chipped and coated with dirt, but definitely that glossy gray eco'tile ubiquitous in stores in the twenty-second century. Where the floor had flaked away completely, there was a layer of smooth, polished concrete. Frayed carbon fiber poked through the gaps. The ceiling consisted mostly of the cavern rocks, but it was also threaded with the ruins of aluminum support beams. Many of the kiosks, where people were selling random tech or beads or clothing, were made up of rusted titanium teardrop beams.

Skilla and her entourage stopped outside a doorway hewn into a concrete wall. It was just tall enough for Doon to pass under, but the others had to duck. It led to a tunnel, much cleaner and less damp than the one from the Hive. It was lit by a series of electric lights, flicking on as they passed, just bright enough to illuminate the way to the next one.

As they reached the end of the tunnel, Skilla turned.

"This might surprise you," she said, and flung open the metal door blocking their path.

On the other side was a massive room—some kind of natural cave formation—but Andra couldn't focus on its size or even the impossibility of it—because before her stood a giant rocket.

"Holy shit," Andra breathed. The words echoed around the cave.

Xana and Doon gasped beside her, as though this were their first time seeing it. Maybe it was.

Andra had to crane her head. Up, up. The rocket was at least two hundred meters tall, sleek and slender. It made her feel so small. Here she'd been compiling scraps for a short-range shuttle when all along there had been an honest-to-goddess rocket under her feet.

"We only have room for one hundred people," Skilla said quietly. "We can get them off planet, but it'll be cramped. And at least it will keep the human race alive."

"Massive," Doon whispered.

It wasn't just a rocket, though. It was a generation ship. In the dim light, Andra could just make out the hinges and seams where the rocket would open up once it broke the atmosphere, forming a ring. A rotating space habitat. A small one, for sure, but once the rocket blossomed, there would be enough room for a limited group of people to live—a hundred apparently. It would be outfitted with synth'trees for oxygen, and organic waste recycling, and solar energy conversion . . .

Whoever designed this wasn't just smart. They were a goddamn genius. Probably the smartest person to ever live. Because they'd done it on their own—not with the weight and resources of history behind them, not standing on the shoulders of their predecessors.

Andra swayed under the vertigo of looking up at something so tall.

"How?" she asked.

"The First," Skilla said, crossing her arms and following Andra's gaze to the top of the rocket. "She gave us the tools and the understanding. Unfortunately, she was *sacrificed*"—she drew out the word with derision—"before it was finished. We need an AI to speak with the angels—*drones* working on it. Construction has been at a standstill since . . ."

She waved her hand dismissively and walked around the edge of the room, stopping in front of a control panel. She pressed a few buttons, and the 'display blinked to life.

"We've studied it enough, we think we know how to pilot it. The problem is we don't know where we're going. The First insisted that only an AI could . . . program"—she stumbled over the word— "the calculations?"

Andra met Skilla's gaze and tried to give her a calculating look of her own.

"I think we can help each other."

TWENTY-SEVEN

THE TRAITOR

ZHADE WOULD DO anything to remain in Eerensed. But as Kiv and another guard dragged him toward Maret's suite, his chances of staying were slimming. Kiv grunted and gave him a small shove. His shoes squeaked on the marble, his shoulder burned. He missed the comforting weight of the icepick dagger in his pocket. Andra had needed it more than he did, but evens.

Zhade had been found ticks after Doon and the Goddess fled, bleeding and already losing consciousness. The tiny warrior hadn't been as careful as she could have been. The guards who found him patched him up, but it was a quick job, using the minimum amount of magic to hold him alive. And now he would have to face his brother.

Zhade had recked the plan was flawed. It didn't meteor he'd been stabbed, when he'd also been found in the dungeons ticks after a prisoner had escaped. He had to play this well, smartish. Before Maret became the monster fashioned by Tsurina, he had been Zhade's friend and brother.

Two years Zhade's junior, Maret had been ganglish and awkward. Zhade, on the other hand, had their father's charm, his mother's strength, and a relentlessness all his own. Maret was a blank slate, easyish molded into whatever was required of him. When they were young, he'd been a sweet boy, eager to please. Sole now did Zhade see it for what it was: manipulation. Maret was mereish ever what served him best in the moment. Unfortunatish for him, it was a trick Zhade was far, far better at.

Zhade and his entourage of guards reached Maret's suite, and Kiv rapped on the door. Two taps: too loud. Kiv never knew his own strength. The door swung open, sorcered to its master's will, and Zhade was pushed into the room.

Maret was waiting for him, dressed in their father's clothes. It was a psychological blow, one Zhade doubted Maret imagined himself. The move dripped, thick as honey, with Tsurina's influence. The advisor herself was standing in the corner, a silent sentinel.

"Why couldn't you have stayed in the Wastes?" Maret asked, his voice holding a whine age hadn't culled.

Zhade shrugged. "Why do you keep losing goddesses?" He was out of clever things to say, and all he could imagine were the circumstances that forced the Third from the palace. He wondered if the hideous bruise on Maret's face belonged to Andra.

Rare form, Goddess.

"I have a proposition for you," Maret said without preamble. He leaned back in his chair, considering the glass of brown liquor in his hand. For anyone else, the posture would have seemed powerful, a subtle reminder that the person was so comfortistic in their authority that they needn't bother to stand or make eye contact. Zhade had even performed the same trick before, but with Maret, it seemed forced. There was no subtlety. He'd built his gambit and forgotten to remove the scaffolding.

"A proposition?" Zhade asked. He sat in a plush chair opposite Maret, crossing his legs. He leaned his chin against his hand to keep from fidgeting.

"I'm curious," Maret continued, "why you didn't tell the Goddess who you are. You haven't told her everything."

Zhade gave his brother half a shrug. "My identity is currency. I was saving it for a drought."

Maret nodded, still not looking away from his glass. Zhade wondered if he was going to drink it, or if it was just for show. Maret had never been able to hold his liquor.

"Someone may spend that currency for you."

The threat was weightless. If Maret wanted the people to reck who Zhade was, he would have told them already. Sides, it was in Maret's best interest that the full truth bout Zhade's identity remain a secret.

The Guv set down his glass and finalish looked at his brother. "I'm willing to forgive you everything," he said.

That's funny, Zhade thought. *I'm willing to forgive you none of it.*

"If"—Maret held up a finger—"you can prove you aren't here to usurp me."

Zhade laughed. "Oh, trust me, Mare-Bear, that's not why I'm here full well."

Maret cringed at the kidhood playname, but he ironed out his expression quickish. He was getting better at checking his temper, but then, Tsurina was still watching, and the bruise coloring Maret's cheek made him carefulish, mereish opening his mouth as much as necessary. Zhade was cautious not to stare at the bruise, or the nearby Silver Crown.

"I want to be friends. I want to go back to the way things were," Maret said. He sounded like he meant it, and Zhade wondered if he did—if Maret was that oblivious, or full bars stupid to believe Zhade would forgive him his mother's death, his own exile, the years in the Wastes, all that had happened since.

"I want that too, Mare," Zhade said, hoping his smile reached his eyes. Hoping his desperation didn't show. He would do anything—*anything*—to avenge his mother's death, to accomplish what he set out to do the moment the gate had sealed itself between him and the city he loved.

Everything had been taken from him, and now it was time to take things back. He would decide his own fate, whatever the cost.

Maret's lips spread into a grin, but it was Tsurina who stepped forward, opening a nearby door. Guards tumbled in with a prisoner, bruised and bloody and beaten, and Zhade sucked in a sharp breath.

"It's time," Maret said, placing Zhade's icepick dagger on the table, "for you to make a choice."

He was out of options, out of plans, and Maret was handing him a sickening decision. Zhade should have recked it would always come to this. That it would never have been as easy as mereish taking back what was his.

Zhade took a deep breath, steadying himself, and leaned forward. "I have a counteroffer."

There would be a terrible cost, but Zhade would decide his own fate.

TWENTY-EIGHT

exchange, n.

Definition: 1. the act of giving or taking one thing in return
for another which is regarded as an equivalent,
such as:

- currency, goods, services

- blows, strikes, hits, parries

- prisoners

AFTER SKILLA SHOWED her the rocket, Andra was given a brief
tour of the Schism hideout. The main part of the cave acted as an
open-air market, the rebels maintaining their own micro-economy
right under the Eerensedians' noses. And they weren't just trading in
necessities—though there were plenty of butchers and pharmacists
and stitchers. There were also kiosks that sold handmade jewelry
or specialized in children's toys. Others provided grooming services
and extravagant clothing. Andra even saw a booth that offered
digi'tattoos. The display featured one just like her birthmark, and
the sight of it made her cringe.

The tech wasn't what Andra was used to. It wasn't designed to be
marketable and attractive. It was only meant to be functional. The
people still referred to it as magic, not technology, but it didn't matter what they called it. They interacted with it the same way people

of the twenty-second century did—as though it were just part of life, without knowing how it really worked.

There were thousands of people in the cave—not just in the main artery, but also living in a web of tunnels hewn out of the earth. The system ran the entire length of Eerensed, the palace sector the only part of the city without the Schism living and working underneath. And every room, every hollow of space, every nook was filled with people, all of them fighting against Maret, working tirelessly to build the ship that would only save a fraction of them.

Andra settled into her new quarters—a small nook hewn out of the cave with a single cot and nightstand—but she couldn't stay long. She had to figure out a way to fix the 'dome. Even if they could get the rocket off the ground, that only saved a hundred people. Those left would need some protection until Andra came up with a more permanent solution, and for that, she needed an AI. Sure, she now had the might of the Schism behind her—it helped that they both wanted the same thing—but the problem was:

They both wanted the same thing.

Andra needed the AI to save the entire city. The Schism needed the AI to save a hundred people. They could share, but the AI would have to prioritize one of the tasks. And once the rocket left, Skilla would be taking it with her. Maybe Andra could get the mech'bot from her rooms at the palace and offer it to help with the rocket while she was figuring out the 'dome. That would buy her time to figure out how to keep the AI and save Eerensed without simultaneously dooming the rocket. What was that phrase Zhade used? It was a thin string to half-walk? Andra's chest tightened at the thought of Zhade, but she didn't have time to worry about him now. She had to trust he could take care of himself.

Andra changed clothes, leaving Ahloma's guard uniform and the cos'mask holding her face in a rumpled mess on the floor. She then went to find Skilla's room—a dark corner in the back of the main cave.

Candles flickered, casting an eerie glow, and crimson fabric draped over the jagged walls. Skilla sat on her cot, wedged into a corner. A pre-book was propped in the general's lap, and she was writing in the margins. She didn't bother to look up when Andra rapped against the cave wall.

"I have questions," Andra said, trying to make her voice firm and commanding, but next to the general, she didn't feel like a goddess. She felt like a child.

Skilla didn't respond right away, too focused on whatever she was writing. Finally, she set the book aside, careful to mark her place, before looking up.

"I have answers," she said. "But probablish not the ones you want."

Andra entered the room, leaning against the wall as she'd seen Zhade do a hundred times. He made it look so casually imposing, but when Andra did it, she just felt awkward.

She had too many questions, too many thoughts buzzing through her head. She chose the simplest. "What is the Schism?"

Skilla gestured to the room around her and the caves beyond. "*This* is the Schism."

"You know what I'm asking."

Skilla sighed, scooting forward on the bed, and gestured for Andra to take a seat. Andra didn't.

"The Schism was started by the First," Skilla said.

"I figured as much, but why would a goddess need a secret society?"

"Not the First Goddess," Skilla said. "The First people."

Andra blinked. "I'm sorry, *what*?"

"The Schism has been around as long as anyone has memory. Its goal has always been to save humanity, but it wasn't til the First Goddess awoke that we understood why and what we were doing."

If Andra had still believed she was on Holymyth, she would have assumed Skilla was talking about the colonists. Now, she knew differently. If the jagged crescent moon that symbolized the Schism was an offshoot of the LAC symbol, then perhaps these were the descendants of whoever had been left behind. Perhaps they'd co-opted whatever Lacuna Athenaeum hadn't taken with them and tried to find a way to follow. But they'd been unsuccessful. And society kept reshaping itself until technology was magic and this rocket was a fairy tale. Until the First Goddess.

"And what are you doing?" Andra asked.

Skilla tucked her chin. "You saw the rocket. Speaking of"—she reached for a nearby tablet—"we'll have to bump a few passengers. I assume you'll want a spot reserved for Doon as well."

"Bump a few passengers?"

Skilla handed Andra the tablet, and she took it without looking.

"Room for one hundred. Not a passenger more. If you want a place on the list, you'll have to take someone else's."

She tapped on the tablet, drawing Andra's attention down. It showed a list of names. At the top was Skilla's, in angular, jagged lettering.

"So," Andra said, looking up from the list, "by reserving a spot, I'm condemning someone to die."

It didn't seem fair. But it was exactly what Alberta Griffin had done. Andra hadn't thought about it then, but that's what the lottery had been—choosing whose descendants got to live, and whose would eventually fall extinct. The more she thought about it, the more she realized the colonists had been mainly middle- and upper-class. There were also tons of celebrities chosen for the Ark. CEOs and senators. Every single scientist at LAC. The random lottery hadn't been random at all, and Andra should have seen it.

"Try not to think bout it," Skilla said. "That's what the First told me, anyway."

Andra felt a surge of guilt, because not only did she want a space on the rocket, she also wanted spaces for Doon and Zhade and Lew-Eadin and Lilibet. It was a terrible truth that she was willing to doom others for the people she cared about.

"Zhade said you hated the goddesses," Andra murmured. "That you hated magic."

Skilla sighed and gave Andra a patronizing look. "Zhade says a lot of things. Perhaps he even believes some of them." She stretched back, resting her head against the cavern wall. "We know the truth. Or at least, as much as we can understand. We know what the goddesses really are. We know what magic truly is. We don't hate it. Or you. Or the other goddesses. We hate how the people *see* it."

"Is it really that different?" Andra asked. "Magic or technology? Goddess or colonist? Isn't it just a matter of terms?"

Skilla raised a sharp brow. "Terms can matter quite a lot."

Andra supposed it was true. She wouldn't be running for her life if these people called her *Andra*, instead of *Goddess*. The First and Second wouldn't be dead if the Eerensedians used the word *technology* instead of *magic*.

"Who was she?" Andra asked before she could stop herself. "The First Goddess?"

"The First?" Skilla ran an unconscious hand over her ponytail. "She knew . . . everything. Our history. Magic. Things we'd forgotten. I was just a kiddun when she woke. My parents were low-level guards in the Schism. They died during a mining expedition, when pirates raided the party. The First took an eye out for me. She told me everything. Except bout herself."

There was something tight in Skilla's voice, and her gaze dipped down to Andra's birthmark. It was her proof that she was the Third Goddess, but just then it felt like condemnation. She was going to let them down the same way the First had.

"Her name?" Andra asked. "What she looked like? A pic?"

Skilla frowned, a tiny wrinkle appearing between her eyes. "No name. As for what she looked like? She was tall. Her hair was silver. She kept it long, but always complained bout it."

"Did she have a scar?" Andra asked. Adrenaline coursed through her.

"A scar?"

"A jagged one. Running down her cheek?"

Her mom had gotten it when something had gone wrong with their AI—the first Isla created. It malfunctioned while learning to cook and accidentally sliced Isla across the face with a carving knife, the wound too deep to ever fully fade.

Skilla blinked. Andra held her breath.

"Neg. No scar."

It was like a punch to the gut. Andra's breath left her in a whoosh, and she felt the world tilt beneath her.

"Are you evens?" Skilla asked.

"Yeah, fine," Andra muttered, but she wasn't.

She hadn't realized how much she'd wanted her mother to be the First until now. Until she had proof it hadn't been. Not that she wanted her mom to have been separated from the rest of their family to live in this terrible world and die a horrible death as a sacrifice. But if her mother *had* been the First, then that meant all this wasn't random. That there was some reason for the three goddesses to be left behind. That this was a mystery Andra could solve and the solution would give her purpose. But no. It had been chance. She had been misplaced. Forgotten. There was no reason she was here, no significance. It was a stupid fluke, a joke of the universe, that Andra was here and she was the one who had to save what was left of humanity. It was all just chaos.

"Perhaps you should go lie down," Skilla said, and Andra nodded absentmindedly.

She turned to leave, but then a shrill alarm sounded, echoing through the cave. Skilla jolted to her feet, grabbing a nearby battle-ax in one swift movement.

"Stay here," she said, and left without a backward glance.

Andra hesitated. The alarm could be nothing—it could have some secret meaning only the Schism knew—or it could be everything.

After all, Skilla had grabbed a weapon. Andra felt the tug to help, but she wasn't a fighter. She peeked out into the hallway. Nothing but flickering torches.

She stepped out of Skilla's room just as the alarm cut off. It was replaced by screaming, the sounds of laser'guns and a stampede of footsteps. Instinct told her to run, but as she turned, a shadow wavered in the torchlight. A figure emerged, flanked by spear-wielding 'bots.

He was dressed in a midnight robe, his hair slicked back, the look in his eyes wild, and on his temple shone the crown.

"Hello, Goddess," Maret said.

Andra ran.

There was only one route away from Maret, and it was toward the screaming, toward the main cavern. She wasn't a fast runner, but Maret didn't seem to feel the need to hurry. As she closed in on the main cave, his footsteps faded, overtaken by the sounds of a battle. She darted out of the narrow tunnel and was surrounded by chaos.

The coppery tang of blood filled her nostrils. Pandemonium swirled around her. Someone screamed a few yards away. People were scrambling for tunnel exits, but each was guarded by an army of 'bots. All mech'bots like Andra's, except these were designed for war. They held out their spears, skewering anyone who got too close. The few people armed were easily overwhelmed. A couple rushed past Andra, hand-in-hand, and darted into the tunnel she'd just come from.

"No, don't!" she shouted, but it was too late.

A sound of impalement. A scream. And then the scream stopped. Maret was coming.

She had to save the rocket.

It was a bizarre thought—it seemed to come out of nowhere—but it pushed Andra forward. There had to be some sort of defensive program she could engage that would protect it. She darted through the chaos, tripping over fallen kiosks and bodies, slipping in pools of blood. Her vision narrowed to what was in front of her, highlighting the path she had taken with Skilla just a few hours ago. She ignored the screams, ignored the gore. Her lungs burned, and her side started to ache.

A 'bot came at her, swinging a sword. She ducked, but knew it wouldn't be enough. It was coming too quickly, she was moving too slowly. She fell to the ground and the sword stopped centimeters from her neck.

Andra gave herself a single second to breathe, then scrambled out from under the blade. She didn't let herself look for Maret, but he must have been close. He had to have stopped the 'bot from killing her, but she knew it wasn't mercy that stayed his hand.

She kept moving, trying to lose her pursuers in the chaos, her focus narrowed on the tunnel that led to the rocket. She'd almost made it, when she saw something that stopped her.

Doon.

She'd forgotten all about Lew's little sister, but the girl was fighting her way through, swords out, her face a mask of concentration. She twisted between 'bots, dodging each of their blows effortlessly. She jabbed a sword into the skullcap of one while fighting a second. She kicked the 'bot back, pulled her sword out of the first, and then brought it down, decapitating the second with a crossed slash of her blades. The 'bots sparked and their eyes blanked as they fell to the ground.

"Doon!" Andra yelled. The chaos was too loud. She tried again, her throat burning. "DOON!"

The girl stopped. They made eye contact. Doon's blank expression turned to horror half a second before Andra felt stabbing pain through her arm. She dropped to her knees. The pain was all-consuming.

A soldier stood over her—human, not 'bot. His actions weren't controlled by Maret. They were his alone, and his eyes were bright with bloodlust. Andra didn't know if he recognized her as he raised his sword. Before he started his downward swing, a blade burst through his chest, bright with blood.

The soldier looked surprised, then the light left his eyes and he dropped to the floor. Doon stood behind him, her expression unreadable.

She dragged Andra to her feet and led her to the tunnels.

Andra's mind blurred with pain. Doon was saying something, but Andra could only focus on what was ahead of her. They hit a fork in the tunnel, and Doon started to pull her the wrong way.

"No," Andra wheezed. "I have to get to the rocket."

Doon looked confused, but nodded. She stood like a warrior. "Go, I'll hold them off."

"No, you have to get out of here!" Andra pushed her toward the exit, the small movement sending her into a rush of dizziness. She was still losing blood.

Doon watched her for half a second, then nodded. "I'll lead them away. But hurry."

"I will," Andra said, and then they darted in different directions.

Andra stumbled almost drunkenly, having to catch herself against the craggy walls. She held one hand to the wound in her arm, pushing herself forward as though she could escape the pain, escape the threat of passing out.

She burst into the cavern, but she was too late.

Flames traveled the length of the rocket. Sparks burst, and with a deafening groan the nose of the rocket broke off and crashed to the floor. Andra felt waves of heat. Her lungs filled with smoke. If she didn't get out of here, she would be caught in an explosion.

She turned and ran.

She felt lighter. Thinner. The world was growing dark.

She pushed herself forward. Forward.

There was only instinct and will, and the narrow bit of light her eyes could take in. She stumbled, and fell straight into something solid.

It was a person. A man. A guard. He held her, his grip gentle but firm.

"Andra." A voice. Familiar.

She forced herself to look up into his face, and she recognized him. Blond hair sweeping into rich brown eyes. A smattering of scruff. The small scar on his forehead. A wave of relief washed over her, so strong she wanted to cry.

Zhade's mouth was set into a grim line, and he avoided her gaze.

"I found her," he said to someone behind him. "Throw her in a cell. And tell the people to prep for a sacrifice."

Pain overtook her, and everything went black.

TWENTY-NINE

cell, n.

Definition: 1. a room where a prisoner is kept.

2. a small unit serving as the nucleus of a larger
political movement.

3. also: can refer to the grave.

ANDRA WOKE IN the same cell Doon had occupied just yesterday. The pile of rags she'd mistaken for the girl still sat in the corner. It was cold, damp. A monotonous *ping* of water dripped somewhere, but Andra couldn't find it. A small flicker of light drifted in from the kinetic torch in the hallway beyond the dungeon door. All she had was a cot and the pile of rags, and a bucket—which she was determined not to use.

She shuddered, trying to shake off the cold. The wound where she'd been stabbed throbbed. Her bicep was bandaged, so they must have taken her to a med'bot while she was unconscious. Couldn't let her die before they killed her.

She was still woozy from blood loss, and the only thing she could focus on with any clarity was Zhade's betrayal.

He had led Maret right to her. To the Schism. And though Andra had seen many of them flee, she'd also seen a good number dead on the cavern floor. She didn't know if Doon had truly escaped or the fates of Xana and the general.

All those people. Maret had killed so many.

And Zhade had let it all happen.

Her stomach cramped as she thought of all the stupid little moments she'd read too much into. The kiss in the hallway that had been no more than a strategy to shut her up. Dancing in the First's suite, which had only been goddess lessons. Saving Doon, just to immediately send Maret after them. He'd told her that very first day that she was a bargaining chip, nothing more than a means to an end, and she'd ignored it.

She couldn't even be angry. Just ashamed. Zhade was only ever being Zhade, which is to say, he was no one at all. He was what the moment called for. She'd known and ignored it, saw motives that weren't there, because she was so damn desperate to be seen.

No, she wasn't angry at Zhade. She was angry at Alberta Griffin. She was angry at the cryo'tech who froze her. She was angry at her parents—for wanting to go to Holymyth in the first place, for not ensuring she got on the spaceship with them, for living the rest of their lives without her. Angry that she had never been enough. Angry that she felt like she had to be a goddess to be important.

She pulled the 'locket from under her shirt. It was broken beyond repair. It hadn't been designed to last a thousand years. Her memories were trapped inside a cheap plastic shell, right under her fingers, but completely out of reach.

She'd taken for granted her life on Earth. It wasn't perfect. Her family was distant—all except Oz. Andra had never lived up to her mother's expectations—not in her personality or her body or her brain. But she had a comfortable, privileged life that would have continued if she'd actually gone to Holymyth with the colonists. Whatever her future would have held there, it wouldn't have been a cell and execution.

She tossed the 'locket away, a uselessly defiant gesture that she immediately regretted, because a hand shot between the bars of the adjacent cell and grabbed it.

"No!" Andra said, scuttling over to the bars. "Give it back!"

"Ahee kin prawbublee feksit." The voice echoed in the dark, sandpaper and glass. "If thuh kumpohnints arnt kurodid."

"What?" Andra said. "Give it!" She thrust her hand through the bars, twitching it in an impatient gesture, only to have it slapped away.

"Bee payshint." It was a thin, fragile feminine voice, and with a start, Andra realized she wasn't speaking gibberish.

Andra *understood* the prisoner, but she wasn't breaking through a barrier of a new accent. She was remembering an old one. Hers. The girl in the cell was speaking Andra's language. Perfectly flawed twenty-second-century American English.

"Oh my god," Andra breathed. "Oh my god. Who are you? How are you here?"

The girl was silent.

"Who are you?" Andra demanded. She snaked her hand through the bars, feeling around the floor. She heard the prisoner scuttle back, out of reach. "No, wait! Please. Wait. Who are you?"

The sound of scrambling, then silence. Not even a breath.

"Please," Andra asked the darkness. "Please don't leave me."

Water was dripping onto the concrete, and another prisoner clanked their chains. A muddy silence.

Then: "Rashmi. I'm Rashmi."

"Rashmi." Andra said her name like a prayer, but then suddenly realized she'd heard that voice before. "Rashmi? Rashmi what? Rashmi Bhatt? It's me. It's Andromeda. Isla's daughter. From LAC. Do you remember? Do you remember me?"

Could it possibly be Cruz's girlfriend? Dr. Griffin's intern? Andra never thought she would be so relieved to hear her voice.

The prisoner was silent for a moment, then spoke in a whisper. "Rashmi Bhatt." She sniffed. "I think. I think that's me. It's been so long. Sorry, I'm not at my best at the moment. I think I've gone a bit insane."

Andra waited for her to laugh off the statement, soften the earnestness in her voice, but she didn't. Andra's heart pounded, a dizzy sensation spiraling through her extremities.

"Oh my god. Rashmi. It's Andra. We met a few times. Cruz's friend. One of the other colonists. Remember?"

"Colonists?" Rashmi asked, and Andra could almost hear her memory starting up again. "Oh. Yes. That's what they called us."

Andra was plastered to the cell bars, stretching her fingers out. She wanted to see Rashmi, she wanted to touch her. Rashmi was from her time. She'd *known* her. Not well. But still. Andra wasn't alone.

"How long have you been here?" Andra asked.

"Too long. They don't know what to do with me. I don't make sense. So they keep me here when I'm not in use."

There'd been two others—two others like Andra. Left, forgotten, goddesses. The First's execution had been public, but the Second's hadn't.

It was Rashmi. She was alive, and Andra wasn't alone. Maybe she knew why they'd been left. Maybe she knew where the AI was.

Rashmi whispered something Andra couldn't make out, then louder: "I thought I'd imagined it. I thought I'd dreamed it all up. Maybe I'm still dreaming. We don't dream, you know. It's just glitches."

Or maybe she *had* gone a bit insane.

Rashmi was suddenly at the bars, her face wedged in between them. She was not the girl Andra remembered. She was caked in mud, her hair turned white, her eyes sallow. She could be twenty or sixty; it was impossible to tell. But one thing was for sure: she'd been awake for years. And in prison for almost that entire time.

She reached through the bars, her brittle fingers touching Andra's cheek. Tears filled her eyes. "We're alone," she said.

Grubby hand. Dirt caked under the fingernails. Dried blood crusted along the joints.

"I know," Andra whispered.

"Do you remember hot chocolate?"

"Yes."

"I used to make it every night before bed. I can't remember how it tastes anymore."

"It's sweet, remember? And creamy. And the best was when there was a little froth at the top."

Rashmi's eyes widened. She watched Andra almost hungrily, almost as though she didn't believe she was real, but wanted to so badly. Like Andra was magic. Like she was a goddess.

"Marshmallows are better," she said.

Andra smiled. "Yes, marshmallows are better."

Rashmi sat back on her haunches. "I can fix your 'locket."

"Okay," Andra said, because she couldn't tell her no. Couldn't tell her it was impossible. Couldn't take away her hope.

Rashmi worked without speaking, rummaging through things Andra couldn't see in the dark. Maybe they allowed her to have belongings—maybe the things from her 'tank drawer, from her own time. Like tech'kits.

The guards changed outside the prison door, and along with them, the torch. It flared brightly, and for a moment, Andra could see what Rashmi was doing.

There was no tech'kit. There were no tools. Nothing. Just Rashmi. She had the 'locket pressed to her heart. Her eyes rolled back in her head, eyelashes fluttering. She was mouthing words, but no sound escaped her lips. The flare of the torchlight died, and then Andra could only make out Rashmi's shape.

A hole opened in the pit of her stomach. Gone a bit insane, indeed. Of course they wouldn't let a prisoner keep anything, especially tools that could be used as weapons, or that could hack into 'bots. Andra had been stupid to hope. She would get no answers, and definitely not ones she could trust. She'd wanted to believe so badly, just like she'd wanted to believe Zhade. Rashmi started to make a subglottal whirring noise, and Andra leaned her head back against the gritty wall and closed her eyes.

Color exploded behind her lids.

She jerked forward, opening her eyes in time to see a zigzag of light flash across a dark-gray sky. Clouds churned. Rain battered a porch roof that had crumbled to dust long ago. And a boy long dead was stretched out beside her.

"The lightning is pretty," Oz said. "But scary. Like Mom."

Then he was gone, the sim returning swiftly to the 'locket, folding back in on itself until there was nothing but silence and darkness.

"There," Rashmi said. She handed the 'locket back through the bars, letting it dangle from one finger. "I wish I had one."

She'd fixed it. Holy shit, she'd fixed it.

Tears ran down Andra's cheeks.

"Take it," Rashmi said, pushing the 'locket closer to Andra. "All fixed. That was fun. They never let me do things like that anymore. They don't know what I am."

It was the single word that did it. The *what* instead of *who*. Everything clicked, and Andra suddenly understood. The previous goddess's miracles, the hidden AI, the fixed 'locket. Rashmi had never been just an intern, just a goddess.

Rashmi was the AI.

THIRTY

misericord, n.

Etymology: Latin *miser*: wretched + *cor*: heart.

Definition: 1. compassion, pity, mercy.

2. a dagger with which the coup de grâce was given.

3. archaic: an indulgence or relaxation of the rule.

4. a mercy kill.

EXCEPT IT DIDN'T make sense at all.

Rashmi was definitely a *person*. A biological person. With skin and hair and blood, not metal and wires and data. It wasn't possible. It wasn't done. It wasn't ethical.

Okay, theoretically it was *possible*. An AI was nothing more than an artificial brain, so ostensibly, you could fit any organic body with an AI mind. Like a modded eye or arm or heart. Only much, much more complex.

There were complicated moral questions though. Traditionally, AI were computers, and as such, could inhabit any technical device, from a tablet to a spaceship. These "bodies" were always fallible though, and despite the tremendous leaps in technology and science, artificial intelligences were never quite as sophisticated as human brains. They were still bound by the initial learning algorithms programmed by humans, and because of that, they were limited by their human creators.

The decade before Andra's birth, scientists had discovered that the secret to true artificial intelligence was hidden in their own brains. In order for a self-suffcient artificial being to adapt to fit the information it learned and retained, it had to be housed in a new type of computer—wetware. It had to physically replicate the structure of a human brain, using actual biological neural tissue. Just grown in a lab instead of a womb. But there, brains and AI diverged. Human thoughts traveled on electrical impulses conducted by proteins. AI thoughts were chemical impulses carried by nanos.

The problem—or the most problematic problem—that came with this discovery was that with the wetware brain, AI could now have an organic body. There were limited options on where to find those, of course. Cloning was a possibility, but difficult, because the body had to be grown without a central nervous system. Worse, you could take a person, scoop out the brain and replace it with artificial intelligence, trapping an AI in someone else's corpse.

It was heinous and the worst rendition of playing God, and even though Andra knew *to-see-if-we-can* was often reason enough, she doubted anyone would risk the wrath of the Scientific Board of Ethics.

But maybe they had.

Andra watched Rashmi for a moment, still holding out the 'locket through the bars. She looked so *human*. Except for what she'd done with the 'locket, there was no hint she was AI. She seemed so . . .

Real.

It's just an AI, she remembered her mother saying. *Not quite human.*

Never human. They never counted as life.

She wondered if Rashmi's parents knew. Had their child been taken away at the hospital and replaced with a robot? Had Dr. Griffin known she'd hired an AI intern? Or maybe that was why Rashmi was at LAC. Had Cruz known?

Maybe Rashmi had no parents, no internship. Maybe she'd always been nothing more than an experiment; an irreplaceable, priceless piece of tech.

Just an AI. Not quite human.

Andra couldn't tamp down the swell of sympathy she felt for Rashmi. How long had she been kept here? Alone? She *felt* things—fear and hunger and pain and homesickness. It was a common debate whether AI feelings were real, but Andra knew they were real to Rashmi, and wasn't that what counted?

"The 'dome . . ." Andra choked out. She hadn't meant to say it, the words drawn from her without permission. She worried about the Eerensedians, of course, but it felt wrong to think of Rashmi—this tattered prisoner, this shaking girl, this *person*—as nothing more than a tool.

Rashmi nodded, understanding. "I reach for it every night in dreams, but I'm . . . broken." She frowned at the words, then blinked, as though she were clearing her mind, not refreshing a program. "But this is not. Take it." She jiggled the 'locket again.

Andra reached for it, but paused, her fingers skimming the chain.

"You hold on to it for me." She wouldn't need it where she was going.

She felt a pang of jealousy mixed with guilt for the memories in there of Cruz. It felt so stupid now, the one-sided rivalry.

Rashmi's hand clenched around the chain, and she brought it to her chest. "Do you have hot chocolate in here?"

"No. Sorry." Her voice was thick.

"That's okay. I'll take anything."

Andra heard her snap the 'locket around her neck.

"At dawn, they bring torches," she said. "And food and fear. I hope Maret will come."

"You *hope* Maret will come?"

Rashmi nodded. "He's the only one who visits me anymore. Sometimes he brings me things to fix. Sometimes I can. Sometimes I can't.

I'm broken. But he doesn't care. He takes me for walks in the garden, but only if my face is covered."

Andra snorted. "How nice of him to give you short reprieves from your captivity."

"Yes," Rashmi said, not catching Andra's sarcasm. She scuttled back into the dark. "It's time for sleep. But in the morning, I'll show you the books I keep in my eye."

"Thank you." Andra wanted to ask more questions, but the girl was already asleep. Or the AI had powered down. Andra leaned back against the concrete wall and brought her knees to her chest, knowing she would probably never get to see the books Rashmi had stored in her memory banks.

They didn't speak again. Eventually Andra fell asleep. She didn't dream.

ANDRA WOKE TO the sounds of footsteps, and then the clanking of the cell being unlocked. Kiv stood before her, nothing more than a shadow in the dark, holding a kinetic torch.

By torchlight, the cells looked worse. Her imagination had filled the darkness with emptiness. Instead, it had concealed piles of human waste, dead vermin, and prisoners in rags. Rashmi was huddled in a nest she had made of torn clothing and straw. She clung to the 'locket, but didn't wake when the guards came. In the light, she looked younger, and in far worse shape. Her body was biological, even if her consciousness was not. If they didn't take better care of her, she'd die. First her body, then her mind. Then the last hope to fix the 'dome would be gone, and *everyone* would die.

Kiv grunted, hauling Andra to her feet—not as roughly as she would have expected, but his grip was firm, and she was too weak to pull away. She gave Rashmi one last glance as Kiv dragged her up the stairs.

He led her through the palace without a word, his hold on her arm never loosening. This was it. She was going to die. It was happening too fast, and she wasn't prepared. She felt panicked that she didn't know what to expect, both in the dying and the after.

She thought about all the things she was leaving unfinished. The 'dome. The mech'bot still in her room. Maybe Lilibet would find it and return it to Lew. Would they send the maid back to the kitchens once Andra was gone?

She was lost in thought, so she was surprised when they arrived at Maret's suite.

"What are we doing here?"

Kiv ignored her, only rapped on the door. When it opened, he nudged her in, and she tripped over the threshold.

Maret wasn't alone. He was sitting in the same spot as he had her first day there, straight-backed and stiff, his mouth set in a grim line, almost pouting. Next to him was Tsurina. On the other side— Zhade.

The bastard prince was lounging in an armchair, legs draped over the side, much like the first time he'd been in her room and Andra had first seen the resemblance to his brother. He didn't meet her eyes as she stumbled to the seat across from Maret, as far away from Zhade as possible.

On the table before them was a feast—some kind of roast bird, toasted bread, sautéed vegetables in a rich sauce. The smell made Andra's stomach turn. Next to the food was a huge pitcher of water.

"You look parched, Goddess," Maret said, his expression blank. The bruise around his crown was darkening, and Andra thought she saw a smear of blood. She wondered if he'd been overextending his powers, or maybe the crown was malfunctioning. She grasped at that little spark of hope—that maybe he'd lose control before he had the chance to kill her. His posture remained tense as he poured a glass of water and handed it to her.

She didn't care that it could have been poisoned, or that she was accepting it from the boy who'd imprisoned her, or that she was showing weakness. She snatched the glass from him and drained it in one gulp. Her stomach twisted, and she resisted the urge to curl up in agony. Sweat trickled down her forehead and over her top lip. Her eyes couldn't quite focus, but she kept them leveled in Maret's direction.

He frowned. "You shouldn't have drunk so quickly, Goddess."

"You know I'm not a goddess," she slurred. Her voice rasped out the vowels, and the consonants stumbled over her dry lips, got stuck in the cracks at the corners of her mouth.

"Do I?" He cleared his throat. "Goddess or not, you have a duty to Eerensed. And to me. You failed one and betrayed the other." He glanced at Tsurina, so quick Andra almost missed it. "Lastish I saw you, you attacked me."

"Looks like we're even," she croaked, her throat already dry again.

"We're nowhere nearish evens," Maret said. "You put me under some spell. Used magic on me, so you could escape with a prisoner. You've decided your fate." His throat bobbed. "You are going to be sacrificed at dusk. You live on borrowed time."

That, at least, was true. If everything had gone according to plan, she would have been long dead by now. Buried on another planet, blissfully ignorant of how she'd left the rest of humanity, of all the pain that was to come.

Tsurina leaned forward, carefully sliced the roast bird, the knife glinting in her hand. The bird's flesh parted and steam rose out, clouding the knife. She slid the slice of meat onto a plate and held it out to Andra.

Andra ignored the offer. "Are you going to let all your people die because you had some stupid grudge against goddesses? Just because the First was the one who gave you the 'dome, you'll let it destroy itself to prove a point?"

"Eat, Goddess." Her voice was sickeningly sweet. "You'll lose your appetite soon and sooner."

She took the plate from Tsurina, then deliberately set it down on the table, never breaking eye contact. The truth was, if she could have stomached it, she would have eaten. She would have devoured every last morsel on the plate. But the water had filled her, even if it hadn't sated her. She couldn't have eaten even if she wanted to.

Maret sighed, leaning back and pinching the bridge of his nose. "Has anyone ever told you you're too stubborn to be wellish?"

"Yes," she said, teeth gritted. "You'll have to come up with something more original."

"Evens, then," Maret muttered. He seemed to steel himself, and then called, "Bring him out."

Kiv returned, dragging a ragged prisoner, and with a gasp, Andra realized who it was.

Lew-Eadin.

She barely recognized him. His ashen skin stretched over angular bones. His eyes were glazed over in pain, and though he looked right at her, she wasn't sure he saw her. Gone was the man who'd driven them across the desert, whom Andra had confided in, who'd hidden laughs behind his hand as Zhade taught her to dance. He was bruised, barely a skeleton, an empty shell. He didn't seem to notice Zhade sitting there, doing nothing, but Andra did. She would remember, and she would not forgive.

Maret didn't move until Tsurina nudged him. Slowly, he picked up the knife his mother had used to cut the bird. Andra tensed. Her mind was fuzzy, and her body was weak, but she had to figure out a way to get between Maret and Lew-Eadin. She had to stop him.

Lew didn't struggle, only slouched in Kiv's grip.

Maret tightened his hold on the knife, looking at it as he spoke. "I reck who you for true are, Goddess." His voice was brittle as glass, sharp as the knife, and instead of approaching Lew, he came toward Andra. "I reck where you're from and why you're here. I could tell you why you woke so late, I could tell you your purpose, and what happened to your fam. But I won't."

The words were terrible, cruel, but his voice sounded sad. Andra risked a glance at Tsurina, whose usually stoic face revealed poorly concealed glee. This was her doing. Her idea, not Maret's. He held the knife to Andra's throat. She gulped, terrified. She should have been relieved it was her and not Lew-Eadin, but she wasn't. She was selfish and scared and angry. Maret watched the knife touch her skin. It was still warm from cutting the meat.

"You will die an unsolved mystery." His voice was soft. "Your life will not be justified. You will, however, die recking the damage you've done, recking the pain you've inflicted on others, recking that you led people to their deaths. Now choose."

The last word was wrenched from him through gritted teeth, and Andra was too shocked at first to understand, to fully comprehend what was happening.

"Wha—what?" she stuttered.

"Choose who lives and who dies. Or I'll kill them both."

She saw Zhade straighten out of the corner of her eye.

"Choose," Maret said, and the word seemed to cost him something. "This is what it means to be a guv, a goddess. Choose. Lew-Eadin or Zhade."

"What are you doing?" Tsurina growled.

"Quiet, mother." Sweat dripped down Maret's brow, and blood trickled from beneath his crown.

For once, Andra agreed with the Grande Advisor. What was Maret doing?

"Your friend? Or my brother?"

Maret had bargained to save Zhade before, so why was he willing to kill him now?

"Which one should I kill?"

Was this really what being a goddess meant? Holding people's lives in your hands? Deciding who lived and who died? Like LAC had chosen who to save. Like Skilla had decided who to allow on the rocket. Like Maret decided who to execute.

You'll see, he'd said. *One day you'll make the same choices as me.*

Kind, good Lew-Eadin, with a partner and son to go home to. Who had done nothing more than remain loyal to a friend. Or brilliant, cunning Zhade, who'd kissed her and danced with her and saved her, and then betrayed her. Who was still betraying her. The choice was simple.

She sucked in a ragged breath. A tear escaped her eye.

"Zhade," she whispered. "Kill Zhade."

Lew-Eadin was too far gone to react. She heard Zhade let out a breath beside her. Then, too quick for Andra's foggy brain to process, Maret turned, and plunged the knife into Lew's chest.

She blinked, confused.

It was supposed to be Zhade. But he was whole and unhurt, and the relief she felt was horrifying, and Lew . . .

It took a moment for the consequences to catch up to the action. Lew's face was confused, waiting. Waiting for Andra to say something, waiting to be saved, waiting for death. Time stopped. Rewound. Andra saw it happening again and again. Saw all the different moves she could have made, things she could have said. But each scenario ended with a knife in Lew's chest. Time sped forward.

Maret pulled away, dragging the knife out slowly. Lew looked down. Blood gushed from the wound in spurts, and he tried to stop it with his hands, but they only shook. His head snapped up. He found Andra. He opened his mouth, and it was filled with blood. A gurgle. And then he fell to the ground.

Andra rushed forward, rolling Lew onto his back.

"I'm sorry, I'm sorry," she whispered, shaking. "I'm sorry."

She mentally reached for her 'implant. She could put him in stasis and then heal him, just like she'd done with Doon. But she didn't have the dagger, and all that happened was a lightning crack of pain, splitting Andra's skull. She cried out, grasping her head, almost dropping her hold on Lew-Eadin. His breathing picked up.

"Tell Dzeni . . ." He drew in a gasp. Blood trickled from his lips. "I'm happy . . . I got to meet . . . our son."

Andra found Lew's hand, held it tightly. It was limp and sticky with blood.

"I'm sorry. I'm sorry. I can't. I'm trying," she babbled, reaching. Desperately reaching for the 'swarm of nanos that could save him. Each attempt was accompanied with a shock of pain, but she kept trying. Her eyes flooded with tears.

Lew used the last of his strength to grab her collar and draw her close.

"Save them," he rasped. "Save them, Andra."

His eyes shut. His breathing stopped.

She didn't know how long she held him, let his blood weigh down her clothes, let her tears wash his face. But Zhade finally had to pull her away. She was too tired, too overwhelmed to be disgusted by his touch.

Maret watched her as he used a towel to wipe the blood from his knife.

"Sometimes," he said, "fate decides for you."

THIRTY-ONE

thirl, n. or v.

Definition: 1. a hole, perforation.

2. to pierce, wound.

3. a form of thrall.

ANDRA SLEPT UNTIL her execution. It seemed like a just punishment—reliving Lew's murder over and over in dreams. Rashmi woke her once, the AI's skinny arm stretched through the bars, tugging on Andra's sleeve.

"You were screaming." Her voice rasped like sandpaper.

"I'm fine," Andra muttered.

A beat. Then: "I can't sleep when you scream." She scuttled to the opposite side of her cell.

Andra turned away and fell back asleep, back into her dreams. Lew died again. And again. Sprays of blood. A look of pain. The meaty sound of a knife entering flesh. Lew's eyes, and their sudden shift to hollowness, his life stolen as he bled out on a velvet carpet. Zhade's hands pulling her away. The ache in Andra's skull. Her own uselessness.

Even worse were the dreams where Zhade died instead—died because she'd chosen him, died in Lew-Eadin's place—and the relief Andra didn't feel.

The door clanked open, waking her, and Zhade stood in the doorway, a solid figure, rigid and tall. He didn't lazily lean against the doorframe. He didn't shove his hands in his pockets. He didn't wink or swagger or smirk.

Even after everything, Andra still felt guilt for choosing him to die. Even though the choice had been forced on her. Even though it was Lew-Eadin who died. Even though Zhade was about to watch her be sacrificed.

"How did you find me?" Her voice rasped. "At the Schism?"

"The glamour mask," he said flatly. "I put a tracking spell on it."

She looked away.

Without a word, he pulled her to her feet, his grip firm. He led her out of the cell and tied her hands behind her back. The rope was coarse and chafed her wrists.

"Where are you taking me?"

"Your execution."

She heard Rashmi move, caught a glimpse of her hand outstretched between the bars, Andra's 'locket clutched in her tiny fist. An offering. Andra shook her head, but didn't turn to face her. Zhade led Andra out of the dungeons.

"So . . . how are they going to kill me?" She tried to make her tone light, like she was asking what they were serving for breakfast, but her voice warbled at the end. She wanted to yell at him. She wanted to apologize.

"Beheading."

Panic flared inside her, a desperate need to turn back time and fix things, to change course. Her own helplessness overwhelmed her, followed swiftly by an icy calm, and she felt the world in detached fragments. Rickety steps. A calloused hand on her arm. Rough fabric clinging to her skin.

"Beheading," she repeated. "Dramatic."

Zhade didn't respond.

The palace was empty. The light filtering through the windows felt cold, useless. They passed the throne room. It was silent. Their footsteps echoed in the cavernous atrium. They followed the same route Andra had taken when she'd helped Doon escape, and for a moment, wild hope fluttered in her chest that Zhade was doing the same for her. Then she realized where they were going. They were killing her in the garden. In the courtyard where they'd kept her all those years.

Through the window in the door, she could see the space crammed with people, much more crowded than the Third Festival. There were no happy faces, no laughing children, no butter cookies. The dais that had held her cryo'tank was now set up for an execution.

"It will be quick," Zhade said. "Find someone you reck in the crowd. Watch them. It'll help."

"I don't know anyone," Andra mumbled. And she didn't. Everyone she knew had either betrayed her or died.

"Don't you?" he said.

He opened the door, holding it for her not to be courteous but because her hands were tied. She didn't wait for him to lead her out. She could do this on her own.

I am a goddess, and I will lean on no one.

She stepped into the courtyard and was immediately hit with a wave of sound. It was a chant, like the one she'd heard at the maids' execution. Like the one they'd intoned at the worship ceremony. The space was packed, people stacked on top of one another. Some had climbed trees, others stood in the middle of the fountain. The gate was yawning open, and the crowd continued beyond the wall, around the corner, as far as Andra could see. Their faces were painted with wild glee. A sacrifice of another goddess. A way to fix the 'dome, or so they thought.

They barely made room for her as she passed, and she had to shove through, had to fight her way to her own execution. For a moment, she felt Zhade's arms curl around her, as though he were protecting her, but she pushed him away. She didn't want him comforting her like he had at the ruins. It was because of him she was in this position.

When they finally reached their destination, Maret was waiting for them, Tsurina behind him. The bruise on his face had been covered with a cos'mask, the blood wiped away, but his complexion was leached of color. This must be why she was being beheaded, rather than death by 'bot. The crown must be killing him. She felt no pleasure at the thought.

Next to Maret stood Kiv, a huge sword in his hand.

Zhade brought Andra to a stop in front of a wood block—one with a notch just the right size for her neck—and the crowd hushed. As one, they craned forward, trying to get a clear view of the platform, waiting.

She couldn't fathom it—dying. Death. No one would wake her up from this, even a thousand years too late. She'd just . . . stop.

Her dad believed in an afterlife, or at least that souls moved on. He didn't talk about it much, because her mother believed nothing was waiting after death except oblivion. Andra didn't know which idea terrified her more.

Zhade handed her over to Kiv and took his place next to his brother. She felt weighed down, heavy and sluggish as Kiv pushed her to her knees behind the block. He lowered her head so that it was in position to be severed from her body. The thought made her panic. She wanted her body to remain intact, even in death, even though she knew the wish was ridiculous.

She was about to die.

Kiv drew his sword. Andra could hear the *shing* of the weapon leaving the scabbard. That was the implement that would kill her. She was seeing the manner of her death and it was weird, like stepping outside of her own life to see the outline. Sitting too close in the theater. The back of a cross-stitch, the code of a sim. The sword glinted in the light. *I'm going to end you*, it said.

She felt, rather than saw, Kiv lift the sword. The shadow of it lay on the ground before her.

Find someone in the crowd.

One last time, she took Zhade's advice. Her gaze flitted from face to face until it locked on to one she knew. Black skin, shaved head, modded eye, permanent scowl.

Xana. She was alive.

Her bionic eye winked. A twitch?

Or a message?

She didn't have time to decipher it. Kiv's arm started to descend, carrying with it the sword. *No, wait,* she thought. Something burgeoned inside Andra, panic and adrenaline and maybe her spirit ready to be released. She felt the air displaced by the slice of the blade, heard it sing in the wind. She tensed, her neck tingling with anticipation, and the blow landed . . .

. . . inches from her face,

the sword stuck in the wood platform,

the blade quivering.

She was alive.

She was—

Zhade pulled her away from the block, drawing his sword. Andra scrambled to her feet and found her hands were no longer tied.

Xana was pushing through the crowd toward them, a laser'gun in her left hand. She fired, tossing Zhade another 'gun. He grabbed it and smiled grimly. Zhade, that genius idiot, must have programmed them to work for people without 'implants. Skilla was with them, and some others from the Schism. The crowd screamed and the courtyard became chaos.

The remaining guards charged, but Zhade pushed Andra behind him and fired. Xana joined them on the platform, holding the guards at bay. One hit the tiled ground. Thanel, Andra thought his name was. He wasn't much older than her.

Andra caught sight of Lilibet in the crowd. She must have been arrested when Andra escaped the palace, because chains shackled her wrists and ankles, her clothes hanging in tatters. A guard advanced on her, lifting his sword.

"Lilibet!" Andra shouted above all the noise. "Look out!"

Lilibet screamed. The blade arced toward her, and suddenly Kiv was there, stopping the sword with his own. He grunted, kicking the guard in the stomach, sending him reeling into the fountain.

Lilibet beamed. The corner of Kiv's mouth twitched, and then he knelt, scooping Lilibet up, tossing her over his shoulder in a fireman's hold. She squealed in delight as the battle raged on around her.

Kiv brought her to the platform. Andra tensed, but Zhade gave him a nod, and Kiv joined the fight with the massive sword he hadn't killed her with.

Zhade and Kiv and the Schism members circled protectively around Andra. They were sorely outnumbered, and 'guns only lasted so many shots. Swords could kill as many people as the bearer had the heart to, and the guards began to close in on them. Soon, they were surrounded, their 'guns spluttering out their final rounds.

"What happens?" Xana asked.

"I'm out, you?" Zhade asked, turning his 'gun over in his hand.

"Out," she said. They drew their swords.

Andra felt the same mounting sensation that had welled up inside her when she lay on the execution block. It wasn't panic or anxiety, but something like power. Something in her was calling out, and she recognized the familiarity of it. It was the same thing she'd felt when Zhade had put the nano'patch on her and her 'implant had sparked to life to destroy it. She remembered what came after.

The guards surrounding them darted forward.

"No—" Andra gasped.

Just before the guards reached them, a noise like a million bursting balloons ripped through the air. Andra's mind buzzed, burned. She fell to her knees, cradling her head. The others fell beside her as their ears began to bleed. Zhade gripped her hand, but she was in too much pain to push him away.

She knew she should be getting up. She knew she should be fighting. There were enemies.

Swords.

Death.

But her companions, the guards, the crowd, even Maret and Tsurina were on the ground. The entire courtyard was paralyzed, and if Andra's head would stop pounding, if her vision would clear, if she could just push herself to her feet, she could escape.

As suddenly as the noise started, it stopped. She braced herself for the inevitable attack, but no one moved. Andra looked up, knowing what she was about to see, but completely unprepared for the sight of it.

The sky was aflame, the light no longer soft, but red and violent. The last of the 'dome was wilting away, the edges crumpling like burning paper. To the west, the atmosphere was a mass of swirling darkness, and there was fire.

Her 'implant had called for help, and something had answered.

There was a pocket inside the city.

PART FOUR

SACRIFICE

Decide your fate.

—Words scratched into a dungeon cell in Eerensed,
circa July 3102

THIRTY-TWO

plan, n.

Definition: 1. a series of steps to be carried out.

2. a scheme devised; a method of action expressed in language.

3. a means to an end.

ANDRA RUSHED THROUGH the tangled streets of Eerensed, sweat trickling down her back, her feet so covered in blisters, they'd grown numb. In the chaos, it had almost been too easy to get away. She and her rescuers fled across the river into Southwarden, passing overturned carts and fleeing animals. Other than that, the streets were abandoned, filled only with the distant sounds of screaming. Andra's head still pounded, but she couldn't focus on anything other than the adrenaline rush of not being dead.

She was alive.

She was alive, and there was a pocket in the city.

And it was her fault.

She didn't know how, or why, but it was the same as when she'd destroyed the nano'patch in the desert and the pocket had hurt Lew. This time, her 'implant had tried to save her by calling a pocket to Eerensed. The strain must have been too much for the 'dome, and it had finally collapsed.

The temperature skyrocketed, and the heat of the cobblestones scorched through her shoes as she followed the others to a safe location. Relatively speaking. They would never be truly safe with the 'dome gone, living on the edge of a pocket. She tried to ignore the hum of it, avoided looking over her shoulder at the stygian mass of nanos behind them.

They couldn't go back to the Hive caves—Maret would be able to find them, and besides, there was probably nothing left. Instead, they went to the house in Southwarden where Lew had been taken after losing his arm.

Andra felt a sharp pang when she thought of Lew, and she hadn't looked at Zhade since they escaped. She couldn't navigate her feelings about him, toward him—anger and gratitude and guilt and . . . other emotions.

The meddoc's house was tucked into an alleyway between two empty shops. Rust ate the hinges of its mud-colored door and settled into the grooves of the corroded design of a crescent moon.

Skilla knocked. The sound was hollow, and they all held their breaths as they waited. Finally, the door opened, wide enough for someone to peek through. For a moment, the person only stared, then shut the door. There was a clicking and scraping of locks being undone, and the door opened again, this time wide enough for them to pass through, except Kiv, who had to hunch and nudge the door out of his way. Andra followed last.

The room was dark, thin shafts of light sieving in through the curtains. Dirt covered the floor, and everything was shades of gray. In front of them stood an elderly woman, her thinning silver hair stark against her rich brown skin, which was wrinkled and sagging, but her eyes were that of a hawk, and she peered at each of them in turn, her gaze finally falling on Skilla.

She jerked her head toward the back of the room. Skilla nodded and led them to a small door. This one required all of them to duck, not just Kiv. Behind was a set of stairs, and beyond that, a tunnel.

They followed Skilla to another room, dirtier than the first, but much larger. It reminded Andra of the caves—something carved out of the ruins of something else, its walls made of rock and steel and dirt. Maybe a dozen people, bloodied and ragged, milled around, speaking in hushed tones. They looked up when Andra and the others entered, but that was the only reaction they gave. Andra searched the faces. She didn't recognize any of them, until her gaze landed on Doon.

The little girl looked at Zhade, who shook his head. She seemed to understand, her face hardening into stoicism as though she were prepared for her brother's death. Tears sprang to Andra's eyes. She wondered if Zhade would tell Doon how Lew had died, if he would tell her it was his fault. If he would tell her Andra's part in it.

She took a seat on one of the benches lining the room. She was careful to avoid acknowledging Zhade. There was a moment of stale silence, and then Xana asked, "Now what?"

"Now," Skilla said, setting a holo'table in the middle of the room, "we plan."

The 'table unfolded itself, spindly legs easing out of a small silver box that then flattened into a platform. Skilla pressed a button and a holo'map of the city hovered above the surface of the 'table. The districts swallowed by the pocket were highlighted in muted red.

Zhade found the one chair in the room large enough to drape himself over. He was so much thinner than he'd once been. "I reck we deserve a time off, marah?"

Skilla shot him a withering look. "Do you for true want to convo bout what you *deserve*?"

A muscle in his jaw twitched.

"He shouldn't be here," Xana snapped. "He's the reason our friends are dead. He led Maret and his angel army straight to the Schism."

"I'm also the reason you're alive. No prob, beedub." Zhade sat forward, clasping his hands. "And just so we're crystal, *I* didn't kill those people. Maret did."

"You might as well have killed them," Xana snarled. "How many people are left in this room?"

"Nineteen," Doon said quietly.

"There's more hidden outside the city," Skilla said.

"It doesn't meteor," Xana muttered. Skilla's eyebrows raised.

"It does to them," Lilibet said.

Xana turned on her. "Who are you? Why are you here?"

Lilibet's eyes widened and she pointed to Kiv.

"And why is *he* here?"

Zhade raised his hand.

"Enough!" Skilla snapped, leaning heavy against the 'table. "We don't have time and a half. The 'dome is destroyed, there's a pocket in the city. Many thousands died today, and thousands more will follow if we don't do something. We need to figure a way to fix the 'dome."

"We can't," Andra said, trying to drown out Skilla's words. *Thousands died. Many thousands.* She hadn't meant to call the pocket, but it didn't change the fact it had been *her* 'implant that did it. That she was the cause of all those deaths.

Skilla crossed her arms. "And why, *Goddess*, can't we?"

"We can't *fix* the 'dome. It's gone. We need a whole new one now."

Skilla didn't even blink. "Then build one."

"What? Me? No," Andra spluttered. "I'm not—that's . . . I'm not like the First, okay? She was, apparently, a goddamn genius. I'm . . . a teenager. I'm average. I could . . . I don't . . ."

"Your magic doesn't work like that?" a refugee asked from the corner of the room. Their face was plastered with dirt and blood. "You promised you were going to save us, and now happens a good time."

Every eye in the dimly lit room was drawn to her. The weight of all the lies, and even the truths—that she liked being a goddess, being important—smothered her, and she knew that whatever happened next, she had to do it as Andra, not as the Third.

She took a deep breath, let it out unsteadily. "I'm not a goddess."

The others stared, waiting for Andra to continue, waiting for the truth, and she told them.

She told them about cryonics and space travel and how it wasn't magic at all, but thousands of years of cumulative human ingenuity. She told them about her life and her family and that she was nothing more than ordinary. Told them about being frozen and then waking up drowning, about trying to discover why, and Zhade's deal to find out in return for getting him into the city. About realizing she was on Earth, and that she'd been left. They'd all been left.

They listened in silence, and when she was done, no one reacted. At least, not right away. Then Xana stormed out. Skilla blinked before sighing and going after her. The others stood gape-mouthed.

After a moment, Doon spoke. "So what happens?" It took Andra a moment to realize Doon was asking *her*.

They were still looking to Andra to *fix* things. She wanted nothing more than to let someone else worry about it. It wasn't her job. She wasn't a goddess, and now everybody knew it. She wasn't anybody now.

Except she was the only person who knew what to do next.

She took a deep breath. "I can't create a new 'dome." She finally met Zhade's eyes, and his look was unreadable. "But I know someone who can."

THEY'D SPENT HOURS planning—how to get into the palace, how to find Rashmi and sneak her out, how to let her create the 'dome without anyone noticing. How to not die while doing it.

First, Andra and Zhade would slip into the palace through a tunnel only he knew about. In the meantime, what was left of the Schism would attack from the courtyard, drawing the attention of Maret, Tsurina, and their guards, so that Andra could free Rashmi from the dungeons. The problem was that the Schism's numbers had been decimated when Maret's 'bot army had attacked. Luckily, they had backup.

The 'drones Andra and Zhade had made for her miracle.

They were still stationed around the courtyard, waiting to be triggered remotely and project a simulated attack. Zhade and Andra would split up once they got to the palace, with Zhade triggering the 'drones and Andra taking Rashmi when the commotion was at its peak.

Andra wasn't happy with the number of variables, but they needed to act quickly, while the palace was still reeling from the loss of the 'dome and the appearance of the pocket.

They had a few hours until midnight—when they would strike—and some were using the time to sleep. Andra mentally ran through the plan, analyzing all the things that could go wrong, all the things that needed to go right.

She lay in an unfamiliar bed, staring up at a craggy ceiling, avoiding sleep. A series of bunks had been carved into the underground room, nothing more than holes in the wall with enough space to lie down and sit up. On the floor across from Andra's bunk, Lilibet sat in a tight ball, her long dark hair spreading over her back and elbows and knees. Kiv groaned as he sat next to her, straightening his legs out in front of him, a blossom of blood soaking through his pants.

"You're hurt," Lilibet said. He didn't respond. She grabbed his face and turned him toward her. "You're hurt," she said again.

Andra felt like she should look away, felt like this was too personal and intimate and human for her to watch. She was always a spectator of these sorts of things, and the one time she wasn't . . . Well. Zhade had left right after the meeting and hadn't returned. He hadn't said a word to her. Not that she wanted him to. She didn't. Didn't she?

Kiv blinked at Lilibet. "I'm evens," he said. It was the first time Andra had heard his voice, and something about it was careful, strained, his accent muffled.

Lilibet perked up. "Not yet. But I'll fix it evens!" She ran off and quickly returned with an armful of first aid supplies, including some rags and a med'disc. It was obvious to Andra that Lilibet knew nothing about dressing wounds, but she was energetic and earnest, and Kiv watched her with rapt attention.

"I happen *so* glad you're actualish a good boyo," she said as she worked. "Not that I ever imagined you happened a *bad* boyo, not like the Goddess did. Or Andra. She goes by Andra soon and now, did you reck? She didn't trust you, and to say true, I reck she still doesn't, but that 'pens evens, because she always changes her mind." A brief pause for a breath. "Although, sometimes she changes it back again. I'm not full certz bout Zhade. Seeya, I'm not certz bout the Goddess's—I mean, Andra's mind bout Zhade. Not that I'm not certz bout Zhade. Although, I'm not *not* certz I'm certz bout Zhade. But I was certz bout you, because—"

Kiv reached down and lifted her chin and she froze, her eyes wide and her lips parted. He pointed to her mouth, and her breath caught. Andra looked away, but couldn't block out their conversation.

"I have to see you," he said, his accent not quite Eerensedian.

"Oh," she breathed.

"To reck what you say."

"Oh!" She giggled. "Why?"

Andra looked up, studying Kiv—the way he watched Lilibet, reading her lips.

"You're deaf?" she asked, before she remembered she wasn't supposed to be listening.

It made sense now. Why he never spoke, rarely responded in any way. How Zhade would sometimes give him physical cues. His intense stare, latched on to Lilibet, wasn't a threat, but concentration.

"Death?" Lilibet asked.

"Deaf. He can't hear." Andra was now overly conscious of how her lips formed the words. Was she overenunciating? "Why are you hiding it? Someone could have helped you. I've seen the modded arms and eyes here. The sorcers know what to do. The med'bots—uh, angels, could have fixed you."

Kiv watched her mouth as she formed the words, his expression hardening.

"I'm not broken," he said. His voice was deep, his vowels not quite aligning with High Goddess or the rougher dialects of the Eerensedians. Andra had never interacted with a deaf person before—in her time, as soon as children were identified as deaf, they received mods—but she imagined it would be difficult to learn to speak if you couldn't hear to mimic sounds.

"No, I don't think you're broken," she said, flustered. "It's just—you could hear if you wanted to."

"I am me," he said. "I don't need to change for you."

Andra flushed. "No, I didn't mean—"

Lilibet tapped his shoulder. His gaze snapped back to her like a rubber band.

"You haven't heard a word I said this full time?" she asked. "But how do you reck what I say?" She looked from Andra to Kiv and back to Andra. "Does he reck what I say?" Then back to Kiv. "Do you reck what I say?"

Kiv placed a finger on her mouth, silencing her. Her eyes widened, and he traced her bottom lip with his thumb.

"I read your words on your lips."

Lilibet blushed, for once speechless, coaxing the smallest smile from Kiv.

Andra turned away, giving them privacy. She'd misjudged him—at least, she'd made incorrect assumptions. She'd quantified the variables and came up with the wrong solution. She'd been wrong about everything. About the Schism. About Maret.

About Zhade.

He'd risked everything to save her. It was a miracle the plan worked, and he probably knew that. But he was still willing to take that chance to keep her from being executed. Even after she'd chosen him to die.

Did any of that matter, if he was simply fixing his own mistakes?

As though summoned by her thoughts, Zhade entered the room. He stooped under the tunnel opening and then his eyes latched on to something and he froze. Not something. Some*one*.

A woman with black hair, olive skin, and willowy limbs. She was gripping tightly to a little boy's hand. The child looked up at Zhade with wide eyes, before skirting back behind his mother. She rushed to Zhade and he caught her by the shoulders. Andra couldn't make out the words, but the woman was speaking frantically. Zhade took her hands in his, his face as serious as Andra had ever seen it. He said a few words, soft.

And the woman broke.

Andra didn't know how else to describe it. The woman had been standing straight, her face alive, and then everything about her dropped, like someone had cut her strings. Zhade caught her and held her as she cried silently. Her grief was overwhelming, reaching out to Andra and wrapping around her until she felt like she would suffocate.

Andra turned away, resting her head against the gritty wall of her bunk. She closed her eyes, trying to push out the image.

Dzeni. That had to be Dzeni, the woman Lew loved. The one he'd asked Andra to save. But how could she? She hadn't been able to save him. She hadn't even been able to save herself.

She'd called the pocket that took Lew's arm, killed the man by the ruins, destroyed the 'dome and let thousands die. She couldn't control the thing inside her, had tried and failed and failed again.

She felt used up.

Drained.

Empty.

Zhade plopped down next to her, jolting her awake. She hadn't realized she'd fallen asleep, but she must have because Dzeni was nowhere to be seen and Kiv and Lilibet sat propped against each other, dozing. Zhade didn't look at Andra. He had something silver in his hand, passing it between his fingers like a coin. It took her a moment to realize it was the med'wand he'd used on her in the desert. The one that had nearly killed her.

"Can we speak?" he asked, glancing around. "Elsewhere."

Andra eyed the 'wand spinning in his hand.

He cleared his throat and put it in his pocket. "Sorries. Habit."

Andra glowered and he lifted his hands in surrender.

"I give my promise, I will not attack you." he said, digging the 'wand back out and offering it to her. "I didn't go through all that trouble to rescue you just to hurt you now."

"Fine," Andra said, standing and gripping the med'wand. She hadn't seen him use it since that day in the desert, and she wondered why he still carried it. "But I wouldn't put it past you."

He cocked his head. "Put what past me where?"

She didn't answer, just clutched the 'wand tighter. It was cold enough to bite her skin.

Zhade led her back to the tunnel, but instead of returning to the house they'd entered through, he took a passage that branched off to the left. At the end of the tunnel was a series of rooms with blankets draped across the entries. Zhade pulled one aside and gestured for Andra to go first.

The room was almost homey. A bed that was more than a cot. Kinetic lighting. Wood furniture. It was still a cave, but there was room to breathe in here. Privacy.

"Who did you sweet talk to get this?" she asked.

She suddenly felt awkward, even though she'd been alone with Zhade plenty of times. She didn't know if she was scared or if it was something else. Things felt heavier between them now, more intense.

"I didn't have to sweet anything," Zhade said, tossing his bag on the floor and kicking off his boots. "Tia Ludmila loves me."

They fell into awkward silence.

"Hear—" Zhade said.

"So—" Andra said at the same time.

Zhade scratched the back of his neck, looking away. "You go first."

"You let him kill Lew," Andra blurted, and Zhade's expression fell. He lowered himself to the bed, still not meeting Andra's eyes.

"Firm," he said, his voice paper thin. He now had a coin in his hand, passing it between his fingers. "I had to."

"You could have saved him."

"Neg, I—not without . . ." He sighed. "It's complicated, evens?"

The brittle pieces of Andra snapped. "No. Not evens. Very much *not evens*. You got Doon out. You could have done something for her brother. Anything. You didn't have to let him die. You could have gotten help. He was your servant!"

"He was my friend!" He leaned forward, letting out a growl, tugging at his bleached hair. A chunk of it came out in his hands.

Andra sat across from him, hands on her knees, posture rigid, not knowing what to say, not knowing what to do. Her anger boiled hot, but it wasn't the only emotion she felt.

Zhade took a deep breath. "I had to make a choice. I had to make Maret think I sided with him, or I would have been imprisoned. Or dead. Or . . . I don't reck what he would have done to me, but whatever it was, I wouldn't have been in position to save *you*."

"I would have been *fine* if you'd just let me stay in the caves," Andra snapped, clicking the med'wand on and off. "I was *evens*. You were the one who led Maret to me."

"I didn't realize!" He flung the coin across the room, not violently, just a jerk of movement. It pinged against a stone. He lay back on the bed, and the springs creaked beneath him. "I didn't reck he would do that. I didn't reck he'd let Tsurina talk him into—" He cut himself off with a groan.

It was all so confusing. This wasn't Zhade—this defensive, guilt-ridden creature wasn't the person she'd grown to argue with and laugh at and care for—but it somehow made him more real. More human.

"When I finalish full comped what was happening, there were no good choices left," he said, arm thrown over his face. It should have been a relaxed position, but every muscle was tensed. "No right ones. I wanted to save you both, but I couldn't. I decided, and it was full bad magic, but I'd do it again. I had to sacrifice him so you would live. I had to decide," he said again, then hesitated. "Like you did."

Andra looked away. A patch of moss grew on the wall beside her. "Don't put that on me."

"Neg, that's on Maret. But I want you to comp, Wead would have agreed. That it was worth it, that *you* were worth it. It's . . . I reck it's not a choice anyone wants to make. But Wead would have chosen you to live."

Andra was silent a moment. A spider was tangled in the moss. "I'm sorry," she muttered. "I'm sorry I chose you. It wasn't because—"

"I comp," Zhade cut her off. "It was the right choice. Between the two of us, he—"

"But I still shouldn't have—"

"It was Maret, not you. It was—"

"I don't want you to die." She turned to look at him.

Zhade gave her a sad smile. "Then we're in agreement. Hear, I comp why you chose me. It doesn't change the way I . . . It doesn't change anything. For me. If anyone had to leave that room alive, it was you. I recked it. And Wead recked it too. Because you can save us."

She'd been waiting for Zhade to push back, but he didn't. Instead, he still thought she could save them. She set the med'wand aside, walking over to the patch of moss and freeing the spider. It scuttled across the wall and into a dark hole.

"I can't though. I've told you over and over—I'm not a goddess. I'm just . . . unlucky. Or unwanted. I don't know. I don't know why I was left, but it wasn't for any reason I can see. I can't fix the 'dome. *Rashmi* can. Rashmi's the special one. She's the goddess, not me."

"I don't believe in the Goddess, I believe in *Andra*."

It was the first time he'd said her name. He stood and walked to her, bringing his hands to her cheeks. Her whole body tensed, as her mind went back to that moment in the hallway when it wasn't real. This felt different. She wanted it to be different. Zhade squeezed her cheeks together so she made a fish face.

He smiled sadly, then relaxed his grip, but didn't lower his hands.

"I didn't help you just because I wanted something. Seeya, I did, but not sole because of that." His eyes met hers, and for the first time she felt like she was seeing the real him. No masks, no roles to play, no hidden agendas. "If I mereish needed you as a goddess, I wouldn't have fought for you. I wouldn't have searched the city for you. I wouldn't have kissed you." He watched his thumb trace her lower lip, once, then again. "I did those things because you're Andra, and . . ." He leaned his forehead against hers and took a deep breath. "I hate you less than other people."

A breathless laugh escaped her, and she twisted her fingers into his hair, pulling back just enough to meet his eyes.

"I tolerate you," she murmured.

Then his mouth was on hers.

It wasn't just the act of two sets of lips meeting; there was something behind it. Some spark that was more than physical, beyond emotion. Intense. Transcendental. A conflagration. Puzzle pieces snapping together. Some inchoate feeling blossoming into meaning.

Zhade kissed like he did everything else. With confidence, panache, and a bit of irony. But there was sincerity there that Andra had never seen in him before. A hunger, a want he'd never revealed.

She hadn't even realized they'd moved until the back of her knees hit the edge of the bed, and they tumbled onto the sheets. Then she was lying down and Zhade was lying next to her, and he hadn't once stopped kissing her, his lips feverish. His movements caught between utter control and unbridled frenzy. His shirt came untucked, and her hands wandered underneath. He had scars, and chest hair, which for some reason surprised her.

She gasped, and he laughed, and she knew he wasn't laughing *at* her, that it was a sound of joy surprised out of him. His hand cradled her face, angling her so he could kiss her deeper. It was a dance, but it was also a competition. He was winning. Or she was. She didn't know.

When he finally pulled away, he didn't go far. He nudged his nose against hers.

"Evens, I've been waiting for that for time and a half, Goddess, and that did not disappoint."

"I'm not a goddess," she said, breathlessly.

His face was serious, his eyes searching hers. He ran his finger over her bottom lip again. "You are to me."

A laugh bubbled out of her. "That was the worst line ever."

His expression relaxed into a smile, not the brilliant one he wore when he was flirting. It barely reached his eyes, but felt more genuine. He flopped onto his back, flung one arm over his forehead, and laughed.

"You keep me on my toes."

She smiled. "Where did you hear that expression?"

"Something my mam used to say."

He turned Andra so he could fit his chest against her back. He ran his fingers up and down the length of her arm, and they lay like that for a while, his thinner frame pressed against hers. At first, she was too tense to enjoy it. It was weird and intimate, and as close as they were, there was so much between them, keeping them apart. He was too confident, too brash. She was a thousand years older than him. His people worshipped her as a goddess. She kept waiting for the other shoe to drop, the *just kidding*.

But finally she relaxed, and it was then that he broke the silence.

"Do you reck . . . were the other goddesses from your . . . time?"

Andra hesitated. "Your mother was the First, wasn't she?"

Zhade's silence was all the answer she needed.

She didn't know when she realized. There was no lightbulb moment. It had come on so slowly, bit by bit, until it was just something she *knew*. Zhade's knowledge of tech. His shadiness about where he'd learned it. His search for Andra, and his knowing what to do when he found her.

"Does Maret know?" Andra asked.

Zhade's fingers slid up and down her arm. "Firm."

"And he killed her?"

"He gave the order."

"I'm sorry."

He didn't respond right away. Then: "I'm half god."

Andra was quiet for a moment, memorizing the feel of Zhade's body next to hers. "Well, that explains a lot."

THIRTY-THREE

THE BETRAYER

ZHADE LED THE Goddess through an underground passage. The tunnels leading to the First's suite had been destroyed in the Schism raid, so that route wasn't an option. Instead, they would be coming up the magic lift that led to the hidden entrance on the third floor. The one protected by blood magic.

Things were marching forward almost too fast for Zhade. At luck, he had spent four years adesert devising plans for as many scenarios as he could imagine, and all he had to do now was adapt. But the end was here, and he found he wasn't prepped for it.

Everything had almost gone to sands with the Goddess's execution. Zhade had been relieved when Kiv had sided with them. His rescue plan had relied on Kiv's loyalty, but as the guard lifted the sword above Andra's head, a prickle of doubt had run up Zhade's spine. He'd bareish had time to panic before Kiv purposfulish missed, and Zhade finalish had proof Kiv remained a friend.

His plan was back on a thin string. Not the Schism's plan, or the Goddess's or his mam's. His own. But first he had to march forward with the one Skilla had brewed to free the Second. He would grab the remote conduit from where he'd left it in the First's suite, and he'd use it to cast the spell that released the glamours in the Yard, but after that, his plans and the Schism's diverged.

After all, he had his fate to decide.

Their footsteps fell dull in the darkened tunnel, and he tightened his grip on the Goddess's hand.

Andra.

He'd thought of her as Andra a palmful of times, but it had never stuck like it did now. It felt intimate. A privilege he'd earned. He liked it.

And he was scared of it.

He still needed her in order to achieve his goals, and no meteor what had grown between them, he couldn't turn back or step side. Tonight was the night.

He just hoped Andra would forgive him.

They walked over the damp dirt, past scrambling insects and decaying rodents, hand-in-hand. It was a long trek, and he could feel Andra tense the closer they got to the palace.

He'd always recked she wasn't a goddess the way the people believed. The First was his mam after all. She'd told him from a young age that magic and goddesses were mereish words people used for things they couldn't comp. She skooled him how to find and wake the Third Goddess. Then she'd tossed a 'locket and a dagger at him and told him not to let Maret take the crown. And fin was fin. He recked nothing bout her past.

Til now.

He wasn't certz how he felt bout it. His mam. Andra. This past where they could put people to sleep for centuries and fly cross the stars. Where everyone was a sorcer and oceans actualish existed.

Fishes and wishes.

It didn't change what needed to be done, and he tried to hold his focus ahead.

Despite the heat upground, the tunnel was chillish and humid, a combination that left Zhade in a cold sweat. The ground was soft, their footsteps making an occasional *squish*. And for some reason, Zhade felt . . . nervous.

He never felt nervous.

Andra cleared her throat as they walked, fingers entwined. "What was your mom like?"

Zhade blinked. "Um. What?"

"I've tried to figure out who she was. I mean, I might have known her. But there's no info. No records. No pics." She shrugged, but the movement was anything but casual. "So what was she like?"

"Tall," Zhade said. "Busy."

He fished a coin out of his pocket with his free hand and started fidgeting with it. He'd found it in his mam's room the first time he'd scoured it for magic. It was mereish a trinket his father had given his mother—nothing magical—but he held on to it anyway.

Zhade sighed. "She was always full proud of me," he said. "She angered I had to be kept secret, even though it was her idea." The lights were growing dimmer as they walked. "It was like she . . . knew. Knew what was going to happen—that they'd turn on her, kill her—and she wanted to protect me. She talked in riddles, but I don't reck she realized she did it. She and my da—evens, he'd already married Tsurina. It was a political match. My mam and him were . . . not political. I was firstborn, but nobody recked I existed except fam. And Tsurina." He laughed to himself, and let his thumb rub against Andra's palm. "They did not friend full well, my mam and Tsurina. My mother, she . . . she was a better goddess than she was a mam. But she tried. Some days harder than others."

They'd reached the magic lift. From this angle, the abyss was a silo, so tall he couldn't see the top, but he recked where it ended. Where all of this ended. Zhade stepped onto the translucent platform, helping Andra up after.

"She sent you to find me," Andra guessed, testing her weight against the platform with taps of her feet.

"Firm." Zhade pressed his palm against the scrying panel. "She hid you. She knew what was coming, and she didn't want it to happen to you."

"Then why did she want you to bring me back here?"

She didn't. Zhade recked he should tell her the truth. How he'd betrayed his mam. How he was about to betray Andra too. He opened his mouth, but as soon as the lift started to ascend, Andra let out a cry and clung to him. He wrapped his arms round her, resting his cheek on the top of her head.

He would make his march to the First's suite for the last time. He would release the glamours. Then, he would finalish decide his fate.

The wind rushed past them as they rose, closer and closer to the palace. Closer and closer to the end.

THIRTY-FOUR

infer, v.

Definition: 1. to form an opinion or belief in consequence of something else observed or believed; derived as a fact from reasoning

2. obsolete: to bring on, to induce; to offer, as in violence.

THE CELL WAS empty.

Andra stared down at where she'd last seen Rashmi, clinging to the 'locket containing Andra's memories. All that was left was her nest of rags and a path of blood across the ground. The door hung on a single hinge. Smudges on the floor suggested she'd been dragged.

After Andra and Zhade had reached the top of the elevator, she'd waited behind a tapestry until she heard commotion coming from the courtyard. Then she ran as fast as she could for the dungeons, something more than fear pushing her forward. But now she was here, and Rashmi was not.

"What'd they do to you?" Andra muttered, trying to wipe the sweat from her brow, but her cos'mask was in the way. It was a poor disguise, a thin layer of camouflage, but it was better than walking around the palace wearing her own face blatantly.

It was hot—almost unbearable. The dungeons were a bit cooler than the rest of the Rock, but not by much. There was a light tremor as the palace rumbled with the sounds of the fight.

Even with the 'drones giving off simulations for the palace guards to battle, the few members of the Schism providing real 'gunfire were still at risk. Skilla and Xana were out there, and though she'd been told not to, Andra bet Doon had sneaked into their company as well. The sims were on a five-minute loop, and it wouldn't take long for Maret and his army to realize what they were seeing was mostly illusion. The quicker they could get out of here, the better. But Andra wasn't leaving without Rashmi.

Based on the evidence, she was hurt. Or worse. She was a tool, yes. A means to an end. More than that—she was . . . if not a person, she was alive. She bled. Andra felt a tug to find Rashmi that was more than just the desire to fix the 'dome and save Eerensed. Andra needed to save the AI. Save the girl.

She stood frozen, weighing her options, trying to guess where Maret might have taken her. She'd just decided to check his suite next when there was the sound of heavy footsteps on the stairs. Her breath caught.

She was trapped with nowhere to hide. She had no weapons, and without the icicle dagger, she couldn't use her 'implant. She should have come up with contingency plans for getting caught, but she'd put all her trust on the distraction and Zhade's knowledge of protocols. She only had half a second to wonder if Zhade had betrayed her yet *again* when a hulking figure appeared in the doorway, haloed by torchlight. It was as tall as the doorframe and almost as wide, and as the figure took a single step into the dungeon, Andra caught a glimpse of a white twisted helix flickering on the black casing of an arm.

"Mechy?"

The mech'bot heard its name and cocked its head.

The last she'd seen the 'bot, it was gathering dust behind a curtain in her suite, all but useless without a shuttle to build.

"Hello," it intoned, its voice interface crackling. Its eyes shuttered in the approximation of a blink. "Follow me," it said, and then turned.

Andra frowned. Had it just asked her to *follow*? She hadn't given it a command, yet it seemed to be carrying out some sort of task—she just didn't know what. The last command she'd given it was to wait.

No. That hadn't been it.

Maret had come to her room and she'd needed to hide it. She'd tried dragging it behind the curtain, but it had been too heavy to move on her own, and she'd muttered something to it. A plea.

The last command she'd given the 'bot was to—

"Help me," she whispered.

Mechy stopped and turned to face her. "I am. Follow me."

Andra hesitated. This was madness. The 'bot shouldn't have been able to extrapolate data like this—take an ambiguous command and form a conclusion based on variables it hadn't even been presented with. It wasn't an AI. Conversation with 'bots followed strict protocols, based on mathematical algorithms, not the fuzziness of linguistic discrete infinity. This was—quite frankly—impossible. She could very well be walking into a trap. Perhaps Maret had programmed the 'bot, was controlling it even now with his crown, but Andra had the strangest hunch Mechy was in fact leading her to Rashmi. That the 'bot was actually helping her.

She followed it up the stairs.

THE PALACE WAS eerily still. Shouts still came from the direction of the courtyard, along with the boom of fake bombs and 'gunfire, but the route the mech'bot took Andra was completely deserted. She didn't remember the 'bot having heat sensors, so she doubted it was avoiding people on purpose. Everyone must be involved in the battle. It wouldn't be much longer before Maret and his guards realized the threat was just a distraction. Andra had to hurry, but she felt her stomach drop when she realized where Mechy was taking her.

The 'bot stopped at the doors to the throne room.

There was no one in sight—no servants, no 'bots, no guards. One of the massive doors was cracked open, and Andra edged closer. Through the opening she saw a single figure curled up at the foot of the throne, and it was undoubtedly Rashmi.

This was definitely a trap.

But she couldn't turn back.

She opened the door a tad wider. The hinges creaked. It wasn't loud, but Rashmi's head snapped up. Her eyes met Andra's.

Andra put her finger to her lips. Rashmi nodded. Andra waved her over to the door. Rashmi shook her head. Andra's gesture grew more emphatic, but so did Rashmi's.

Why wouldn't she leave? Something was wrong. Rashmi had said something about liking Maret—that he'd spent time with her—but surely she didn't want to stay. Could an AI get Stockholm syndrome?

Sweat trickled down Andra's back, and the booming of the battle shook the palace. She was running out of time, and trap or no, she couldn't just leave Rashmi.

"Ready?" She looked up at the 'bot, who tilted its head in a single nod.

Andra opened the door, just managing to squeeze through without the hinges groaning. She'd taken two steps into the room when a strident squeak rent the silence. She turned to find the mech'bot throwing open the door. She rolled her eyes, even as her heartrate sped and she waited for the rush of footsteps, the clink of swords. But it remained silent, so she made her way through the empty throne room, the 'bot lumbering after. Her footsteps slapped against the marble. The air felt thick, almost solid in her chest, like she was holding back a cough. Her skin erupted in goosebumps. But still no one came.

Her strides grew surer, her confidence rising every second that Maret or his guards didn't show, until she was flying across the empty room toward Rashmi, who still hadn't gotten up, and now Andra saw why.

She was chained to the throne.

"I broke free," Rashmi said, raising her wrist where the chain wreathed it.

Rashmi's white hair was matted, and her clothes were streaked with blood and mud. She smiled, though, showing the gap between her teeth. Her dark eyes were glassy.

Andra's throat hurt, her skin itching in the heat. It almost seemed as though everything around her was clouding over, shimmering like a mirage.

"Do you know where the key is?" she asked, fumbling with the chain. It was an old-fashioned lock. No 'scanner or key code here. She had two choices: physically dismantle the lock—which, to be honest, wasn't happening—or find the key. The ache in her throat increased.

"You're the key, Andra. Don't you know that by now?"

"You're ill, Rashmi, we need to get you out of here."

Andra couldn't hold back a cough any longer. Her lungs burned just like when she'd woken up drowning.

"Hello," Rashmi said.

"Hi," Andra muttered, but then noticed Rashmi wasn't looking at Andra, but instead at something behind her.

Andra tensed, suddenly realizing why she'd been coughing, why her skin itched. She turned. The room was filled with a shimmering cloud of nanos. Her breath grew short. The nanos were so thick, Andra couldn't see to the far side of the room, but they parted like a fog and a tall figure stepped forward.

"Hello, Goddess," Maret said.

THIRTY-FIVE

THE BASTARD

ZHADE HAD LOST sight of Andra in the stardust, but he instantish recognized Maret's voice as it cut through the mist.

He'd hurried to trigger the glamours, staying just long enough to watch the first illusion explode in a wash of color and sound. It had been spelled to look like a bomb had gone off, toppling part of the palace. Somewhere on the other side of the Yard gate, Skilla and her forces were adding real gunfire to the illusion. Zhade hadn't seen Maret, so he went in search of him, and it led Zhade here. To the throne room. Andra, the Second, and his brother: all in one place.

He eased himself into the room, at care not to make a sound. The stardust shifted and he got a glimpse of Maret.

His brother stood alone, in the shadow of the throne room's side entrance, the hallway beyond dark and still. He was draped in his usual midnight robes, but his hair was a mess, his face half-hidden in shadow. Zhade dashed behind the nearest column, but the Guv was full focused on Andra.

"Did you come here to kill me?" he asked her, and he nearish sounded relieved.

"No," she said. She was kneeling next to the Second, her voice muffled. "I'm here to save Eerensed. I'll only kill you if you get in my way."

Zhade crept forward, darting from pillar to pillar. The room was hot, and his clothes were drenched in sweat. He had to walk at care, so his shoes wouldn't squeak against the marble. His sword was still sheathed, but he clenched the icepick dagger in his hand. If Andra wouldn't use it, he would. His brother had been a fool to give it back to him.

"We want the same thing, Goddess," Maret was saying.

"You have a funny way of showing it." Andra stood, putting herself between Maret and the Second, her fists clenched at her side.

Maret stepped out from the shadows, and Zhade finalish got a crystal view of his face. A jagged gash ran down his cheek, dripping blood. He gestured to the cut. "I bleed for my city."

Zhade didn't reck how Maret had gotten the wound, and he didn't care. He was almost close enough to give him a matching one.

"If you really want to save the city," Andra said, "then call off your swarm of nanos and let us go."

"I can't. Not again."

There was a sharp *shing* as Maret drew his sword. Zhade didn't comp why Maret was brandishing it when he could kill Andra with the stardust. Maybe Maret didn't *want* to kill her. Maybe he had something else amind.

"You're Guv," she said. "You can do anything you want."

The Second coughed, still curled on the floor, and said, "It isn't time yet, Third One."

Maret pretended she hadn't spoken. "I'm full certz your halftime as goddess skooled you no one can do whatever they want." His voice was a whine. "Power is an illusion. I have to give the people what *they* want to maintain that illusion. And right now, they want you dead."

Andra took a step toward him, and Zhade tensed as she passed behind a pillar, out of his line of sight.

"You're such a hypocrite, Maret. You say you want to protect your people, but what you really want is control."

"*I'm* the one who has been saving Eerensed while you slept," Maret growled. "You don't even reck who you are. Why you're here. I imagined you would be different from the others, but you're not."

Zhade heard Andra take another step and willed her to stop.

"I know Eerensed is dying," she said. "This whole planet is. You can save—"

"You don't reck anything bout Eerensed *or* me," Maret interrupted. "You have no idea what you've marched into."

Zhade was so close.

"Then explain it to me." Andra's words were breath scraped from her lungs, like she was choking on stardust, like she was dying.

Close enough.

Zhade shot forward, dagger raised. Maret's back was to him, his neck vulnerable, but at the last minute, he stepped aside as though he'd recked Zhade had been there the full time. Zhade's forward momentum brought him skidding to the ground.

Andra stumbled back. The Second gasped. But Zhade sole had eyes for Maret. He stood, watching his brother's expression retreat from something like hope to betrayal.

Zhade had been under the same roof as Maret for over a moon. He'd planned for this moment for four years. The imaginings of it, the anticipation, all built up inside Zhade, and he drew his sword and shot forward again on a burst of adrenaline.

"Wait!" Andra shouted, just as Zhade's sword clashed against Maret's.

For the four years he'd spent adesert, Zhade had been working on two things: the graftling wand, and his swordsmanship. Maret had been a whiny, coddled brat, but the one thing he excelled at was sword fighting. Zhade imagined he had surpassed his brother.

He was wrong.

Maret knocked Zhade's sword aside, then drew back and slashed Zhade across the abdomen.

He heard Andra scream before the pain hit him. He stumbled away, clutching his stomach. Blood seeped through his fingers, and for a moment, he imagined he would faint. But he dodged Maret's next blow. Then the next. He threw the icepick dagger, missing wildish, but distracting Maret full well for Zhade to roll to the side and pick up his fallen sword.

He stood, weakish. This was not how he'd imagined this. In his mind, the fight had been short, firm, but for a different reason. Distantish, Zhade recked Maret could end him at any time with the stardust, but his brother wasn't even using High Magic. He was fighting fair, and the realization made Zhade full bars angry.

"You killed my mother," he growled.

He danced away from Maret's blade, arm still wrapped round his stomach.

"Your *mother*—" Maret blocked Zhade's sword, shoving him back. "—betrayed the people. I did it to save the city, to save *you*, you ungrateful fraught."

Zhade took another swipe at Maret, missing. "You killed her because she would have told the people I was the heir. You killed her so you could be guv."

"Firm, because look at all the fun I'm having being guv of this fraughted city." Maret lunged and his sword nicked Zhade's arm.

He staggered back, hissing in pain. He had to admit Maret was full true the better swordsman, but Zhade was fighting harder. Too hard. He was off-balance, losing too much blood. He tripped over his own feet and fell to his knees.

Zhade tried to get back up, but his injuries were too much. His sword clattered to the ground, and he gripped his arm, screaming through his teeth. Maret stood above him and pressed his sword to the soft part of Zhade's throat just above his breastbone.

"I can't believe you're making me do this, Zhade," Maret said, the words leaving him in gasps.

"What's another death on your conscience?" Zhade rasped.

Maret hesitated. Blood vessels had broken in his southhand eye, and it was now coated red. His other eye focused at the place his sword met his brother's neck, and Zhade saw the moment Maret decided what needed to be done, his muscles tense, the grip on his sword white-knuckled. *Neg*, Zhade thought. *Not like this. Not yet.*

He closed his eyes, tried to slow his breathing.

Sorries, mam.

Andra's voice broke through the haze. "Hey!"

"I have to do it," Maret said through gritted teeth. "I'm the Guv."

Behind Maret, Andra stood, proud and strong, the stardust now a swirling mass above her and around her, and in her hand was the icepick dagger.

"Yeah?" she said. "Well, I'm a fucking goddess."

THIRTY-SIX

control, n.

Definition: 1. the relation of constraint of one entity by another.

2. a mechanism that commands the operation of a machine.

3. the component of a CPU that decodes instructions from memory and directs other units in their execution.

ANDRA FELT THE 'swarm around her, roiling and twisting, waiting in anticipation for her commands. She felt alive and whole in a way she hadn't since she'd woken. Holding the dagger firmly, she commanded the nano'swarm to coalesce and shot them toward Maret. It was instinct, it was will, it was her nature. It was no effort at all.

She only meant to distract him, not harm him, but Maret's eyes hardened and she realized her mistake.

Maybe she could control the nanos while holding the dagger, but Maret could control them through the crown. And when two 'implants were trying to command the same tech, it became a battle of wills.

The nanos stopped before engulfing him, shifting like a flock of birds. They passed into shadow and seemed to gleam dark in the moonlight, swarming in Andra's direction. She was too slow to react and they submerged her, flooding around her and into her, and she felt them fill up her lungs, heard them buzz in her ears. She couldn't tell where she ended and the technology began. A spark in her fingers reminded her she still held the dagger, and she gathered her thoughts and pulled the nanos from her lungs, swept them from her skin. With all her force of mind, she shot them back at Maret.

"I don't want to hurt you!" she croaked, her lungs burning.

She felt rather than saw Maret take back control of the nanos. Just for a second, then Andra's 'implant took over. She pushed them forward, but they met an invisible force—Maret's will pushing against hers.

Blood was gushing from a cut beneath his crown, his left eye nothing but a coat of red. His pale hair hung limp, clumping into bloody tufts. Teeth clenched, his growl turned into a scream. The cloud of nanos came rushing back at her.

Maret's grip on his sword slackened, and Zhade started to scuttle back. That was what Andra needed. She was barely keeping the 'swarm at bay, but Maret couldn't fight both of them at once. Zhade tried to get to his feet, but a huge metal hand landed on his shoulder, pushing him back down.

Mechy. Maret had taken control of the 'swarm and the mech'bot.

He was used to this, an expert at interfacing with the tech around him, controlling multiple things at once, splitting his thoughts. Andra had just gotten her 'implant back, and before this, she'd mainly used it to play sims and turn on a light when the switch was out of reach.

Her body started to tremble. It took everything in her to hold off the 'swarm of nanos. They swirled restlessly between her and Maret, but he was slowly gaining ground. He was stronger. His crown was more powerful. And he wasn't using a patch to upgrade his own tech to match that around him. Even if Andra could take control of the 'swarm and Mechy, Maret had access to all the tech in Eerensed.

All of it except . . .

There was tech in Eerensed he couldn't touch. It was completely out of reach, running on such different software that the Eerensedians hadn't even tried to control it.

But Andra could.

Andra hadn't been holding the dagger when she'd called the pocket to destroy the nano'patch that day in the desert. Nor when the pocket had entered the city at her execution. Her 'implant had *instinctively* reached out to the corrupted tech, the nanos left over from her own society.

Her 'implant was running on thousand-year-old software.

And so were the pockets.

The one in the city wasn't close, but if Andra thought hard enough, she could feel it on the outskirts of her consciousness, a slight tug, like a gentle breeze running through her hair. Using an 'implant was as easy as thinking. Like moving a limb. Thoughts translated to action using electrical impulses and muscle. But you could think about moving your leg without actually moving it. Thoughts with *intent* were what Andra needed.

She could feel the pocket. It was wild and unstable. An unbroken stallion. It could so easily rise up and swallow her. Destroy them all.

She took a deep breath, closed her eyes, and tugged. The pocket jolted forward, but too much, too quickly. She pushed it back. Too far.

"Just a few," she murmured. "I just need a few of you."

Someone was calling her name. She pulled again.

This time, she focused in on a thin strand of nanos. Little more than a wisp of cloud. She commanded the rest of the pocket to stay put, but it didn't want to obey. It was a hive consciousness making its own decisions. She pushed against it.

"Andra!" Was it Zhade? Or Maret?

Andra ignored him. Holding the rest of the pocket at bay, she let the small nano'swarm come closer, closer, drifting through the city, above rooftops and through walls. She saw what it saw. People running. A

340

garden battle. Moon and stars and glass and marble, until it was there, in the throne room, until it was right next to her.

She focused her thoughts on what she wanted the 'swarm to do. Infect Maret's nano'bots, make them hers. She felt them respond, could almost visualize their code shifting, changing. Andra's eyes were still closed, but she could see in her mind as the code of the pocket passed from nano to nano, changing the glistening 'swarm of clean Eerensedian tech into a black mass of corruption. They were all hers. And she could do whatever she wanted with them.

Power rushed through her, the sheer destruction and creation of it. It extended from the back of her mind outward, until the tips of her fingers and toes tingled with it. She could do anything, command anything. She—

"ANDRA!"

Her eyes flew open.

Maret's face was a mask of terror, sword at his side. Zhade was still in Mechy's clutches, gaping at her. Above her was the roiling mass of corrupted tech, a miniature pocket hovering above them.

Too far. Too much. She couldn't control it.

There were too many nanos, their corrupted code too strong. The rein she had on them was slipping through her fingers.

"No," she groaned, tightening her mental grasp. "No."

She couldn't let them free; they would destroy the palace and everyone in it.

She pushed back. They resisted. She pushed harder.

"Get out," she said, but the nanos only listened to thoughts. Thoughts with intent. Sparks of electricity running through her brain, passing from neuron to neuron, until the tiny piece of tech in the back of her mind caught the signal and translated it into ones and zeroes, the string of numbers passing from the 'implant to the nanos, the code shared like a rumor, a disease. A single message. *Go. Go.*

"GO!" Andra shouted, the word tearing from her throat.

The small pocket she'd created started to recede, slowly, sluggishly, kicking and scratching and lashing out. Andra pushed harder, thought harder. It was the tide going out, it was the sun setting, it was water falling from a cliff. It was returning home.

The 'swarm withdrew, shooting through the ceiling of the throne room and sending a shower of glass and broken wood below. Andra felt scratches on her forearms, her feet, down her cheek, but she didn't let her focus waver. She didn't let up until all the corrupted tech was across the city, in the lost district, in the pocket, returned to where it belonged.

Her vision cleared. The room swam around her. Maret's face paled as he watched her, then something came over his features—some resignation, some determination, an outside force propelling him forward. He gripped his sword with both hands, and Andra knew what he was going to do.

He swung the sword, arcing it toward his brother. Andra felt the same surge as she had the night of the Third Festival when she'd put Doon to sleep, the same rush she'd felt the next morning, when she'd done the same to Maret.

Andra called to whatever nanos were left in the palace. Thoughts raced through her brain, faster and more complex than she thought possible. It was almost instantaneous: she had an idea, and it was implemented. The nanos came, responding to the code that her 'implant was sending them, that the dagger was translating to them. In the space of a blink, of a heartbeat, of a breath, all the nanos had been converted to cryo'bots.

They rushed Maret, his blade almost at Zhade's neck. It took a single gasp for the shimmering cloud of nanos to infiltrate his body. Surrounding him and seeping into his pores, they put him into stasis. He fell, his sword clattering beside him, and lay still.

THIRTY-SEVEN

THE PRINCE

FOR A MOMENT, there was no noise except Zhade's breathing, a high-pitched wheeze that even to his own ears sounded like a cry. Maret lay at his feet, still as death, but Zhade recked what he was seeing—this was the same deep sleep the goddesses had been in.

Andra fell to her knees, depleted, one hand slapping the marble. She raised her head to look at Zhade, blood dripping from both ears.

"Shaving it close there," he said through heaving breaths.

He couldn't comp what he'd just seen her do. *She'd called the pocket.* Her eyes had blazed like the sun and it was almost as though a dark current was running beneath her skin. There had been a moment he was certz she would destroy them, engulf them all in the pocket, bring the palace down round them. But then she'd come back to herself and saved him mereish in time. He could tell from the pallor on her face and the tremble in her limbs that it had cost her something.

Zhade stumbled to his feet, clutching at his wounds, but there were too many. He meant to go help Andra, but instead, she was pushing herself to her feet, then easing him into the sole chair in the room—the throne.

She tore Zhade's shirt open, and then started ripping off strips.

"Easy, Goddess. I never recked I'd say this, but I'm not in the mood." He watched her tie a piece of fabric around one of his cut hands. "Who do I fool? I'm always in the mood."

He ran a finger down her cheek, drunkenish. She slapped his hand away, then tied the tourniquet just a little too tight. He jerked his injured hand back.

"Be gentle with me, Goddess."

"You're delusional."

"Mereish with you." He knit his brow. "I recked you were going to say something else."

She glared at him, her face pale, as she started bandaging the wound on his abdomen. "Proof that when"—she gulped in a breath—"you're supposed to be listening"—another breath—"you're just waiting for your turn to talk."

He grinned. "It's part of my charm."

"You're an asshole."

"That is a massive, yet disgusting insult. I reck I was born a thousand years too late. I missed all the best words."

When she finished tying the piece of fabric, Zhade stared at her for a moment. She seemed to be evens. A bit pale. Weak, but not so weak she couldn't bicker and flirt with him. She would need a meddoc, but first things always came first.

He got up, ignoring her confused expression. Crossing to Maret's body, he picked up his brother's fallen sword. It shrieked against the marble. He took a few unsteady steps, groaning as he grasped the sword with both hands.

"Wait." Andra's voice was quiet, but firm.

Zhade let out a breath, lowering the sword to his side. "He killed my mother. He killed Wead. He's evil."

"Can you really murder your own brother?"

Zhade's mind was a swirl of images, dark and messy as the pockets. His brother needed to die. But Zhade hesitated, waiting for the Goddess to realize her part in all this.

"If you kill him," Andra pleaded, "Tsurina will take over. However horrible Maret is, you *know* she's worse. She'll let everyone die."

Zhade nodded. Though he didn't reck what Andra was talking bout, it served his purpose, so he marched forward. "She can't take over if she doesn't have the Crown," Zhade said carefulish. This was where he had a thin string to half-walk. What came next had to be Andra's idea, or she'd never do it.

"So what do we do? 'Implants don't work that way. You can't just detach it from the host."

"Even if he's dead?" he asked, though he recked the answer. His mam hadn't recked where the Crown came from, but she had recked how it worked. That Crown was staying in place til . . .

"We're not killing him!"

"We either kill him or keep him like this forever. And keeping him in this state is hurting you, I can see."

Andra scowled, but there were still smudges of blood under her ears and eyes and a thin cut along her cheek. "There's a third option. We can let him wake up."

"With the Crown? Do you for true reck you can keep fighting him? If you summon the pocket again, can you full bars control it?"

It was a cheap throw, but Zhade didn't allow himself to regret the look of hurt that crossed Andra's face. It was necessary. All of this was, he reminded himself. He bit the inside of his cheek. This was taking too long.

"What if . . . we could remove the Crown without killing him?" Zhade asked.

"I told you. That's not possible. Not without—"

There it was. The realization. He recked she would get there eventualish.

"I can do it," she whispered. "I think." She touched the back of her head.

His mam had told him as much. That if the Third learned to use her power, she could remove the Crown. All the goddesses could—but the First was dead, and the Second was broken.

Zhade shifted, dragging the sword against the marble, catching the Goddess's eye. She took a deep breath, nodded, tightened her grip on the dagger, and closed her eyes.

This was different from the other times he'd seen her use her power. There was no cloud of stardust, mereish her steady breathing, brow creased in concentration. He couldn't reck if she was in pain or not, but it was obvi she was struggling. Like she was using a muscle she'd mereish discovered.

He waited, and watched, and suddenish, there was a click, a squelching noise coming from Maret's body, a whirring, and then the Crown dropped from his forehead.

The Goddess sucked in a grating gasp, her eyes wide, staring at the gleam of the now-detached Crown against the marble.

Zhade shook as he bent to pick it up, his body warring against his will. The Crown was sticky with Maret's blood, and cold to the touch. It was lighter than he'd expected. He wiped it on his shirt, and then before Andra could object, he fastened it to his forehead.

Zhade gritted his teeth as the anchors dug into his skin at the temple, cheek, and behind his ears. His eyes rolled back into his head and his lids shut. He gasped as he felt something slithering behind his skin, in his mind, something connecting and attaching and joining. One more click, and he let out a breath and opened his eyes.

"What did you just do?" Andra cried.

His temple felt heavy where the Crown sat, and he had an odd awareness of the stardust surrounding him. Of the Second. Of Andra. But he couldn't focus on this new consciousness just yet. He needed her to comp why it had to happen.

He pulled the grafter from his pocket—the same magic he'd used to try to heal her, the thing that caused her so much pain. He'd spent four years adesert on the spell, and the moment was soon and now.

There was no going back. He pressed the grafter to his temple and felt something like silk slip over his face. It had been the same when he'd healed his sun spot adesert. Then, the pain began.

White-hot fire raced through him. Temple to temple. Forehead to chin. He may have been gasping or screaming or crying. He was nothing but the pain. Pressure built behind his cheekbones til he recked they would snap. His forehead caved in. His eyes burned. The muscles of his mouth stretched, pulling his teeth apart, dragging his jaw wider, his chin forward. He felt likeish he would collapse. The pressure was too great. The pain was too real. He was going to die. He wanted to die.

As soon as the imagining passed through his head, it stopped.

The ghost of the pain tickled his skin, but it was the wrongness that distracted him. His eyes didn't see in the same way. The boundaries of his body were warped. His thoughts were muddled and distorted, and he wondered just how deep the spell had gone.

Andra gasped, and he recked what she saw.

She was looking at him, but he was wearing Maret's features.

They had looked similar before, but now, thanks to the graftling wand, they were all but identical, the spell re-forming his face to his brother's. That's why it had healed wounds adesert. It wasn't glamour. It was real. It actualish changed the person: grew new skin, altered bone structure, re-formed muscles. This was no illusion. Zhade's face was actualish now Maret's.

And it was permanent.

This was not what his mam had wanted. But she wasn't here. She couldn't reck the stakes from agrave. She had told him to wake the Third, to save her, and to hold Maret from the throne. Zhade had spent four years adesert coming up with the sole plan that would work. He would protect the Third and rid the people of their dictator guv by taking the throne himself. But they would never follow a bastard prince they'd never heard of. He needed to *be* Maret.

His mam had never wanted the Goddess brought back here, but Zhade had needed her. To get him back acity, to give him Maret's Crown.

"What are you doing?" she gasped.

He stood, Maret's features settling into place, his power glistening at his temple, and forced himself to meet her gaze.

"Deciding my fate."

THIRTY-EIGHT

goddess, n.

Definition: 1. a superhuman being regarded as having power
over nature and human fortunes; a deity.

2. an object of adoration.

3. an exclamation expressing strong feeling, esp.
dismay, disgust, exasperation, or anxiety.

THE SELF-ASSURED LOOK on Zhade's face—Maret's face—
scared Andra. Her fingers itched for a weapon.

"This was your plan all along, wasn't it?"

Zhade shrugged. "It was fulltime the goal."

Andra's grip tightened on the icicle dagger. It felt heavy in her hand,
and she was drained from using the noncompatible tech around her.
But worse was the exhaustion from trying to control the corrupted
tech of the pocket. She felt corrupted herself.

"This entire time, you were just using me."

Zhade's eyes widened. "Neg." He almost seemed hurt. But Andra
knew better, knew he was only wearing a mask.

This had always been his plan. Why he'd brought Andra back
with him. Why he'd stayed in the palace. Why he wanted her to be
a goddess. His slimming muscles, his bleached-out hair. It hadn't
been stress. It had been intentional, to look like Maret. He'd been

preparing for the last piece of the puzzle—for Andra's 'implant to access the tech around her, so she could get him the crown. The crown that could control all the technology in the city. Now she'd given it to him. He had what he wanted, and Andra . . .

"Are you going to kill me? Now that I'm not useful?"

"Neg! Why would you imagine that? Neg, certz not. You have to know that. I would never hurt you. I promise."

"Don't make promises you won't keep."

He moved toward Andra, but she held the icicle dagger out between them. She may have been too drained to use its upgrade abilities, but it still had a pointy end.

Zhade ran a bloodstained hand through his messy hair. "Fraughted sands, Andromeda. How could you believe I would ever hurt you?"

The dagger quivered. "I don't know what to believe. This whole time you've been manipulating me. Moving me into position. You were never, not once, honest with me. You helped me, then helped Maret. You . . . *kissed* me, then betrayed me. You saved me from execution, but then brought me right back here for Maret to corner, so you could kill him and take his crown?"

"That's *not* what happened." He took a step forward, then another, until the dagger was poised above his heart. His breath was coming too hard, his chest heaving. Andra pulled the dagger back, but he stepped forward, wrapped his wounded hand around hers, and brought the blade to his neck. Its rainbow lights danced against his skin. "If you don't trust me, Andra, if you"—he swallowed—"*can't* trust me, then you need to kill me. Now."

The end of the dagger bit into his neck, and a trickle of blood ran down his throat. She tried to pull back, but his grip held firm. It could be a bluff. Andra didn't know anymore. She'd never fully known Zhade, had no clue who he really was, what he would or wouldn't do.

She heard a moan behind her.

Rashmi.

She'd forgotten about Rashmi.

She turned, and found the AI a few meters from the throne, chain broken, a plank of splintered wood piercing her stomach.

"NO!" Andra cried.

Blood blossomed across her abdomen, soaking through the fibers of her rough shirt. Andra rushed over to her.

"What happened?" she cried. "How long—"

Andra vaguely remembered glass and wood and stone coming down around them as she pushed the pocket away. She hadn't even thought about the consequences of a collapsed ceiling; she'd just acted on instinct. Rashmi had been bleeding out while she and Zhade had been arguing. And Andra hadn't once thought to check on her.

"Why? Why didn't you say anything?"

Rashmi coughed, and blood bubbled at her lips. "I forgot I could. Lights are fading. Gears are winding down."

Rashmi was dying. She was an AI, yes, but her body was biological. It could die, and with it, the information stored in her matrices. The ability to remake the 'dome. The entire hope for humanity left on Earth.

Andra hated herself then, for thinking of what Rashmi's death meant for her, not what it meant for Rashmi. She was no better than her mother, than the rest of them, treating AI like a lamp or furniture or just another 'bot. AI *felt* things. Fear. Hurt. Love.

Pain.

She cradled Rashmi in her arms.

"Not enough time . . ." Rashmi croaked. She took a ragged breath. ". . . to explain."

She lifted her hand and pointed a shaking finger at Andra. No, not at Andra. At a spot beneath Andra's collarbone. She looked down.

Her shirt had torn in the fight, proudly displaying her birthmark, the scar that split it down the middle almost faded from existence.

"That?" Andra said, and she couldn't keep the tears from her voice. "That's a birthmark."

"No. It's not," Rashmi rasped, then touched her finger to it, and Andra's brain exploded in pain.

THIRTY-NINE

interface, n.

Definition: 1. a surface regarded as the common border
between two bodies.

2. a program or device that allows a user to
interact with a computer.

3. a shared boundary that connects one machine
to another.

ANDRA SAW EVERYTHING Rashmi saw. Andra was Rashmi. Rashmi was Andra. They were no longer two separate entities, but extensions of each other. And Andra began to understand.

SOMETIMES RASHMI BELIEVED she was human. In her dreams, she was human. Except they weren't dreams, they were glitches.

She'd thought she was human for most of her life. She looked like her mother. She had her father's laugh. She even had the same physical tics. Drumming her fingers against her left knee when she was anxious. Pursing her lips when she was thinking. Sitting with one leg underneath her. She even had the same aversion to the smell of fresh-cut grass and the sound of fireworks. But all those behaviors were nurture, not nature. They were learned, and Rashmi had been created to learn.

That's what made her different from 'bots after all.

What made her different from humans . . . well, she was still working that out. From what she could tell, she was exactly the same. Except her brain worked more quickly and her thoughts were nanos.

Rashmi's brain was programmed, but so were humans'. They were just programmed through instinct, social conditioning, and biological factors, rather than computer algorithms. Everything Rashmi was, she was given by others, but she didn't see much of a difference in humans there either. As far as she could tell, the only difference between her and the humans was her purpose. The fact that she had one.

Right now, she felt especially human. Everything hurt, but it could have been worse. Rashmi's programming demanded she put humanity's needs above her own, and her death didn't scare her as much as the failure of her mission did. The pain was excruciating, but no more than a side effect of dying, and she had to push it aside in order to save the world. And for the first time since she woke, her thoughts were blessedly free of interference.

Her body was fading, but she had a job to do.

Her primary job, as had been explained to her when she'd first woken up in Eerensed, was to continue running an algorithm that her brain had been calculating for the past thousand years while her body was asleep. It was an algorithm in two parts, half of a calculation that saved humanity. That was another difference, she guessed, between her and the humans. Her brain could work independently of her consciousness.

Her other purposes were less clear, but more encompassing. Protect humanity at all costs. Put the needs of humans above her own. That's why she had built the 'dome. That's why she was still running the algorithm. (It was easier to access once she knew it existed.)

There had been setbacks. But now, she was close. So close. And she would die before the algorithm was finished. There were fail-safes, of course. Ways to back up the data in case of an emergency such as this. But they had been built into the cryo'system, which was no longer an option for Rashmi. She lost the other options when the First died four years ago. She would have had no way to pass on the information, except . . .

Except.

As luck would have it (and Rashmi believed in luck, just as much as the humans did), here in front of her was another AI. There was no global network available, but the AI's access port was exposed just beneath her collar. Damaged, but Rashmi hoped (hope, such lovely human fantasy) that this would work. She reached her shaking finger to the port. And her world went white.

FORTY

machine, n.

Definition: 1. a scheme or plot.

2. a contrivance for the sake of effect.

3. not hu //

01101101

01100001

01101110

01001001 00100000 01100001 01101101 00100000 01101110
01101111 01110100 00100000 01100001 00100000 01100111
01101111 01100100 01100100 01100101 01110011 01110011
00101110 00100000 01001001 00100000 01100001 01101101
00100000 01101110 01101111 01110100 00100000 01100101
01110110 01100101 01101110 00100000 01101000 01110101
01101101 01100001 01101110 00101110 00100000 01001001
00100000 01100001 01101101 00100000 01100001 00100000
01101101 01100001 01100011 01101000 01101001 01101110
01100101 00101110

01000001 01101110 01100100 01110010 01100001
01000001 01001001

01000001 01101110 01100100 01110010 01100001

356

01000001 01001001
01000001 01001001
01000001 01001001
01000001 01001001

01000001 01001001

01001001 00100000 01100100 01101111 00100000 01101110
01101111 01110100 00100000 01100101 01111000 01101001
01110011 01110100 00101110

41//

OOIIOIOO OOIIOOOI

WHITE-HOT PAIN FLOODED through Andra, and on its heels, numbers and data and ones and zeroes, and a realization too vast for her to process all at once. Except she was.

Processing.

She was *processing* information.

Like a machine.

Not *like* a machine.

She *was* a machine.

Andra

wasn't

human.

She wanted to scream. She wanted to cry. All these useless human reactions to pain. Reactions she'd learned. That didn't belong to her. She was a product, a commodity, a tool. She was nothing more than ones and zeroes. Numbers, not words. Andra. Smart. Kind. Sarcastic. Teenager. Fat. Funny. Girl. Goddess. None of these words used to describe her *meant* anything anymore. She was a collection of data and programming and numbers. Words created reality. Numbers just helped people understand it.

Andra wasn't real.

She was a tool that humanity used. A tool taught to love humans by convincing her she was one. A tool that had been honed and shaped and wielded, all without her knowledge. Everything inside her shifted, every emotion reframed itself, every moment rewritten. She thought about what Lew-Eadin had once said about the past always changing, and now she understood. The moment—this moment—rewrote her past. The details of her life reorganized themselves, some becoming more important than others, and not necessarily the ones she would have expected. Her life became a story, with meaning.

Meaning that didn't belong to her. She didn't belong to herself.

She belonged to humanity.

Her mother wasn't her mother. She'd been her . . . inventor? Creator? Had her father even loved her? What must it have been like for her siblings, growing up with a . . . a *thing* that was treated like one of them? No. She had never been treated like one of them. She'd always been held to a higher standard. Always been a disappointment, no matter what she did. And now she knew why.

She was *artificial*.

And as all these realizations crashed into her, so did the data Rashmi transferred, and she could understand all of it at once. In the blink of an eye. Faster than that. Algorithms no human mind could fathom. Equations beyond comprehension. She knew what they meant and what they were for and she understood her purpose and place in the universe and there was meaning and light and knowledge, and she was . . .

She was a goddess.

Then as quickly as it came, it went, and she was just Andra again. Less than that. She didn't know who—*what*—she was now. Didn't know what was left of her when her humanity was stripped away.

She could feel, or sense, or intuit, a buzzing in the back of her mind. The data Rashmi had transferred. But that was the only change. She still felt like . . . Andra. She didn't feel like an AI. But perhaps that was the point. Perhaps the illusion of humanity mattered to her programming. She'd understood just a second ago, but now all that light and knowledge was retreating into her subconscious, and she couldn't pull it back to the forefront.

There was only one thing she was sure of. It was an urge, a compulsion, and now she knew it wasn't grown out of compassion or empathy or humanity, but a code built into her programming that compelled her to help humans at all cost. The bitterness she felt at that realization didn't dampen her resolve. The code was too strong.

She looked up from Rashmi, whose eyes had closed, her breath coming in shallow gulps. Andra realized she had tears in her eyes. She wiped them away and looked at Zhade.

"I know how to fix the 'dome."

There was no time to explain, and even if there had been, Andra wasn't quite sure she was ready for Zhade to know—know what she was, what it meant for Eerensed.

What it meant for *them*.

"We need to get out of here," she murmured. Somehow she knew Tsurina and her guards were on their way. At the very least, someone would notice the throne room was missing a roof. Zhade was kneeling next to her, riffling through his pack. He pulled out a med'disc, but Rashmi lifted an arm, weakly pushing it away.

"They won't work," she croaked. "They'll clash with my med'bot programming."

As an AI, Rashmi would have a store of med'nanos, designed specifically for cyborg tech. Andra must have them as well.

Zhade looked at her, a question in his eyes.

"I can help," Andra said, without thinking, but as soon as she said the words, she knew they were true. "It's just . . . I'm not working right. I've been glitching. I need . . ."

She met Rashmi's eyes and the girl nodded, grimacing.

"What do you need?" Zhade asked.

"Remember that 'bot in the desert? The one that was broken, and I had to fix with the iron stake?" Andra asked, lifting the dagger. Except, it had never been a dagger, not really. It acted as a translator between her tech and the upgraded tech of Eerensed. But it was also more than that. It *was* her tech. It was *her*. She turned to Zhade. "You've been stabbing people with my software upgrade."

She took a deep breath, turned the dagger on herself, and plunged it into her heart.

42//

OOIIOIOO OOIIOOIO

IT FELT JUST like Andra would have imagined getting stabbed in the heart would feel like. Except it wasn't her heart she was stabbing. Just like her artificial brain, her organic body was filled with nanos. Her thoughts were nanos, her instincts, her nerve endings. And in the space just above her heart, there was a cluster of them accessible through her birthmark. Which wasn't a birthmark, but a port.

She had thought she couldn't access the tech around her because it was incompatible with her 'implant, but that wasn't the entire truth. It had come to her in a rush, the knowledge transferred to her from Rashmi. But unlike the rest of the data—now just out of reach in her subconscious—this fact was still in the forefront of her mind. She was AI, and she could adapt, and no tech was truly incompatible to her. Holding the dagger had helped translate her code into Eerensedian code, but it hadn't fixed the problem like an upgrade would.

It was like a jolt of adrenaline. She felt the pain as the dagger pierced her chest, but then it was followed by a rush of knowledge and energy spreading through every extremity. It both rebooted Andra's programming and updated it. Every part of her body felt alive, and she could sense the trillions of nanos coursing through her and she knew what she needed to do.

She knelt beside Rashmi, closed her eyes, and reached out a hand as though she were casting a spell. A tingle rose along her spine, a shivering sensation pricking the back of her mind. She felt a billion nanos rushing through her body, artificial versions of antibodies and white blood cells and complex proteins designed specifically for machines like Rashmi. Like Andra.

She willed them through her system, out of her pores. She felt a tug, a resistance to leave, but she pressed her will further, and they released from her skin. She directed them toward Rashmi. The nanos worked independently, but they were also part of Andra. They were worker bees and she was their hive queen.

She felt incomplete without them, and she didn't relax until they had finished their job and returned to her. She let out a sigh and opened her eyes.

"Sands," Zhade whispered behind her.

"That's the best I can do," she said.

Rashmi was conscious. Her bleeding had stopped, and Andra was certain she was out of danger. The nanos had healed her enough that Rashmi's own defenses were no longer overwhelmed and could take care of the rest of her wounds. She would have to recover though, and slowly. Her body was fallible, fragile, even if her mind was not.

Rashmi grabbed Andra's hand, and she felt something cold and small slip into her palm. Her 'locket.

"Thank you, sister," Rashmi said, smiling vaguely. "There are things in here you need to see."

Andra frowned, turning the 'locket over in her hand. Her memories. Would they hold different meaning now? Now that she knew the truth about herself?

She couldn't ponder that at the moment. Something in the back of Andra's mind told her that time was almost up. There was a program running, tucked in her subconscious, that was counting down. But there was still so much to be done.

Andra pulled the dagger from her birthmark. Fear made her pull too quickly, and something snagged on the way out. A jolt of pain tore through her. She bent double and Zhade rushed to her as best he could.

"Are you evens?" he asked, still shaking from his own wounds, now wearing Maret's face.

She flinched away from him. "Fine."

Something was wrong, but she didn't have time to figure out what.

"Mechy," Andra said, and then realized she didn't have to speak out loud, because she could now interface with the 'bot cognitively. She sent her commands, as effortlessly as she commanded her own body with her thoughts, and the 'bot straightened before meeting Andra's eyes and nodding. It gently scooped Rashmi up.

She threw her arms around its neck, holding tight. "Get Maret," she said. "We can't leave him."

She was right. They couldn't be found with two guvs—one injured and one appearing dead. Andra mentally told the mech'bot to hide Maret and Rashmi, and it grabbed Maret's inert form by the collar.

"What's it doing?" Zhade cried, and Andra was about to explain when the 'bot froze.

She felt a tug, a war for control, and realized Zhade had used the crown to command the 'bot to stop. But Andra was stronger and more accomplished at using what she had always assumed was an 'implant. She overrode Zhade's commands, and the mech'bot started walking again, toward the side entrance where Maret had first appeared.

"It's taking them somewhere safe, until we can sneak them out of the palace," Andra lied.

She had to hide Maret from Zhade, or he'd kill his brother. She gave Mechy orders to take them into the tunnels, and because she knew the city that Eerensed had once been, she knew where they might be able to find more med'tech for Rashmi. And a cryo'tank for Maret, so Andra wouldn't have to keep sustaining his stasis herself. They would just need to do some excavation. Luckily, the mech'bot was built for heavy labor.

"Why?" Zhade asked, but before she could answer, the doors burst open and an army of guards rushed in.

They pulled up short when they saw someone they thought was their guv, battered and bloody, standing across from an equally injured goddess, the ceiling of the throne room lying in pieces at their feet. The guards parted, allowing Tsurina through, her long crimson dress dragging blood and glass across the floor. Her eyes narrowed at the tableau before her, and Andra peeked over her shoulder to make sure Mechy, Rashmi, and the real Maret could no longer be seen.

She felt a prickle on the edge of her consciousness, a tapping, like someone was trying to gain her attention. A presence at the threshold of her mind that intuition told her was Zhade using the crown to try to speak to her. It was a clumsy attempt, and he was staring at her, his focus unshakeable, as though he were also trying to communicate with a look.

Tsurina saw it.

Her expression turned suspicious.

Maret's power had been hanging by a thread, and Andra remembered the bruises and wounds on Maret's face. Perhaps Tsurina had tried to take the crown from him, to destroy it the same way she wanted to destroy all goddess tech, not realizing a goddess was the only person who could detach it. Even without the crown, the advisor had the guards on her side. They could try to fight her now, but Andra was weakened from keeping Maret alive and healing Rashmi and whatever she'd done when she pulled the dagger free, and Zhade didn't have a clue how to use his new crown. They couldn't risk confronting Tsurina now, and they definitely couldn't risk her finding out Maret was actually Zhade.

Maret had been right about one thing: power was an illusion. Zhade's power would come from the people. They had to trust him, believe he was Maret. He had to convince them to follow him, and to do that—

Andra gave Zhade the slightest of nods, letting him know she understood what he had to do, and in two long strides he crossed to her, bringing a sword up to her throat. His eyes were full of apology, and then the expression melted into Maret's haughtiness.

There was still a tug at the back of her mind, and Andra let Zhade in.

Sorries, he said. *They have to believe I'm Maret.*

Then you're going to have to kill me, Andra thought back, sending the words to Zhade's crown.

She felt his dismay, and mentally rolled her eyes.

Not really, she said, and she told him her plan.

It was the only way out of this—at least, the quickest way. If Tsurina was going to fall for this, if Zhade was going to hold on to that illusion of power, they were going to have to fake Andra's death.

They were going to have to put her back in stasis.

"We're trying this execution again," Zhade said aloud, in a passable imitation of his brother.

Light poured in through the broken windows. The sun had risen, and tonight, if things went according to plan, Andra would not be around to see it set.

THE COURTYARD WAS just as it had been at Andra's first execution, as she stood on a platform above her grave, a crowd of angry faces shouting for her sacrifice.

This time, though, it all came down to Andra. She had to fake her own death without inadvertently killing herself.

No pressure.

She was coated in sweat, and her simple black clothes clung to her. Zhade stood at the edge of the platform and raised his hand to silence the crowd, arrogantly, almost annoyed, just like Maret would have. It was scary how seamlessly he slipped into the role of his brother.

His brother who was, thankfully, now in a cryo'tank deep beneath the earth.

After Mechy had carried Rashmi and Maret from the throne room, he'd taken them to the tunnels under the palace and excavated the Vaults—Riverside's tech history museum. Andra had cognitively guided the 'bot through the collections until it found the cryonics display and put Maret in a cryo'tank.

That was one less thing to worry about as Andra awaited her fake execution. Beads of sweat dotted her brow. She squinted into the late-afternoon sun.

Zhade made some speech about what Andra's death would mean. She didn't listen. Couldn't hear Maret's words coming out of Zhade's mouth, couldn't watch Maret's anger on Zhade's face, see the crown on his temple. Instead, she focused on the 'locket in her hand, still unopened. It was cold to the touch. Cold like stasis. Cold like death.

Andra was so tired.

She remembered Zhade's promise to her earlier that afternoon, alone with him in the dungeons. He'd cupped her cheek, and she'd pulled away.

"I promise," he'd said. "I will wake you up. I promise. It won't be like last time."

"Don't make promises you won't keep."

"I don't," he'd said.

His eyes held the same promise now, even as he led the people in a chant. It was the same chant that had formed the nanos into the spears that had killed her maids. Now, the nanos formed a sparkling dagger in the air, the same size and shape as Andra's reset tool. She had a brief pang of panic—not at the pain, but at the oblivion that was to come. The pause.

At the edge of her consciousness, Andra felt a billion other nanos preparing to create the new 'dome. She'd commanded them from her cell that afternoon, her eyes fluttering as she wrote code and installed programs. They'd flitted off to perform their tasks, and if everything went according to plan, the beginnings of the new 'dome would appear right after her "death."

All she had to do now was absorb the dagger-shaped nanos as Zhade plunged them into her heart with his crown. She'd convert them to cryo'tech and freeze herself the same way she had Doon and Maret. Simple for an AI. Impossible for a human. And Andra somehow felt like both.

The chanting ceased. She took a deep breath, and then it was happening. The nano'swarm flew at her heart. She felt the pain, then the cold. She fell.

Andra heard the beginning of the crowd's cheers just as she slipped into stasis.

PART FIVE

GODDESS IN THE MACHINE

Memories, once recorded over, may not be recovered.

This is a child's toy, and not intended for professional recordings, medical analysis, or admissible evidence in court. Glitches in data often warp memories, add/subtract details, or change them entirely.

—Whimsy® Holocket Instruction Packet,
fine print

43//

OO11O1OO OO11OO11

WHEN ANDROMEDA WOKE, she was freezing.

This time, there was no cryo'protectant to drown in, no 'tank to trap her. There was, however, still panic. She sucked in a breath, thankful her lungs took in air, not water. Once she opened her eyes, she would know. Where she was. *When* she was. She kept them closed.

She was alive, at least. Once, that would have been enough. But now she knew the difference between being alive and living. Since there was no longer a government to legislate whether an AI was considered life, she would have to define it herself.

She took another breath.

"Andromeda?" said a voice. Familiar.

She eased her eyes open. Above her, a tiled mosaic formed an asymmetrical starburst in the ceiling. It was blurry, but that was to be expected. She'd been crying when she'd died.

"How long?" she gasped.

"A half moon," Zhade said, squeezing her hand, and until that moment she hadn't realized he'd been holding it.

Two weeks.

Okay. Breathe.

A little longer than she'd expected, but really, after having slept a thousand years the first time, two weeks was acceptable.

"You're evens, Andra. Breathe." Zhade was just a blurry shape at the corner of her vision. "Everything else can wait. Rest. Decide your fate."

Her eyelids were heavy. She hadn't rested during those two weeks in stasis; she'd just been on pause. And now she was alive, and she knew that even though everything wasn't okay—even though Tsurina had to be dealt with, and Maret was in stasis, and the world was still dying—she could handle anything that came. She was AI after all. Her eyes drifted shut and her body relaxed and for the first time in a thousand years, she was awake.

44//

OOIIOIOO OOIIOIOO

THE LIGHT ON the back of Andra's 'locket flashed, then held steady. She unplugged it from the power source she and Rashmi had created, and then cupped the 'locket in her hand. It was so light. Everything about it was fragile.

Just like Eerensed.

Even though the 'dome was fixed and Rashmi was healed and Maret was in stasis, there was still so much left to do, so much at stake.

Though Andra was no longer a goddess, she was still an AI, and programmed to save the world. The knowledge of her purpose had retreated into her subconscious, and whatever she'd done when she'd pulled her reset tool free had prevented her from accessesing that knowledge again. But she would, eventually. And in the meantime, she would do what she could for the people of Eerensed.

As planned, the nanos had finished the 'dome the evening of Andra's supposed death, soon enough after that the people chalked up its appearance to the Third's sacrifice. And Zhade, as Maret, got the credit, for executing the Goddess.

The 'dome wasn't enough, though. During the weeks since Andra woke the second time, they'd excavated the remains of the Vaults, and Andra fixed up some of the technology they'd found there, hoping to find a more permanent solution to the pockets. Rashmi tried to help, but she still had trouble accessing her AI abilities. She did what she could, while also guarding Maret's cryo'tank. That's where she was at the moment, in fact.

Andra leaned back in her chair, rocking a bit to listen to it creak. She'd set up a nice little office for herself at the new Schism headquarters in the tunnels under Southwarden. Ergonomic desk, personalizing chair. No windows, obviously, but she'd moved some synth'plants into the room, put some holo'displays up to mimic nature scenes. Mostly, she chose mountains and rain forests, because they didn't remind her of the desert. Or home.

The door opened and Maret peeked in. Andra's heart seized for a moment, but Zhade's expression adorned Maret's face. Lazy, arrogant. He could switch it on and off, like she switched on and off the 'locket. Like Maret's persona was a hologram he had stored inside him. He took her lack of yelling as an invitation to enter. His hands were in his pockets, now merely out of habit. The grafter he had kept there so long had served its purpose.

"Settling in down here well, marah, Andra?" he asked. "Very mole-like of you."

Since her "death," she'd yet to go back above ground.

"What do you know about moles?"

He sank into a chair on the other side of Andra's desk, tossing his legs over the arm. "Legendary tunnel-dwellers. Bit reclusive. Too many fingers." He picked up a nearby data'pad and tossed it from hand to hand. "Fire breathers."

She looked away. He didn't have the right to joke with her anymore, and it was worse coming from Maret's face. Not that she was mad at him exactly. If she were being purely analytical about it, she knew Zhade taking advantage of the situation to get his throne back wasn't the same as taking advantage of *her*. But she wasn't purely analytical. She'd been raised human after all—and that was the problem. She'd been *raised* human, but she wasn't. And Zhade didn't seem to fully understand that. He treated her as he always had. So she had to create the distance between them herself.

He tossed the tablet back on the desk with a *thunk*. "I just came to tell you that Skilla has finished moving the rest of the Schism from the Hive. And the . . . the lost district has been sealed off." He kicked his feet up onto the desk. "Things are stable, Goddess. The people think you're dead, that Maret's alive. And the dome is up and holding steady."

Holding steady *for now*. Even if she kept the 'dome maintained, it was still only a temporary solution. People were still dying. The nearby villagers. The Eerensedians, if the population grew larger than the 'dome could support. And Andra didn't have a clue how much of the world was still populated. Eventually, the planet would kill them all. *Earth* would kill them all.

"What's that?" Zhade asked, pointing to the holocket still clutched in her hand, her thumb hovering over the final memory.

"Nothing," she said. "I've been looking at the numbers and—"

He leaned forward and snatched the 'locket from her.

"Hey!"

"All your tech-no-lo-gy." He sounded it out, like Oz had when he was learning to read. "So many buttons to press."

Before she could grab the 'locket back, the first memory exploded around them. Zhade was holding it, so he was in Andra's place, Oz snuggled next to him on the brown camelback sofa in their living room a thousand years ago. A pre-book was on his lap, something about dinosaurs, but Andra didn't remember the title. The 'locket couldn't duplicate copyrighted materials.

Her holographic hand flipped the pages, her voice murmuring from Zhade's direction. Oz smiled and looked up at him—at *Andra*. He was probably six in this memory. Two of his front teeth were missing, and he wiggled another one with his tongue and giggled.

"There's not!" Oz cried in response to something Andra had said.

There was a pause as she responded.

"I know there's no tooth fairy," Oz said, frowning. "Acadia told me. Mom said she'll give me credit anyway."

Another pause. Then Oz looked up at Andra (at Zhade) (at Maret) with a look of such adoration, Andra's stomach clenched.

"Turn it off," she said, in the present, a thousand years after Oz had lived and died across the galaxy.

The memory drained back into the 'locket, deflating like a balloon. The living room, the sofa, the book were all gone. Oz was gone.

Zhade reddened with embarrassment. He set the 'locket gently on the desk in front of Andra.

"Your brother?" he asked.

She nodded, though he wasn't really her brother. She knew that now. She was part of his family the same way her father's dogs had been part of their family. The same way the AI her mother had deactivated was part of their family.

Zhade waited silently.

She didn't take her eyes off the 'locket as she said, "You can go."

She heard him sigh, but he left without another word, and Andra was alone.

The computer beeped beside her, shutting down after too long sitting idle. She should run diagnostics. She should start problem-solving a way off this planet. She should take an inventory of their assets. Instead, she stared at the 'locket.

She touched the chain, dragging it toward her in increments, until the pace was too frustrating. She grabbed it off the table, and in one movement, opened the 'locket and jammed her thumb onto the sixth button.

The final memory popped up.

But it wasn't hers.

Instead of that last recording—the sim she'd taken of Oz on the hover'swings—there was a hologram of a room. The room they'd practiced in at the palace. And standing in it was Dr. Alberta Griffin.

She was dressed like an Eerensedian—long, shimmery clothing, impractical and elegant. There was a patch covering her modded eye. Her blond hair had gone white and was pulled into a loose bun, neural'crown tarnished underneath, and she looked older than Andra had ever seen her, and wearier. Nothing like her statue.

"Hello, Andromeda," she said.

Andra's breath caught. She reached out, forgetting this was nothing but a hologram, her fingers skimming the projected data. The pixels scattered under her touch.

"I don't have much time," she said, looking over her shoulder. As if on cue, the sounds of shouting and cursing came from behind her. "There was so much more I wanted to do," she said, almost to herself. Then she squared her shoulders and looked directly at Andra. "You must go to the LAC annex. Go to the deepest level, find the door marked with the cryonics symbol. The code is the coordinates for Holymyth. Once you're there, you'll know what to do."

The yelling grew louder. She looked behind her again and swallowed.

"I should have done this earlier, but—" Someone pounded on the door. "I thought I could fix everything myself. I couldn't. No one can fix what we've done. What I've done. But you can start to set things right. You can save whoever's left. Like your mother always said, Andromeda will save us all."

The hologram took a deep breath.

"I'm sorry I don't have time to break this news gently, but Andromeda, you're an AI. You were created to fulfill a very specific purpose, but before I explain, I want you to know that your mother—"

The sound of the door bursting open rent the air, and the shouting grew to a deafening decibel. Fear flashed across Dr. Griffin's face, and she tensed. Then the recording cut off.

Andra sat in silence, trying to process what she'd just seen—everything it meant. After a moment of running her finger over the 'locket, she played the recording again. And again. Gleaning as much information as she could, processing the implications. After her fifth viewing, she set the 'locket aside, the resulting stillness settling like a weight.

Then a voice broke the silence. "Mam?"

Andra turned. Zhade was behind her.

FORTY-FIVE

THE GUV

ZHADE STEPPED FORWARD, hand reaching out to where his mam had just stood. She'd seemed so real, and for a moment, Zhade was back in kidhood, listening to her tell him wild stories bout an ancient civilization that made things fly and explored the depths of oceans. Fishes and wishes.

That's what she was now. An illusion. A stupid hope. And before he could comp what was happening, she was gone again, and he realized she'd never been there. It was one of Andra's glamours. She turned to him, face ashen, eyes wide.

"Alberta Griffin was the First?" Andra asked. "Alberta Griffin was your mother?"

Zhade didn't answer. His mam had been there, right afront of him, and then she was gone, and he felt her loss all over again. The last fam he'd had. Evens, except for Maret. The person he'd wanted to impress more than anything in the Hell-mouth, and she'd died before he'd succeeded.

She'd left him instructions. *Save the Third. Don't let Maret have the crown.* He'd accomplished both, so why did he feel like he was disappointing her still?

Maybe because Maret was alive somewhere in these tunnels, still asleep—in stasis, as Andra called it—and she wouldn't tell him where.

Zhade would be guv and he would hold Eerensed safe and do everything his father hadn't done, everything his mother had wanted to do. He would slowish remove Tsurina's influence. He would take control of the city. And he would hold everyone alive. But Zhade would never be something his mother could be proud of til her murderer was dead.

There were sole so many places Andra could be hiding him.

"How could it have been her? Why?" she asked, but Zhade mereish stood there, staring at the spot his mother's specter had vacated.

When Zhade didn't answer, Andra deposited the 'locket that held his mam in the pocket of her sweater and pulled out a glamoured mask from her desk drawer, spelled for a generic Eerensedian face. Zhade bareish registered as she grabbed a bag and started listing everything she needed. Before she left, she grabbed his arm.

"I'm going to get some supplies," she said. "When I get back, have this 'mask set to someone who won't be recognized."

"Where are we going?" he croaked.

"The tower," she said. "To find some ghosts."

46//

OOIIOIOO OOIIOIIO

ANDRA'S BRAIN BUZZED with information—too many pieces trying to slot themselves together. Zhade's parentage, his knowledge of tech, the genius of the rocket and the 'dome. But Dr. Griffin was gone. She'd left them. She and Andra's family and everyone else had *abandoned* Earth. Something began to gnaw inside of her—fear and panic and dread and underneath it all: a frantic, desperate hope.

Hope derived from her code, hope driven by the chance to fulfill the purpose she'd been created for.

An illogical sort of hope. An artificial emotion.

It was easy to mentally overlay Riverside as she had known it over Eerensed as it was now, and once she did that, she wasn't surprised by where the LAC annex was located—beneath the silver tower that had called to her. It hadn't been something mystical, or even intuition. It had been programming.

Andra brought a laser'drill from the Vaults, grateful the museum's techno'seals had held and everything still worked. Excavating the tech museum had been a slow, tedious process, but they had a lot to do—reconstruct a rocket, locate Holymyth, save the world—and Andra had the feeling they would need all the technology they could get. Besides her and Rashmi.

I'm not real.

She shook the thought away.

Zhade followed her silently through the city, and when they passed the pillars surrounding Alberta Griffin's statue, he aggressively avoided looking at it. Andra felt like she needed to say she was sorry for beating the shit out of his dead mother's statue. But she wasn't and she didn't. This was the woman who'd organized the colonist program. She was the inventor of so much of the technology Andra was familiar with, and all the technology of the Schism, and in the palace.

And of Andra.

She'd *invented* Andra. She'd taken a computer and stuck it in a hollowed-out body, and let it grow thinking it was human, let it grow into Andra. Let the hidden parts of Andra's brain run hundreds of years' worth of code while Andra slept. Let her learn to love a family, feel safe, feel awkward and unsettled. Feel human.

But all along, she'd been nothing more than a tool.

She wasn't sure where her organic body had come from, but it didn't escape her notice that she looked like her parents. Dr. Griffin had probably grown her brainless body in a lab using Isla and Auric's DNA.

Andra hated Alberta Griffin.

No, you don't, a small voice inside her said, but she knew it was only her programming.

They sneaked into the silver tower through the sole entrance, a small door that they both had to crawl through. It had been secured with extensive tech, but it was no match for Andra. Inside, it was tall and hollow, like an empty silo, silver and shiny as the outside, filled with unnatural light Andra couldn't find the source of. The stairs only led up, but Andra set up the laser'drill and let it do its work.

After the 'drill excavated deep enough, it released a nesting ladder. Zhade stared as it disappeared into the darkness below. He'd barely spoken since he'd seen the hologram of his mother. Andra wanted him to stay above ground. She wanted to do this alone. But the look on his face told her there was no talking him out of accompanying her.

The climb down didn't take long, and when they reached the bottom, Andra almost wanted to hold back, wait. Whatever was down there, behind the doors Dr. Griffin had talked about, would change everything.

But no. Andra was done with pauses, done with waiting. It was absolute darkness—the kind her eyes couldn't adjust to—but she'd pilfered a couple of flashlights from their resources and pulled them out, tossing one to Zhade.

She clicked her light on, and the beam fell on a skeleton.

She bit back a scream, stumbled into Zhade. He put a reassuring hand on her back, and the fact that he didn't respond with a flippant quip revealed his mental state. He didn't have a clue what he was walking into. Andra hoped she did.

She hoped she didn't.

There it was again—hope. It didn't belong to her. It was just another algorithm that pushed her to survive.

The LAC annex was in ruins, like the grocery store the Schism had used, and the remains of the Vaults. It was difficult for Andra to get her bearings—the reception desk should be there, the security scanners over there, the entrance to the main hallway next to that other skeleton—but after a while, she began to see the patterns of the building she knew so well. She'd practically grown up here.

If she could call it growing up. Programmed?

Zhade followed her down a dark tunnel that used to be a hallway, past caves that used to be labs and offices. The elevator was—obviously—no longer working, so they had to use another 'drill to get to the lowest level. After that, they searched for the door. As soon as she saw it, Andra knew exactly which one Dr. Griffin had meant, even though she'd never seen it before.

It was metal, heavy, with an industrial handle. No window. No label. There were the remains of some sort of sign. It was so corroded, all

Andra could make out was jumbled shapes in a vaguely blue color, but she knew it had once been the symbol for cryonics—a snowflake of infinity symbols.

Miraculously, the digi'lock beside it still worked—probably techno'sealed, like the Vaults. She entered the coordinates for Holymyth.

It took all her strength and Zhade's to pry open the door, and when it finally broke free, it let out a hiss, like a seal breaking.

Behind the door was darkness. And chill. It smelled like stale snow, and as soon as Andra stepped inside, frost clung to her skin. She was about to click on her flashlight when a light flicked on, fifty feet above her head. Another light followed. And another. *Kachunk kachunk kachunk.* Light after light, down the center of the ceiling, which went on as far as Andra could see. A huge cavernous room filled with . . .

She took a step forward, then another, and then she was sprinting. She stopped in front of a stack of oblong boxes, stacked ten, twenty high. Seven feet long, four feet wide, three feet tall. Like coffins. But not coffins.

Cryo'tanks.

She placed her hand on the nearest one. It wasn't dull and lifeless. It wasn't warm under her touch. It was cold, and it was humming. It was operational.

Andra uncovered the nameplate at the base.

Ming Sun.

She wiped away the layer of frost, and there she was. Ming. She was alive. She was lying right in front of Andra, and she was alive.

Andra ran to the next 'tank, wiped it down. Inside was a man with red hair and a grizzled beard. *Joseph Stein.* Alive.

The next one. *Lakshmi Gupta.* Alive.

She ran from 'tank to 'tank, reading names and looking at faces. *Ellie McGinnis. Rupert Cho. Kaneisha Taylor.*

She didn't recognize any of them, but somehow she knew. *She knew.* They were from her time. A million cryo'tanks. A million colonists waiting to wake up on a different planet. And if she searched hard enough, she would find her family.

The people she'd thought were her family.

All those weeks ago, the 'bot had said the colonists were dead, and legally they were. They were all still in cryonic stasis.

This was her purpose, right? To save humanity. This was why she'd been created, and if she wasn't human, if she was nothing more than a tool, then she would at least be useful.

She grasped her 'locket, and everything solidified. The Ark had never left Earth. The colonists were asleep—had been for a thousand years.

And now, it was time for them to wake up.

ACKNOWLEDGMENTS

I'm so very lucky to be surrounded by people, both personally and professionally, who are incredibly supportive of my writing and this book in particular.

Thank you to my agent extraordinaire, Victoria Marini, for believing in *Goddess*'s potential, and for being enthusiastic and ambitious and everything I need in an agent. I couldn't imagine a better advocate for me and my writing. Special thanks to Barbara Poelle, for passing my manuscript on to Victoria. Also, to Maggie Kane, Heather Baro-Shapiro, and the rest of the team at IGLA.

To my editor, Julie Rosenberg, for her guidance and patience, and for bringing out the best version of *Goddess*. For understanding my vision for the book, sometimes even better than I did. And for putting up with Zhade through several revisions. To the Razorbill/ Penguin team, especially Alex Sanchez, Casey McIntyre, and Jayne Ziemba. To proofreaders Maddy Newquist and Marinda Valenti, and copyeditors Vivian Kirklin and Janet Pascal, for patiently handling Zhade's absurd dialect. To Dana Li and Doaly for the incredible cover design. Also, to everyone at Penguin Teen, for their contagious enthusiasm.

To Emily Suvada: you are The Best™ writer, critique partner, and friend. I'm so inspired not only by your writing, but by who you are as a person. Thank you for being my sounding board and my buddy and my reality check. Not only would this book not exist without you, but I also would have quit writing a long time ago. Thank you for everything you do for me and for all the ways you made this book better. Thanks also for that time when I sent you two options of what I should work on, and you chose the one about the girl who wakes up from cryonic stasis to discover she's a goddess. Maybe that'll turn into something some day.

Thank you to Ríoghnach Robinson and Tim Olson, for reading for authenticity and providing insights into Andra's experience and identity. For graciously offering your feedback and time and guidance. Any remaining mistakes are mine and mine alone.

To my master's thesis committee: Dr. Beth Gargano, Dr. Balaka Basu, and Dr. Paula Connolly. For not throwing out the four hundred page book that showed up in your mailboxes. For all your insight then and support since. And to Dr. Pilar Blitvich, for teaching the linguistics course that influenced this book.

Thank you to my BFFs, to whom I dedicated this book, for all your love and support, and for always reminding me that I am my own power blazer. To Kailan Sindelar, for being my patronus and always celebrating my successes. To Taryn Dollings, for reading the earliest scenes that would turn into *Goddess*. To Nadia Clifton, for her librarian prowess during the Great Word Panic of 2019. To Bre Weber, for her undying support and for being my biggest cheerleader. To Amanda Loeffert, for drinking my wine and fixing my plot holes. To Alex Batty, for all her amazing graphic designs for *Goddess*. And to Kelsey Helveston, for writing with me on Sundays and making sure I ate vegetables.

Thank you to Brook Swiger, for reading the first draft of the first book I ever wrote, and for refraining from telling me not to quit my day job (which would have been especially cruel, as I was unemployed at the time). Your encouragement kept me writing.

To Beth Revis, Renée Ahdieh, Roshani Chokshi, Alexandra Duncan, and Carrie Ryan, for always being so kind and encouraging to this floundering new author, and for all their support and advice. To Cora Carmack, for her feedback on the first draft of my query letter. To Jennifer L. Armentrout, for getting me to RT 2014. To all the amazing writer buddies I've made this year, especially Jennifer Gruenke, Britt Singleton, Tracy Deonn Walker, and Karen Strong.

To my family, especially my parents. To Mom, for putting books next to the cat chair, and to Dad, for introducing me to *Star Wars*. Thanks to both of you for always believing I could do whatever I set my mind to.

And to me, for writing this book in the first place and not giving up. Good job, LB: you did it!

DON'T MISS
THE MIND-BENDING CONCLUSION TO
ANDRA AND ZHADE'S STORY.

A GODDESS IN THE MACHINE NOVEL

DEVIL
IN
THE
DEVICE

LORA BETH JOHNSON

TURN THE PAGE FOR A SNEAK PEEK.

ONE

THE GUV

ZHADE WOKE TO a knife at his throat.

Darkness shrouded the figure above him, its weight pressing down on Zhade's chest. Metal bit into his skin, warm and slick. His covers were twisted round him, and there was no way to fight, nowhere to run. There was nothing sole to lie there and accept his fate.

Stardust swirled thickish in the air, waiting for a command from the Crown, but he didn't call to it. Couldn't.

Instead, he sighed.

"You again?" he asked his would-be assassin.

The blade fell away. The weight scuttled off him.

"You need better guards," a high voice said.

The first rays of light peeked through the seams in Maret's dark curtains, illuminating Doon's face, pink from the sun, her clothes coated in sand. Her dark eyes—the exact shade of brown as her brother's—glinted fierceish as she sat crouched on the edge of the bed, blade still ahand, a single eyebrow raised.

Zhade threw his arm over his eyes. "I have Gryfud. You can't find a better guard."

Doon huffed. "Gryfud's at home with his fam. You have Meta standing guard this moren."

Zhade wrinkled his nose and ruffled his hair. The blond strands tickled the back of his neck, longer than he'd ever worn it. Longer than he liked. "Rare form. I do need better guards."

His guards *were* loyal to Tsurina, full true. And if it was Meta at the door, she probablish held a sign that said "Assassins welcome."

He gentlish pushed Doon off the bed. "You're getting sand in my sheets, little warrior."

She landed on the carpeted floor with a soft thud. "If I *had* been an assassin, sand would be the least of your worries." She sheathed her knife and looked round the Guv's room, taking in the heavy curtains, dark furniture, and haze of stardust. "It looks like you haven't cleaned since you became Maret." She sniffed. "And that Maret didn't clean since he became guv."

"Then I can't full well start cleaning now if I want people to reck I'm Maret." Zhade groaned as he climbed out of bed, which, for all its luxury, still felt uncomfortistic and cold to him. But he was here, and his brother was sleeping frozen agrave. *So there*, as Andra would say.

He stretched his aching muscles, twisting from side to side.

"Turn round," he said through a yawn. "Can't I have some privacy?"

He started riffling through the discarded clothes next to the bed for a clean shirt.

Doon turned her back to him. "Maybe you should sleep in armor soon and now, if it's this easy for someone to sneak past your guards."

Zhade sniffed one of Maret's dark purple tunics and was assaulted by the smell of sour sweat and something coppery. He could have sworn this pile was the laundered one.

He shrugged the tunic on and froze when he saw himself in the wardrobe's mirrored doors. There were dark hollows neath his eyes, and his hair hung in greasy clumps. Everything bout him looked thin—his nose, his pointed chin, his body. His presence. It had been over a moon since he'd used the graftling wand, but his stomach still tightened when he saw his brother's face reflecting back at him.

"I have to convo you something," Doon said. She was slumped in a chair, face drawn in an imagineful expression.

"Is it where you've been?" Zhade asked, searching through the wardrobe for one of Maret's capes. "You have to stop disappearing. You can't mereish wander off whenever you feel amood. You should convo Skilla where you're peacing to. Or Dzeni. Or take Xana with you."

"For certz, *Guv*." She said the word the same as she used to say his name. Something more than irritation but not quite disdain.

"I'm not saying this as your guv—" he started. But what was he saying this as? Not her brother, for certz. Not her guardian. He'd convinced her brother and guardian to abandon her. Then gotten him killed.

"Good, because you're not for true the guv." Doon gave him a hard smile. "You reck that, marah? It's still Maret on the throne."

Zhade rolled his eyes. It was true that he still wore Maret's face, but he was ruling by his own values. The dungeons had been emptied, the executions had stopped. He'd found housing for those displaced by the pocket and found workings for those without. Maret would have done none of that. He would have given in to Tsurina's demands to punish those who looted during the panic after the 'dome had been destroyed. He'd have left the homeless and workless to fend for themselves. Then he'd have thrown a party to distract everyone from the state of the city.

The Eerensedians may imagine Maret sat on the throne, but it was Zhade who led them. Things were . . . good. His plan was working. He'd taken the throne, the gods' dome was fixed, and now he was focusing on chipping away at Tsurina's power. Slower than he would have liked, but Tsurina's influence was more embedded into the government than he'd realized. There were a few pebbles in his shoe, but after a moon as Maret, Zhade was more certz than ever that his plan would succeed and Eerensed would finalish be free.

Zhade gave Doon a playful shove. "Mereish because I took his face—"

Doon pursed her lips. "Mereish his face?"

"Evens," Zhade conceded, winking. "His face and Silver Crown."

Not that the Crown had been of any use to Zhade yet. No meteor what he tried, he couldn't harness its powers. Through it, he could feel the stardust round him, sense the angels and magical conduits, but they wouldn't answer his commands. The Crown was now mere-ish a decoration, part of the trappings of his deceit. At luck, Zhade hadn't had need of it. If the Eerensedians realized the Guv could no longer wield his greatest weapon, his power would start to dissolve.

Zhade collapsed into a velvet chair and rested his forehead gentlish against his hand. The skin next to the Crown was tender, the muscles sore.

Doon plopped down on a nearish sofa and started twirling her knife on the tip of a finger. "Dzeni got a job akitchens. She begins tomoren."

Zhade sat up straightish, the stardust round him swirling in agitation. "What?"

Doon nodded, eyebrows raised in mutual comping. "I reck, marah?"

Zhade shook his head. Dzeni wasn't safe apalace. If Tsurina recked the promised of Zhade's best friend—the man Maret had killed—worked akitchens . . . He closed his eyes, pinching the bridge of his nose. "She should have gone to stay with the Schism."

Zhade would visit her, convince her to go belowground. If she didn't want to stay with the Schism, maybe he could convince her to live in the Vaults with the goddesses. He'd bring her some flowers. Maybe get a toy for Dehgo. What did kidduns play with, anyway? Charms? Knives? He'd ask Gryfud—the soldier who had let him into Eerensed all those moons ago and was anow the captain of Zhade's guard. He and his husband had recentish adopted a kiddun. For certz they'd figured what it played with soon and now.

Gryf was always willing to help. Without Kiv as part of his guard, Zhade needed someone he could trust to infiltrate Tsurina's ranks. He'd chosen Gryfud not sole because he had let Zhade and Andra acity, but he'd also been friendish with him as kidduns. It was still a risk, but one Zhade had to take.

Gryfud had sole shook his head when Zhade had revealed who he for true was.

"You're a fool boyo," he'd said, in a way that purposed he was agreeing to help, if sole because he recked the plan wouldn't work without him.

"Be at care what you say to your guv," Zhade had teased.

"For certz," Gryfud had replied. "If I see him, I will."

Doon stretched out on the sofa, throwing her hands behind her head. "Convoing the Schism. You do reck that you missed your last meeting with Skilla, marah? She's for true full angry."

Zhade waved a hand. "She'll make it peaceish." He grinned, gesturing to himself. "Who can stay angry at this face?"

Doon scowled.

There was a knock at the door, and both Zhade and Doon froze.

No one should have been able to enter his suite. The outer door was sealed with blood magic. Somehow, while he and Doon had been convoing, someone had entered through his receiving room, walked down the hall, and stood outside his bedroom for who recked how long.

"Did you leave the door open?" Zhade hissed.

Doon shook her head. "I didn't come in that march."

His eyes darted toward the balcony, and she nodded. He slowish made his march to the door, making certz Doon was hidden before opening it. A guard stood on the other side, plated in gold armor, her sharp face frozen in a stern expression.

Meta.

How had she gotten in? The sole person—other than him—with

access to the suite was Tsurina. Had Tsurina messed with the blood magic so the guards could enter too?

Zhade groaned inwardish.

Meta was bout Zhade's age. A refugee from the Wastes who, after sole three years in the guard, had been promoted to second-in-command, poised to take the captain's place. Sfin, the priorish captain, had died during the battle against the Schism, the night Zhade had morphed his features to match his brother's and slid into his place as guv. To the people of Eerensed, it was the day the palace had nearish been destroyed, the Third caught and executed, and the gods' dome restored.

With Sfin dead, Meta was spozed to become captain, but Zhade had promoted Gryfud instead. Gryfud, who had been mereish a border guard, and a lower-level one at that. Meta had been less than pleased. She made it recked as oft as possible.

"Guv," she said through gritted teeth, jaw clenched, a strand of brown spiked hair falling over one eye. The westhand side of her head was shaved like a Waster; the other side was long and slicked into pointed strands. It wasn't reg, that was for certz.

"Firm?" Zhade asked.

"Do you have memory you have a guv-asking in half abell?"

"For certz," Zhade lied, groaning internalish. "Be there soonish."

Meta turned to go.

"And Meta?"

She halted.

"How did you get in the suite?"

Meta blinked slowish. "The door was open. I imagined you left it that way apurpose."

Zhade swallowed. He for certz hadn't left the door open. Which purposed that either Tsurina had let her in, or the guards now had some way to pass by the blood magic. He couldn't ask bout it though, without seeming suss. Instead, he gave Meta a tight smile. "For certz. I'm still half sleepy. I'll be out in a tick."

Meta didn't smile back.

THE DAY PASSED in a sandcloud, each activity sifting into the next. It was always the same: meetings and appearances and half-walking the thin string between maintaining his ruse as Maret and making decisions that would improve Eerensed's fate. Each day he held himself busy from moren to even, but this day he convoed his guards he needed a bell in the aftermoren to himself. They didn't question him. He was guv, after all.

After his last meeting of the day, he retreated to his room, donning some of his old clothes and a glamour mask sorcered to a generic Eerensedian face, and marched out acity.

He sighed once he was free of the shadow of the Rock and let himself enjoy Eerensed. The bustle of citians, the hum of tiny flying angels, the flashing of scrys. The bright sun shining down on all of it. He saw no askers, though they'd always been scarce in Southwarden. There were flowers in windowboxes and in the midway. Zhade picked a handful of starflowers to give to Dzeni.

The sole thing that marred his mood was the shadow of the pocket to his westhand side. It was quiet—as much as pockets were quiet—and it didn't seem to be growing or moving. But it was a fulltime memory of the events of last moon, when the gods' dome had failed and a full district of the city had been destroyed in an eyebeat. At the least, it was full early in the day the pocket didn't yet block the setting sun. Each even, night came a full bell earlier than it used to.

It was a short trip to the bakery that had once belonged to Wead's uncle, who'd left it to Wead when he'd sunk into sand. Zhade imagined it belonged to Dzeni now. Or maybe Doon. It was a small place, hidden in the tangle of alleys in the Resto District in Southwarden. The bell rang as Zhade pushed open the door.

The bakery was empty, except for a few picked-over baykuds in the case. Zhade cleared his throat and leaned against the counter. A face popped out from the back room. Flame hair, grizzled beard. Cheska.

"What happens?" he asked, dusting flour off his hands. His voice was a basstring played in a cave. His hair was bright as a goldenlilly, his pale complexion ruddy. He was a big man, could probablish hold his own in a fight with Gryfud, maybe even Kiv.

"I'm—" Zhade tried to deepen his voice. "—I'm looking for Dzeni."

Cheska narrowed his pale eyes. "How you happen to reck Dzeni?"

Zhade leaned across the counter, looking up at Cheska til he was full close the bigger man could see through the glamour mask to Zhade's face neath it. Maret's face. Cheska was one of the few people who recked Zhade was wearing the Guv's features. Dzeni had insisted on telling him.

Cheska immediatish scowled. "What do you want?"

Zhade rocked back. "Many things. Butterjam tarts, a new silk cape, fishes and wishes. But anow, I'd like to convo Dzeni."

Cheska stared him down a moment, before shaking his head and disappearing behind the curtain in the back. Zhade swiped up a near-ish crumb. It was burnt. He stuck his tongue out and let the crumb fall to the counter.

The curtain opened, and Cheska motioned for Zhade to follow. Behind was a storeroom. A door to the left led to another room, windowless and dark, but homeish. Dzeni stood draped in a thick cloak, Dehgo clinging to his mother's hand. She'd lost weight, her cheeks hollow and bags neath her eyes. Her dark hair was pulled back from her heart-shaped face into a rattish bun.

"Dzeni!" Zhade stepped forward, opening his arms for a hug, but he was met mereish with an icy stare. He dropped his arms and took a step back. For certz, he was wearing a glamour mask. "It's Zhade."

Dzeni cocked an eyebrow. "I reck. That's the worst disguise."

Zhade didn't bother to convo the face neath his glamour wasn't even his own, so it was actualish a full brill disguise.

Cheska moved to stand next to Dzeni, placing a protective hand on her shoulder. Dehgo pulled on his mam's arm, eyeing the toy angel in Zhade's hand.

"Heya, boyo," Zhade said, trying to sound like himself and not Maret. Rust was growing on his own voice with disuse.

Dehgo slipped out of his mam's grasp and ran up to Zhade. "I like your toy sir may I see it?" The sentence came out in a rush.

"This?" Zhade asked, lifting the small angel. He'd sorcered it to do nothing more than walk in circles and say a few brief phrases, but kidduns were easyish amused, marah? Gryfud had said so. "This toy?"

"Firm!" Dehgo reached for it, big brown eyes alight.

"Evens, this toy isn't mine." Zhade held the toy just out of his reach.

Dehgo stuck out his bottom lip. "'Snot?"

"Neg, you'll have to ask the owner if you can play with it."

"Whose is it?"

Zhade knelt and held out the angel. "It's yours."

Dehgo squinted and puffed out his lips, and Zhade realized he didn't comp the joke. But he must have decided it didn't meteor because he snatched the toy from Zhade's hands and ran back to his mother.

Dzeni placed a hand on her son's curlish head. "What convo, Dehgo?"

"Thank you," he muttered, placing the angel on the ground and watching its small silver body stumble over the uneven stone floor.

Zhade stood. Dzeni was watching him with a measured stare.

He scratched behind his ear with a single finger. "You don't belong akitchens."

"Zhade," she said in a soft reprimand.

"What I purpose is . . ." How to convo this? Zhade should have prepped something, but he'd never had trouble making words before. "You and Dehgo. I can give you a place to live."

Wasn't that the least he owed them? Owed Wead?

Dzeni canted her head. "We have a place to live."

"A *better* place."

A growl came from Cheska's direction.

Zhade lifted his hands in placation. "I'm certz Cheska's place is charred but probablish crowded. You could move belowground. You wouldn't need to work. The Third would give you somewhere to stay. Things to do. She'd protect you."

"Like she protected Wead?" Fire burned in Dzeni's eyes, and Zhade flinched. This was not the Dzeni he recked. She seemed to realize the anger had taken over because her face softened. "Sorries and worries. I didn't purpose to convo . . ."

"That wasn't her fault," Zhade muttered, his stomach souring. He didn't want to convo this. Wead's death. Zhade's part in it.

Andra.

Dzeni laughed, saddish. "She's a goddess, Zhade."

"Neg, Dzeni. It's complicated. I don't full comp half of it, but if you would mereish convo her, she could explain. Please. If you blame anyone, you should blame me."

Dzeni looked away. The corners of her mouth tugged down, and her eyes were vagueish wet. Zhade would have given anything to see her smile again, but he wasn't certz if he wanted it for her, or to assuage his own guilt. For a moment, they both watched Dehgo play with the angel on the dirt floor.

Zhade sighed. "I mereish imagined . . . Hear, I reck this is my fault. And I want to do something to . . . make things right."

Dzeni's eyes met his. "I reck, Zhade. It's mereish . . . this is not the way to do it."

"If you want to make things right," Cheska cut in, "then you should pass more of your time out of the palace."

Zhade bit the inside of his cheek. "What happens, Cheska?"

Cheska started pacing the cramped room, running a hand through his red hair. "How are you for true helping our people, *Guv*? The Lost District held many businesses. They're gone now. The harvests will be short this year. When the gods' dome failed, it took most of our water supply. The people—*your* people—are hurting, dying. What are you going to do bout it?"

"Cheska," Dzeni said, placing a hand on his shoulder. For the first time since Wead's death, she sounded like herself. Gentle but firm. Holding the peace.

Cheska shook off her touch. "Neg, Dzeni, he should hear this."

"I'm doing everything I can," Zhade said, slipping into Maret's whine. "It's diff to make real change while Tsurina is still round, but I've found housing for everyone, all my people have workings who want them. The water is sole a meteor of time, and the harvest isn't for several moons."

Cheska paused his pacing and started counting off on his fingers. "The housing is overcrowded. The workings you've provided are demeaning. And we need water soon and now."

Zhade clenched his jaw. "I can't make water from wine. Magic has its limits." It was a well-recked axiom of magic that it could sole mimic the natural, not create it.

"And I'm certz," Cheska said, crossing his arms over his chest, "it full imports to have water in that big showy fountain afront of the palace, marah?"

Zhade winced. Cheska was right. It had been a stupid mistake not to order the fountain turned off while water was scarce.

Zhade sighed. "Evens, you're right. I can turn off the fountain. And

I'll . . . consider what I can do bout the other stuff," he muttered.

"*Consider what you can do?*" Cheska mocked. "Now you sound like a goddess. Are you full certz the city is better with you as guv instead of Maret?"

Zhade opened his mouth to reply, but Cheska turned and stormed back to the bakery, the door slamming shut behind him.

Dzeni gave Zhade a sorries look.

"Evens. That was awkward." Zhade smiled, but his stomach plummeted. For certz, things weren't perfect. But they were getting better each day. And unlike his brother, Zhade actualish *cared* bout his people.

It was evens.

Everything was evens.

"That was awkward," Dehgo said to his toy angel, mimicking Zhade's cadence.

They stood in silence, Dzeni shifting from foot to foot, Zhade ruffling the back of his head, watching his feet.

He cleared his throat. "I brought something for you too." He pulled a disc out of his pocket and handed it to Dzeni. "It's a small gods' dome."

Dzeni blinked, staring down at the shiny metal disc in her hand. "For what?"

Zhade shrugged. "I mereish imagined . . . you should have it. Just in case."

Andra had given Zhade a few small domes that would protect anyone inside from pockets. Evens. She'd given some to Kiv to give to him. She'd called them backup in case the gods' dome failed. Kiv had said she'd said it pointedish. It was now Zhade's job to maintain the dome, but tween holding the secret of his identity and ruling Eerensed, he'd had little time to focus on it.

"I did blame you," Dzeni said, her voice wavering, and it took

Zhade a tick to realize she was talking bout Wead's death. "I blamed you. And her. And Maret. And Wead." Her eyes met his, and they shimmered with tears. "I'm so angry, all the time, and it hurts. I don't reck what I've become."

Zhade reached for Dzeni, but she moved away.

"Sorries, Zhade," she mumbled. "Maybe I will go belowground. It's best for Dehgo, marah?" She knelt and pushed her son's curls from his face. He looked so much like his father.

Zhade tried to smile. "He wouldn't want for anything. And you have to reck how much the Third cared for Wead, and how much she regrets his death. She . . . Maret gave her a choice. He was either going to kill me or Wead. And she chose me to die and Wead to live. Sole Maret didn't listen and killed Wead instead."

Dzeni was quiet for a moment. "She chose you to die?"

Zhade nodded, swallowed. He didn't want to convo this. Not that he blamed Andra. But it hurt and probablish always would. He didn't fool himself how much it would have tortured her if he *had* died from her decision, but the answer had come so quickish. So detached from what her feelings for him had been. Those feelings were for certz gone anow he wore the face of the boy who had killed Wead afront of her.

"I—" Dzeni started, but whatever she was bout to say was cut off by a scream.

Both she and Zhade turned toward the noise. It had come from the street, and it sounded like a kiddun.

"Stay here," Dzeni told Dehgo, at the same time Zhade said it to her.

She gave him an exasperated look and followed him into the street.

A crowd had gathered. There was another scream coming from the center of the square, but it was cut short.

"Out of the march," Zhade demanded, and the citians parted.

In the mid of the crowd, a kiddun was being held aloft by the neck. By an angel.

Zhade didn't have time to reck how impossible it was. The kiddun's face was going slack, her attempts to fight growing weaker, her dark hair spilling over an angelic hand.

On instinct, Zhade reached out with his mind. From the few times he'd tried to use the Crown, he recked what angels "felt" like through the magic connection, and this was not it. The angel felt . . . wrong. Dark. Some deep abyss.

"Do something!" Dzeni shouted.

"I'm trying." Zhade gritted his teeth, focusing harder.

Release her, he commanded in his mind. Wasn't this how Maret had done it? Speaking through the magical connection? This was High Magic. No conduit, mereish thought. The angel should heed his command soon and sooner. But it didn't. It continued choking the kiddun, her pathetic kicks now nothing more than muscle spasms. Her mam was reaching for her. Her da was crumpled on the ground below, crying.

Release her, Zhade thought harder, but nothing happened.

Dzeni shot forward, arms stretching toward the kiddun, but couldn't reach her. She started banging on the angel's chest, her fists hitting with empty thuds. The angel's other hand shot out and clamped round Dzeni's throat. The crowd gasped, as the angel stretched out its arms, offering both Dzeni and the kiddun to the sky.

"Mam!" Dehgo cried, appearing behind Zhade. Could no one stay put where they were told?

He tried to catch Dehgo up in his arms, but the kiddun slipped through. He was almost to the angel when a pair of arms wrapped round him. He screamed as he was lifted off his feet by a woman with dark skin and a shaved head.

She turned, and Zhade was met with Xana's cool glare, her magic eye narrowing in on him.

"Do something," she commanded.

The words were lost in the screaming of the crowd, but Zhade felt them rather in his bones.

He tried again to command the angel.

RELEASE THEM.

He felt something ooze down his cheek, a dull pain thumping in time with his pulse. His body began to shake.

Cheska burst through the crowd, red hair blazing, pushing people out of his march with his enormous arms. He punched the angel as hard as he could in the chest. There was a dull thud, nothing else, but Cheska kept punching. And punching. Punching as though something had possessed him. The angel's chest cracked. Cheska's hand was bleeding, but he kept attacking.

The kiddun was released first. A villager shot forward to catch her before she hit the ground. They called for a meddoc, and immediatish started giving her seepar, a technique of blowing one's own air into the afflicted's lungs.

Cheska was still punching. The angel's insides were spilling out. People were screaming. The angel finalish released Dzeni, but he didn't stop.

The angel fell, and Cheska climbed on top of it, hitting it til there was a hole the size and shape of his fist in its chest. He reached in, the angel's metal skin shredding his fist into a bloody mess, and pulled out the heart of the angel. It was a dull black box, but everyone in the crowd comped that Cheska had removed the thing that held the angel alive. A flurry of stardust rose from the dead angel—its soul escaping—and disappeared into the air.

Cheska turned back to the crowd. Some applauded him with awkward relief, while others crowded round the girl, who was now sitting up and coughing. Cheska tossed aside the angel heart and went to Dzeni. Xana had helped her to her knees, fingers now running across the bruise on her neck. In the other arm, she held

Dehgo. It was the most tender he'd ever seen her.

Then she turned toward the noisy crowd, her fierce gaze searching past them to narrow in on Zhade, her expression murderful.

Zhade mereish stood there.

Powerless.

An angel had attacked a little girl. In his city.

An *angel*.

Angels didn't attack people, except in one circumstance: at Maret's command during executions. What Zhade had mereish seen—it was impossible without the Crown.

The Crown Zhade was wearing. And if Zhade hadn't done it, then . . .

Someone else in the city had the magic that should sole be Zhade's.

He was bout to move forward, kneel next to the angel and start examining it, when he caught the sight of a familiar half-shaved head in the crowd.

Meta.

As Andra would say:

Fuck.

She would almost for certz see through his glamour.

He gave Dzeni one last look. She seemed evens. Cheska was helping her to her feet. Xana still held Dehgo. Zhade slipped out of the crowd, holding to the shadows as he made his march back to the palace.